I0672417

The Third King

By Daphne C. Murrell

Copyright © 2016 by Daphne C. Murrell

Front cover design by Taylor Cash.

All rights reserved.

This book or parts thereof may not be reproduced in any form, stored in any retrieval system, or transmitted in any form by any means without prior written permission of the author, except as provided by United States of America copyright law.

This book is a work of fiction. Names, descriptions, entities and incidents included in the story are products of the author's imagination. Any resemblance to actual persons, events and entities is entirely coincidental.

PUBLISHED IN THE UNITED STATES OF AMERICA

Mountain Paradise Publishers.

ISBN-13: 978-0692648551 (Mountain Paradise Publishers)

ISBN-10: 0692648550

Dedication

This book is dedicated to the princesses in my life: Melody, Charis, Bretta and Isla, just to remind you that dreams really can come true.

Acknowledgments

Many thanks to Pat Nelson, Nancy Denny and
Chris Newton for their help.

A big, huge, massive thanks to Taylor Cash
for designing the "Blue Steed."

And thanks to Rick for listening…

Because sometimes we just need a good fairy-tale …

Once upon a time …

❧ Chapter One ❧

The king slammed his hand on the table, and all three boys jumped to attention in their chairs. Five-year old Andrew Braisogn knew not to wiggle as he blankly stared at the ancient map his father had spread out before him and his two brothers. Charts and kingdoms paled in comparison to tonight's annual Royal Christmas Ball. His older brothers, George, thirteen, and Peter, ten, slowly slid back in the oversized seats and crossed their arms again. Why had Christopher Braisogn chosen tonight to discuss matters of kingship and land with his sons?

"Braisognia," he further dictated, "will eventually belong to one of you. One of you," he panned each boy and pointed a straight, stern finger, "will rule as king in my place."

"Why can't we all just share it?" Peter yawned as he slumped deeper into his chair.

"Because in Braisognia we have one king. He is the leader of the military, the leader of the people, and the leader of the congress."

George scrunched his freckled nose. "Why do we need a military? We haven't had a war in over a hundred and fifty years."

His father's gaze became perturbed. "Why do you think we've had no war in all that time? Because we have an impenetrable army! Our military is unmatched for such a small nation! No one would dare attempt to overtake Braisognia for fear of utter defeat and humiliation! If we are to remain safe and independent, we must continue to be strong and invincible. We must be ruled by a leader with a heart sworn to defend those who serve him."

Andrew was lost again. He comprehended half the words his father used, so his mind wandered once more. All he could think of was the evening to come. The dinner, the music and the dancing were always exciting, but those were not what had captivated his heart. The sparkling green eyes, the gently upturned nose, and the mischievous smile—all hiding an imaginary world he could never tap on his own—loomed before him. Evangeline. Just her name set his heart to thumping! Though he knew he had seen her before somewhere, all his memories focused on last year's ball. Beneath the tables they had hidden in caves and swum in perilous oceans. They had hunted dragons in horrid forests and built cabins with decorated empty boxes. They had tiptoed between ornate pillars pretending to save the kingdom from dark plans and evil marauders.

Then the clock had struck midnight. The ball ended, the guests left, and his world crashed into reality again. He had cried himself to sleep, deep into the loneliness of the other three hundred sixty-four nights. In his brief life he had never known such adventure, and he often drifted back to that night of memories when the cold, staunch existence at the palace became unbearable. Would he see her tonight? He cautiously moved his hand behind his back and crossed his fingers.

"But I don't want to be king!" Peter bolted from his chair. "I want to be a fireman! I don't want to fight men! I want to fight fires!"

"If you are king," his father snapped, "you will own the firehouses. You can ride with the firemen anytime you like. You can do anything you wish. You would be king!"

"But I want to live there and slide down the poles and wash the engines and—"

"Enough! You are royalty! You are not a ... a ... lowly fireman!"

"But I don't want to be royalty!"

"You do not have a choice!" his father's voice boomed. "You are royalty! It's in your blood!"

"Then get it out, please!" Peter hovered on the verge of tears.

His father glared, dark eyes brooding as a vein throbbed on his forehead.

Peter cowered back into his chair and stammered, "I don't want to fight men." His lip quivered. "I don't want to fight anyone."

His father mumbled as he looked at the map, "It's a good thing you're second in line to the crown, then."

George, putting his head down, sneered under his breath. "Great. Just great."

"What was that?"

He glanced up and shook his head. "Nothing, Father. Nothing at all."

"I should hope not. You three have no idea what awaits you. It is a life of privilege and honor, of duty and heroism. Any boy in this kingdom would gladly trade places with you. Remember that. Understand?"

George and Peter nodded obligingly, but Andrew was lost chasing dragons again. A smile had eased upon his face as he wondered what adventures awaited him this evening.

His father wrongly interpreted the grin. "You, my youngest, may be the only one who truly understands the greatness that awaits you." He gently tousled the dark head of hair with pride.

Andrew flinched, startled at his father's rare touch. His whimsical smile instantly faded.

U U U

The royal family strode down the corridor toward the banquet hall, the sound of their heels reverberating against the marble floor. Andrew found comfort in his mother's presence, something he never felt with his father. Julia Braisogn's cropped blond hair was meticulously set beneath the golden tiara, and her flowing gown of dark green and maroon taffeta exuded Christmas. His stomach flipped again. This was the best night of the year. Bearing the formalities of greeting the guests in the receiving line would be worth it if Evangeline was waiting for him at the children's table, her eyes glowing full of exotic plans for the evening.

Andrew thought his father and brothers looked striking in their military attire. In five years he would also don the Braisognian uniform. The tassels on his father's shoulders had always fascinated him, and he recalled once, during one of the few times he could remember being in his father's lap, he'd been allowed to touch them softly as they endured a long, boring speech. He had studied the strong angles and faint lines of his father's face framed by the dark hair and punctuated by deep brown eyes. His father, tall and strong, had seemed oblivious to Andrew's wiggling that day. Only the occasional glance and raised eyebrow of his mother reminded him to remain still and quiet.

Instinctively he reached his hand up to hers, and she responded with a warm smile. If they had been alone, she would have spoken sweet words to him and praised him for doing well in his lessons, especially with music. She would have told him how handsome his dark hair and eyes were and to always remember how special he was. His father became angry when she petted him, so when she squeezed his hand he understood she still believed all those things but wouldn't speak of them tonight.

Four guards stood in front of the doors to the great hall. Julia surveyed her husband's appearance and removed an almost invisible piece of lint.

"Congratulations, Christopher." Her voice was void of emotion. "You managed a straight tie for the first time in fifteen years. Perhaps that alone is cause enough for celebration tonight."

The king lifted an eyebrow then sighed. "The only cause for celebration will be when this blasted thing is ended and put away for another year."

"Don't be so cynical. It's all part of being king, which means you love it."

"Sometimes I wonder."

She then turned her blue eyes toward her older sons. "You are too handsome to possibly be my little boys," she smiled. "Oh! That's right!" she giggled as she straightened Peter's tie, "You're practically grown now, aren't you?"

George stared hard at her as she tried to calm the cowlick at the crown of his golden hair. She licked her fingers and pressed firmly on the unruly strands.

"Mother, it's never helped before. My hair is my hair, and unless I cut it all off, those things will always and forever keep sticking up."

"That might not be a bad idea. When you start summer maneuvers you'll have to get it shaved anyway," his father suggested, again with the eyebrow raised.

"Not shaved," George said, "just clipped. I will never shave my head."

"Me either," red-headed Peter agreed.

Christopher looked down at Andrew, pausing for his response, but the boy's thoughts were so far away that he never acknowledged his father. He waited eagerly for the doors to open so they could parade through, shake a myriad of hands, and be released for the rest of the night.

"Are you ready, your majesty?" the guard asked the king.

Christopher sighed again. "I suppose. Do I have a choice?"

"No," Julia noted, and turned to the guard. "We're ready." She stepped two paces behind her husband, a practice she had grown accustomed to from the day of their marriage.

Before he could take another breath, Andrew heard the announcer's voice boom through loudspeakers, "Lords and Ladies of the kingdom, I present to you the hosts of tonight's celebration, his royal highness, King Christopher Braisogn and his lovely wife, Queen Julia Lamonte Cordova Braisogn." The room exploded with applause.

Andrew was light-headed with anticipation as two guards released the locks to the massive doors and strained them open for the family. The king walked through first, followed by the queen and their sons in successive order. They took their places without delay and greeted their guests. Andrew watched his brothers carefully to know which were family with whom he should shake hands, and which were also dignitaries to whom he must bow. But when Lord James Dorvain and his wife, Lady Giselle Montevo Dorvain approached, Andrew could not help himself. He broke line by only a stride and peeked around those in front of him. There she was—Evangeline, his angel, his savior for the night, for the year. Her smile revealed two missing teeth right in the front. She gave him a small wave, and he felt as if he were floating.

"Andrew!" Peter whispered sternly. "Get back in your place!"

He took a step back in line, but his heart was racing again.

♕ ♕ ♕

As Evangeline took him on a tour of her imagination, two guards followed them in and out of dreams and through the halls of the palace. They had lost the other children long ago to cakes and canapés and games and dances, but Andrew and Evangeline moved on to other worlds. When he saw the guards glance at their watches, he struggled against the sinking feeling in his stomach. Soon it would be midnight and their adventures would fade away. He would have to be a prince again, a whole other year, before he could lose himself in Evangeline's exotic lands once more.

"I know!" Her excitement pulsed through him. "Let's pretend you're the king of this kingdom, and I am a great lady with a beautiful blue horse!"

Andrew halted. Peter's words came back to him. "I don't want to be king. I want to be a fireman."

She furrowed her brows and cocked her head to the side. "Silly, if you're the king, you can be anything you want."

He shook his head. That wasn't true. "No, I can't, and I really don't want to be king. You be the queen and let me be a knight with the blue horse."

A gap-toothed smile creased her face as she reached for his hand. "You be the king, and I'll be your queen. You can ride our horse whenever you want, and you can put out all the fires in the kingdom, and I will rule while you're away."

He considered it for a moment. "You would be my queen?"

She nodded and squeezed his hand. "And you can always do whatever you want."

"Can I have a red horse like a fire engine?"

"You can have anything you want. You're the king!"

He closed his eyes and imagined riding upon a red steed with Queen Evangeline following on her blue horse. He smiled, feeling his cheeks grow warm. "I'd rather ride with you on your blue one."

She leaned into his ear and whispered, "Then let's go, my king."

♕ ♕ ♕

Tears burned Andrew's cheeks. The excitement that had filled him before the ball had melted into bitter loss. He was again alone in his massive room. Maybe if he closed his eyes and drifted off to sleep, he would be transported back to his kingdom with Evangeline, and they could ride her blue horse through the forests—laughing, singing, dancing—and maybe this time, just maybe, he would never wake up.

ᛞ Chapter Two ᚲ

(Five Years Later)

Andrew carefully tied his tie for the fourth time—it still wasn't right. Why had he not been more attentive when old Alfred—his steward or tutor or whatever he was exactly—had explained the various twists and turns necessary for a perfect uniform? Had Alfred ever been in the military? Of course he had. Every male in Braisognia was required to serve. Andrew chuckled. He couldn't imagine the man holding a gun and crawling in trenches.

There went the yelling again. He wondered if all families were like that. Recently, it seemed as though George could do nothing right, and his father constantly berated him regardless of how small the issue. Andrew tried to ignore the present argument, but George's room was next to his, and he had left the door slightly ajar when he had gone in to see if his brother would help him with his tie. George had yelled and told him to leave his room, so Andrew had crept back softly.

"I will not!" the eldest brother yelled loud enough for every word to be clearly heard.

Andrew crept to the door hoping to shut it completely. This was his favorite night of the year and he didn't want the sounds of a restless eighteen year-old and a disapproving father to haunt his evening. He wanted only pleasant thoughts when he saw Evangeline. He longed to escape again.

"You have no valid reason to do this!" his father bellowed.

"I am a human being! That is my reason!"

"You are a prince and first in line to this kingdom! I will not allow you to walk out on this—your duty, your legacy and your destiny!"

"I don't want this destiny! I don't want to be king! I never have wanted it!"

"It is not a matter of want!" he thundered. "It is a matter of duty and honor!"

"I am not a man of duty! I am my own man!"

Silence. Andrew wanted to shut the door, but the deafening quiet after such a storm would magnify the sound of its closing. He even held his breath hoping they wouldn't notice him slinking in its crack.

Finally his father spoke. "You are no man." Andrew knew he was gritting his teeth by the sound of his voice. It happened often lately. "You are a spineless, dishonorable snake."

"Call me what you want," George conceded, "but you will not call me king."

More silence.

"You don't deserve to wear that uniform," Christopher continued. "You're nothing more than a traitor. I should make you take it off before you face the crowd tonight who believes you'll be crowned their next ruler, but you still have to serve your two years. Maybe that will make a man of you yet."

"I don't intend to serve either."

This statement scared Andrew. He braced himself for an explosive reaction. Every man had to give two years to the military either after high school or college. Anyone refusing to do so would be imprisoned.

But the king remained controlled. "Surely I don't have to remind you that you have no choice in this."

Andrew couldn't breathe. He couldn't imagine George would go to prison rather than give his two years.

"When I complete high school I plan to leave the country … for good."

The conversation had softened, but the young boy was worried. He needed to hear whatever was said next. Moving his head to the split in the door, he tried to see his father or George. Neither was in his line of vision.

"If you leave," Christopher seethed, "you can never return. You wouldn't do that to your mother."

George took a deep breath. "I don't want to, but there is no other option for me. I'm a pacifist. I don't believe in war or guns or bombs. If there were none, there would be no war."

"It would seem you have stuck your proverbial head in the sand. There are guns and bombs and wars. And if we do not protect our nation from these vile things, then we will be overrun by them. This strip of land is priceless and strategically located in the eyes of the world. Every power would love nothing more than to overtake us and force us to become a military buffer on this continent. I don't fight because I want to fight. I fight because I don't want to fight. I fight to protect what is the personification of peace. I prepare for war to keep war from invading this peaceful soil, this peaceful kingdom. I have no desire to kill, but I have no desire to be killed or to see my countrymen killed."

"Then don't!" George pleaded. "Stop the fighting! Make treaties ... or do whatever it takes to stop the fighting!"

Andrew heard steps and then the sound of the door opening before his father said one last thing.

"This is whatever it takes, George. I wish the whole world thought as you do, but it doesn't. We will forever have enemies desiring to rip away our freedom, and I intend to make sure that never happens. I'm sorry I somehow raised you to be so blind and selfish that you can't grasp that."

"Don't be," George said snidely. "You ... didn't raise me. The generals and tutors and coaches raised me. Perhaps that's why I find it so hard to believe as you do. I've never actually heard from your own mouth until today why you've always been such a warmonger. Had you taught me that on your knee while growing up, it might have been more believable and a little easier to swallow than it is right now."

There were no more words. The king left the room, and the sound of the door echoed a boom throughout the hallway. Andrew eased his own door shut and trudged slowly back to the mirror, attempting the tie once more. He wondered if he would really leave. He knew George hated their father, but he adored their mother. Could he walk away and leave the family forever because he detested one more than he loved the other?

♛ ♛ ♛

"Show me your room," Evangeline whispered as they walked through the empty corridors later that night.

"Really?" Andrew couldn't imagine why she would want to see his room.

"Yes," she beamed. "It would be so grand to see a prince's bedroom."

He shrugged. "If you really want to—there's nothing very interesting there."

She followed him closely as he led her through the twists and turns to his room. Had he put all his things away? Was his closet door shut? Were the pillows arranged on his bed? What if she needed to use the restroom? Had he put the seat down? He had heard women laughingly complain about men not doing that. Of course he hadn't put the seat down! He was the only person who ever used his restroom. He halted.

"What's wrong?" she asked, nearly running into him.

He peeked back at her. "You don't have to use the restroom, do you?"

"No, silly," she giggled. "Why?"

He sighed with relief. "It's just up here—my bedroom, I mean."

The last hallway seemed to go on forever. He, George and Peter all had bedrooms on this floor along with a small gym where they were required to do hours of strenuous workouts each week. Andrew walked up to his door and hesitated. Suddenly he felt as though he was being invaded. This was his room, his abode. Few seldom came in here. His mother would stop by on occasion to sit and talk with him. George and his father never entered the room. Alfred, whatever Alfred was, often came to the door to fetch him for his lessons or a meal, but seldom did he enter. The maids came in regularly, but they wouldn't speak socially to him. They would curtsey and ask his permission to clean the room, to which he always agreed, then leave immediately when they finished. Peter used to come in often, but he seldom did anymore.

"Are you alright?" Evangeline asked as they paused before his door.

"I don't know. I've never brought anyone in here before … not a friend … you know … no one like that. My guitar teacher came in here once, but that's all."

"Good," she smiled at him. "I like being special."

That was all the encouragement he needed, because she indeed was special. He opened the door, reached for the light, and proudly motioned her into the expanse.

"Wow," she breathed out softly. "It's so big." She gazed over at him. "Everything in this building is so big."

Building—that was not a word he had ever used for the palace. That made it sound cold and uninteresting. She strolled around and took in all the details, not touching anything as though she were in an expensive shop. For some reason he really wanted her to like it. It seemed important that she be pleased. She looked out the windows, each one, and finally reached out her fingers to run them across pieces of furniture. It was almost as if she was absorbing the room into her mind.

"What do you think?" he asked hesitantly. She wasn't smiling, but she wasn't frowning. He was desperate to know if she approved.

"I don't know. I guess I expected that since you were a prince, you could decorate it any way you wanted."

He was confused. "I have a tree," he told her as he pointed near the sitting area of the massive room toward a ten-foot decorated Christmas tree.

"I don't mean holiday decorations," she smiled. "I guess I thought you would have forests painted on your walls and blue horses. I imagined you would escape in here from the rest of the building, and it would be your special hideaway where the real you could play and run away."

Escape? There was no escape here in the palace. Every minute of every day was scheduled. Escape was sleep, not play. The closest thing to play Andrew ever did was mock battles during training sessions. And even then there were no children … just Andrew and five military personnel who would play exaggerated forms of hide and seek.

"Are your walls painted?" he wondered.

She smiled big and nodded. "I have purple skies and butterflies. I imagine that they can carry me wherever I want to go. Sometimes they even bring me here to see you, but I never thought of your room like this." She turned back at him. "It will be ..." she hesitated, "... hard to come fly back here again."

"No!" he nearly panicked. "Don't stop! Just keep pretending it looks like you always wanted it to look!"

She shook her head. "I want to, but I don't think I can." Her smile began to fade. "It looks like everywhere else in this building. I didn't think you ... well ..." She grew silent.

Suddenly his eyes grew wide. "I know!" he called to her in excitement. "There is a special place I go sometimes! I could take you there!"

"A secret place?" she asked in awe.

"Very secret."

"I want to see it! Maybe I can fly there?"

"It has a window." He was animated as he tried to describe it. "A very big window in a very strange room. You and your butterflies could come right in."

He motioned her to follow him and then walked quickly in and out of hallways. When he turned down the last hall, he bubbled with anticipation. A small set of stairs stood out alone in the corridor leading up to a door that was half-size. Perhaps a three year-old could walk through it, but they would have to duck and crawl. His heart pounded.

"You'll like this place," he whispered as he climbed the steps and reached up to open the half-door. "Wait." He stuck his hand into his pocket and pulled out his phone. "There's no lights. This will get us through the little tunnel, and then the light from the window will be enough when we get inside."

Evangeline pulled the bulk of her fancy dress up above her knees so she could crawl through the dark passage with more ease. They crept about six feet before the room opened up. When she finally emerged, she gasped in delight. "It's amazing!"

The room was nothing more than leftover space from when the palace had been added onto. It was small, and there were no straight walls or floors or ceilings. Everything was angled in some strange way, and she marveled at its oddness. The window was indeed large and beautiful, and rays poured into the room from the floodlights surrounding the palace. When Andrew saw her expression, he crossed his arms proudly and began beaming.

"Can you fly here?" he asked as she walked carefully on the angled floor to the window.

"Absolutely!" Her eyes were wide with wonder. "Every night maybe."

"Really?" He couldn't believe his luck.

"But only at night," she said with a serious look. "People would see me come in the daytime and give our hiding place away."

"Not if you flew from the forest." He pointed back toward the thick woods beyond the palace grounds.

She looked back at him. "You're right. I could come anytime!"

She gazed around and noticed a few plastic animals and figures lying around the small room. She reached down and picked up a small horse that had been colored blue with a marker. She smiled.

"My horse," she said as she held it up to the window. "I never thought of coloring one blue. I just always imagined it to be that way."

"Then take it with you," he insisted. "I can color another one." He shyly looked away. "And maybe you could ride your blue horse over sometime and still be my queen ... if you wanted."

Suddenly a loud pounding echoed through the room.

"Mr. Andrew!" yelled Alfred's familiar voice. "Are you in there, sir? We lost you!"

Andrew rolled his eyes, but Evangeline panicked.

"They've found our secret room," she said with deep disappointment. "We can never be alone now."

Andrew looked at her and set his jaw like he often saw his father do. "Yes, we can. I am the king of this room, and you are the queen. If I say we are to be alone, then we can be alone."

She cocked her head to the side again and began to grin.

"Alfred," Andrew called out as he got on his knees and yelled through the passage. "I am in here and I want to be left alone."

"But what of Miss Evangeline?" Alfred questioned. "Is she with you?"

Andrew looked to her. If she wanted to be kept secret, he would lie for her. He would do anything for her.

She dropped down beside him and shouted into the passageway, "I'm here too, and we'll be out in a minute. We've found a dreadful dragon and King Andrew has injured him horribly. If we can heal him now, he will forever be indebted to us, and he will protect us from the other terrible creatures in this palace. Can you not be patient just a little while and give us time to possibly save the kingdom?"

There was a stretch of silence as the children waited. Andrew raised his eyebrows as the quiet drew on.

"Uh, yes, Miss Evangeline," Alfred said.

"That would be *Queen* Evangeline," Andrew reminded him.

"Oh, okay," Alfred stammered. "Queen Evangeline and King Andrew, you may remain with your ... um ... your dragon for a little while longer, but I fear your presence will be missed in the um ... ballroom ... should you delay a long while."

Evangeline smiled at her king.

"Very well, Alfred," Andrew yelled back. "We'll try to speed up the process, but dragons can be very hard to get along with when they've been hurt."

"I understand, sir, but fathers can be very hard to get along with when their children have been lost."

♉ ♉ ♉

For the first time Andrew could remember, he didn't cry after the ball. Even as his clock registered two thirty in the morning, his head was still spinning from the memories. He would now have a special place to go to escape, and he knew Evangeline would be there whenever he wanted, even if it was only in his mind.

For the first time Evangeline could remember, her father didn't carry her into her room from the limousine and put her to bed after the late Christmas ball. She walked up the steps to their home then down the hall to her room. She gently took the blue-colored horse and set it on the stand beside her bed.

"I will fly to you every day, King Andrew, and we will meet in our special room."

She lazily closed her eyes and imagined that she had mounted her strong, blue steed. She then whispered softly as she felt her body drifting, "To the palace, dear steed, to see my friend again."

❧ Chapter Three ❧

(Five Years Later)

Andrew should have felt proud as he stared into the mirror. His uniform now held several medals and colors, evidence of his proficiency in areas that made his father beam. He had tied his tie perfectly in only a matter of seconds. His thick hair had grown down past his neck, and many a magazine had commented on how his dark, wavy locks had set him apart as the most handsome of the Braisognian princes. He had anticipated his father complaining about its length, but all he noted was that it would come off when he served his duty. "Let him enjoy looking like a pretty girl all he wants right now. The military will make a man of him one day."

Every other Christmas he had been overcome with excitement. This was still his favorite night of the year. He knew as soon as formalities were over, he and Evangeline would eat quickly, perhaps grab a couple of dances, and then sneak off to their secret room to catch up on the past year. If he had been a normal teenager he could have called or texted or e-mailed her. But he was not a normal anything, and now his life was about to change in ways he had never imagined, never hoped for, in fact, in ways he had only feared. He would have to tell her, but he wondered if he was even allowed. Years of royal living had taught him that many things were never to be spoken of, but he had always told her everything—only her. She was, in truth, his only friend.

But could he tell her this? Should he tell her this? He hated his family right now for dropping this on him right before the Christmas Ball. Why not tomorrow or after the holidays? Why had he been sitting in the same room when the argument had begun? He had planned to leave earlier to shower and dress in anticipation of the night, but when Peter walked in, he wanted to spend a few moments around his often absent brother. Little did he know how those moments would drastically change his life.

Andrew joined his mother, father and Peter in the corridor behind the massive doors. No one was speaking, not even Julia. He could tell she had been crying, and he dare not ask why. He knew. He could have cried himself, but had discovered long ago that crying accomplished nothing except to give his father another reason to be angry with his weakling sons. The youngest prince had learned to manage pain, both mental and physical, in amazing ways. The king had voiced that he believed he was truly the strongest of the Braisogn boys, but Andrew knew differently.

Christopher impatiently glanced at his watch and fisted his hands in frustration. George and his wife, Lynette, had not shown yet. Andrew almost wished they wouldn't, for that would be one more pound of stress to add to the already tense situation. He had feared George would leave the country and never return, but Julia somehow convinced him there were other ways to serve in the military besides fighting, and he was free to abdicate the throne if he truly did not want to rule. So George kept records during his two years, refused the crown, and married Lynette of non-royal blood, all of which made it clear that Peter was now to be king.

"There they are," Julia whispered in relief. "I told you they would be here."

"I didn't doubt their coming," Christopher scorned. "I doubted their coming on time."

"And in both cases you were wrong," she countered as she went to greet her oldest son and his very pregnant wife.

The doors were finally opened, the family was announced, and they marched in regally with Julia two paces behind her husband. Andrew graciously took his place at the end of the receiving line and bowed and smiled and shook hands and hugged, but tonight there was no joy in his heart. In fact, he was so oppressed by the turn of events that he almost wished he could go back to his room and go to bed. But then he saw her.

Evangeline looked more like her mother each year, the beauty that stole the heart of a royal and forever doomed him to a life without pure honor. Giselle Montevo's mother, Evangeline's grandmother, had been one of only a handful to break the ranks of blood lines with an affair, and the first to ever marry outside the royal families. It didn't take long for all to realize she had been pregnant, and that the marriage was simply the result of a tawdry relationship with a non-royal. The royals felt she deserved the scorn and disgrace it had brought upon her. However, Giselle, the daughter of that union, was a bit of a paradox for the upper crust. Because she was half-royal and half common, no one knew how to draw the lines as to where she could and could not go. Fortunately for Giselle, she found the royal life to be arrogant, pretentious and distasteful. Rather than care if royalty accepted her, she chose to give her life helping the needy, the orphaned, and those much less fortunate than she ever imagined being. This was great for the royal side of the kingdom. They didn't have to ignore her because she just disappeared into a commoner's life. During high school she spent all her time working and volunteering for centers and camps for the impoverished, and she deliberately chose a commoner's college rather than attempt to attend one of the elite royal universities. All was simple and easy until James Dorvain entered the scene.

James was a promising royal and masterful law student at the most elite university in the kingdom. Even though his plans were to become a personal lawyer for hire, his ability was so amazing that the military offered him incredible rewards if he would promise to study and work for them once his education was complete. He loved the military, and even more, he loved military law. All was moving well until he took a field trip while in a class on handling issues dealing with the many fatherless children of Braisognia. It was then that he met who many had called the most beautiful maiden in the kingdom—Giselle Montevo. He had heard of her before, the child scorned, her unmatched beauty, and how sad the royals were that she could never be a part of *their world* because of her mother's impure marriage. But it only took the first of six weeks volunteering by her side with the unfortunate orphaned children for James Dorvain to realize that this woman, royal or not, was the most incredible creature he had ever met. By the end of the summer, they married. Again, a royal, James Dorvain, and a non-royal, a commoner, Giselle Montevo, had allowed the blood lines to become polluted … lines which had been held firm for centuries.

It had been quite a scandal, and the entire kingdom buzzed that Giselle had become pregnant. Surely that would be the only reason for James to give up his honor and the honor of his future children over a woman. They admired him for his integrity, but when their first child, Evangeline, was born six years later, the rumor mongers realized that indeed it must have been the love he so fiercely professed for her.

At forty her beauty had not faded an ounce, and even though many looked down on James for marrying out of the royal line, no one doubted why any longer. However, their only child, Evangeline, was now the subject of many discussions. James—greatly respected and needed as the chief counsel for the military and all its dealings—was a man everyone wanted to keep above reproach. He was still invited to royal events and treated with all the respect of royalty. No one dared speak to him of Giselle being common, but it was spoken among the royals plenty. And as Evangeline matured, the dilemma of how the royal lines should treat her was growing also. She was allowed to stay in private royal schools during her primary and now secondary education, but what would happen when the time came for college? So far, no commoner had ever been allowed into a royal university. And though Evangeline was not fully common, she was most definitely not fully royal.

For the first time ever in the family of a king, George Braisogn had done the same. He didn't have to formally abdicate the throne. His marriage to Lynnette officially made him no longer eligible to rule. Thus, the crown now went to the second in line—impulsive Peter Braisogn. Many royals, including the king himself, believed that the blame could be partially placed on Giselle's mother who deliberately chose to have an illicit relationship and then marry outside of her pure bloodline. James Dorvain received the rest of the blame for choosing to marry Giselle, officially a non-royal. Thus Evangeline was now a poison for any red-blooded male nobleman. Her beauty matched her mother's, and she continually rubbed elbows with those of pure royal breeding.

As the line passed, Andrew only had eyes for Evangeline. As soon as he caught her gaze, she smiled, waved, and motioned behind their backs for her parents to move on. The corners of his mouth turned up slightly and he was glad now that he was here—the earlier events of the day could almost be erased. When she finally reached him, he wished she would throw her arms around him and hug him tightly, but they gave each other the proper greeting.

"There's something wrong with you tonight," she noted gently as she leaned in. "I can see it all over your face. You will tell me, won't you?"

"Perhaps I just had a bad lunch."

She frowned as she gazed into his eyes. "Are you okay?"

"We'll talk later," he told her as he edged closer so Peter wouldn't hear. "But we must be careful this time."

She smiled and all his fears melted as she said, "Aren't we always, my king?"

He swallowed hard as his father scowled at the exchange. He imagined the king was thankful the two only saw each other once a year.

Andrew could barely stomach the dinner. He was not a fan of fowl, and he disliked pheasant the most. Then at times like tonight, when his insides were tied in millions of knots, just the thought of eating the bird made him nauseous. The fruits were delicious, and he had twice asked a waiter to bring him another helping. The third time the server wanted to hesitate, and Andrew realized he was requesting something already prepared to fill a plate not yet served—yet the prince was asking. How would one tell him that only so many helpings of food per person had been made, and he had already taken two more than what was allotted him? He blushed in humiliation.

"Here," Evangeline said as she pushed her plate beside his. "Give me your bird and you can have my fruit. My mother hates pheasant so we never eat it—I love it. I'll gorge myself on it so it will last me the year, and you can continue your practice tonight of playing vegetarian."

"Thank you," he said genuinely as he scraped the fruit from her plate. "I don't care if I ever eat pheasant again."

"I'll tell my mother that in case you ever come to visit. She won't try to impress you by cooking something so elaborate."

"She cooks?" he asked in surprise. "Your mother?"

"Of course!" She laughed. "Well, at least most of the time, especially at night. Does your mother never cook?"

Now Andrew laughed. "Are you serious? Julia? Cook?"

She just shrugged as she took the pheasant from his plate and dragged it to hers. "I thought all women cooked. It's fun actually."

"Do you cook?"

"Of course. In fact, there are many nights that all three of us are in the kitchen preparing different things for the meal. It's kind of a fun family thing."

He couldn't imagine a family doing anything fun, especially cooking. No one in his family even went into a kitchen. "What kind of things do you cook?"

She shook her head. "I can't believe it's been a whole year since I've seen you and we're sitting here talking about cooking … especially when I know there's something really huge you have to tell me."

Reality was back. It was indeed huge, and he needed to get the burden off his chest. Somehow she had the ability to turn his mountains into blessings, and he was hoping beyond hope that she could this time too.

"Eat your fruit, royal boy," she nudged him as she took her fork and picked at the bird. "Then we'll hope for a decent song to dance to, and I can follow you through this crazy maze of a palace to our secret room."

Thankfully the band was good about playing a wide variety of music, and it wasn't long before a popular song all the kids loved was starting. Evangeline didn't wait for Andrew to suggest a dance. As the teenagers and older kids began to flood the floor, she grabbed his hand and pulled him from the table.

"I take it we're dancing now?" he asked as she towed him toward the front of the room.

"Well, I am," she said glancing back, "with or without you."

He did like the song and knew it well. Music was about the only contact he had with the real world beyond the palace walls. In fact, music was his escape. But the only dancing Andrew had ever been taught was ballroom dancing. And though there was plenty of that offered tonight, the teenagers never joined. As others all around danced with freedom and glee to the song, he felt self-conscious and out of place. He looked up to his guitar teacher, the lead singer and guitarist for the band, and the man smiled with a nod to assure him he looked fine. Mr. Skantar knew Andrew's insecurities, and he was almost as much a counselor as a tutor.

When the song finished, the younger crowd cheered with delight. They all assumed the band would play another pop song since they were out there waiting, but instead, Mr. Skantar began to talk.

"I suppose you're all wanting a little more of that, huh?" he asked with a silly grin.

The group screamed in agreement.

"How about we try something really bold?"

They yelled out again.

"Bet you didn't know this," he said as he took off his guitar, "but one of your Braisognian princes happens to be quite the guitarist."

The crowd cheered again, but Andrew could feel his face growing warm. Mr. Skantar had asked him just this week during his lesson what was the point of learning to play if he never performed. He had agreed but said he went nowhere that he could play, so what was the point of discussing it. It never occurred to him that the man would make an opportunity.

"He already looks like a rock star with all that pretty black hair," the teacher continued.

Now the crowd knew the prince to which he was referring.

"I'll bet if you'd just give him a little encouragement, you could get him to come up here and dazzle you with quite a proficient performance of *Save Your Love*. His voice isn't half bad either."

The girls screamed, but Evangeline gave him a warm smile. She drew herself beside him and spoke above the crowd. "Here's your chance, prince. Dazzle us."

He shook his head as his hands grew clammy. "I'm not ready to play in public. I never planned to play in public. This could be extremely humiliating."

"Or it could be amazingly exhilarating."

He knew his eyes gave away his fear.

"Don't play for them then," she said directly into his ear. "Just play for me. I promise you, no matter what happens, I will be dazzled."

"Andrew! Andrew! Andrew!" the crowd chanted as Mr. Skantar encouraged the frenzy.

He knew at this point if he declined it would be humiliating for everyone. He couldn't see his father, but he could imagine his expression. He really had no choice. He looked at Evangeline, and she simply nodded and mouthed the words, "Dazzle me, prince—dazzle me."

He threw his hands into the air and walked toward the stage. The crowd screamed even louder. If he totally blew it, then he blew it. He had played and sang the song again and again, and if he couldn't do it out here in front of this crowd, just like Mr. Skantar said, what was the point?

His teacher shook his hand and handed him a guitar as he said, "You can do this. You've played for years, Andrew. Let your father see there's more to you than guns and uniforms."

He nodded, not with confidence, but with hope that if his teacher believed in him enough to do something this public, then surely he could do it. He placed the guitar around his neck, tuned the low string to a drop D, and then looked out toward the crowd.

"You do realize," he told them, "that I've never in my life played with a band?"

"You rock, Andrew!" yelled a girl from the floor.

"That has yet to be decided," he chuckled into the microphone. The crowd laughed with him.

"Count it off, I guess," he said as he looked back at the drummer.

"One … two … three … four …"

And the song began.

Christopher Braisogn watched nervously as his son calmly handled the crowd during this moment of total surprise and awkwardness. He could care less about his guitar playing or his singing. It was the manner in which Andrew approached it that astonished him. The boy, only fifteen, was humble, yet displayed a likeable quality as he faced the people—making the crowd want to hear him all the more. As the music began, however, and he began to glide his fingers effortlessly around the strings, the king realized for the first time how extraordinary this son truly was. This was a boy who was not only studious, not only strong in military prowess and physical conditioning, but had an artistic and gentle side that endeared him to the people. If allowed to be king, Andrew Braisogn could quite possibly be the ruler to go down in history as the most loved and cherished king ever of this kingdom.

🎖 🎖 🎖

Sneaking from the ballroom proved to be a bigger challenge than before as everyone sought out the prince to tell him how wonderful his performance had been. He finally noticed Evangeline motioning to him from one of the side doors, making sure he saw her leave. He then excused himself to the restroom, left through the same side door, and found her waiting just outside.

"I would have gone on," she said as they hurried down one of the halls, "but I had no idea where to even start trying to find that room. I couldn't find a bathroom here if the signs didn't point it out."

"We'd better hurry," he said turning down another corridor. "People will start looking for us any minute now."

"Us?" she laughed. "There isn't anyone in there looking for me!"

"Lucky you."

He led her through a few unexpected doors and hallways in an attempt to stay away from main areas where someone might spot them. At last they rounded the final corner that held the steps leading up to the half door.

"You go first," she told him, out of breath from the run. "If someone sees me standing out here it won't matter."

He leapt up all four steps in one jump and flung open the door. Quickly dropping to his knees, he began the crawl through the short passage to the oddly shaped room. Once inside, he leaned against the straightest wall he could find next to the window. He heard the outer door shut and then the rustling of layers on her clothing as she made her way through the tunnel.

"Whew," she breathed out, plopping down beside him trying to catch her breath. "I think we made it. In fact, I didn't even see security back there."

He grinned and shook his head. "They're there ... somewhere. I guarantee the cameras followed us and someone has reported our exact destination ... as if they didn't already know."

"Cameras?" Her eyes grew wide. "We're being watched by cameras?" She searched the dimly lit room.

"Not in here. It wouldn't be worth the effort. Plus, I think ... at least I hope ... that the staff believes I should have a little privacy now and then. No cameras in my room, no cameras here. They're havens, more or less."

"Thank goodness," she said doubtfully, still looking around uneasily. At last she turned her attention to him and smiled. "That was pretty amazing."

He shrugged. "Escaping? Or are you referring to your incredible feat of crawling through a hole with layers of taffeta?"

She lightly punched him. "No, silly, I'm talking about you. What you did back there was very amazing."

He hoped she couldn't see him blushing but knew his expression had to show self-consciousness.

"You definitely dazzled me," she reached to his chin and lifted his head. "You dazzled everyone in there."

He sighed and shook his head. "So what?" he said in a defeated tone.

"So what? I had no idea you were such a fine musician. I knew you played and sang, but I wasn't prepared for that. I'm serious—you dazzled us tonight."

He leaned his head against the wall and closed his eyes. "But what does it matter? My music isn't what I'll be remembered for ... not what I'm being groomed for."

"You don't know that. You're really quite exceptional. And I should know! I go to a privileged school where kids pay unbelievable amounts of money to take lessons ... and I've never heard any of them come close to what you did up there tonight. You can be whatever you want!"

"Right ... if only ..."

"Come on. Stop pouting. You did great!"

"I'm not pouting!" he blurted out from frustration.

She looked at him more in surprise than shock.

"Well, maybe I am, but not for the reasons you think. I'm not pouting because I feel like I did a lousy job. I'm ... well ... pouting, I suppose, because that can never be me. I can't fulfill that part of my life."

"For crying out loud, Andrew, you're a prince! You can do anything you want."

He sighed heavily. "Apparently that isn't to be my destiny."

She leaned against one of the crooked walls and crossed her arms. "Something's happened—that's what you wanted to tell me when I first saw you tonight, isn't it?"

He nodded and closed his eyes in emotional weariness. He knew this conversation shouldn't be taking place, but he was on immeasurable overload from its reality, and he needed a sympathetic ear, not another person telling him that to fulfill his duty was an honor.

"Peter had a meeting with Mother and Father this afternoon. I had the misfortune of being there too," he began. "It's hard to believe a person's life can change so fast within a matter of minutes. He didn't even beat around the bush. He just spat out that his girlfriend, Kayla, was pregnant, that he intended to marry her, and that he too would be abdicating the throne."

She gasped, "What? You're not joking, are you?"

"I wish. Father immediately began offering alternatives. I couldn't believe the things he was saying. His first suggestion was abortion."

"But that's illegal in Braisognia."

He smirked. "Nothing is illegal when you're king. Sad statement isn't it."

"Well, I hate to say it, but if you've got the money, it's readily available. I know some girls who ... well ... anyway."

"Peter would have nothing to do with that."

"Good for him."

"Then Father suggested that Peter keep her—you know, set her and the baby up in a luxurious apartment somewhere, give her some kind of allowance, basically hush money, and then he marry a royal."

"That is the stupidest law in this whole kingdom! It has caused my parents so much grief!"

"It's causing me plenty of grief right now! I have two brothers, heirs to the throne ahead of me, who literally gave up the crown over it."

She reached over, took his hand, and squeezed it hard. "I know this sounds crazy—and please don't take it the wrong way—but who would have ever thought that you would be king ... third in line? Now that's unheard of."

"No heir in the eight hundred year history of Braisognia has ever abdicated, much less married a non-royal, and now it's happened twice in the same generation."

He found comfort with his hand in hers. She understood. No one else could imagine what a horrible turn of events this was for him. Most would perceive it as a stroke of luck, but for Andrew this was his worst nightmare coming true. All he had ever looked forward to was one day having a normal life, a life away from the microscope, a life where he was free to roam and explore and express himself anyway he wanted. He dreamed of a life where his words weren't weighed, his actions weren't based on ridiculous and ancient protocol, where he could plan his own days, do as he pleased, and never worry about making a massive blunder that would be plastered across the pages of the nation's tabloids.

She finally broke the long silence. "The press will have a field day with this—the second royal in one family to give up the throne. Peter is gonna cause a big ruckus."

"Yeah ... I know." He ran his fingers threw his long locks. "And then every eye will turn ..." he didn't finish the sentence—he just pointed to himself. "What will the last prince do?"

Still holding his hand, she now cupped it with her other one. "He'll do just fine."

He slowly turned his head to look at her, holding back the tears burning his eyes.

"Andrew, look at the positive."

He raised his eyebrows.

"You have the opportunity to change this kingdom for the better, to write history here, for Braisognia, and perhaps even the world. You'll have the power that no other individual here can have. Thousands would pay untold sums to trade places with you, but they can't. And the reason is clear—God has chosen you, my friend, to take this role."

He shut his eyes again and let his head fall back against the wall. This was one area they did not agree on—God. The royal family was very religious, but Evangeline took it to a deeper level than he had ever known. She believed God was more personal than ethereal, and she had often encouraged him to read Scripture for himself to discover who God really was.

"I would love to argue with you there," he confessed, "but I won't, because it seems that too many impossibilities have happened in order to put me in this position." He looked at her soberly. "That doesn't make me very pleased with God if it's the case—I don't want to be king."

"You're like David," she smiled sweetly. "He was a gentle heart, a musician, a sensitive and compassionate spirit. Most would have chosen any one of his older brothers as king, but God chose David because of his heart. Perhaps that's why God has chosen you."

22

Again there were tears skirting the edge of his eyes. She squeezed his hands and offered an assuring smile. "You'll make a wonderful king."

He shook his head doubtfully.

"I promise." Her confidence seemed unshakeable. "I know you will. You may not see it yet, but I've seen it all along."

✺ Chapter Four ✺

(Four Months Later)

Utterly exhausted, Evangeline left her car and climbed the steps to the portico of her house. Tennis practice had been brutal. In fact, if she could, she would quit. Days like today made it no fun. She liked playing, but she hated competition. Even more, she hated when the coach became angry because of a loss and forced them to practice and drill to the point of misery. She would love to leave the sport altogether, but her father would never allow it. His motto was that once you started something, you finished—you never quit. It was a noble thought and she knew he would never back down. She resigned herself to two more years of torment under the coach whom all her teammates referred to as *Hitler* behind her back.

"Hey, sweetheart," her mother called out as she walked inside. "Did you have a good day?"

"No," she said frankly. "And you?"

"Well, apparently it was much better than yours. Want to talk about it?"

"Just tennis," she grunted as she dropped her gym bag and book satchel beside the table. "Enough said."

Her mother nodded and handed her an envelope. "You got something from the palace today. It looks official."

Evangeline took the envelope and examined the outside carefully. "Pretty color." She slid her finger beneath the seal and opened it with no enthusiasm. She couldn't imagine it being something genuinely important. Perhaps congratulations for making straight A's again or for leading her tennis team to participate in the national competition. The palace was good about recognizing their youth for outstanding achievements. She pulled out the card and walked over to the light to read the fancy, embossed writing.

"Wow," she said slowly as she read silently.

"Really? Wow?" her mother asked curiously. "What is it?"

24

"Apparently Prince Andrew is going to have a big sixteenth birthday bash, and I made the list."

Her mother frowned. "What's the date? You'll probably have a tennis meet."

"Oh gee, let's see—a day in the heat hitting my brains out for the Third Reich or a chance to go to the palace and actually participate in something fun? I don't see your point there, Mother."

Giselle Dorvain didn't look amused. "Check your calendar before you R.S.V.P. You do have prior obligations in certain areas that should receive priority if they conflict."

"I won't miss Andrew's party. I'm sure he had to argue with Lucifer himself to get me invited. I won't disappoint him."

"You're not a royal, Evie." As if she ever needed reminding. "This will not be like the Christmas Ball where you can ride on your father's coattails. You'll be there on your own and people will …"

"I don't care about people."

"For heaven's sake, Evie …"

"I'll be there for Andrew." She was firm. "I'm his friend … his best friend … maybe even his only friend."

"But that's not by your personal choice. He's put you there, and it's not fair."

"But it's a fact. What would you have me do? Ignore him? Just leave him all alone because now he's going to be king and I'm only a half-breed? The rest of this kingdom can look at blood all they want, but I'll choose to look at the heart forever and always. Maybe one day someone will see the stupidity of this whole separation of classes and realize that people are people and every person should be valued for what they contribute and not who their parents are."

"Don't you think I, of all people, understand that? But matters of the heart can't always be controlled. I never meant to let your father fall in love with me! I pushed him away as hard as I could. But when someone loves you that deeply and that strongly … you can't … you don't just …" She paused and sighed. "You would give your life, your reputation, your everything for that kind of love."

Evangeline turned to the window, refusing to respond to her mother's words.

"You are beautiful, full of life, vivacious, enchanting, intelligent, and easy to talk to," Giselle continued. "How could anyone ever compete with that? Yet, at some point, he'll have to either turn away from you, or totally destroy the royal family and lineage. That's a burden, my dear daughter, you don't want to bear … even for the sake of love. I honestly can't stomach the thought of how all this can eventually hurt you … devastate you."

She looked back at her mother, her expression softer. "This isn't about me. Even if Andrew someday would actually choose me over the crown, I wouldn't allow it. I would never bring that kind of scorn on his name … his name … Andrew … not the stupid Braisogn royal family. He will one day make a great king and do great things for this nation, but right now his heart is tender, and his world is so small. My friendship is something he desperately needs to help him know who he is and what he can do and be." She clutched the envelope to her heart. "Because of that, I'll always be there for him … but I would never … never … marry him and cost him the crown."

Evangeline headed down the hallway and shut herself away in her room.

James Dorvain entered from the den where he had heard the whole conversation. "Why do you do that to her?"

Giselle shook her head. "All I want is to protect her. She thinks she's in control, and that one day she'll just let go of him and all will be fine."

"And maybe she will," he replied as he wrapped his arms around his wife. "She's a smart girl."

"With a huge heart—James, he will be king. He cannot marry her in any way, shape or form."

"And they both know that."

"But what you know and what you feel are totally different." She turned to him. "You should understand that better than anyone. Andrew is … remarkable. He's handsome and gentle and artistic … how do you find someone else to ever surpass that? He's all Evie could ever want but can never have. Every man that comes into her life after him will never be enough if she doesn't move on now … while she's still young … and not so deeply into it yet."

James knew his wife was right. He should have done the same thing with her. As soon as he realized he was attracted to her he should have moved on and never talked with her that second time. But something within her compelled him to go back again and again. It was so much more than her beauty. She captivated every inch of him, and finally he chose to forego the passing of his royal heritage for the love of a woman. It had been an unmatched scandal in the kingdom, and rumors were large after the marriage. Their greatest misfortune, Giselle's inability to conceive easily, had actually been their salvation. No one could imagine he would have married her for any other reason except pregnancy. But it took six years before Evangeline came, and after that they never conceived again.

"She'll be hurt," she breathed out sadly. "And it will go on and on and on. You don't forget a young man like Andrew Braisogn."

"We don't know that she loves him. She claims they're just friends, and now that she knows he'll be king and there's no hope for her, surely she'll guard her heart."

"Hmmm," she moaned as she buried her head into his shoulder. "You can't guard your heart, not really. You can disguise it perhaps, but you can never truly protect it. You just can't."

As she lay on her bed, Evangeline thoughtfully read through the invitation again and again. There was no way it could have been easy for him to get her invited. He must have made promises or threats to get his father to agree. She knew her mother was right—she should decline the invite, make up an excuse, and be done with the whole friendship. She also knew Amy and Jenna would be invited too, her best friends, and they would decline if she asked them. The three of them could have a non-birthday party and poke fun of the royals instead. As much fun as that seemed, the thought of devastating Andrew by refusing to go erased the idea completely. She couldn't deliberately hurt him—he lived with that every day of his life. No, she would go, so would Amy and Jenna, and they would dress up and laugh and pretend it was the party of a lifetime. And no one would suggest that she was giving just another piece of her heart away to a guy who could never fully accept it.

� ♟ ♟

"They're here," James called down the hall to his daughter. "The limo is pulling up the drive now. Do you need me to tell them to wait or are you ready?"

Evangeline had been especially nervous and attentive to her appearance for this party, and James was beginning to fear that perhaps his wife had been right—she felt more for Andrew than just friendship

"I'm ready!" she yelled from her bedroom. "I can't find my tote! Have you seen it, Daddy?"

Looking around the room he spied it on the breakfast table. "It's in here, Evie—on the table."

She burst through the door in a very unladylike manner, but the sight of her in that dress, long hair curled to perfection, make-up accentuating her naturally beautiful features, her father knew no girl tonight would compare. This was becoming a recipe for disaster. Giselle followed her, a more mature mirror of her daughter, but every bit as beautiful. And Evangeline, like her mother, had a heart and spirit that couldn't be matched. How could anyone possibly know her and not adore her? Well, that was easy. Just like her mother, she was not bred of full royal blood. Tonight there would be many whispers about her invitation, and like her mother, she would ignore them and chalk up the gossip to silly ignorance and inane traditions. The only problem was that Andrew Braisogn would see this vision step into the room, and like every other party, he would only have eyes for her. One day, however, those eyes would have to turn elsewhere in order for him to be king.

"Thank you, Daddy," Evangeline replied breathlessly as she ran for the table to grab her purse. "Do I look okay? Do you think this green is a good color?" She was rushing about and speaking purely from nerves.

Her father grabbed her arm and made her stop. "You look more beautiful than ever," he observed soberly. "I'm serious."

She paused and gazed into his face, her green eyes matching her dress perfectly. "Thank you." She hugged him and then began rushing again. "Don't wait up!" she yelled as she bounded for the door.

Her parents watched as she climbed into the limo with her two best friends and waved as it pulled away. They couldn't see through the glass but just assumed she was waving back. They sighed as the gate opened and let the long car pass.

"I'm worried," he confessed for the first time.

"No kidding."

♕ ♕ ♕

The forty-five minute ride to the palace for the three girls was filled with more excitement than usual which meant an abundance of giggling and yakking. Amy and Jenna were pure royals, and the fact that they were best friends with Evangeline gave the snobs a good subject they could always pontificate if nothing outright negative was happening in their world. Seeing that Evangeline was the only mixed-blood ever allowed to royal affairs, no one was sure how to handle her schooling. Royals went to private schools—commoners went to state schools. Evangeline was neither. To force her into a state school would be an insult to her father, a royal lawyer for the military. But to allow her into a private royal school would be … well … who knew because it had never been done. James Dorvain hadn't waited for a discussion or vote. When it was time for her to begin her education, he registered her for the most prestigious school in the kingdom, paid his fee for the first year, and that was that.

If only the rest of her life could have been that easy.

"Do you think you'll be able to sneak away again?" Jenna asked her with wide eyes and a knowing grin.

"Yes!" Amy chimed in. "To that weird little room you always go to!"

Evangeline shook her head. "I don't imagine we can get away with it tonight. He's going to be the center of attention. I'll probably be lucky if we even speak. In fact, I still can't believe I was invited. I'm sure he had to move heaven and earth to make it happen. You know every eye in the palace will be watching."

"Did the other two have sixteenth parties?" Jenna changed the subject.

She despised the fact that people judged her friend more on silly blood lines than personhood and character. There was no more wonderful creature in all of Braisognia than Evangeline Dorvain, and Jenna had no issue proclaiming that openly on a regular basis.

"I think Peter did," Amy tried to remember. "Isn't that the party where some of the kids got a little wild and started tying tablecloths to the top story banisters?"

Jenna cackled. "Yes! That's right! That was hilarious! I remember my sister talking about it!"

Evangeline remained quiet as they continued the banter. Jenna tried to keep things light, but she knew her friend was dwelling on whether or not she would get to speak with the prince. She knew it would be devastating if she was kept from him all night. No matter what, Jenna was determined to stay by her side and keep up the laughter, unless, of course, Andrew requested her presence elsewhere.

ဆာ Chapter Five ဿ

He had managed to avoid the military uniform. It had cost him favor with his father who had claimed he should be proud to wear it anywhere at any time, but Andrew was sick of it. The military had become his life since he was to eventually be its commander. Rather than fight it like George, he gave up to fate and immersed himself in the practices and disciplines. That alone made his father proud. He actually felt sorry for his brothers who never received any sort of acceptance from the king whatsoever. Their choices in abdicating and marriage had made them an anathema.

But tonight Andrew had no desire to think about the military or the kingdom or the crown or his destiny. He had only one thought on his mind—Evangeline. At Christmas she had been more beautiful than anyone he had ever seen in his life, even the ladies in magazines and the occasional movie he might be allowed to watch. But it wasn't just her beauty that captivated him, it was who she was. She was the one person in his world who seemed to understand him—the one person who could touch him somehow in places that others didn't know existed. She was almost like his missing piece. There was a part of her that completed the great void that sank down inside him when the maps and maneuvers and books and programs and protocol were put aside for a moment. She was always there, somehow floating inside his mind, telling him he was wonderful and capable and chosen. Sometimes her words were all that kept him from going crazy in this life that had been dictated to him.

He straightened the tie on his tux and reached for the paper laying on his dressing table which he had carefully prepared. He folded it, placed it gently in his inner pocket, and then patted it warmly. This was the only reason he had agreed to the party.

The young prince had insisted there be no receiving line. As hundreds of guests made their way into the party, he greeted as many as he could, but kept his eye open for only one. He had wanted to ask security to alert him when she arrived, but that would have raised havoc in the palace. Alfred had always reported their sneaking away during the Christmas balls, and Andrew had always received a reprimand for abandoning the great hall during the evening. If he set anyone on watch, his father would have probably found a way to thwart it and cause even greater confusion in the process. His only hope was to keep his eyes peeled toward the entrance and find her as soon as she entered the ballroom.

People were everywhere—teenagers were everywhere. Hardly any actually spoke to the prince since he knew so few personally. He wasn't schooled with them and wasn't allowed to participate socially in any way. He knew many guys from summer military maneuvers, but even then he was kept in his own quarters during the evening and night hours when most of the camaraderie occurred. A few nodded and spoke, but even at military camp they had to refer to him as his royal highness, so no one knew what to do with him on a personal level. He really didn't care. Socializing to him was just another game. If he needed to smile, he smiled, if he needed to bow, he bowed, if he needed to shake hands, shake, if he needed to carry on meaningless conversation for the sake of being polite, he was a master at it. But it all drained him to the point of headaches at night, and he was hoping with all that was in him that tonight there would be no headaches, only sweet memories of his sixteenth birthday being spent with the most beautiful girl in the world.

There she was! He watched as she entered the room at the top of the split staircase, having more elegance than any queen could exhibit. He immediately noticed the green of her dress would match the green in her eyes. Two girls were with her, obviously thrilled to be at the party, pointing out various decorations and amenities created specifically for this event. But Evangeline was different. She was poised, deliberate, and scanning the room. His heart stopped—was she looking for him?

He quickly made his way toward the entrance, following her with his eyes, hoping not to run into any one along the way. When she disappeared at the bottom of the stairs, he found himself praying that the girls wouldn't lead her quickly to some far away table where he would lose her forever in the night.

"Don't go far, Evangeline," he pleaded under his breath. "Please stay at the bottom—please don't run off."

He moved quicker now, not caring if he hit anyone or not. Most moved out of his way because they wouldn't know what to say to him anyway. He was more like an untouchable celebrity than a peer. Generally that bothered him, but tonight he was thankful. He stopped making eye contact and moved faster, hoping he would reach the stairs before she could be pulled away.

Boom! He had run into someone quite hard this time. He looked up immediately to apologize and nearly fell in a dead faint. Evangeline! "Hello," he managed to say. "I was hoping to find you before you …" He could say no more.

And as though she read his mind, she replied, "I wasn't going anywhere. I would have waited here all night if I had to."

He smiled in relief and just stared for a moment. She was a vision from somewhere out of this world, perhaps even heaven. Her beauty had doubled, if possible, since Christmas. He couldn't speak as he held her gaze.

The silence between them was awkward, so she smiled warmly, reached inconspicuously for his lapel and spoke into his ear, "I'm not sure what I should do. Am I here for you … or am I just here?"

He jerked himself into reality and remembered the paper in his pocket. He quickly opened his coat and pulled it out with shaking fingers, again praying they could pull this off. "Here." He handed it to her. "Try to leave around eight from the west entrance." He motioned his head toward the door knowing the palace always confused her. "I'll leave shortly after that and meet you there."

She clasped the paper tightly and put it inside her tote. "I'll do it," she smiled again with a wink.

"Ok," he nodded. "Eight."

"You'd better mingle," she suggested as she reached up and pretended to straighten his already perfect tie.

"I know."

She watched him slowly walk away and then took deep breaths to calm herself. This was crazy. She now realized this whole party was about her. He had found her and they would go off alone. He would pour out his heart to her—only her—and she would give even more of herself to him— just like every other time they were together. Then she would leave, again knowing there would be no future and no hope of anything other than secret meetings until they grew up and got on with their lives which would be a kingdom of blood apart.

"So what happened?" Jenna asked excitedly as she and Amy grabbed her and pulled her toward a table.

They sat and Evangeline reached into her purse for the folded paper.

"What did he say?" Amy wanted to know. "Come on! Tell us!"

"Hang on," she shushed them as she unfolded the note. Her smile grew.

"What is that?" Jenna asked. "A letter?"

She shook her head and grinned. "It's a map."

"To the secret room?" Jenna wondered as she scooted next to her to see.

"Exactly. I'm to leave at eight and then meet him there as soon as he can get away."

Amy nearly squealed. "Oh … my … gosh! This is unbelievable!"

Jenna grabbed Evangeline's arm and shook her head. "You'd better be careful. You know this can't lead to anything … serious."

Her eyes glanced between her friends and she slowly nodded. She knew, her friends knew, Andrew knew, the whole kingdom knew. "I'm just his friend," she tried to convince them as well as herself. "We all know that."

Amy took her hand. "No. We all wish we knew that, but the truth is …"

Evangeline put up her hand to silence the conversation. "I am his friend … and that's all I'll ever be."

"Right," Amy said doubtfully.

♛ ♛ ♛

Evangeline followed the map carefully, taking note of each direction he had written. She marveled how fluid and artistic his handwriting was. She had traced the letters with her own finger as she waited for eight o'clock. His instructions were very detailed, even down to certain scars on the floor or walls. Before long she was standing at the short stairs, staring at the small doorway that led to the room, or more aptly, that led to her heart.

"He's already there …" a voice spoke from behind her, "… waiting for you."

She turned abruptly. Alfred.

"You know this can't continue," he told her.

She hoped the startle had not cost her some composure. She wanted to quip something smart and sassy to him, but chose instead to simply smile and walk up the stairs. "Good night, Mr. Alfred," she offered with a wave as she closed the door behind her.

She caught her breath before crawling through the tunnel. Alfred always had a way of looking at her with marked disapproval. Of course she was used to that from most people she was around, but Alfred was more or less Andrew's protector. His disapproval could possibly bring consequences.

"You're here," Andrew grinned as he reached for her hand to help her through the opening. "I didn't think you'd ever come."

"You told me to leave at eight and that you'd be here later! And Alfred met me in the hallway before coming in. He sort of reminds me of an old buzzard."

He chuckled. "Me too. But I couldn't stand the boredom out there."

"You're kidding! You have the best band in the world playing your party and you're bored?"

He looked at her from a dim corner and sighed. "Yes"

She settled against one of the oddly angled walls and closed her eyes to collect her thoughts. "What are we doing here, Andrew?" She looked over at him and cocked her head to the side. "I probably shouldn't have come, but I couldn't bear not showing up after you managed to get me an invitation. I imagine you had to go through hell and back to get me invited."

He nodded, but still grinned. "You have no idea."

"Oh, yes, I do. I live my life every day. You only have to deal with it once a year, well, twice this year."

"I don't care—it's my birthday, and the only thing I could think of that I really wanted was to be with you again … for just a little while." He looked at her and his smile faded. "I need someone other than my father and the staff to tell me I can do this … that I can be king … someone I can trust." His eyes pleaded. "There's only you."

Her heart ached for him. Here was a boy who seemed to have it all, but the weight that it carried was too much for him to bear.

"Is that all you wanted?" she teased. "I can deliver that with no problem. Convincing you that you're the best man for the job is a no-brainer."

He folded his arms and leaned against the wall as he shook his handsome head. "How do you say that so easily? Is it because you really believe it or because you know that's what I need to hear." The disillusion in his voice was strong.

"Andrew, look at me."

He looked slowly and with great defeat.

"I would never, could never, lie to you. I respect you too much to do that. I have no desire to just tell you what you want to hear. I have nothing to gain from that."

Deep vulnerability shone in his eyes. "Why do you always come to me? Why do we cling to these meetings as though they were our very life?"

She shook her head. She was about to lie, the very thing she had just promised she would never do. "Not *we*, Andrew. *You. You* cling to them. I have a very full life outside this palace. I go to school, I play tennis, I attempt to play violin—rather pathetically—I go to church, I go to friends' houses and I cook and laugh and play with my parents. You, Andrew, are not my life." She tried to pretend it was true. "And you only live for these meetings because it connects you to something outside of your life. It won't always be like this."

She expected her words to hurt him, but they didn't seem to.

"I hope it won't," he admitted. "I hope someday I have other friends, but with you it's always been so easy. I couldn't imagine celebrating this birthday and you not being a part of it. I think it might have ruined my life if you hadn't showed."

"Well, I'm glad I came then," she reasoned lightly. "That's a heavy burden for someone to bear. I could have ruined your life?"

"Absolutely. So you probably just saved the kingdom, you know."

She snickered. "I feel the burden lifted then. Glad to know I've been of some good tonight."

They sat in silence for awhile and basked in being together again. No matter what she had just said, they both knew their connection was deep.

"So what does the boy who has everything want for his birthday?" she finally questioned in the quietness.

He sighed again. "I don't imagine there's really anything tangible I want. It's true, you know, what you just said. I have everything in the sense of the material. It's the immaterial that evades me, and yet that's what I most want."

"You speak a little too deep for a sixteen year old. I don't think I can fill the immaterial very well."

He looked over at her. "You already have." He nodded. "This is what I wanted most, and you're here. Wish granted."

"Nope—not good enough. Come on! It's your sixteenth birthday! There's got to be something you really want. Forget stuff for a moment. I know you've got the world at your feet. Let's pretend I'm a magic fairy and can grant you three wishes. What would you ask for?"

He raised an eyebrow. "Any limitations?"

"I'm a magic fairy! Please! Don't insult me. Of course there are no limitations. I can do anything. Just name it."

He ran his hand through his flowing dark hair as he considered it— oblivious that she wished she could take her fingers and feel the soft locks as well. His good looks were talked about throughout the kingdom, and as she stared into his thoughtful face, so many desires swirled within her. She closed her eyes hoping to erase them.

"Okay," he said turning back to her. "No limitations?"

"None."

He took a deep breath. "If I could have just one thing, it would be to be normal."

"Normal? Are you telling me that you're abnormal?"

He smirked. "Good heavens, how much more abnormal can one be? I can't leave my home, I can't go to a store, I just turned sixteen and can't drive a car. I'm going to be king and it will all get even worse. I'm the epitome of abnormal."

She reached over and gently touched the tip of his nose with her index finger as she whispered, "Wish granted. Now tell me—what are you going to do as a normal person?"

He paused to reflect again, but she was overcome with how her finger touching his nose had spread an ache of desire throughout her body.

"I would actually play soccer with a real team, not just a coach and a few security guards. I would drive to your house tomorrow and let you beat me in tennis."

Her eyebrows flew up. "Let me beat you?"

"You think you're so good at it. I play with a personal coach twice a week. I imagine I would have to let you win."

She shook her head. "Well, since all this is just a wish, have at it. But it would be quite a task for you to beat me."

"I would go shopping," he continued. "Everywhere. I would go to every kind of store imaginable and just look at stuff and touch it and see how it worked. I would go to a restaurant and order pizza! And I would sit there and wait for it to come to my table instead of walking into a room with everything already prepared."

"Would you go alone?"

He smiled. "Never. I would never do anything alone if I were *normal*. I would always have friends and be surrounded by people who knew me well … like you."

She gently pinched his arm. "You wouldn't like me because I would beat you at tennis."

"Okay, a lot of friends, but you wouldn't be there because you challenged my manhood on the court."

"Good. You can finish your wish now."

"And a movie! I would actually go to a theater and watch a movie … a real movie, not something I have to see to help bolster my education or increase my knowledge of the military. I would just watch something that was a pure fairy tale."

"You don't see the latest movies here?"

"Are you kidding? That's squandering time and brain-power. There are so many better ways to fill my time than watching garbage like that."

The reality of his condition began to sink into her mind again. If she could, she would love to sneak him out and take him away from this world. But she couldn't. This was his life—royalty, kingship—and it was his destiny. And in his life there would never be a place for her.

"Okay," she said as she shifted on the odd floor trying to find a reasonably comfortable position. "Wish number one is granted and you're normal and have done all these other normal things. What about wishes two and three?"

He leaned back and folded his arms again. "If I were normal, I can't imagine wanting anything else." He paused and stared at her again. "Every dream would come true. What more could I want?"

"I don't know … something. Normal isn't all it's cracked up to be.

There's got to be something else you want."

He turned his head down now as he fidgeted with his untied tie. "Maybe there is, but maybe I don't have the nerve to say it."

"Oh, please," she groaned. "You're the future king. What could you possibly not have the nerve to say?"

"Hey, I thought I was just normal at the moment!"

She put her hands up in mock surrender. "Sorry. Okay, what else does this *normal* boy want?"

His gaze now became slowly more intense. The smile faded, but his stare deepened. He traced her face with his eyes and then he swallowed hard. He started to speak, but changed his mind and shook his head.

"What?" she whispered. She knew the pretending was over now. "You can tell me, Andrew."

He fixed his eyes on hers in a way that nearly melted her.

"It's okay," she assured him. "You've told me many things over the years. I've kept them all right here." She touched her heart. "No one knows … not Amy or Jenna … not even my parents."

He licked his lips and closed his eyes in what appeared to be pain.

"Andrew," she reached for his hand. It was cold and clammy, but his eyes looked back at her fiercely this time. "What is it?"

His hand reached up to her face. He touched the line of her jaw, the bridge of her nose, and ran his hand down the side of her cheek. "If I could have but one wish for a lifetime, it would be to kiss the most beautiful person I will ever know. Just once. Nothing long, nothing intense, nothing even passionate. Just to connect with you like that one time … it would be … it would be every wish, every dream … everything coming true in one moment."

Her heart jumped into her throat and felt as though it would leap out at any second. He could not have just asked that.

She hesitated to answer. "I … I … don't know if I can." She was so torn. "I've never kissed anyone before. It would probably be a miserable disaster."

His hand still held her face as her hand tightened around his.

He softly said, "I've never kissed anyone either. I wouldn't know if it was good or bad or worthy or … miserable." He then smiled. "But whatever it might be, it would have to be perfect, because it would be a wish … granted."

She made herself breathe. If she kissed him, her heart would forever be his. Did she refuse and save herself, or did she give in to the only wish she could ever truly grant him?

He removed his hands and scooted back toward the wall. "I'm sorry. I asked too much. I told you I shouldn't say it."

"No," she assured him. "You don't understand. It just seems so … I don't know … awkward. We're just friends. If I kissed you, I don't know if we could just …"

His eyes were closed in humiliation.

"Andrew … don't," she pleaded. "It was okay to ask. It really was. I'm just uncomfortable. I don't know how to kiss anyone. And it would be my first kiss and what if I … messed up …"

He was looking out the window and the flush on his cheeks was bright. Protecting her heart was pointless. He would always own it, no matter if they kissed or not. He would always be her one love, and she could never have him. Why double the misery? If one kiss would make this birthday the most memorable, then why hold back? What could it hurt?

Everything.

She leaned into him, pulled his face back to hers, and waited until he looked into her eyes again. She reached her fingers into his hair and felt the softness she had often longed to touch.

He reiterated with a whisper, "You don't have to. I shouldn't have asked."

She looked slowly down his face and wished she had some kind of experience to draw from, but she had only seen movies. She doubted she could come anywhere close to that.

"Wish granted," she smiled as she leaned into him and gently touched her lips to his.

Neither one moved. They sat absolutely still, afraid to even breathe. For the first time Evangeline knew why her father would throw away his royalty for the love of a woman. Then Andrew whispered her name and drew himself deeper into the kiss. She wanted to scream for him to stop because she knew this would be all there ever was between them, but the connection was too strong. Instead she reached her other hand up to his neck and pulled him even closer. He put one hand behind her waist and the other behind her head as he slowly laid her down against the angled floor. Part of her was scared she was doing it all wrong and that at some moment he would catch his breath and start laughing, but the desire within her drove her hungrily to continue.

When he finally pulled away, she was shocked at what she saw. He was above her, looking down at her with tears streaming off the end of his nose.

"Are you okay?" she asked immediately as she reached up to wipe the tears. "Was it that bad?"

He closed his eyes and a few more tears squeezed out. "How can you even ask that?" He looked down at her again. "Was that not the most incredible thing you've ever experienced in your life?"

She smiled slightly. "So it wasn't … miserable?"

He didn't answer. He leaned down to kiss her again. This time she didn't feel so self-conscious, but her heart was aching. As wonderful as this was at this moment for this one night, it would be over and her life would never be the same. How could there ever be anyone above Andrew?

She pulled away and looked at him with all the pain she knew would come, "I can't do this." She could now feel her own tears and understood the source of his.

"I know," he groaned as he forced himself to sit up. She followed, smoothing out her long hair as she tried to regain her composure.

"I'll never forget you," he spoke through the shadows. "I'll never forget this." He looked at her, but there was no more pain in his face—there was actually peace. "I'll look back at this and remember it when I'm sitting alone in my room at maneuvers, or playing soccer with a handful of grown men who could care less, or laying alone in my bed at night." He reached up to touch her face again. "I'll remember that this is how it feels to be really alive … and to be really touched by someone who really matters." He gave his most handsome smile. "Thank you."

She smiled as a blush warmed her cheeks. "So I didn't do too badly then?"

"Never—you will always be the best … always."

"But you know we can't do this again."

"I know," he nodded. "Believe me, I know."

Amy and Jenna didn't pry much during the limo ride home. Evangeline had told them she and Andrew had talked about all that was coming up for him, and how he was trying to face it bravely but regretting he could never have any kind of normal life. She had encouraged him, and now she was tired. She imagined she would sleep the entire forty-five minutes back. It looked like she was sleeping, but in her mind she was replaying her first and last kiss. Her emotions went from sublime to despair over and over again. This night had been the apex of her life. Everything else would now be meaningless compared to Andrew Braisogn.

❧ Chapter Six ☙

Evangeline had finished the last exam of her first semester in college. It was a brutal first term because of her need to take as many classes possible in the fall so the spring term would be easy and minimal—tennis would have to be the main focus. Because Braisognia was such a small nation, the majority of their college matches took place outside the country. There was much travel, much playing, much missing classes, and not a lot of time for studying, especially catching up if one ever fell behind.

She turned in her exam and began bundling up to face the bitter, cold walk back to the dorm. Amy had left yesterday after lunch since her exams were finished. Jenna had one more this morning, but was still packing when Evangeline went to take her last. She wondered if she could have survived this semester had she not roomed with Jenna and Amy. She had imagined college being loads of fun with a little studying in between, and it was for most of the students. But when Evangeline had applied to Brigdon University, a royal school, she was immediately denied because of her mixed heritage. Her first instinct was not to go. She told her parents she would apply somewhere else and just move on with her life, but her father had refused to accept the no.

It wasn't long before Brigdon was made aware of Evangeline's intense talent on the tennis court, and soon they were falling all over themselves offering her scholarships galore to come. This was the habit of universities in Braisognia. Royals were royals and commoners were commoners, and never the twain shall meet, except in the cases of national competition and talent. Exceptional commoners might be considered worthy of being placed in royal schools if their abilities held the possibility of bringing the nation recognition. Evangeline fell into this category, and she was one of only a handful to actually be accepted and attend. The only problem was that she hated playing tennis, and even more, she hated the way the snobs at Brigdon looked down at her, talked down to her, and tried to make her life miserable by being there.

As she passed through the parking lot to the dorm she noticed Jenna's car still there. Good. No one would bounce into the room to say something derogatory if she was around. She had taken on the self-proclaimed elite in Evangeline's behalf, and with her sharp wit and biting tongue, cut them down to size many times. Evangeline had asked her to stop, told her it didn't matter, but in truth she was relieved to have her. Amy was sweet, and she generally just cringed during the attacks. But the three of them spent most of their time together in their room as though they were back in high school and all was well.

"How'd you do?" Jenna asked from her bed where she sat looking through a magazine.

"Who cares?" Evangeline placed her backpack on a desk and glanced around to see if there was anything she had left undone.

"I care," her friend replied with a smug smile. "If you fail out your first semester, all this sarcastic wit I've thrown out the past four months will be for nothing."

"Twenty-one hours," Evangeline sighed. "That sounded like a lot even before I knew what it meant."

"But only twelve next term. Plus you get to tour the world! Do you not see how lucky you are?"

Evangeline gave her a glare, but Jenna only broke out in laughter. It was all just farce, and she had to laugh slightly with her. She thanked God daily for her friends who were true and devoted.

Driving the two hour trip home gave her too much time to think. She couldn't help comparing herself to Andrew in all of this. She had heard him describe many times being trapped in a situation he had no desire to fulfill, but because of duty he would stay the course and give his life to be a man of integrity ... and royalty. Her only sin was really no fault of hers. It all went back to her grandmother, a royal who married a commoner, and then to her mother, a mixed-blood who had married a royal. And here she was— a third generation outcast with great ability and an honorable father no one wanted to publicly disgrace, but who everyone despised in secret. If she defected to the commoners, the royals would win. But if she fought the tide and persisted in her planned course, perhaps she could be the first to break a barrier that should have never been placed there to begin with.

Andrew. She tried not to think of him. Last year—their senior year—at the Christmas ball, things had been vastly different. They did sit together and talk throughout the evening, but they never went to their secret room and never mentioned his birthday. All night she had wanted to throw her arms around him and plead with him to take her away somewhere, anywhere—but they both remained composed and calm as though nothing had transpired between them. They conversed with those around them and appeared normal and cordial all night long.

This year's ball would be a week from tonight, and she was dreading it. In fact, she was seriously considering not going. She had dealt with pretense on such a deep level all semester long that she had no desire to play the game with Andrew again. If she said the word, Amy and Jenna would come over and stay with her, and they could laugh and talk and play all night until her parents returned. In fact, even her parents would probably decline to go also … if she asked.

But what of Andrew? Would he need her again this year? Was he merely on top of his life last year and trying to be his own man? Would it be like that again or would he be the old insecure, hopeless boy he had always been year after year before? What if this year he really needed to talk and they snuck away to their room so he could bare his soul one last time. What would happen if she didn't show? Would he feel forsaken?

"Augh!" she screamed out, slamming her fist against the steering wheel. "This is so unfair! How can I let you do this to me, Andrew Braisogn?"

She wanted nothing to do with him on one hand, and on the other, she obsessed about him constantly.

⚕ ⚕ ⚕

Giselle threw open the door and plunged down the steps of the porch into the thickening snow without a jacket or even shoes to greet her daughter. Evangeline had barely opened the car door when her mother pulled her out, wrapped her in her arms and held her tightly.

"It's so good to have you back," Giselle nearly cried. "You cannot know how hard this semester has been for us."

Evangeline pulled back and looked at her, "I have somewhat of an idea, believe me."

"You only think you do. It's ten times worse for the parents, you know? We want to give everyone a piece of our mind, and we do, in our own heads … every day …"

She looked down at her mother's sock feet. "You're gonna catch pneumonia and die if you don't get inside. And exactly how do expect me to go on without my mother? What possessed you to run out here in the snow like this?"

"You, my dear! Only you!"

⚕ ⚕ ⚕

The first week with her parents was wonderful. For brief minutes she could forget her life at Brigdon and pretend all was normal again. *Normal.* That's what Andrew had wished. She understood now more than ever how he felt. Cooking dinner, watching television, playing games as a family again renewed the grounding she needed to face the next term. She wasn't looking forward to it, but her parents gave her a real sense of who she was—rather than who she wasn't. She would play hard these next few months and show the nation who she was also. She may be mixed in her blood, but she would pound every royal into humiliation that stood across the net from her this coming season, and her name would be known throughout the continent before spring was finished.

Preparing for the Christmas ball on Friday was an emotional roller coaster. She knew Jenna and Amy would be there if she needed them, but she also knew they would keep their distance if the prince were to pay her any attention. She actually hoped he would be aloof and inattentive. It would be easier to ignore him and move on with her life than to have another heartfelt talk about his deepest issues again. She had her own issues for the first time, and she would probably be incapable of any encouragement toward him seeing that in one sense he really was the enemy—he was the epitome of royalty.

The trip in the limo was filled with playful banter between all three Dorvains. Her parents had managed to handle their own scandal with dignity and passion. She imagined that because of all they had to fight in order to be together, it gave them a reason to keep their love strong and connected. She had never seen any couple so deeply committed. Many royal marriages at their time had still been arranged. In fact, her father had been promised to another when he ran off to marry Giselle. It was one of many scourges they had faced. Yet here they were, twenty-three years later, as in love as ever, as alive as ever, when so many had tried to destroy them. Evangeline took heart. She had great examples set before her and she would not cave to the silliness that monopolized this nation. She would rise above it and make her own mark and show the kingdom that she would not be excluded by their snobberies and ludicrous judgments.

The Braisogns were already greeting guests when she arrived. The king was aging and sober, his queen cordial and polite, but neither ever emitting a true smile. George and his wife were more intent on showing off their toddler son, an obvious source of disdain for the king. Peter and his wife with their daughter were definitely uncomfortable being there. But Andrew stood taller and broader than Evangeline could remember—his hair long and dark, wavy and shining. He now wore a thin, trimmed beard, and his uniform glowed with medals and ribbons. For the first time in her life she felt truly unworthy of his attention and wished she hadn't come. Why would such a man of honor, although only eighteen, have anything to do with her, a mixed-blooded young woman whose only hope in life was to succeed at a sport she hated simply to rise above her own scorn? She turned to leave but her father caught her arm.

"Don't bow to this pressure, Evie," he said warmly. "You're above the scandal they all want to pretend is there."

She looked at her parents, her mother's arm wrapped tightly around her father's, and then glanced back to the Braisogns, the queen standing a good yard from her husband. Whose life did she really want? She turned back in line. Her father was right. She would be above them in her character, but her heart would die again when she would shake Andrew's hand in formality and pretend that nothing had ever passed between them.

As she watched the royal family, there were many dynamics to observe. The king seemed bored with the whole evening. He seldom even offered a smile. The queen kept her distance from him on the platform, but her reception was definitely cordial and warm. George and his wife obviously didn't want to be there, but their animated two-year-old kept them busy. Peter held his one-year-old daughter with great pride, but he and his wife would only offer their hands if they were greeted, and sad to say, they seldom were.

Then Andrew saw her. His face lit up and he gave a slight salute. She hated that he even acknowledged her. Now everything she felt for him, thought about him, had shared with him came flooding through her. It was more than an emotional rush—it was every bit as physical as adrenaline poured within her. Why couldn't he just ignore her? Why couldn't he pretend she was just another person passing through the line? He kept his eyes on her as person after person passed by and admired him.

"Miss Dorvain," the king greeted Evangeline. "I hear you may put Braisognia on the map some day in the world of tennis."

She was astonished. The king had never spoken to her in the past. "I will try, your majesty," she smiled as she shook his hand.

"I hope so," he replied, smiling slightly himself. "It seems that as a small country, sports are not at all our forte. I don't imagine we'll ever do much in the Olympics or with any team games. But the talk is that you have the talent to go to the top."

"We'll see," she stated cautiously. "I intend to finish my education first. I can't play tennis my entire life."

"But of course. You're a wise young woman. Best of luck these next years."

"Thank you."

Evangeline hoped her breathing was calmer than the pounding of her heart. The king had just put intense pressure on her—exactly what she didn't need as she faced the next semester.

As if the queen could read her mind, Julia took her hand and said,

"You're an amazing young lady. Just stay the course. You'll be fine."

"Thank you."

She immediately extended herself to George and Lynette. They shook hands with grateful smiles at being acknowledged, and she made on over their little Braxton who was truly the cutest toddler she'd ever seen. She greeted Peter and Kayla with sincere warmth and marveled at their beautiful angel of a daughter, but the whole time her heart was pulling her toward Andrew. When she finally faced him and extended her hand, he took it, but drew her into a gentle hug. He seemed so much bigger now. His arms were strong as they held her briefly, but she was melting again, something she swore wouldn't happen.

"Save me a seat at your table," he whispered in her ear before pulling back.

She had to look up at him for the first time ever. Never before had they not stood eye to eye.

"If you insist," she tried to tease.

"I insist. We must discuss our first semesters."

"I guess yours was better than mine," she slipped—already giving too much away.

His grin turned into a compassionate smile. "We'll talk."

When he finally joined her at their seats, he reached briefly beneath the table and squeezed her hand, then let it go. How could he do this to her? He had to know how she felt—but what did he feel? Even their friendship was taboo, and probably everyone in the room was noting that he was sitting next to the mixed-blood yet again.

She tried to eat her pheasant, but tonight there was no appetite for anything. She really wanted to leave … alone. Jenna and Amy sat on her other side, and they managed to keep the conversation going, but she was acutely aware of only Andrew.

"Do you want to leave? Go somewhere so we can talk freely?" he asked her early in the evening.

She looked at him in surprise. "Are you serious?"

He smiled again, showing a confidence she had never before seen in him. "Yes."

She looked around the room and noted the doors to one of the balconies. The weather had warmed significantly. They could stand outside for a brief time and exchange a few stories before the cold got to them.

"How about outside?" she suggested.

He raised his eyebrows. "Are you serious? We would freeze to death … especially you in that dress. I wouldn't want to be held responsible for that."

She closed her eyes a moment. The truth was she really didn't want to be alone with him.

"We are sanctioned tonight," he informed her.

"What on earth does that mean?"

"Come on," he took her hand and led her up from the seat. "I'll tell you in a minute."

The last time they had been in the secret room, Evangeline had given her first and hopefully only kiss to him. She was literally trembling from the memories as she crawled through the passage. What was she doing here with him again? She wasn't even sure if she could trust him anymore. What if he wanted more tonight? Could she refuse him? Was her heart strong enough to deny the only man she could ever …

"No!" she suddenly objected as she responded to her thoughts.

Andrew, already through the tunnel and inside the room, looked back inside. "What?"

She sighed and repeated, "No." She stopped crawling. "I can't do this with you, Andrew. I can't be in here with you and just pretend …"

"It's all okay," he assured her as he reached out his hand. "Just come on in. I'm not going to … nothing improper is going to happen. We're just going to talk."

Easy for him to say. His heart isn't flipping around in emotional distraught. It wasn't really him that she didn't trust—it was her own condition. She was weak and vulnerable and confused and frustrated. She crept on through and tried to arrange her long gown into a comfortable position as she sat against a leaning wall.

"You look beautiful tonight, as always," he began.

She closed her eyes again and shook her head. "I don't really care, Andrew. I don't want to be here with you … in this room again."

"I know, and I don't blame you, but I couldn't resist. Father told me to do everything I could tonight to make sure you pursue this whole tennis thing."

She looked up at him in astonishment. "For real?"

"I don't know exactly what he had in mind, but if it allows me to spend some uninterrupted time with you without the glaring eyes of the palace beating down on us, it's greatly worth it."

"For you maybe, but not me. I can't just throw this … this … relationship … whatever it is we have … around, back and forth, up and down, side to side … again and again." She looked at him eye to eye. "It tears me apart inside, Andrew. The last time we were here …"

"I know," he assured her as he took her hand. "I'm sorry about all that. It shouldn't have happened. It bound us together in a way that we should never be bound, but it wouldn't have mattered one way or the other. Whether we kissed or talked or did anything else, we are what we are, we feel what we feel, and that's that. It can't change and we can't change." He smiled. "It was wonderful, and no matter what happens down the road, I'll never forget it … I guess you won't either."

She sighed. "Never."

"But we have tonight," he cheered. "No one is stalking the halls, and we can talk as long as we want."

He began. His first term in college had been amazing. He was living in a highly secure apartment complex and was escorted by four guards everywhere he went. To others it seemed a little odd having security ever present, but eventually people got used to it. He was almost *normal* for the first time in his life. He had friends and acquaintances, and he went to *approved* movies and played on the soccer team with guys his age, and he excelled at everything. People knew him for his abilities rather than just being the prince and future king—and he felt enlivened by it all.

"I suppose there are a lot of … women … too?" She didn't want to be jealous, but it was hard.

"I don't even go there. What's the point? I have some friends who are girls, but why start something? If I marry, it has to be someone who passes through all the hoops. The average girl would be crucified as queen … especially by my father."

"If you marry?"

"Why should I? Who cares? As long as I lead this nation militarily and veto all the stupid legislation at the advice of my political counselors, I'll be fine. Even with the military I've got generals who've been commanding since before my father was king!" He shifted toward her and explained, "I'm a figurehead, really—that's all it boils down to."

"Is that what you believe now? That you have no responsibility to the crown? You're just some monkey who shows up at all the right times and waves to the people?"

"No, that would be the future queen." He laughed.

"Who are you!" she bellowed as if in distress. "I can't believe what you're saying! You have the opportunity to change the course of this nation … to be a part of world leadership … and you're treating it all like some big joke! A year and a half ago you held the burden of it all on your shoulders … it nearly broke you … now you're laughing it off as though it's just some trite role you have to step into! What are you doing?"

"I'm enjoying my life. For the first time since I was born I'm actually living. I know it won't last. Right now everyone is accommodating me so when these four years of freedom are over I can go back to my prison and be everything I'm supposed to be again. Until then, I don't want to care. I'll study, I'll continue with military maneuvers and training, I'll do whatever I have to do to keep the powers that be happy, but I will enjoy these four years for all they are. I'm not going to dwell on what happens then. I'm only thinking about what happens now."

She nodded as a lump grew in her throat. "So you stick your head in the sand and glide through all of this." She glared at him. "And you even let them use you to get to me? How stupid of me to assume you cared about me at all."

She turned to the tunnel.

"No!" he yelled as he grabbed her arm.

"Please let me go. I don't want to be in here with you. You've just desecrated every memory I have of this room."

"No," he said more gently, "please understand."

She stopped and sat, but stayed near the tunnel.

"My head is not in the sand," he assured her. "And no one is using me to get to you. I'm using them to be with you."

"Either way, I don't like it. I really would rather leave right now."

He reached for her hand. "Please don't leave."

"Give me one good reason. You have no idea what my life has been like this fall. While you've been living it up and reveling in the praises of your peers, I've been studying my brains out with twenty-one hours and enduring the scorns and scourges of *your* peers. They've made it clear that I'm not a part of their world and never will be. My only hope in this pathetic little narrow-minded kingdom you'll one day rule, is to go pro and let all these people who judge me be honored by my success. I hate them! I hate tennis!" She let out a sob which made her even angrier. "All I want is to follow in my mother's footsteps and help children who have no chance in this pitiful nation because they were born with the wrong blood." She wiped her face. "I want to finish my schooling and then help kids. That's all I want." She was trembling now.

He removed his jacket and wrapped it around her shoulders as he pulled her to him.

"You realize though," he tried to console, "that if you succeed with this tennis thing, it will put them all to shame. You can thumb your nose at them and prove them all to be as shallow and narrow-minded as they really are."

She didn't want to take comfort in his arms, but it was too tempting. She let herself get lost in the strength of his embrace, but not in his words.

She asked him, "Do you really think that's what I want out of life? Some dismal revenge? I want people to remember me for having a huge heart, for reaching out to those who had no hope or future, for moving beyond boundaries. Shoot, let them remember me for moving the boundaries period. What good is there in vengeance? What does it really accomplish?"

"I'll tell you what it accomplishes," he said as he turned her chin to face him. "It gives you the platform to carry out your heart's desire. You succeed in tennis, and you can get any endorsement, any amount of money and time and workers to do anything you want. You could build your own center, and it would be your enemies, your criticizers who would foot the bill. Everyone would swallow their feeble pride and bow at your feet, and that would be a first in this kingdom. And you might be remembered in the beginning as the only Braisognian to break the barrier of professional sports, but in the end it would be your heart that would shine through it all." He stared at her deeply, and she could see the old Andrew again. "They would all see who you really are ... they would see you as I see you ... know you as I know you. They would realize how foolish all of this is ... and realize that you are the representation of all that is truly noble and good and right in this kingdom—that you are a product of love and determination, and not blood and traditions."

She closed her eyes and leaned into his shoulder. He was warm and tender again. "But blood and traditions will continue to rule unless you make the changes."

"I'll try, Evangeline, but I'm only one man against hundreds of years."

"But you will be king. And the king is more than a figurehead. Screw your brain back on right and take life seriously, Andrew. Stop building fences in this kingdom and start building bridges."

♛ ♛ ♛

No one spoke of the ball for the rest of Evangeline's vacation at home. They focused only on each other. Her mother had several heart-to-heart discussions with her, encouraging her to find her soul's mission and then set out to accomplish it. She told her not to be swayed by others' opinions, regardless of who all the *others* might be. She needed to do what she felt she was put here by God to do. That included looking at her talents and her options, and not neglecting any, but using them all for the glory of God to achieve a life filled with passion for what she loved most.

With that in mind, she determined to tackle the next semester with a different point of view. She would welcome the scorn and then play it out on the court. She would work harder than ever before to make sure she rose to the highest possible ranks in the world of tennis. She would stop hating the sport, but rather embrace it as the one tool to bring her to the place where her mixed heritage would no longer be a cross, but rather a door to open in a nation split by silly traditions. She would be the catalyst. That would be her goal.

ഇ Chapter Seven ೞ

(2 ½ Years Later)

Andrew grinned at the young soldiers with their buzzed heads. One advantage to being a college officer was that he could now keep his hair ... and his beard. He liked them both, and so did everyone else. It seemed to be his outstanding feature whenever he was mentioned in the paper or on the news. Even many officers were beginning to mimic his look as displays of allegiance to the coming king.

Having finished his third year of political studies, he was only one away from returning to the humdrum of palace life. He dreaded it, but even worse was that he was five years away from being crowned. He knew his first few years would require little more of him than just making simple decisions on which his counselors would advise, but he wanted to appear competent and confident in all he did. He didn't want to be a figurehead—he wanted to be the king.

As he oversaw the obstacle course, he noticed Max, his security advisor, walking toward him. He was the closest thing to a real friend that Andrew had. He was only five years older than the prince, but he had a sober grasp on the importance of protecting him. He also had the appearance of being a friend because of his age, so if a possible attempt ever occurred, most would never assume that Max was in charge of his security. His allegiance was fierce, and Andrew honestly believed Max understood his misery and plight.

"What's up?" he asked as he sweated through the uniform in the hot July sun. "What brings you all the way out here? Just looking to hone up on your course skills?"

"Hardly," Max spoke soberly as he looked to the ground.

This concerned him. Max was an in your face, eye to eye kind of guy. To not face him meant something severe. "Oh, boy. What is it?"

50

"Let's walk." Max rubbed the beading sweat from his forehead and motioned him away from the course.

"No. Whatever it is, I'd rather you tell me straight on. I don't need to walk." He had never seen him so unbalanced or hesitant to speak.

"Wow," he stalled. "There's no easy way to do this. So ... I'll be straight. It relates to Miss Dorvain."

Andrew's heart fell. Max knew about his feelings toward Evangeline. In fact, only Max knew. Not even she knew how he really felt. He believed it would be cruel to tell her knowing he could never act on them. He assumed if she didn't know the entire truth, he could never reject her.

"Her mother ... had an aneurism on the brain two days ago. It was major ... severe. She remained in a vegetative state for several hours and then passed away."

"What?" His heart nearly stopped. "When did she ... die?"

"That night," he replied softly.

"And I'm just finding out?"

"I just found out. Apparently everyone felt it would be best to keep this from you until just before the funeral. It's at two o'clock this afternoon, and you are, of course, expected to attend."

He literally felt the blood rush from his head. As his knees began to buckle, Max reached out and immediately bolstered him up.

"You okay?"

"What do you think?" Andrew knelt to the ground and got his head as low as he could.

"Let's get back to your room and you can shower and change. A jet will take us to the palace as soon as you're ready."

♛ ♛ ♛

James Dorvain couldn't believe the gall of the senator to demand a conference with him just three hours prior to his wife's funeral. Dexter Braisogn had insisted it was high priority to meet with him immediately, no matter the day's schedule. This conference couldn't wait and there would be no discussion about it. James stormed into the man's office without knocking, red-faced and angry, the first emotion other than relentless grief he had felt in two days.

"This had better be a matter of national security that somehow only I can handle in order to justify what you're doing," he warned. Looking around the room he realized they weren't alone. John Kiln, his own personal lawyer, and Richard Carvell, a highly paid lawyer for many senators and royals were seated in the room also.

"What is this?" he demanded to know.

"First," Dexter began, "let me offer my deepest condolences concerning your wife."

"Mine too," John said as he stood.

Richard nodded in acknowledgement, but he wouldn't stand. In fact, he looked pale, almost sick.

"I don't care about condolences," James quipped in anger. "Right now I have a twenty-year-old daughter who hasn't eaten in two days and is grieving herself sick. My wife will be six feet under in a few hours and whatever you gentlemen have cooked up here had better be worth pulling me away from what matters most at this moment in time."

"It is," Dexter assured him. "Please take a seat and we'll get on with this as quickly as possible. I have a press conference scheduled at eleven thirty to make this public, so we don't have a whole lot of time."

Richard now stood and tried to speak. "Dex, surely there is a better way to handle all of this than to ..."

"Enough!" Dexter silenced him. "I have lived with this too long, and had I followed my conscience rather than your self-obsessed advice, we wouldn't be in this position right now!"

"A position *you* are forcing," Richard reminded him.

James Dorvain pounded his fist on the desk. "Would you please get to the point!"

"Right away," the aged senator said as he sat behind the desk and motioned for Richard to return to his own seat. The lawyer dropped in despair.

"First, you have to understand my timing," Dexter began. "It seems awful, and I wanted to do this right after Eloise died two years ago, but I was persuaded to let her death pass and to give this some time before pursuing it." He gave his lawyer a harsh glance. "Unfortunately, it was too much time. And now my hand is forced in a most embarrassing way, but I will get this burden off my back once and for all. I won't remain a hypocrite as so many have in this kingdom."

James was still clueless. "So unburden yourself and let me return to my daughter ... please."

"The bottom line," he continued as his own face began to pale, "is that Giselle was my daughter. I was already engaged to Eloise when Gillian, Giselle's mother and I ... well ... ended our relationship. I had been arranged to marry Eloise years before. I was up for my first term as senator in the House of Royals. If I broke my engagement to Eloise and married a very pregnant Gillian ... well ... I think you get the picture. I was a spineless worm, and my pathetic decisions cast a curse on the only child I would ever have. Eloise couldn't bear children, so every year that I watched Giselle grow and eventually turn into a beautiful and accomplished young woman, it would eat me up inside. I wanted to come clean years ago, but Eloise pleaded with me to not humiliate her through all of this. It was my mistake—not hers."

James' body began to shake. "So you allowed Giselle, and now Evangeline, to live with humiliation instead?"

"I have no valid excuse. You have every right to do or say anything you feel right now—and I would deserve it all."

"But what of Montevo, Giselle's ... well ... the man she thought was her father?"

"He was an honorable commoner, a better man than I could ever hope to be. He married her, loved her, raised Giselle as his own, and was condemned for much in the process. Yet the truth was that he merely covered my mistake and allowed me to succeed in immeasurable ways."

James leaned his head back against the stately seat and stared at the ceiling. All these years his girls were ostracized by the royals when in reality they were every bit as royal as the rest.

He looked at the senator in unbelief. "And you plan to make this public?"

Dexter tapped a folder on his desk. "This contains all the legal documents necessary to confirm both Giselle and Evangeline are my descendants. They are signed and notarized. At eleven thirty I'll make the announcement public on television, resign my post in the senate, and hopefully your wife—my daughter—will be buried in the Capital Gardens where she belongs."

James didn't reach for the folder. He still couldn't believe what he had heard. His Giselle, whom he had given up so much for, and Evangeline, who had also borne the brunt of this lie, would now be released from the biggest scorn a person could bear in this kingdom ... and his wife would never know.

"I wish Giselle could have had this choice to make herself," he mourned. "I doubt she would have chosen to be placed there."

"From what I know of her, you're probably right," Dexter agreed. "But I think she should be placed there as a reminder of the foolishness this country has allowed all these years. She was a gracious and spirited soul, a woman above reproach who gave herself to caring for others rather than stewing in self-pity. I consider it an honor to claim her as my daughter, yet I bear that honor with the greatest shame and disgrace a man can carry."

"As well you should," James proclaimed as he stood. He took the folder and looked at his lawyer. "John, you knew about this?"

"About an hour ago," John confirmed. "I've been supervising the signing. It's all legal. Giselle is officially a royal ... and now so is Evangeline."

James had nothing more to say. He was angry and hurt, and only wanted to grab Dexter by the collar, drag him across the desk, and beat him until every ounce of life drained from his body. But he also knew what this had cost the multi-termed senator—he had just lost his life in Braisognia.

Turning to go he looked back across the desk. "What do you intend to do after all this?"

"Leave the country, I suppose. I can't imagine finding favor with much of anybody after this. The royals will hate me for exposing their hypocrisy—the commoners will hate me for allowing it to plague Gillian and Giselle and young Evangeline. I could hole myself up in my mansion and live comfortably in solitude for the rest of my life, but that doesn't seem very appealing either."

James nodded in understanding. "I need to leave. I have some changes in arrangements to make before the funeral."

Dexter nodded.

"By the way," he added, "I do thank you for what you're doing right now, but I will despise you forever for what it cost those I loved the most."

"Of course," he nodded sadly with understanding.

🎖 🎖 🎖

Evangeline couldn't believe she was able to hold it together at this moment. She stood as tall as she could next to her father at the Capital Gardens as the minister said the final words over her mother's casket. She was vaguely aware of Andrew's presence across the field, but she was more involved in processing all that had just happened. She was a royal. A *royal.* They would despise her now more than ever because all their hatred was unfounded. Even as she grieved the loss of her mother, a part of her longed to run to the casket, turn to the crowd, and yell judgment on everyone present.

"Are you okay?" her father asked as the minister suggested they bow for the final prayer.

"You can't possibly have just asked me that."

He smiled for the first time in two days. "You are the strongest woman alive and you have just been given your wings. Do you know what your mother would say?"

She shook her head.

"She would say, fly, baby, fly—nothing can stop you now."

"And that's exactly what I intend to do."

🎖 🎖 🎖

"You cannot be serious!" Christopher Braisogn shrieked at his youngest son. "This could all be a huge hoax! I refuse to allow you to crawl to that girl's house and assume everything is acceptable now just because someone has claimed her to be of royal descent!"

"What?" Andrew spun around and faced his father. "Is that why you think I'm going there? You think I'm going to propose marriage? Are you out of your mind?"

This statement took his father by surprise. He thought that was exactly why he was headed to the Dorvain house. "Why are you going then?"

"Because for 20 years she has been my dearest friend, my closest, and many times my only confidante. She has stood by me and told me I would be the greatest king ever in this nation, and she did it all under the judgmental sneers of her own kind. I wouldn't dare offer her the position of queen in this pathetic kingdom—it doesn't deserve her. She's better than any of us. She now has the world at her feet and can do anything she wants, even without tennis. Why would I assume she would give it all up for the ball and chain that life here would be for her? I'll never give her that chance. I'm merely going to comfort a friend who just lost her mother, not just any mother, but a caring, involved, and passionate mother for whom this kingdom also isn't worthy."

Andrew bolted from the room, grabbed his keys and told Max, "I'm leaving now. If you want a security team to follow, you'll have to catch up."

♊ ♊ ♊

"Colonel Dorvain," came the call from the gate box.

James got up from the couch and went to answer. "Yes."

"You have a visitor."

"From the list?"

"No sir, but I wouldn't be comfortable turning him away."

"Really? Who is it?"

"The prince—Andrew Braisogn."

Already. James assumed he would show up when he found out Evangeline was a royal, but he didn't think it would be this soon. At least give her time to grieve her mother before dragging her away into his life. He had his speech well-prepared when the young man drove up in the black sports car, but Andrew spoke first.

"I'm not here for the reason you think," he began.

"Oh, I doubt that," James replied. "I can imagine exactly why you're here."

"I bet you can, but you're wrong. I've already been accused of improper motives once today. I'd rather not have to explain this to you too at the moment. I'm here to see Evangeline."

"I don't know if that's wise," he said as he stood between the prince and the door to the house. "Give her some time to deal with all of this—the death of her mother, the bestowing of royalty—before you barrel in there and ask her to give it all up and follow you to the throne."

Andrew shook his head with hurt. "Thank you for condemning me as a fool just like my father. He doesn't know me at all, and neither do you, Colonel. I would never dream of asking Evangeline to throw her life away. After finally finding her freedom, why would I propose that she become imprisoned in the pitiful life I'll have to live year after year after year? I'm here because your daughter has been my deepest, truest friend for many years, and for the first time I have the honor of comforting her."

James slowly stood aside. Perhaps Andrew was nobler than he had thought. "Inside … down the hallway to the left. Her room is the second door on the right."

Andrew walked up the steps and into the house. It had a cozy warmth about it he had never experienced before. Pictures lined the wooden walls, mail was piled on the breakfast table, and dishes were stacked in the kitchen. He wished he had time to linger and take it all in, but he needed to see Evangeline.

He knocked on her door and waited patiently for a reply. To his surprise, it was opened by one of her friends.

"Wo," a dark-headed girl replied as she stood stunned in the doorway. "I didn't expect you."

"May I speak with Evangeline?"

She glared at him suspiciously, obviously very protective of her friend.

"I'm only here to bring my condolences," he assured her. "Nothing more—I promise."

"Who is it, Jenna?" he heard Evangeline's weary, broken voice ask.

She opened the door all the way to reveal the visitor. The other girl's jaw dropped. She jumped up from the bed beside her friend and stood speechless.

"Andrew?" Evangeline asked in unbelief.

The second girl walked toward the door. "I think Jenna and I will go now."

"You call us if you need us," the brunette said firmly. "I mean it." She gave Andrew a hard stare as she passed him on the way out.

He held up his hands in innocence. "It's not what you think."

She replied, "I hope not. I assumed you were classier than that."

"Believe me, I am."

He was immediately moved to grief when he finally got a good look at Evangeline. Her make-up was smeared, her eyes were swollen and red, and her body was thinner than he had ever seen before. He approached her bed slowly and then lowered himself beside her.

"I have absolutely nothing to say other than I'm sorry," he began. "I'm sorry for all of this—for losing your mother, for the idiocy of Dexter Braisogn and every other royal in this kingdom. I just wanted to come here personally because I couldn't get to you at the funeral. I tried, but it was impossible. And even if I did, what could I say in such a short moment to really express what I feel?"

"I understood. It was okay, Andrew. You didn't have to come all the way here to tell me that."

"Yes, I did. You've been there for me time and time again. You've lifted me up more than you could ever know … and never asked for anything in return. And I've taken more from you than I know you wanted to give."

"It's really okay."

"No! You don't deserve this!" He wanted to hold her but didn't want her to misunderstand. "I wish I could just take your hand and tell you all this will pass and when you come out on the other side you'll soar. But I don't want you to think I'm asking anything from you—I won't do that to you. You're above me and my kind, Evangeline. I would never ask you to settle for a life with me—a prison. I want you to know that."

He now did take her hand. "I'm here because I only want to bring you some kind of comfort in the midst of all this misery. I want to make you feel like you can go on—just like you made me feel when I thought my world was caving in. And heavens, for helping me get my head screwed on straight … how do I make up for all that you've done?" He pulled her to him. "That's why I'm here—I only want to be a friend to you for the first time."

Evangeline fell into his shoulder and began to weep. Everything she was facing at the moment was too big to process, but somehow having him here did bring a release. She clung to his shirt and let herself explode with anguish and bitterness at all she had suffered. It was so much to bear at one time, but having him hold and assure her that she could go on was comforting. She understood what he was saying. He wouldn't declare any feelings for her, and he wouldn't marry her because he wouldn't let her be subjected to that kind of confinement. She could handle that much easier than knowing she could never be with him simply because of a bloodline.

As she pulled herself together, she began to tell him years of pent up frustrations. He was there as her friend, so she unloaded it all. She talked for hours, on into the night. He only listened and consoled. She shared her dreams and her fears, her anger and her hurt, her confusion and her passion … all of it flowed forth, wave after wave. She was almost embarrassed at her rambling, but she had held so much back from him over the years that once she started, she couldn't stop.

"You want something to eat?" her father asked them as he peeked inside the open door. "I've already fed your security team."

Andrew looked at him in surprise. "Really? They usually handle their own needs."

"They told me as much. We have a ton of food here people have prepared from the church. Evie and I could never eat it all. I thought you must be getting hungry. It's nearly ten o'clock."

Andrew looked at Evangeline. "Are you hungry?"

She shook her head.

"Evie," James pled in a low, concerned voice. "You've got to eat."

Andrew looked back at her and she saw worry in his eyes. He reached out his hand. "Come on. Show me how this is done … eating other people's food. I'm not at all familiar with that."

She smiled and took his hand.

They ate and looked at pictures around the house. Father and daughter explained each photo and how significant it was in their life as a family. Andrew ached that he had missed all of this. He wondered if it were even possible to raise a real family in the palace. He wished he had come here years ago and seen what had made her who she was. This was what he had missed, and what he would always miss in his life.

Evangeline followed him out to the car well after midnight to say goodbye. The security team had already loaded the black van and was waiting for him by the gate.

"Thank you," she said in the darkness, barely able to see him from the light on the porch. "Consider yourself officially noble and friendly after this. You were what I needed today more than anything else."

He nodded. She could tell he didn't want to leave.

"I want you to make me a promise," she said as she took his strong hands in hers.

"Anything."

"Please marry for love," she implored. "If you don't do anything else, at least do that. It will cover a multitude of wretchedness with everything else you'll have to face."

He chuckled. "You say that as though it's actually possible. There's nothing I want more in this life than to marry the woman I love, but that won't … that can't happen. I wouldn't do that to anyone I truly loved."

She wished she could see his dark eyes and read his face. She knew what he was saying and loved him even more for it, but that familiar ache she always had when they parted was back. She lifted her hands and softly caressed his beard. He would sacrifice his happiness to let her accomplish her dreams. She could marry him now, but is that what she really wanted? Did she love him more than she loved her freedom? But then, would she ever really be free if her heart was always tied to his?

"I wish my head were clear," she confessed.

"Your head is never clear," he laughed as he pulled her to him. "And it never will be. There's too much going on in there and it always mingles with your heart. You'll just have to play your life by ear."

There was so much she wanted to say, so many things they should talk through, but he had made his stand, and she was somewhat relieved because of it. As the thoughts jumbled around in her mind, she found herself pulling his face down to hers. She kissed him for the second time in her life. If he was walking away for good, she wanted one more moment of him. He warmly responded and pulled her closer than she imagined possible. Many others had given up love for great causes, and she had to let him know how she felt one last time.

"Why did you have to go and do that?" he asked breathlessly as he buried his lips in her hair.

"I don't know. Maybe I just needed us to be sure we could walk away."

He kissed her again, his hands rubbing the muscles in her arms as he ran them up and down slowly. "You've just made me more unsure than I've ever been in my life."

"Good," she smiled through another kiss. "We're even then, and I know you'll never forget me."

"Like I could ever do that."

❧ Chapter Eight ☙

(2 Years Later)

Evangeline stretched mindfully in the locker room as she awaited the call to come to the court. Her coach, Terry Smith, very blond, very handsome, and very American, paced the area like a caged cat. They had timed her going pro for this very moment—The French Open. She wasn't at all surprised to be here at this time. This was exactly what she had worked for, exactly what she had planned, and now she was ready to complete this first step in her life mission.

"Okay," Terry pestered as he glanced at his watch. "Let's go over this one last time. First …"

"This is my medium," she spoke before he could finish.

He looked sharply at her. "You seem so smug about all of it. Do you realize what's about to happen? A virtual unknown is playing in the finals at the French Open and taking on the number one seeded player in the world. You haven't even been pro for a year, and you totally skipped the Australian!"

"I know exactly what's about to happen," she said nonchalantly as she continued to stretch, "and if you'll remember, this is exactly how we planned it. We carefully chose our circuit, made it to the French, and I'm about to take on Stephanie Bartko, the unbeatable American who pounds every point to death. Does that sum it up well enough for you?"

"Ugh!" he moaned. "I'll admit I've never seen anyone train or focus as much as you—it's actually been a little bit scary."

"So what are you worried about—that I'll lose?"

"For crying out loud, Evie!" His frustration at her calm approach to this match was clear. "It really doesn't matter at this point! You made it to the finals. But I want to see you stay alive and give this girl a run for her money! When this match is over, I don't care if she wins, I just want people to say

60

you gave her a good fight."

"Sit down, Terry. Let me lay it all out for you. Clay is my medium. I'm not a pounder—I play with finesse. I carefully strategize each shot and place the ball in the least likely place for my opponent to return it. Stephanie is pure strength. She drives a player farther and farther back until at last the ball simply cannot be reached." She grinned as she leaned down into his face. "But we are on clay," she whispered. "Her balls will be slowed in a major way, and I intend to be aggressive in every shot I make. Stephanie Bartko will not pound me to the line today like she has every other player in the world. She will not wear me down. In fact, every error I make will be because I was aggressive trying to throw her off balance and break her rhythm."

"You sound like it's all in the bag."

"It is. I'll come to the net every single serve she sends me. She'll either have to lob it over my head or try to get it past my reach. I don't have her height or build to play her game, so I'll make her play mine. I'll serve every single serve with a spin—I'll back drop every ball possible and draw her to the net against her will. She can pound it back as best she can, but she'll have no rhythm today."

A page came into the locker room. "They're ready, Miss Dorvain."

"Then so am I," she grinned as she grabbed her bag.

♛ ♛ ♛

Andrew hoped to watch the match by himself, but he had learned a valuable lesson about leadership. Contrary to his father's philosophy, he found the men respected him and trusted him more if he allowed himself to be personal with them. So when they suggested they watch the game together in his room on the large screened television, he obliged.

He longed to have called Evangeline and wish her luck, but it would have been a major act to accomplish. He had no contact with anyone except those with whom secured phones or internet addresses had been given. The closer it came to his coronation, the higher his security became.

He sat uneasily watching the match, but it didn't take long for even soldiers who cared nothing about tennis to pile into his room. Evie Dorvain was calculatingly slaughtering the reigning tennis champion, Stephanie Bartko. When the first set went down six to zero for Evangeline, he struggled to keep his composure. He jumped to his feet at one point and yelled in pure delight. Soon all the soldiers were chanting her name. When she wiped out the second set at another six zero, clenching the title, no one in the room could contain their enthusiasm. A Braisognian had just won a world sports tournament for the first time in history.

As expected, the king called his son immediately.

"Yes, Father, I watched every second of it," Andrew confirmed over the phone.

"Straight sets, six zero, six zero ... I had no idea something so skinny could be so powerful."

"You've never seen her muscles." He remembered the night after her mother's funeral when he had felt her arms while saying goodbye. "Apparently she trains incessantly."

"Well, when she made the semi-finals I thought we should do something to acknowledge that, but to take the title, frankly, I'm stunned. I don't quite know what would be adequate for something like this. A banquet? An award? A program of some sort in her honor? You know her, Andrew, what do you think she would want?"

There was a first—Christopher Braisogn asking advice from his son.

"My first thought is not something so huge that she gets overwhelmed by numbers. Maybe give her an award at a press conference outside one of the balconies at the palace. That way people could be there to see it live if they wanted, but she wouldn't have to actually be part of the crowd. Then we could have a small, more intimate meal with her inside. Invite her father ... perhaps her friends? The royal family, of course, would attend."

"Hmmm, that sounds good, really good. I'll put my people on it right away." His father paused. "Have you spoken with her ... lately?"

"Right," he muttered sardonically. "I just call her up regularly on our secure lines and chat away."

"I never know anything where she's concerned."

"You know everything where she's concerned." His response was laced with bitterness. "The last time I saw her was Christmas. The only time I ever contacted her outside the palace was when her mother died. You know everything, believe me."

♉ ♉ ♉

"So you're nervous about going to the palace to receive this nutsy award," Terry complained after the limo picked them up from the airport. "You weren't nervous about playing the world's number one player, but you're nervous about meeting the king?"

Evangeline shook her head. "I've met the king ... many times."

"Then what's with the mood? You look horrible. I'm glad at the moment all those rumors about us aren't true. I'd be scared to death to be your lover with that expression."

She punched him for that one. "Do you know why there are so many unfounded rumors about us—why the press has tried to peg us together romantically from the day you signed on as my coach?"

"Because they'd like to see you happy ... maybe?"

"No," she snapped flatly. "Because of Andrew Braisogn."

He shook his head. "I'm sorry, but I have no clue who that is. I've met so many Braisogns since moving here I can't keep them straight. That is so weird. You don't walk around America meeting all these people who have the last name America. I wonder about all the inbreeding going on here."

"Hmph ... me too." She looked out the window trying to find comfort in the familiar scenery of her homeland. This would be very different from any visit prior. She was now a national hero rather than a scandal of false circumstance. "Andrew Braisogn is the prince—the man in line to be king in a few short years."

"And so the press is putting us together because of him?"

"He and I have been ... close ... in the past," she tried to explain. Terry was so American that she knew he would get the wrong idea if she didn't go into detail. "When we first became friends, my family heritage was in question. You know ... the whole royal/commoner baloney."

"Right, and then the thing happened where you found out you and your mom were royal all along."

"Yes, causing a big stink in the whole class division system. And my winning the French Open will now make it all even worse because the very people who hounded and humiliated me will now be reluctantly kissing up to me ... and that includes the king, Andrew's father."

"What about the queen? Will she struggle with the kissing up?"

"She's a non-entity here. Watch when they enter a room—she's literally a yard behind him the whole time. That's her place in the kingdom, somewhere in the back just bearing him children with her royal blood."

"Wow, I can see where all that attitude descended from now, but it doesn't explain why the king would discourage a friendship or anything deeper with the prince. Why would the press try so hard to make it look like we're cavorting all over the world?"

"I'm sure it's all part of the king's PR plan. If he can make it look like I'm philandering with the sexy American, it would cast doubts on my integrity as well as make Andrew believe there's another man in my life. All of that together should discourage him from ever considering me ... well ... you know ..."

"Another man? Is Andrew the first man then? You were in love with the future king of this crazy country and you never told me?"

"No," she countered firmly. "We were friends. For too many years he couldn't even consider a relationship with me other than that, then when all the truth about my grandfather came out, it almost made the scandal worse. Only now people couldn't talk openly. They had to hide their comments because ... well ... blood is blood."

"My brain is spinning with all this," he griped as he shook his blond locks around. "So why are we having a supposed fling on the front pages of your press if you and Andrew are just friends?"

She sighed and gazed back out the window. "His father wants to pick the next queen. He wants to be in control. He wants Andrew to be as miserable and cold as he is."

"And is he?"

"Not so far, at least not since last Christmas."

The crowd outside the palace was massive. A path had been made for the limos to bring in the few selected guests, but no one knew which one would carry Evie Dorvain. She was aware of this and wanted to make sure the people saw what they came for. She reached for the button that opened the roof.

"What are you doing?" Terry asked as she pulled off her heels.

"These people came here to see me today—I want to make sure they get a good look."

"But ... is it safe? What if someone wanted to shoot you?"

"The only people here today that would want to shoot me are lining up inside the palace right now to shake my hand. There's no safer place at the moment than through this roof waving at that crowd."

She shot up through the top and the people immediately began to scream. She waved and blew kisses until the limo disappeared behind the gate.

Old Alfred, tall, lanky, thick glasses and gray, met Evangeline and Terry at the door. He looked as unhappy and constipated as ever.

"You're late, Miss Dorvain," he politely grumbled in his monotone manner.

"I'm fine, and you, Alfred?" she quipped sarcastically.

"I did not mean to be rude," he supposedly apologized with a bow, "but there is a press conference awaiting you. Everything and everyone is in place ... except you, of course."

"If that's the case, then my guess is you really were being rude."

Evangeline walked by Alfred, and Terry tried to keep from snickering. There were many things he liked about Evie, and her sharp wit was one. But she was too pristine for him. In fact, the rumors flying around about them bothered him intensely. Evie was beautiful beyond compare, and she was gracious and determined, but the best word he could use to describe her was noble, and he didn't need a noble woman in his life. He wondered what the king could possibly have against a girl who would obviously be a great queen for this country.

Evangeline was ushered to the open balcony doors where a podium and microphone were standing. The king was fisting his hands and grinding his jaw as the queen talked with an attendant. Andrew was standing leisurely, his hands behind his back. When she saw him she nearly gasped. He seemed to grow taller and broader each time she laid eyes on him.

"What about me?" Terry asked the security around them. "I was just asked here to eat. I don't have to go out there, do I?"

Alfred replied, "No, sir, Mr. Smith. If you will follow me I will take you to where the others are awaiting the luncheon."

Andrew brightened immediately when he saw Evangeline and motioned for her to stand beside him. As she took her spot he placed his hand in the small of her back and leaned into her as he softly said, "Glad you could make it."

"I thought a grand entrance would be more appropriate," she whispered back.

The king walked over to her and offered his hand. She took it, gave a small curtsy and then apologized. "I hope I didn't delay the conference by too much. Jet lag is a real killer for me."

"Not at all," he assured smoothly. "This is a celebration of your accomplishment. We would have waited all day and night if necessary."

"Looks like you were prepared for the worst then, so this can't be too bad."

Andrew snickered.

"Shall we begin?" Christopher suggested.

"Certainly," she nodded. "Is there anything I need to know about any of this, or do I just go with the flow?"

"Flow … that will be all that's needed," the king assured her.

Christopher motioned the press that he was ready to begin.

ᛒᚩ Chapter Nine ᚳᚫ

The luncheon was actually marvelous for Evangeline. She knew it had to be Andrew's plan because she couldn't imagine the king capable of putting together something so wonderful in her honor. Her father was there, her best friends Jenna and Amy were there along with their fiancés, her college and high school coaches were there, and then the king, queen and Andrew. The royal couple left first, soon followed by her school coaches. Her father and friends lingered much longer, but then they were ready to head home. Terry left when James Dorvain exited—it was finally down to just Andrew and Evangeline.

"You look great in yellow," he told her after the last person left. "I always imagined green to be your color, but yellow against that tan is striking."

She blushed. She didn't want to flirt with him—she just wanted to talk awhile.

"And you look so dashing in your … military blue," she purred. "You know what? I don't remember ever seeing you in anything other than formal attire except for that day you came to visit me at my house. You were wearing a red polo with blue jeans and loafers." She smiled. "I'm afraid red may be more of your color than blue."

"I'll be sure to let the military know that when I head back to maneuvers." He reached for her hand. "Let's go to the parlor. We'll be more comfortable there."

She walked with him to the next room which contained several couches and lavish pieces of decorative furniture. He motioned her to have a seat on a plush piece as he sat opposite her. They just stared at each other for a moment.

"This is very different," she finally confessed. "I'm not sure how to behave. We're not sneaking around to strange rooms to talk, and I just had lunch at the palace in my honor. Am I dreaming?"

"Were you dreaming when you took on Stephanie Bartko at the French Open and beat her in straight sets?"

She looked directly at him and declared, "No. That was very real. I think I might still have the sweat to prove it."

"Hah, you didn't sweat the entire game. I've never seen that woman look so pathetic. How did you manage that?"

"Partly clay. I knew it could slow her game significantly if I could keep her on the run—so that's what I did."

"And to think I believed at one time I could have killed you in tennis. I'm glad we never had the chance to actually play."

"I would probably have let you win."

He shook his head. "I deserve that." He grinned with great charm. "I could be very trite and ask how you're doing and how your life is, but it appears as though you're much focused and doing quite well."

"For the most part that's true. I'm completely honed in on tennis for the time being, but am only using it for a greater means."

"Charity?"

"More or less. Not just charity, but helping kids in general. I believe if a child has someone to believe in them and something to hope for, they can rise above any circumstance. I hope the French Open is only the beginning."

"Wimbledon?" He raised an eyebrow.

"That's my next stop," she smiled confidently. "Braisognia would definitely be on the bigger map instead of everyone thinking my win at the French was just a fluke. If I could take Wimbledon this year, well, let's just say it would seal my reputation here significantly."

"Oh, it's sealed already, I assure you. But what about the U.S. Open? Surely you don't think you can take on Stephanie Bartko there? She would slam you around that court like a …"

"We'll deal with Wimbledon and the grass first. I'll think about the U.S. when the time comes."

"Fair enough, but it won't keep me from being nervous for you."

She giggled. "What is with you men? Terry was climbing the walls before the match, scared to death I was going to be humiliated. I tried to assure him I was very confident in my game, but he seemed to think I was being foolish."

Andrew looked away.

"What?" she wondered at his response.

He just shook his head and smirked.

"What is it?" she repeated.

He sighed and ran his fingers through his long hair. "The coach, huh," he mumbled. "I guess as a coach he's very adequate … taking you to a world championship in such a short time."

"He's done fairly well once I convinced him that I wasn't out to develop a style but rather to just beat everyone I played."

"Isn't that the idea?"

"Not always. People have a tendency to play to their strengths, lean on what they're really good at. I think that's kind of what life is like in general for most people."

He cocked his head and smiled as he asked, "But not you?"

She firmly shook her head. "Not at all. My goal is to beat each player by disarming their strengths. I spend many hours scouring footage of potential opponents. I learn what makes them tick, how they move, their most likely returns to certain shots, and then I literally play every point with the plan of throwing them off so they're just trying to get the ball back over the net."

"That sounds scary. I have no desire to be opposite you on a court any longer. Doesn't all that thinking deter you from being ... well ... I don't know, on top of your game?"

She smiled. "You tell me. Did I seem off of my game at the French Open against the most ominous woman player in the world?"

"She didn't intimidate you at all, did she?"

"No, because I disarmed her."

"You certainly did ... highly impressing the world ... and Braisognia in the process."

She shrugged. "If only I could find the ability to disarm people in real life."

"You're kidding, right? Are you not aware of what just happened here today? My father threw a press conference and royal luncheon in your honor! Would you not consider that disarming?"

She snickered sarcastically at his suggestion. "I disarmed nothing where your father is concerned. If anything, I just caused him to build a greater wall. He would have loved to have stamped me out of this kingdom years ago."

"You're wrong! He's tickled pink! You're the hero of the day here."

"Of the day. Nothing could irk him more than to realize *I'm* the one who put this nation on the world's map. Now he has to bow to me for the sake of his nation's reputation, and I can guarantee it sickens him."

"I imagine you're right, but at least he's smart enough to know that distancing himself from you would be the worse decision of his royal legacy. And if you win Wimbledon ..."

"If? What do you mean *if?*"

"... If ...," he continued, "you were to win Wimbledon, my father would have to eat his pride in a larger dose than any of us could imagine."

"Ugh! What I hate most about all of this is that it still boils down to the stupid, arrogant divisions in this ridiculous system! And what makes it so infuriating is that I have no legitimate cause to be hated by your father or the rest of the self-righteous snobs in this kingdom! I'm legally a royal, disdained and shunned by my own because of a royal-initiated lie, and now hatefully ingratiated by all of them who would much rather have seen me disappear than succeed. The truth is—those who loved me for who I was before all the disclosure at my mother's death are the only ones who still love me now. The ones who were proud of me before ..." she sighed and paused, "... are the only ones who are truly proud of me now." She gazed at him with frustration. "Everyone else is playing a game. It's called, *Watch the girl until she crashes and burns and then we can all laugh at her rather than celebrate with her.* I can guarantee your father is pleased I won the French, but he'll be seething when I win Wimbledon, and he'll be exploding, privately of course, when I win the U.S. Open. You watch ... I know the evil side of the royals—I've lived with it all my life."

He smiled and held up his arms as he laughed. "So what? I've lived with it all my life too, but my future lies with it ... in a big way. I can either give into it, you know, succumb to it and be defeated by it all ... just sucked into that evil, or," he leaned over to her and whispered, "I can tolerate it ... and eventually dominate it."

She leaned toward him and whispered back, "You will be king. You will have the legal authority to dominate it."

"Yes," he continued softly, "but you have something even greater than that—you will disarm it."

She giggled. "Why are we whispering about all of this?" She looked up and around at the ceiling. "Are we being watched?"

"I just wanted a good excuse to get closer to you, plus I thought it would make a great effect—make you listen to me harder."

Was he flirting, she wondered. He always managed to somehow. "Why would you want to get closer to me?"

"To see if you smelled like the cologne your tennis coach had splashed all over himself."

She sat up abruptly. "What? What is that supposed to insinuate?"

"I read the papers. I watch the news. Everyone except for you guys seems to think there's some romantical hanky-panky going on."

He was jealous? She grinned. "Romantical? Is that even a word?"

"Well, it's the best I could come up with. Everybody claims something's a-spark between you. All these awkward pictures manage to appear ... seemingly romantic, thus *romantical*. But you guys always deny everything. In fact, I think the coach even used the word terrified concerning how he felt about you. I keep thinking, if something is actually going on, why are they denying it? But everyone I know seems to think it's just one of those celebrity things, and you all are simply trying to keep it quiet."

"That's ridiculous! If I was in a relationship with somebody, why would

I hide it?" She looked at him, and then smiled. "Unless it was you. I'd have to hide it—I would fear for my life."

He leaned back on the couch. "So you're telling me, honestly, there's nothing going on with you two? Nothing at all?"

"Never has been, never will be. He really doesn't like me that much. He likes that I win, but not how I win. Every time I walk out on a court he becomes a nervous wreck. We actually got a good laugh when all of the rumors started. He thinks I'm too good."

"Too good? What does that mean?"

"Too idealistic, too confident, too over-the-top for him."

"But you're beautiful," he added. "Maybe that's the problem ... you're better looking than him."

She laughed and slapped his knee, "That's it! He can't handle the competition!" Then she stopped laughing and frowned. "Maybe that's why he keeps telling me to change my style? Perhaps he actually wants me to lose?"

"So, I guess this whole romance was cooked up by my father. Apparently there's no truth in it, you guys keep denying it, but the rumors just won't die. It spells Christopher Braisogn all over it."

"That was my first thought when it hit the papers to begin with," she agreed. "Terry said it was a typical thing, but I told him it was more than that. He laughed it off ... even posed for some of those pictures. That didn't help."

"My father still thinks I'm gonna lose my head and chase after you. I told him I could never do that to you—I made it clear after your mother's funeral. I also told *you* that after your mother's funeral. My decision will never change. As much as I think you would be a huge asset to this palace ... to this kingdom ... I wouldn't lock that chain onto your life for anything."

She half-nodded, but then looked at him with wonder. "Asset to the palace ... to the kingdom ... what about you? I wouldn't want to be chased after simply because I might be some asset to something else."

He smiled. "You wonder if you would somehow be good for me, if you would perhaps change my life for the better, if you would brighten my days and alter the miserable course destiny has somehow chosen for me? Is that it?"

She was humiliated now. "Dang it," she whispered, hoping he wouldn't hear. She closed her eyes and shook her head. "No. I said I wouldn't do this."

"Do what? Remind me of my misery?"

She didn't respond.

He shook his head as he explained, "Do you think I've suddenly become oblivious to my plight? Believe me—it's always before me, perhaps now more than ever. For awhile, at least, I could convince myself that for the most part … the nation, the people … thought I would be a welcomed change as king. Then I heard the rumors … the coined phrase to describe my impending rulership."

She had heard several herself. "What phrase?"

He took a deep breath and said with disdain, "The third king."

She shuddered. She had heard it many times and had defended him about it at every mention. "You are not the third king."

"Of course I am. The first two in line to the throne abdicate? Let's just shove the little one right on up." He sighed. "The third king. No matter what I do or how well I might possibly rule, I'll always be the only king on the Braisognian throne not by right, but by default."

"You are not on the throne by default," she insisted. "You're the heir to the Braisognian dynasty! It's not your fault that your brothers chose to bow to their own selfishness! You are nobler than any man in this kingdom!"

"Easy to say, hard to convince," he continued with the now gloomy attitude. "Face it—we claim to be a constitutional monarchy. We hold elections. We have two houses—common and royal. But the reality is that the king has fifty-one percent of the vote. The elected officials hold no true authority except to argue over governmental decisions and hope they can be the ones to convince the king to see their side of the fence. This nation is at the mercy of whoever wears the crown, and that's nothing more than a joke. And depending on who rules, it's either a good joke or a bad joke, and it goes on and on for years and years."

"But you will be the king!" she tried to emphasize again.

"Yes!" he exclaimed in exasperation. "The third king!"

"Andrew," she said more calmly, but firmly, "you will be the king."

He stared at her sternly. "Yes, I know. We have established that … over and over again."

He wasn't getting it. She leaned in again and hesitated before she whispered lowly, "Yes, and as king," she paused again, "you can do anything you want … change anything you want." She held her stare on him hoping he would understand.

He slowly wrinkled his brow as he leaned into her and asked as hushed as possible, "Are you suggesting that I consider changing the years of royal protocol and rule that have governed this nation for centuries?"

She shrugged. "I'm not suggesting anything at all." She continued the quiet tone. "I'm just reminding you that, obviously, when you become king, you'll have the power to do … or change … anything … *anything* … you consider unfair, unjust or undeserved."

He bit his lip and nodded slowly.

"Again," she whispered even softer, "I'm not suggesting anything to you. I just think you consider your power more a plight than a privilege.

You might need to begin regarding things in a different light … just … you know … ponder the possibilities."

His eyes darkened as though his brain was rushing with ideas he had never before envisioned. "Why is it that on my own I always feel forced to be something I'm not, but with you I always come away with a strength to be everything I truly want to be inside?"

☸ ☸ ☸

James Dorvain knew something about his daughter's visit with the prince had kept her quiet for several days. He had hoped she would take a rest from tennis after the French Open, but she and Terry were on the court behind the Dorvain house pounding away at balls. Usually there was much arguing between the two. James had laughed at the rumors in the papers concerning a possible romance. Had any press ever observed a practice session, they would have quickly dismissed the idea. But today there was no dialogue at all. Occasionally they would stop, the coach would make a suggestion, she would nod, and they would start up again. Something was definitely not right.

After a shower and a light supper, Evangeline found herself on the back deck staring into the twilight. She was still disturbed about her visit with Andrew.

"There you are," her father said as he walked through the double doors carrying two small plates with cobbler and ice cream. "You disappeared on me after the meal. The cook made some fresh strawberry cobbler—your favorite."

She didn't even look up as she answered, "No cobbler—I'm in training."

"Yes, I know," he spoke as he sat beside her and offered the dessert anyway. "But with as little as you've eaten the past few days, you could have several helpings of this and it would only do you good."

She looked toward him now and gave a tired smile. "I guess I do seem to be having a bad week."

"Anything to do with your trip to the palace?"

Dipping her spoon into the heap of ice cream and warm cobbler, she brought a small portion up to her lips. She relished the sweet flavor of pure sugar and bleached flour. "Actually," she began to explain as she finished the first bite, "it has everything to do with my trip to the palace." Without looking at her father she confessed, "I'm afraid that perhaps I did something inappropriate while with Andrew the other day."

Her father's face showed alarm. "And what exactly have you done?"

She took another bite, letting the flavors melt together in her mouth before continuing. "I might have suggested to him that he use his power to change … change things he felt were not … oh … fair."

"I don't see anything inappropriate with that."

"You don't know what he was considering unfair at that particular moment."

He took his time before asking, "And what exactly was he considering at that moment?"

She put down the cobbler and stood from her seat. Walking over to the railing she leaned her hands on top. "He was sympathizing with those who have called him the third king."

James winced. "He's heard that?"

She nodded.

He joined her at the railing. "I'm still lost as to the inappropriateness of all this."

"He said it wasn't right that one person should have fifty-one percent of the power in a nation that basically claimed to be a democracy. He called it a joke. And he feels right now that this is how most people in Braisognia view him."

"And you suggested … what exactly?"

"I only reminded him that as king he had the power to change anything he wanted." She looked back at her father with a guilty frown. "I think I emphasized the anything again … maybe too much."

James squinted as he placed his own cobbler on the rail. "I see." He paused and looked out toward the growing darkness. "Is it possible that anyone other than Andrew heard you make this suggestion to him?"

"I was whispering very, very softly."

"Hmmm …" He looked worried. "Do you know what could happen if someone else heard you, or if it ever got back to certain people what you might have suggested there?"

She only nodded.

"I don't believe Andrew would speak of it to anyone," he said hopefully.

"He wouldn't. I know that." She sighed. "But like you said, if anyone … *anyone* … heard it … somehow, well, I could be in …"

"More trouble than you could imagine."

"Yep."

James put his hand to his chin and began to stroll a bit. "I know Andrew would ever endanger you—he would keep every word you said in complete confidence." He stopped and turned to her. "But you were in the palace—it has high security. Many things have been said there that were never meant to reach certain ears, but somehow they always managed to find out. Just how softly did you whisper?" he asked weakly.

"Very …"

ᴆ Chapter Ten ᴃ

(July)

The entire nation of Braisognia held a collective breath as Wimbledon geared up for the final women's match. It was likely that every television in the kingdom was tuned into the game. Andrew had managed to watch the entire tournament by himself even though he was in the midst of summer military maneuvers, the most intense of the year. There had been several suggestions that he join them to view the final championship match, but he threw out an excuse about needing to do a bit more planning for the next day's exercises.

He had hoped Evangeline would do well in the tournament but never imagined she could make it to the finals again. He had recorded every match and took note of her unnerving tenacity against each opponent. It was almost as if she could read their every move and counter it with uncanny precision. He had laughed to himself many times at the idea that he had thought in the past they might meet some time during the year and play a little tennis as an excuse to get together. He would have been disgraced unless she would have shown mercy and allowed him some kind of advantage.

He sat nervously before the large screen and even chewed a hangnail, something for which his father would have seriously reprimanded him. He swallowed hard as the players were announced and the camera immediately darted to Evangeline. Every time he saw her, even throughout this tournament, her beauty stunned him. He couldn't imagine anyone on earth more lovely. Was it possible he was so in love with her that he was merely blinded to everyone else? He had considered abdicating many times, and she was the main reason. He could handle all the ups and downs of kingship, but the thought of not spending the rest of his life with her was daunting. Yet he had always known he wouldn't.

He was amazed at her confidence as she waved to the screaming crowd in the packed stadium. He was embarrassed that the only Braisognian sitting in her box was her father. In fact, it seemed mortifying to Andrew that no more than James Dorvain and Terry Smith were there for her support. The king or queen at least, even better, both should have been there to represent the nation. He wondered why his father, so vain and arrogant, wasn't there glorying in the utter success of his kingdom at this moment. He could guess. His father probably didn't believe she could win again. Even though she had taken out the number one player in straight sets at the French, Wimbledon was a much faster court. Stephanie would stuff the ball down Evangeline's throat every chance she got. His father also probably had no desire to have to honor her again publicly. In his mind, Andrew imagined, once was more than enough, and to show public support would be a major admittance to the grand mistakes possible in this society ruled by bloodlines.

As Evangeline removed her racket and took her place at the end of the court, Andrew's heart beat faster. He knew to the rest of the nation this match was only about Braisognia. But for him, it had nothing to do with his country—this was about her. He seriously doubted she could take down Stephanie a second time. The woman had dominated women's tennis since she was eighteen, and no one had come close to threatening her. She was Amazonian in size and strength, and she devastated all who came against her in the game. Evangeline had used a serve-and-volley format against her at the French Open, and even though that would be the classic approach to play here on the grass, the merciless champion would be more than prepared to throw her every curve imaginable. He tried to catch his breath and relax as he anticipated the possible slaughter of the petite girl that held his heart.

Stephanie looked fierce and determined as she bounced the ball several times before taking her service stance. The camera shifted to Evangeline who actually displayed a small smile as she shuffled in anticipation of the first serve.

"Don't look so cocky," he whispered as he started back on the hangnail. "She's out to eat your lunch today. She has everything to prove."

The first serve flew over the net, and to everyone's surprise, Stephanie, in a drastic switch to the characteristic serve-and-volley style, ran to the net, extremely atypical for her. Andrew grimaced knowing Evangeline couldn't have been prepared for that move, yet seconds later he sat stunned as she returned the ball, whizzing it so opposite of Stephanie's stance that had she even attempted to run it down she would have never made it. The first thought that came to his mind as the crowd roared and Stephanie's jaw dropped, was that his father at this moment was probably using the worst form of profanity anyone could imagine.

(September)

Evangeline couldn't believe Andrew would be at the U.S. Open, sitting in her box beside Terry and her father, as she once again played the formidable Stephanie Bartko. After taking the American down for a second time in straight sets at Wimbledon, it would have been a sorry display of national neglect had no one significant shown for the final in New York. She couldn't fathom the king allowing Andrew to be the representative. He must despise her more than she thought to let the prince be the one to represent Braisognia before the eyes of the world. Then again, once the world saw the handsomeness of the prince, perhaps it would be even more enamored with the small country. Maybe Christopher Braisogn had some method to his madness after all.

Terry had refused to allow Andrew and Evangeline meet before the match. He was superstitious as well as scared out of his wits something would distract her from the game at hand. This match would be very different. This was Stephanie's home court, and this was her medium. No one had ever won a single match against her here, and very few could imagine that the tiny girl from the tiny country could dethrone Stephanie on her own turf. Wimbledon had been humiliating for the brutal champion who had changed her game deliberately to serve-and-volley assuming that Evie would have played as she had at the French. But during the entire match Evie had only approached the net an unbelievable five times. The crowd had been stunned at how Evangeline Dorvain managed to dictate every point and was never caught off guard or forced to error on any level.

As the two players entered the arena in New York, again Evangeline's manner was calm and confident. Stephanie, however, for the first time in all the years she had played, looked anxious and unsure. Even with the past two Grand Slam finals going to the Braisognian, the commentators still didn't give her much hope against the American on this court in this city. The prediction was that she would slam Evie to the ground, pounding every ball until exhaustion finally would steal away the final title of the series.

Evangeline removed her racket and immediately crossed the court to where her box and trio of people sat. She bowed low before the prince at which the cameras and crowd went wild. The display of loyalty to royalty was something Americans didn't often see, and they cheered for whom they considered the underdog at this match. Terry nearly went into a panic as he now was worried that Evangeline would only be thinking about the hunky prince sitting next to him rather than focusing on Stephanie Bartko.

♗ ♗ ♗

Once the match and awards were finished, Andrew was at last escorted to the locker room where Evangeline sat, obviously drained and weary from the tournament. This had been the toughest for her yet because it really appeared that her picks in the draw were designed to be more difficult and hopefully take her out before the finals. As Andrew walked in, she sat on a bench with her face buried in a towel. He stepped toward her and wondered exactly how to greet her this time. They had never met in such a private, informal setting.

"Hey, champ," he spoke softly as he approached the bench. "You okay?"

She immediately looked up, threw the towel down and ran into his arms. "I can't believe you're really here," she said as she fell into him. "I wanted to speak to you before the whole thing started, but dum-dum Terry about had a cow over it."

"He told me." He moved her back so he could see her face. "Still beautiful, even drenched in sweat."

She giggled. "Maybe drenched in sweat, but also a Grand Slam champion again."

"I can't believe you slaughtered her like that. Where did all this come from? How did this little Braisognian beauty manage to take on the world's most ruthless player and hack her to pieces?"

"I explained all that to you a few months ago. Were you not listening to me?"

He took her hands and looked deep into her eyes. "I hang onto every word you ever say to me."

She believed him. His stare was intense as he squeezed her hands.

"You know what?" she smiled and looked up at him. "We're not under the watchful eyes of Albert or any other palace employee right now."

He motioned to the door with his head. "Well, Max is right over there, but we can pretend he's invisible if you like."

"But Max is not a palace employee—he's yours ... loyal to you."

He nodded. "I see what you mean."

"Do you have a whole security team traveling with you?"

"Yes. It was quite a job to get me here."

"Enough to cover us all going out tonight to celebrate? I've got a small team myself. We could call the club and let them know we're coming and to reserve a hidden place."

"Seriously?" His eyes grew wide with excitement. "I haven't been out anywhere since my college days."

"It's a sports bar," she explained as she walked back toward the bench to gather her belongings. "I've been there several times the past couple of weeks ... just to get away from the grind of the game and the boredom of hotel walls. Everyone's been very considerate and supportive. With our security combined I imagine it could be doable."

He grinned wide. "Let me get Max over here and you can go over the details with him." He turned to go, but came back immediately and kissed her quickly on the cheek.

"What was that for?"

"For the best day of my life."

ᕼ ᕼ ᕼ

Security had everything honed down perfectly so when Andrew, Evangeline, Terry and James stepped out of the limousine at the establishment, the flow into the building and to the table was smooth. Many cheered when she walked in, and Andrew was mesmerized by the idea that this was the first time he had ever been anywhere that it wasn't about him or his family. As they walked through to their table, congratulations were offered and drinks were lifted in her honor. He had to continually put out of his mind the thoughts of what a perfect queen she would make. He had known that long ago but had also long ago decided that no one so wonderfully free should ever wear such chains.

They sat, they ordered, they laughed and they danced. In America it was almost as if they didn't exist in the royal world. On occasion someone would take notice and speak to them, but for the most part they were left alone.

"I am absolutely swimming in hilarity right now," he spoke into her ear as they danced to the live music. "I have never in my life experienced anything like this."

"The bar?" she grinned up at him. "Or holding me this close in public?"

He shook his head at her and just held her closer. "Everything. Absolutely everything."

Later that evening, Andrew, James and Evie sat in her hotel suite and continued the celebration. Andrew had never spent much time with her father prior to this. They had shaken hands at public events and royal gatherings, and had been in meetings of the military several times, but to sit and talk had never happened. Andrew was envious of the closeness the father and daughter shared. She sat snuggled next to him on the couch, and much of their conversation was laced with playful banter as James revealed silly things she had done over the years. He was a man with intense compassion and love, and Andrew marveled at how approachable and gentle his demeanor was. He had never met any man like him before.

It was also enlightening to see Evangeline in a setting that didn't center on Andrew or his problems or his fears or his insecurities. This night was all about her, and she graciously took it in stride. No one would ever know that she had just won a third Grand Slam title for women's tennis in her first year of going pro. He was thankful his father hadn't come—the mood would have been drastically different. There would have been the unnatural formality that exuded from Christopher Braisogn, and laughing would have been pretentious if at all. The pleasant, relaxed serenity surrounding them in the room was a breath of fresh air into the stale, humdrum life he had always known.

"I suppose I should leave you two to talk alone for awhile," James yawned as he stood from the couch and stretched his arms wide. "I know these moments are rare for you."

Andrew was shocked. He never imagined her father would leave them unaccompanied in her room. "Are you sure?"

James raised his eyebrows. "I was ... should I not be?"

Evangeline laughed just as she had all night. "You can trust him, Daddy. He's an honorable fellow."

He looked to his daughter. "But can I trust you?"

She thought on it for a moment then replied, "It really doesn't matter. Andrew is not a man easily persuaded."

James shook his head as he walked to the door. "I hope not. It's tense enough watching you play international tennis. Worrying with royal family issues would be ten times worse."

She laughed again as she followed him to the door and gave a large hug. "I love you, Daddy. Good night."

"Good night, sweetheart." He gave a wave to Andrew. "Good night."

"You too, sir"

She came back to the sitting area and plopped down on the couch where she and her father had been sitting. She smiled at him, but he could see the exhaustion in her eyes.

"I probably should go too," he told her, not really wanting to. "You've got to be close to collapsing after all the playing you've done the past weeks."

"This is nothing. I practice many more hours every day leading up to all this. True, Stephanie is a challenge, but as long as I can keep her running she doesn't have much time to send me all over the court."

"I don't know how you do that," he said still astonished by her game. "She scares me to just look at her, and when she plays, she's vicious. You literally make her look like she doesn't have a clue what she's doing out there."

"That's my job."

"I hope one day I can carry my job out as well as you have yours."

"You will. You'll be unmatched in your kingship."

"Unmatched, perhaps, but that doesn't mean necessarily for the better."

She studied him with a puzzled look. "What is it about being king that worries you so much? What are you afraid that you won't do well?"

He sat back and thought. He had never been posed that question before.

She added, "Don't contemplate your answer to me. Don't try to phrase it or explain it just so. Tell me what was at the front of your mind and the top of your heart when I asked."

He raised his eyebrows and confessed, "That's very foreign to me. I have to be guarded and contemplative at all times. I can't afford to have my mouth go off like a loose cannon."

"I say you can't afford to not speak your mind on occasion—that's why you have me." The corners of her mouth lifted slightly.

"Yes … that is why I have you, isn't it?" His heart needed her more than he ever wanted to admit.

"So, shoot off that cannon," she insisted. "Bombard me with all that you can't say to anyone else."

He was tempted to do that, let her hear everything he kept bottled inside, but the night had been too perfect. He didn't want to spoil it with doom and gloom. He wanted to remember this rare trip as something unspoiled, something untouched by his moodiness. He didn't want to bring his father here by conversation, and he didn't want to bring his pathetic destiny either by dwelling on anything other than how wonderful this woman truly was.

"Nope," he asserted. "Not gonna do it."

She looked surprised. "Why? That's what friends are for."

He came and sat next to her on the couch, feeling almost guilty for taking the place her father had shared just a few minutes earlier. "Sometimes that's what friends are for, but sometimes friends are for just being there … just being in another person's life for a particular moment." He smiled down at her. "I'm here to celebrate all of this accomplishment you've managed to achieve, and I don't really feel like, want to, or desire to chat about anything to do with Braisognia."

She put her arms around him and hugged him as warmly as she had her father. "Thank you, then." She pulled back and quickly noted, "Not for not telling me, but for being here today to share this with me."

He sighed. "I wish I could share everything with you—just call you sometimes and tell you what I did or didn't do. Or drive down to your house every now and then and learn how to cook with you and your father. I would even settle for letting you demolish me in a game of tennis once a month if it meant I could be with you … like tonight … like right now." He leaned back on the couch and closed his eyes. "This has been the best night of my life. I don't recall ever being so relaxed and settled. Why is nothing in my life like this? Why is it that the only time I can really be me … is when I'm with you?"

She frowned. "I wish you could free yourself to be who you want to be. Just because all these expectations and demands are dropped at your feet doesn't mean you have to conform to them."

"My father would think …," he hesitated, "… my father …" He looked at her helplessly. "You know I despise him? The thing I hate most about being king is him. Yet the very reason I choose to be king and not abdicate is him … to save his reputation and his pride. What a slap it would be to so devastate him by not having a single heir willing to follow his rule. And yet no matter what I do, it's not right in his eyes. He is so far superior to me that I can only hope—and I use that sarcastically—only hope to attain to his level someday."

She threw her hands up in exasperation. "Why do you let him win like that? Why do you give him that power? If you know you can never please him, not because it isn't possible but because he won't allow it, why do you worry? Why can't you just move on and be yourself? And if he despises who you are so much …"

He finished her sentence, "… tell him to find another king?"

She calmed down. "Perhaps … but that's not what I was going to say. I was going to say that if he despises you so much then stop trying to please him." She took his hand into both of hers. "I don't think your father is capable of truly admiring anyone other than himself. I think he somehow feels that if anyone ever measures up to his expectations, then he's no longer superior." She rubbed her fingers softly over his skin. "Don't let him instill that idea into your gentle, tender soul, Andrew. Superior doesn't mean always being the best at everything. Many times superior means seeing the best in everyone else."

"He's never once told me he loves me."

She gasped.

"I see you and your father and I wonder what it would be like to have that kind of acceptance from anyone."

"I accept you like that, Andrew."

"But you're not a real part of my life. When my world turns upside down, I can't expect to see you at the end of day and know I can just unload it before you and find peace and calm and then pick it back up the next day when I leave. I have silence and darkness …" he sighed again, "… and here we are talking about me when that was the last thing I wanted to do tonight."

"It's really okay. I'm just helping you drop that burden for a little while." She let go of his hand and propped her head up as she asked, "So what did you want to do tonight then if not discuss your dismal life?"

"Anything. Just even turn on the television and watch mindless programming as I sit next to you. Laugh at what we see, discuss what we think about it. What do normal people do when they watch television?"

She thought for a second. "Laugh, I suppose, and discuss what they think about it."

As much as he enjoyed just being with her and watching her beside him, the television had been a bad idea. She was so tired that as soon as she was not engaged in dialogue, she fell asleep. He had thought of leaving, but being beside her, having her lean on his shoulder as she slept, filled him with such tranquility, he didn't dare move. He adjusted so he could stare at her face, and he stayed another two hours, just basking in complete contentment.

God, he prayed softly for the first time in his life, *Thank you for her ... for the few moments all these years that You let her blow through my life with her presence. I sometimes wonder if I could have managed to continue without those times of being near her ... breathing in her freshness, her vitality. Please protect her, and one day give her someone who will love her just as much as I do and care for her as she deserves.*

೫ Chapter Eleven ೬

(Christmas)

"Evie," her father said sternly, "must I insist you not go to the ball?"

She looked at her father with hot, red cheeks and shook her head. "I won't miss it." She rubbed her forehead. "At least I'm not throwing up anymore."

"You have a fever, sweetheart ... a high one." He tried to talk sense through her stubbornness. "I can send a message to him through a general to explain how sick you are and then invite him to come later on during the season—perhaps some time after Christmas."

She shook her head adamantly. "No. I'm going tonight, and that's final. Put your generals and your threats away." She was still speaking nonsense from the fever.

"I'm not threatening you. You can't even think clearly. How do you expect to sit, eat, visit ... endure? How do you expect to last through the evening?"

She got up from the table and headed to her room. "I'm getting ready. I'll see you when I'm done."

☿ ☿ ☿

When Andrew saw her, he immediately knew something was wrong. He wavered between waiting for her in the receiving line or going to her and insisting she sit somewhere until the welcoming was over. He knew if he left the line, his father would make the entire night uncomfortable. He figured the best option was to wait. If she had made it this far, she could make it the next few minutes.

As soon as the Dorvains got to him, James explained she had the flu and a high temperature, but had refused to stay home. If there was anything he could do to see that she was taken care of during the evening, the colonel would be most appreciative. No other word was needed. Andrew immediately ushered her to the expansive parlor room where they had talked after the French Open luncheon, and had her lay on one of the couches. He asked for their food to be brought to them there.

"Sir," Alfred garbled in his monotone voice, "this is highly irregular, and your father will find it …"

"Offensive?" Andrew suggested.

The old man nodded.

"You've done your job, Alfred. You've again reminded me of my duty, my place, protocol, royal expectations … do I need to go on?"

"No, sir."

"Then you may leave."

The lanky buzzard bowed and exited the room as a waiter wheeled a cart with their food through the doors.

"Evangeline?" Andrew asked as he removed the cover from her plate. "Are you hungry? It's pheasant."

She opened her eyes and attempted a smile. Her cheeks were so red and her eyes so watery that he found himself nearly sick over how pitiful she looked.

"I'm not at all hungry," she said weakly, "but I'm dying of thirst."

"Got it," he said immediately as he reached for a glass of ice water. He helped her sit and then handed her the drink. He noticed she was shivering. "Are you cold?"

"I've been cold since I left the house. I should have brought a blanket with me in the limo."

"I'll have one here in a second." He pulled out his phone and punched in Max. "Could you have someone bring a blanket in here for Miss Dorvain? She's very chilled at the moment." He clicked off the phone. "One blanket on the way."

She reached up and tenderly ran her hand down his beard. "You're very sweet to do all this."

He wanted to tell her she was insane for having come in this condition, but he didn't have the heart. "And you were very sweet to come see me tonight even though you're miserably sick." He took her hand in his. It felt like fire. "You're burning up!"

"No, I'm freezing."

When the blanket came, he carefully began to unfold it so he could cover her and hopefully stop the chills, but before he could spread it over her she asked, "Sit beside me?"

Easing himself next to her on the end of the couch, she dropped on her side and placed her head in his lap. He pulled the blanket over her as best he could and rested his arm on top of her.

"Nice," she smiled through her weariness. "We should have done this every Christmas instead of trying to maintain appearances in the ballroom."

"Ha! Had we done this every year, my father would have burned the room down."

'Father, father, father," she moaned. "I get so tired of your pathetic attitude toward your father. He is such a little man, and you are so much greater in character ..."

"He's king!"

"Not because he deserves it, but because he was handed it."

"I hope he never hears you say that."

She waved it off. "I don't want to talk about your father. Let's talk about better things tonight. He bores me. He's so predictable and unmovable."

"Agreed. What should we make the first topic of discussion tonight?"

She rolled to her back and looked up at him. Even when sick she was beautiful. "Let's discuss us."

He was a bit shocked. They never talked about *us*. Generally they avoided that subject altogether. "What about us?" he queried cautiously. "I thought we had agreed there was no us."

"Please," she griped as she closed her puffy eyes. "We've agreed on many things, but that doesn't make them valid. And no matter how much we try to ignore the future, it's still looming there ... that big, dark cloud, ready to burst and storm our little dreams to pieces."

"What dark cloud?"

"What dark cloud? Are you kidding? The cloud that reminds us you'll be king a little over a year from now ... that next Christmas you'll be either engaged or married to some other woman whom the royals consider worthy of the title queen. Next year this time I'll never be alone with you again, never hear your heart ... never ... goodness, Andrew ... never be held by you again, or touched, much less kissed."

"We only kissed twice."

"I know," she groaned again. She opened her eyes and looked up at him. "And they were wonderful. I've relived those moments more than you could know."

"Believe me, I know."

"No, you don't," she said emphatically. "You cannot possibly know what I feel for you, how I feel about you, how much of my time is spent thinking about you and wondering what you're doing and hoping I'll get to see you again soon."

He did understand. Why would she think he didn't?

She continued to ramble. "And sometimes I just sit and imagine what life could be like if I could just tell you all this. Would you change your mind about me? Would you think me worthy enough to ..."

"Hang on," he stopped her. "Don't ever doubt your worthiness for anything in this kingdom. I told you long ago why I would never chain you to this palace."

She yawned. "Do you really think me so weak?"

"No! I don't think you're weak in any way! You're the strongest person I know!"

"You can tell me that a million times, but then you treat me as though somehow I might break if I had to …"

"Evangeline," he spoke more softly, "perhaps I do. But it's not that you would break emotionally—it's your spirit that would be broken. I can't bear the thought of watching you implode because your wings have been clipped in order to keep you inside this cage. You're a person who should always be free … and I won't let you turn away from that because of me."

She sighed and closed her tired eyes as her body continued to shake with chills. "So, my prince, you'll marry another and live happily ever after, I suppose?"

"Hardly. Maybe I won't marry at all."

She laughed. "Right. So instead of being the third king, you can be known as the bachelor king! I'm sure that would go over well with all the royals."

"Why not? Perhaps one can rule better with no wifely distractions constantly tugging at his heels."

"Wonderful idea," she slurred. "I'm sure you're well acquainted with Royal Protocol, Section Seven."

He thought for a moment. He had to be well versed on it … somewhere in the back of his mind. He had been drilled and drilled over protocol since he was ten years old. The truth was that he had never been good at citing sections because he had honestly never cared.

"Of course," he responded, even though he wasn't able to clearly put a mental finger on it. "But protocol isn't exactly my favorite thing."

"Good luck with that, being king and all."

That sat quietly for a bit. She drifted in and out of sleep, but for the most part she just lay still with her eyes closed, seeming to savor what were likely to be her last moments alone with him.

Then she started again. "You do know that I love you, don't you?"

He melted. "Why are you telling me this? It isn't fair."

"I just need you to know how important you've been to me all these years. I tried to make myself believe for a long time that I didn't really care for you, but that everything I did was just because I knew you needed a friend. I justified myself as your friend. But the reality is that I think I've always loved you … deeply. I don't remember ever not loving you."

He wanted to admit he felt the same, and that he had often wondered if anyone in the world but Evangeline and his mother had truly loved him. He knew they were the only people he had ever loved, and that no matter who he might marry for the sake of the kingdom, he could never love another as long as this incredible woman remained in his memory.

But he said nothing. He wasn't sure if she was even aware of what she was saying. She was guarded and careful when it came to discussing them, yet tonight, as the fever raged, she was speaking too freely. Whether she was cognizant of her words or not, it broke his heart to hear her confess her feelings, for he assuredly felt the same, and he knew how a part of him would die when he could no longer be with her on any level. He realized now she would be just as devastated, and that hurt him above everything.

"Andrew?" came a voice from the door.

He looked behind the couch to the opening to see Max standing next to an old college friend.

"Jimmy Newell?" he asked.

Jimmy stepped on in. "Hey guy, what's been going on?"

Andrew motioned for him to have a seat and assured Max all was well.

"I see you have your hands full," Jimmy commented as he sat across from them.

"She's pretty sick tonight. I think she's finally asleep though."

"I thought you and her were … you know … not gonna keep this thing up."

"We're not actually. This isn't at all what it looks like."

Jimmy looked closely at her. "She really is very beautiful. I never got a good look at her while we were in school, but I knew you were smitten with her. I can see why."

"Yeah, well, things haven't changed."

"Why not? She's a national hero now, as famous as anyone in the royal family. In fact, she's probably more popular than any of you guys at the moment. It's like an open invitation for you."

He shook his head. "I don't want her to live this life. You of all people know how frustrating and invasive it is."

His old friend shrugged. "She kind of is living that life already, don't you think?" He immediately changed the subject. "I sort of need a favor."

"Good," Andrew grinned. "I need to throw my royal weight around a bit. What can I do?"

He reached inside his coat and produced an envelope. "I've been wasting a lot of time since I graduated college and got out of the military. Traveled a lot, experienced a lot, and basically lived like a rich vagabond."

"Sounds promising."

"Well, it was fun while it lasted."

"And it's all over now?"

Jimmy bit his lip, nodded, and explained, "I'm gonna get married."

"Wow! And this means your fun is over?"

He shrugged. "Perhaps a new kind of fun will ensue."

"Let's hope."

"Well, first thing is—I need to get an actual job. That's where you come in."

"Thus the envelope?"

"Yep. I need a reference, someone who will impress them in a big way considering I've done nothing but flounder and wander for the past while."

"What kind of position?" Andrew asked as he reached for the envelope.

"Public Relations for the Greenleaf company."

He raised his eyebrows. "Big stuff. How did you manage that?"

"My father was in the right place at the right time and they agreed to give me an interview. During said interview I might have dropped a royal name hoping to further my chances, and rather than take my word for it they wondered if perhaps I could persuade you to fill out a reference form for me ... not that they didn't believe me or anything."

"She must be pretty important for you to jump through all these hoops to get a suit and tie job."

He nodded slightly. "She's ... worth it, you might say." He glanced down at Evangeline and added, "She's no Evie Dorvain ... in the sense of how taken you are with her. But she would make a good wife for me, and I probably should get my life going now."

"As good a time as any."

"That's what I keep telling myself."

ဆာ Chapter Twelve ၈

(Two Weeks Later)

"If I must," Christopher Braisogn seethed, "I will simply forbid you to go!"

Andrew gave him a smirk and shook his head. "Do you really believe you can insist on anything and I'll just drop to my knees and do it?"

"I'm your father," he growled through gritted teeth, "and more importantly, I'm your king."

"Yes, and you've always seemed to be those in that order—king first, father second."

"Do not be impertinent with me!"

"What kind of father has this discussion with a grown son? In four months I'll be twenty-four and one year away from my coronation. Do you have no sympathy for me at all? Do you have no desire for me to find even a small amount of pleasure in life?"

His father slammed his hands together. "Being king is great pleasure! No! I have no sympathy for such weak attitudes that would have you tromping around with those who would ruin your reputation and be the cause of your ridicule and scorn!"

"The Dorvains are some of the most honorable people in the kingdom. Their only downfall was at the hands of royal lies."

"Enough!" His eyes burned with disgust. "I forbid you to go! And if you do, you do so at your own risk!"

"And what will you do, Father? Take the throne away from me? Is that your threat? If so, I'll gladly release myself from that wretched burden. You have two sons whom you've already driven away. Do you wish me to do the same?"

"I had nothing to do with Peter and George removing themselves from their duties—they chose dishonor all on their own."

"Are you really that blind? You actually believe you had nothing to do with their hatred of the throne? And is that your desire for me also? Be the third son to abdicate?" He took a bold step toward his father. "I believe you have run out of heirs, your majesty—so don't threaten me."

Christopher's jaw tightened as the vein in his forehead pulsed. "You will not marry that woman and bring her into this palace."

Andrew shook his head in astonishment. "I thought I'd made that clear years ago. No, I will not make Evangeline stoop to living inside this prison of protocol and pretense."

"She's not worthy to even kiss the grounds here!"

He desperately wanted to hit his father, to lay him on the floor, but he wouldn't draw blood over her name. Instead, he simply said, "No, father, we don't deserve to even be in her presence."

♉ ♉ ♉

Andrew felt a pang of guilt as he watched the black van follow his car to the Dorvain estate. His security should have the privilege of being home with their families during the holiday season, but the invitation to spend New Year's with Evangeline and James Dorvain had occupied his every thought. She had been so sick at the Christmas Ball that they had visited very little, and what few things they had discussed, she seemed barely rational. The one thing she had said that couldn't escape his obsession was that this would probably be the last time they could spend together alone. He knew the pressure was on for him to marry within the next year. He had looked over several prospects his father had chosen, but the thought of being with anyone other than Evangeline was sickening. He hoped if he could spend these few last days with her this year, he could let her go for good and then move on with all he must do in preparation to take the crown.

As the gate to the estate opened, his heart raced. This would be better than the U.S. Open had been. He would be in their home, and he would get a small taste of normal living for the first time ever.

Pulling up to the front of the house in the circular drive, Evangeline ran out the large front door and down the steps to his car. She jumped up and down as she waited for him to unbuckle his seatbelt and unlock the door.

"I cannot believe you're here!" she screamed as she threw her arms around him and rocked back and forth. "We're going to have the most awesome time of our lives this week!"

He pulled her back so he could see into those green eyes. "That's what I'm banking on."

"You have no idea all I've planned for you this week," she began as she took his arm and led him up the steps. "And to start it out, you're going to

90

help me cook dinner tonight."

He stopped. "I've never cooked anything in my life."

She pulled him on toward the door. "I know—that's what will make this so much fun! You may never want to go back to royal living again after a week with me."

He knew she was teasing, but he also knew there could be no truer statement in the world. This was the life he had always wanted—normal—and with her. He was agreeing to live it for one week so he could finally put it all behind him and move on.

She settled him into the guest room just across the hall from hers, and she showed him the rest of the house to familiarize him with his home for the week. She encouraged him to explore as much as he liked and feel free to ask any questions about anything he found. The last stop on the tour was the large back deck which covered half the length of the house. It overlooked three different surfaced tennis courts, a large courtyard, several flower gardens and a pond. The deck itself had several pieces of furniture, an outdoor dinette, and a swing. She motioned for him to join her as she dropped into it causing it to sway back and forth.

"I love your home," he admitted as he plopped beside her, "inside and out. I could probably just pull a cot out here and sleep for the week."

She shook her head. "Not this time of the year. It's mild today but that's unseasonal. They're predicting snow tomorrow, so this will probably be the end of swinging for the week … maybe even the month."

"Perhaps," he sighed contentedly, "but I brought some very warm clothes including a thick jacket. I may not sleep out here, but I'll definitely swing out here again."

She took his hand and smiled. "I can't believe you're actually here. I've dreamed of this so many times but never thought it could really happen."

"Your father is a hard man to resist," he grinned. "Had you sent the invitation yourself, I probably wouldn't be here. My father forbade me to come, if you can imagine that."

"Good old Dad."

Preparing supper was quite an adventure for the completely inexperienced prince. He had never so much as even poured milk into his own cereal bowl. Evangeline, however, was a patient teacher. The meal was simple—spaghetti—and the preparation not too challenging. She worked with him browning the beef and then helped with slicing the vegetables and preparing the sauce. They tore lettuce for a salad, buttered bread for baking, and then put on the pasta. It was ready exactly at six o'clock when James walked into the house.

After supper, all three cleaned the kitchen and then went into the den that looked out to the deck. Evangeline had been right—it was too cold to venture outside again, but the fire James had built made the cozy room just as inviting as the freedom of the outdoors had been earlier. They talked for nearly four hours when Andrew realized he could barely keep his eyes open. They said their goodnights and each left for their own room.

As he lay in bed, his thoughts swimming together from exhaustion at being up so late, he couldn't help but think that Evangeline was just across the hall. This one evening at her house had been better than anything he had ever done in his life. In fact, this had been his best day ever.

♉ ♉ ♉

The next morning Andrew awoke feeling refreshed and rested, but the house was unusually cool. He pulled on some warm clothes and then slowly made his way out the door and to the bathroom. When finished, he heard no noises, so he assumed everyone was still in bed. He wasn't quite sure what to do since his regular routine was to head for the dining room in the palace and have breakfast. He slowly made his way back to the den to wait on his hosts to get out of bed.

As he rounded the corner from the hallway, he heard a quiet voice. He slowed and then peeked into the room. There he saw Evangeline on her knees before the fireplace with a book opened before her. He noticed she was talking, eyes closed, and he looked around to see if her father was with her. No one else was there. She then looked down to the book, read a few sentences out loud, and closed her eyes, talking again. It suddenly dawned on him that she must be praying and the book in front of her was most likely the Bible. He immediately pulled himself back into the hallway and leaned against the wall. He felt guilty for intruding into her devotion, but it hadn't been on purpose.

"Andrew?" she called out softly.

He closed his eyes and grimaced. He was embarrassed now. He hadn't meant to interrupt her.

"Yes," he replied weakly. "It's me." He stayed in the hallway. "I didn't mean to disrupt you."

He heard footsteps creak across the wooden floor. Within seconds she appeared before him holding a coffee mug. Her smile was warm, and her beauty breathtaking as she had on no make-up and her long hair fell free and slightly disheveled down her back and around her arms.

"You didn't disrupt me," she assured him. "I've been here for an hour … just waiting on you. I didn't want to make any breakfast until you got up so I could know what you prefer."

"What I prefer? I don't have any preferences. I just eat whatever is put before me."

She looped her arm in his and led him toward the kitchen. "Well, if you did have some preferences, what would you ask for?"

He honestly didn't know. This was never an option for him. "What do you prefer for breakfast?"

"I don't know that you would care for my typical breakfast."

"Let me be the judge of that."

They walked into the kitchen and stopped at the coffeemaker. "First, I'll get started on my second cup. Then I usually have one of these lovely, large, honey, bran and nut muffins … slathered with butter, of course, since I'm not in training."

"Of course," he nodded as he watched her fill her mug.

"Would you like some coffee?"

"I believe I would. A little bit of caffeine would do me some good about now."

She reached into the cabinet and handed him a mug, then got a fresh spoon to add the condiments. He shook his head.

"I drink it black," he told her.

She frowned. "That's nasty. So does Jenna. I don't know how you can stand it."

"Well, it really began in defiance. At the palace the staff adds everything before you get it. The first time I actually drank coffee, the server asked how I would like it prepared. I had read in a book about some really tough guy drinking it black, so I just told her I liked mine black. Of course, everyone at the table, Father, Mother, the brothers, all gave me this look of shock. I figured then it was going to be bad—really bad—but I was determined to drink it like that for the rest of my life."

Her jaw dropped. "That's the craziest thing I've ever heard."

"Had you watched it, it would have been the craziest thing you'd ever seen." He laughed slightly. "When I tasted it, I thought I was going to choke, but I resolved to act like it was the best thing to ever go down my throat. I drank half the cup within a minute, forcing each swallow but trying to make it look easy."

"Did it work? Did they buy it?"

"Apparently. No one said another word about it, and every morning they bring me my coffee … black."

She took his mug from his hands and smiled mischievously. "Let me surprise you, then, and doctor it up with some cream and sugar … just this once. You may hate yourself for what you've been missing all these years."

"Just so you know," Evangeline explained as they began to prepare dinner the next evening, "Amy's fiancé broke off their engagement on Christmas Eve. She took the position as my PR person after the U.S. Open

… things had gotten so crazy and out of hand that I had to hire someone. She's good at it, so I gave her the job. Her man," she slithered the word out with repulsion, "complained that it took too much time away from him and he wasn't willing to share her with the rest of the world anymore. He gave her an ultimatum." She looked up at him and shook her head in disgust. "She chose me. I invited her over tonight to try and cheer her up."

Andrew put down his knife and squinted. "Is he a jerk? Why would anyone give someone they love an ultimatum like that?"

"Yes, he's a jerk."

As six o'clock neared, Amy showed up, and Andrew remembered her from several occasions over the years when she had been with Evangeline. He knew they had been introduced, but he had never cared. His focus had always been on Evangeline and he simply recognized her friends out of courtesy. Amy's sandy brown hair, hazel eyes and plain dress made her appear very drab at the moment, but he recalled the many formal events at which he had seen her and knew a beauty lurked beneath the present depressive exterior.

When James arrived, the four of them sat at the breakfast nook for dinner. They had yet to take a meal in the formal dining room and Andrew was beginning to wonder if it was ever used. Tonight's meal of baked chicken had been a bit more elaborate in its preparation, but she had managed to walk him through it, and he felt he was becoming quite proficient at this cooking thing. But what would it matter? As soon as he returned to the palace, he would fall right back into the same routine he had known for the past twenty-three years.

After dinner, rather than spending the time in talk as the previous night, they sat in the den, fireplace roaring, and played a fierce game of cards. He found himself laughing often at the competitive natures of the other three. To him, this was nothing more than meaningless fun, but to them it seemed as though the fate of the world hinged on the outcome of each round. It was through all the give and take that he was able to see Amy's true personality shine. She had a low key, dry sense of humor and seemed to know Evangeline inside-out. To James she was just another daughter, and as the evening grew later, the sillier they became. Andrew knew this was the most he had ever laughed at one time in his entire life. This had to be the best day of his life.

✂ Chapter Thirteen ✂

The following morning, New Year's Eve, Andrew sneaked out of his room in only his sock feet. If Evangeline was already up like yesterday, he didn't want to disturb her again. He wondered why they kept their house so cold at night as he made his way into the kitchen. The coffee had already been made, so he reached into the cabinet for a mug. He was overwhelmed by the assortment. There wasn't a matching cup to be found. Apparently they chose coffee mugs as souvenirs from the many places they had visited over the years. This should be an easy choice, just reach into the shelf and grab the first one, but there were so many. He looked over the collection and finally decided on a black one with the words U.S. Open on the side. That was the only one he could find a connection with at the moment.

Like it matters, he mumbled to himself as he poured the coffee. *I wonder if I've ever had to make such a hard decision before.* He chuckled. *Maybe this is the secret behind royalty—we aren't waited on hand and foot because of position, but rather because of stupidity and indecisiveness.*

He was amused with his thinking as he began to spoon in the cream and sugar. Evangeline had offered him a fresh spoon yesterday morning, but he really didn't mind sharing hers. Being with her at her own home surrounded by two people who knew her best had only enhanced who he'd always imagined her to be. It had taken him a while, but he finally felt relaxed being there and being around her. Of course, she was easy to be around every time they had met, but they had always been so limited that there had seldom been time for awkwardness. Here in the unhurried atmosphere of her house there were times of occasional silence and nothingness. At first he would just stare at her, amazed again by her beauty and liveliness, which would always become embarrassing when she realized he was staring. But that was passing now.

He padded quietly down the hallway and peeked carefully into the den. She was there again, before the fire with her Bible. She wasn't kneeling this time but was sitting Indian style, her eyes closed and her lips moving in prayer. He suddenly felt guilty about intruding at this special time, but he was fascinated. She had always talked about God as though he were a most trusted friend, and now he knew why. Apparently it was her habit to get up each morning and meet with Him like this. He really wanted to know what she was saying and how she did it, but he didn't want to interfere. She was always talking to him about God, so surely she wouldn't mind if he asked her to share this morning with him.

"Evangeline?" he interrupted softly as he rounded the corner fully.

She opened her eyes and looked over at him with her warmest smile. "I see you found the coffee."

He held up his mug as he walked over to join her on the floor.

"Is it black or did you add to it today?" she wondered.

He took a swallow and replied, "Added to. It's really a pleasant change. This will give me something new to look forward to as I wake up each day." He looked down at her Bible and asked, "So what do you do when you come in here like this in the mornings?"

She leaned back on her hands. "It's the time I set aside to meet with my Heavenly Father specifically. I talk with Him all day long, and I think on His words too, but this just gets me off on the right foot."

He put down his mug and picked up her Bible. "How do you do it? Pray … and stuff like that?"

"Prayer is sometimes a word that over-spiritualizes what it really means. So many people think of prayer as something formal and planned, but really it's nothing more than a conversation with the Lord."

"I've had a few of those conversations, but nothing like what you're doing right here." He looked at the page in her Bible. "And what do you do with this?"

"It's God's Word to me." She took the book and placed her finger down to a specific verse. "God's heart and mind are in these pages. So when I come to Him to hear Him speak, this is where I find that." She began to read, *"Make sure that nobody pays back wrong for wrong, but always try to be kind to each other and to everyone else. Be joyful always; pray continually, give thanks in all circumstances, for this is God's will for you in Christ Jesus.* That says a whole lot to me right now." She looked up into his eyes. "I want to give Amy's ex a real piece of my mind. What he did was miserable, and I want him to pay for it—I want him to suffer the same way that she's suffering." She looked back at the fire. "And when I came to the Lord this morning, I told Him that."

Andrew choked on her statement as he swallowed some coffee. "You told God that?" He couldn't imagine being so bold or familiar with God.

"Why shouldn't I? He already knows that's what's in my head. I didn't come to Him and tell Him to make a way for me to rip that man's arms off. I just poured out my heart and then asked Him what the right response might be."

"And He told you this verse?"

"Not exactly ... but sort of. I've read this many times, and as I was talking with Him those were the words that came to mind ... *make sure nobody pays back wrong for wrong.* So I turned to that passage and read it aloud. It was exactly what I needed to hear."

"And this is what you do every morning ... tell God things and then try to find answers in the Bible?"

She shook her head. "Every morning is different. Many mornings I'm not seeking answers—I'm just seeking Him. I'll read aloud something from the book of Psalms and pray it back to Him." She tried to explain it clearly. "Like the twenty-third Psalm. You know that one, don't you?"

"The Lord is my Shepherd?"

"Right! I might turn to that chapter and pray, *Lord, You are my Shepherd ... my guide, protector, the One who cares for me. I shall not want ... there's nothing in my life that You won't provide right when I need it. I can trust You with that.* And then I go on down the verses." She closed her Bible and placed it beside her. "Sometimes I do spend a lot of my time talking about specific circumstances or people, and sometimes I just talk to Him about Him ... or about me." She smiled up at Andrew and added, "And I talk to Him a lot about you."

His cheeks warmed. "I'm glad. I need all the prayer I can get."

"Then you should do this every morning too. That's how we get to know God personally. He longs for us to come to Him and fellowship with Him ... not just pray formal things in the presence of others."

He nodded. This really did make sense. He had never thought he could form good enough prayers, but Evangeline's perspective was very different from what he had heard in church or at various meetings.

"You wanna try?" she asked with a pleading smile.

"In front of you?" He shook his head.

"No. I'd leave and go make us some breakfast. You could have the fire and the Bible all to yourself for a few minutes."

He half-shrugged, not completely sure he wanted to try, but not at all against it. "Okay. Could you give me a good Psalm to start with? I really only know the twenty-third Psalm ... I'd like something fresh and different."

"Oh, that's easy." She picked up her Bible, flipped through the pages and handed it to him. "Just begin with the first one. You can start out by saying," she pointed to the first verse, *"Lord, you said a man is blessed if he doesn't walk in the counsel of the wicked. Give me wisdom to know those who are wicked and those who are good. Show me those in my life that would seek my downfall, and reveal those who would be encouragers of truth and righteousness.* See … it's that simple. And maybe someone will come to mind that you think needs prayer according to these verses … someone who is wicked … or someone who isn't and has pointed you to the truth."

He took the Bible uneasily. His heart was nowhere near as pure as hers, but then again, if he sought after God like she did, perhaps God would change His life to be more like hers.

❦ ❦ ❦

"Want to ride?" Evangeline asked Andrew on the last morning of his full day at the Dorvain residence.

"Ride?" he repeated as he poured sugar into his coffee. "Ride what? Scooters? Skates?"

"Horses, silly," she slapped his arm.

"You have horses? Where?"

"Stables." She motioned back behind the house as she lifted the mug to her lips.

"Stables? I've never seen any stables back there."

She finished her swallow and said, "There's a lot you haven't seen here. You're in for a major treat today." She then grinned and added, "This might possibly be the best day of your life."

After breakfast, she packed a basket of food and took him down to the garage where she revealed some sort of dune buggy in which they would ride to the stables. She zipped from the garage in the unusual contraption and followed a well worn, gravel-covered path through the woods until the red and white stables appeared. He had lost his stomach twice on a couple of humps as she took them at high speed, screaming shrilly when the buggy caught air. He never stopped being amazed at her. He had observed her at her most elegant each year at the Christmas ball, yet had seen her decimate opponents on the tennis court by wailing a racket with remarkable accuracy. He'd watched her prepare a gourmet meal with great finesse and care, and had now just experienced careless abandon as she tore over the rocky road in an open-air machine, laughing the entire way.

As they walked through the door of the front stable, he removed his gloves and blew warm breath into his freezing hands. "I think I need to thaw before I jump on a beast and start racing through this icy air again."

"Stop being such a wimp," she scolded with a punch as she hurried toward a particular stall. "I promise not to go too fast so the wind chill will be tolerable for you."

"I'm not a wimp," he grumbled, "just sane and sensible."

"Hmph," she muttered as she opened the door to the stall.

98

"How is my Prince-ey this glorious morning?" she cooed as she stepped up to a beautiful, pure white creature.

Andrew gasped in delight. "What an incredible animal! How long have you had him?" He inspected the horse with approval as he looked over every inch.

"Got him my sixteenth birthday." She reached into her pocket and pulled out an apple and a pocketknife. "I named him after you, you know?"

He was taken back. "Seriously? Prince-ey? That's what you call me behind my back?"

She sliced a piece of apple and Prince took it eagerly. "Slow down, baby," she giggled. "I've brought a real prince with me today. Mind your manners." She then looked to Andrew. "It's just Prince, but somehow the - ey got added on over the years."

"Does the prince get to ride Prince?"

She shook her head. "You get to ride the blue one."

The ride that morning was indeed leisurely. Prince was a spirited horse and begged for Evangeline to let him loose, but she kept the pace slow and steady as they traveled in and out of trails and paths, up and down hills and vales, and finally stopped at a breathtaking river with a small waterfall at its mouth.

"Is this yours?" he asked in awe as they dismounted and dropped the reins.

"This …" she held out her hands and spun around like a dancer, "… is my most favorite place in the world."

He could see why. "I think it might be mine too. This is breathtaking."

"I thought you might like it. I was afraid it was gonna be too cold to make it up here before you left, and I'll confess to maybe being a little selfish in my praying. I kept asking God for just one day so you could experience this."

"Well … amen," he spoke reverently.

While she untied the basket of food, he walked around the area and marveled at its unmatched natural beauty. Snow-covered Braisognian Mountains set the background and then melted into a rolling valley which he imagined contained thousands of wildflowers in the spring. A river ran through the valley and dropped off the fifteen foot rock wall in a rushing waterfall that filled a stony pool before making its way to other parts unknown. He looked back and noted the lean-to building near an obvious fire pit with much wood piled nearby.

"What do you do here?" he wondered out loud, more from sheer awe than curiosity.

"Everything," she piped happily as she placed the basket in the shelter and headed to the logs for wood. "Sleep, swim, cook …" she giggled again,

"… and even skinny-dipped a few times."

He looked at her and shrugged. "As opposed to what? Fat dipping?"

"Good one! I've never heard that before."

"Seriously, what is skinny dipping? I'm not familiar with that term."

She frowned. "You really don't know what I'm talking about?"

He shook his head.

"Well," she looked embarrassed, "in the summers, when it would be unmercifully hot, and Jenna and Amy and I would ride out here, we would …" She paused and looked back at him. "Never mind." She gestured as though she were brushing the thought away and simply added, "We would swim."

"This must be indescribable in the summer!"

She grabbed a couple of logs from the stack. "That's exactly what it is—indescribable."

"Hand me those," he motioned toward the wood as he pointed to her arms. "Do you have kindling or do we need to gather some?"

She hesitated, cocking her head in uncertainty. "You know how to build a fire?"

He laughed as he shook his head in mock abhorrence. "I've been in the military since I was ten years old. I've not only been trained in survival, I've taught it. Do I seem totally helpless to you?"

She tossed him the wood. "Well, you can't cook."

"No, but I can tell you which berries and leaves are not poisonous, and I can make a fire that will last for days."

She turned back to the pile for more logs and muttered, "A couple of hours will do."

He masterfully set the wood and then walked around the trees to locate smaller sticks and brush to add beneath. Once all was set, he looked to her and asked, "Where are the matches?"

"Matches?"

"Or lighter … whichever you brought."

"I thought *Mr. Survival* would just rub a couple of sticks together to get things going." Her smile was impish.

He grinned as he held out his hand. "If I had to, perhaps, but that would take way more energy and time than I'm willing to put into it. And seeing that you were the one planning on starting this—believing me too inept to help—I'm assuming you brought something."

"Maybe I was going to rub some sticks together."

She was still toying with him, and he loved it. After spending the week with her and her father and her friends, they had become very comfortable with each other, and the give and take happening now was something there had never been time for in the past. He tried not to think about the reality that he was leaving tomorrow, but it was a looming cloud over his heart.

And as he sat next to her by the fire, eating sandwiches she had made and fruit she had cut, and then roasting marshmallows she had put on the end of a stick, he longed for one more day with her.

"What's with the shelter?" he asked pointing toward the lean-to. "Keep you out of the rain?"

"More for sleeping," she explained as she bit into a charred marshmallow. "Daddy and I would come up here often and camp. Sometimes Jenna and Amy and I would, but they didn't care much for sleeping outdoors."

"And you do?"

She licked the sticky from her fingers and nodded. "Love it."

"What about your mother?"

"Mom made it clear that the whole camping thing was purely a father/daughter pursuit. She rode out here with us a few times and we would picnic. I think she actually swam with us only once." She giggled at the memory. "She was so timid about sliding down the waterfall. It took us a good twenty minutes to talk her into it. She screamed the whole way down."

"Did she like it?" He was amazed. In his wildest imaginations he couldn't envision his mother or father attempting such a thing.

Another laugh. "Not sure. She was hilarious about it all when she surfaced, but she wouldn't do it again. She said once was enough and was glad she could say she had done it."

He nodded and looked toward the falls. "Do you still miss her ... much, I mean?"

She sighed. "How could I not? She was like glue ... seeping into all the cracks of our lives and sticking everything together so you could see how it all belonged. With her gone, it seems like there are so many holes and gaps I can't make sense of. I can tell Daddy about them, but he's always so logical in his approach. He explains what I should do and why I should do it ... or not do it."

"And that's not right?"

"Sometimes a woman doesn't need logic."

"What does she need ... sometimes?"

She patted his knee as if consoling him. "When you do get married, try to understand that sometimes we pathetic females get so wrapped up in our feelings that reason and logic are impossible to see. What we want ... or need—don't know if you can even separate those two with us—is validation."

"But what if the things you're feeling are ... uh ... misguided?"

She scowled at him. "My point exactly. If we feel it, it's real ... whether right or wrong, logical or not ... it's still very much alive and screaming to be recognized. You guys have this ability to somehow flip the reasoning switch in your brains and it manages to shut off all the emotional mumbo-jumbo." She pointed her finger in his face. "We don't do that … can't do that. If we feel it, well, we have to deal with it. And if we don't … just suppress it all … that doesn't mean it's gone. All that means is that it was swallowed into one of our emotional stomachs and will continue to emit indigestion until we spew it back up and deal with it. That could be twenty minutes …" she stared hard at him, "… or twenty years."

His eyes grew wide. "You're scaring me. I've heard women were complicated, but never imagined why. You never seem to be like that."

She laughed again. "Of course not! I can't afford to be like that with you. What do I have with you? Two or three hours a year? I haven't spent enough time with you to hate you yet!"

"Hate me? What?"

"Absolutely! At some point, if we were together much, I would have to hate you a little bit."

"Hate me? Isn't that a bit severe? Could you maybe just not like me as much?"

"Call it what you want, Princey, but there are two emotions—love and hate. There may be many variances on the scale between them, but you either lean toward one or the other. No sense in sugar-coating it."

"Could you hate me one moment and love me the next?"

She looked amused. "I could love you and hate you at the same time."

He shook his head and released a deep breath. "Sometimes you scare me."

"Good!"

⚲ ⚲ ⚲

The cloud of his leaving was thick and heavy that night as they sat on the couch before the fireplace sipping hot cocoa. James had just gone to bed, and Andrew and Evangeline remained silent as they realized this would probably be the last time they would ever be alone together. So often during that week he would waver between just giving up the throne and leaving the country with this woman, or asking her to accept the prison of kingship with him and bind her to living miserably ever after. Then he would gain a grip on his emotions, allow his logic to take over, and dismiss all thoughts of changing their destinies.

"I need to thank you for this week," he finally began. "You can't imagine how it's strengthened me and opened my eyes."

Her brow furrowed. "That's not what I was going for. I was just hoping to let you have a good time and relax."

"Oh, mission accomplished there, but you gave me way more than that." He collected his thoughts hoping to express clearly what he meant.

"Before this week, being king was just about taking my fated place in this kingdom. I've never seen it as a real responsibility to actually do anything. I know that sounds crazy, but I have no agenda. My life is all I've ever known. Even with the military … it's all about protecting and defending Braisognia. But why? My life has been miserable! Why would I want to protect and defend this life … this country?"

"But this week I saw something. I saw real freedom—I saw real love. I laughed, cooked, lived like a family … I enjoyed the fruits of your father's labor. Riding out to that piece of land today and just sitting there thinking you could retreat to this anytime you wanted … and have done that, year after year … I realized *this* is what I'm protecting. As king, my goal is to see that you and your father, your neighbors, the people of this nation, can continue to know that next week that chunk of land will still belong to you … and you'll still have the peace and freedom to build a fire, slide down a waterfall, and sleep in a lean-to when your children come along."

He put down his mug, took her hand and turned her towards him.

"I have clarity for the first time," he said soberly. "I needed it. I'll never have *this*, Evangeline, but I can keep *this* for you. When I wonder if it's worth the sacrifice of my life and my comfort and my freedom, I can look back at this week and know that it is."

Tears pooled in her eyes and she whispered, "You can have this too if you want it."

He tried to smile as he shook his head.

"Why do you have to be so stubborn?" She continued to whisper. "What if I don't mind the sacrifice?"

He closed his eyes. "It would destroy you. You've only felt the surface of the wrath of royals, but you have no idea what it's like to drown in their blood every day. I won't do that to you."

She sighed and removed her hand from his as she turned away to wipe her eyes.

"You would grow to hate me," he tried to explain as though reading her mind. "You don't belong behind those sterile, cold, white walls … and I'm not just referring to the material walls." He turned her face toward him. "You belong here … in this world. You need to be able to ride Prince through your forests to your waterfall, not through a walled off pasture followed by teams of security and photographers scrutinizing your every move."

She turned her face to the fire. "You seem so sure about what you think I need. My heart would beg to differ."

He ran the back of his hand down the side of her face and lost himself in the beauty of her profile glowing from the embers. "I'll have to hope that as much as you hate me right now for this, you'll find room to still love me for it in the future."

She looked back at him, but without smiling. "I could never hate you." She shook her head. "Never."

Trying to lighten the mood, he grinned and offered, "Yes, you can. Remember? You can love and hate me at the same time."

❧ Chapter Fourteen ❧

There was no question that the woman sitting across the table from Andrew was beautiful. Her Arabian complexion and flowing black hair, however, couldn't disguise the frustration of resolve that glared through her amber eyes—she was being forced to marry also. His father was pushing him to choose a bride and had become downright volatile over Andrew's languid approach to marriage. The truth was he had already decided not to marry. He couldn't bring himself to be united with anyone when his entire being was so overcome with Evangeline—it always would be. No matter if he married and even fathered children with another woman, he would still love only one woman to whom he had given his heart years ago.

"I have nothing against you," he said tenderly. "I only met with you to appease my father's hounding."

"I understand." Her accent was thick, but her language skills were impeccable. "Lucky for you, you may pick and choose whom you want to marry. I am not as blessed."

"Well, pick and choose within boundaries," he corrected. "My lot isn't much better than yours."

She shook her head defiantly. "You are a man—your lot is significantly better than mine. As a princess, I have been raised to be educated and smart, strong and confident, yet because I am a woman, I must be married off to some royalty not of my own choosing." She glared at him. "You are the youngest of my prospects. The next prince in line that my father approves of is fifty-something. I can think and reason and converse with the most intelligent men in this world, but my lot, as you call it, reduces down to whatever man finds me pleasing enough to welcome me into his harem."

He blushed in embarrassment. "I'm sorry. I didn't mean to be insensitive. I was just trying to … relate." He paused before adding, "And I will have no harem."

She smiled slightly and shook her head. "You are a good man, Andrew, and a handsome one. You are sweet and humble … not something you find in a prince. I would be lucky to be your wife, but I will never love you. I love another. So take that into consideration before you make your decision."

His eyes grew wide. "You're in love with someone? Really?"

She sighed and rolled her eyes from sheer annoyance. "And he is a prince!" She rammed her fist on the table. "But my father does not choose him for me because he will not rule!"

"Well, tell your father …"

"To murder me?" she quickly interrupted. "Do you realize that is what could happen if I insist on controlling my own destiny? My fate lies at the whims of illogical men."

He chuckled and this angered her more.

"You find this humorous?" she asked with disgust.

"No!" he replied quickly as he put up his hands in defense. "It's just that I was recently told that men are logical and women are not. It struck me as funny that you turned it around."

"Augh!" she nearly screamed. "Do you know the one thing that causes a man to lose his logical mind—the one thing that drives him to throw all reason out with the garbage and think like a fool?"

He shrugged and guessed, "Love?"

"Ha! I should be so lucky! Hardly!" She then softened her voice and looked directly into his eyes. "Power."

He nodded. That was his father in a nutshell.

She sneered. "It is more intoxicating than liquor, money, sex … or all three put together."

♊ ♊ ♊

Terry Smith was exhausted from trying to handle Evangeline's hostility on the practice court. Whatever had upset her the past few weeks had translated into more fierce determination. He hadn't imagined that was possible, but he had borne the brunt of it, and he was spent from trying to keep up.

"I have an idea," he offered sarcastically as they left the court for the day and headed up toward the house. "Forget playing the women this year on the circuit. You could terrorize the men the way you've been going."

She said nothing as she zipped her last racket inside its case while walking briskly up the path. She wasn't even winded from the workout.

"I sometimes wonder if you're human," he continued. "It's like you've got some robotic brain in there that sends commands to your arms and legs, and wham! You send that ball with such precision and speed that no one could hit it."

Without looking at him she merely replied, "Isn't that the idea? Is that not what I'm supposed to do?"

"Well, yeah … but it's so … um … heartless."

She stopped abruptly and turned to glare at him. "Since when did someone's heart become the purpose of this game? If I start playing with my heart then I stop winning."

"Maybe … but it doesn't mean you have to become a beast in the process."

She seemed to ignore his comments as she hurried toward the steps of the deck.

He continued trying to break her cold demeanor, "You know the Australians are quite put out by you. You've skipped their tournament two years in a row."

"Bless their hearts," she mumbled without feeling.

"For heaven's sake, Evie! What is wrong with you?"

She spun around and stared at him, still seeming unmoved. "I will not let this competition rule my life. I reserve the right to have one month to call my own, and I choose the winter holidays to do that. I want one time during the year that I can relax and enjoy my family, my friends, no training, no dieting, no working out … just actually enjoy living for a few, brief days. If the Australians want me to play in their tournament, they can either change the date or get over it. My guess is they'll get over it—I suggest you do the same."

♟ ♟ ♟

Cassity Braisogn was not what Andrew would call pretty. The best description he could come up with was *impeccable*. She was a career military woman with a perfectly ironed uniform, flawless hair, manicured nails, and unblemished make-up. He tried to concentrate on whatever the conversation was, but his mind kept wondering just how closely related they actually might be. Surely his father had considered that when choosing her as a prospective bride. She was seven years older than he, but her royal pedigree and military record made her the perfect choice to be queen … at least according to Christopher Braisogn.

"So … what about you?" she asked as she paused from whatever she had been discussing to take a sip of her drink.

He blushed. He had no idea what she had just said.

"Uh … well … I don't really know." He wondered if that even made sense.

She shrugged her straight shoulders and began to cut her meat into exact sized chunks. "The truth is one heir is plenty enough if the child is a boy. I do suppose a girl could inherit the throne, but in the eight hundred years of Braisognian history that has never even come into question. All first children have been males. It's not that I'm defiantly opposed to more than one child, but grooming one to rule is a daunting task. I would have to give up my military position anyway as queen, but I'm definitely not the motherly-nurturing type."

No disagreement there. He also wondered if this woman actually thought he was going to marry her. He hadn't even called her to set up the dinner. When he greeted her at the door of the palace, he had called her Cathy, not totally sure he had met her before. She reminded him of previous occasions where they had talked, and just the monotony of her voice brought back the memories. He imagined Evangeline sitting next to him watching the evening's exchange. They would have had to avoid looking at each other to keep from breaking out in hysteria at the whole scene.

"So you would be fine with one child?" she continued pursuing the point.

He took a deep breath before speaking. He didn't want to hurt this woman, but he was finding it hard not to despise her presumptiveness. "I'm not sure what all you and my father discussed. All I've done here tonight is agree to take a meal with you. I'm not considering marrying you or anyone, for that matter, right now. Children is a subject I would gladly discuss if it was a possibility that we might marry. It's just a bit ..." he hesitated. What would be the best word choice? "It's a bit premature at the moment."

"I understand," she replied in her typical businesslike manner. "But before you do consider me as queen, I want to be up front with you concerning the subject of children. I really want only one child. If I had any power, I would strongly urge all couples to consider that." She raised an eyebrow at him. "You might want to reflect on making that a law when you become king."

♕ ♕ ♕

James Dorvain had begun to worry about his daughter. Her obsession with tennis had become unnatural. She seldom talked, seldom read, seldom watched television or did anything. She would wake up in the morning, train from breakfast until lunch, eat lunch, and then train from lunch until supper. After supper, she would shower, sit alone on the back deck, and then go to bed early. He had very little time to spend with her as he dealt with the many tedious legal affairs the military seemed enmeshed with the past several weeks. But tonight he was determined to break through the shell and make her pull out for a breath of reality.

"Have some hot cocoa," he said as he handed her a mug and joined her on the swing.

"Thanks, but no. I'm in training."

"I don't care," he told her as he continued offering the cup. "I don't care if you ever win a game again, and I certainly don't think one small mug of delicious cocoa is going to demolish your winning streak."

She smiled and took the drink.

"So what's going on with you?" he began. "Night after night you come out here and sit in the cool air and do nothing."

She took another sip. "Not nothing … thinking."

"Thinking about what? That's an awful lot of thinking you've been doing."

"My future." There was a long pause. "I really do hate tennis, you know."

He laughed and patted her leg. "Fine career you've chosen for yourself then!"

She shook her head. "I didn't choose this—it chose me. And I've been determined to bleed every last drop of it that I can, but I want to stop after this year."

"Has its blood gone dry?" He was trying to be cute.

"I've gone dry, Daddy," she whispered through a small choking sob.

He suddenly realized this condition she was in was seriously hurting her. "Baby," he said softly as he put his arm around her and pulled her close. "Why didn't you tell me? What all is going on inside that pretty little head of yours."

She wiped a tear. "I don't like beating people, Daddy. I want to help people. I want to be the inspiration that drives them to be better than they ever thought they could be. I don't want to be this person who walks out on a court and kills another's dreams. Every match I win, somebody else has to lose."

"And this bothers you?"

"It's destroying me. I actually feel sorry for Stephanie Bartko. Do you realize the woman won't even talk to me? I don't blame her. I've ruined her life for the moment. But the thing that's so sad is that I don't really care about winning. I do it all because I hate the Braisognian snobs, and I want them to eat their words and hatefulness toward me, toward my mother … toward you."

"I've fought my battles—you can take me out of your little avenging rampages."

He could tell she was trying to force a smile, but apparently there was no happiness in her life for the moment.

"Mom told me to use my tennis as a stepping stone for greater things."

She looked at her father in the moonlight and told him, "I'm ready to do greater things, Daddy. I want to retire after the U.S. Open."

U U U

Andrew had to give his father credit for at least trying to rise above the fiasco with Cassity Braisogn. This time he had chosen an incredible European beauty. She was definitely poised and lady-like and made Cassity appear more like a pit bull than a woman. Tondra, a princess with a last name he still couldn't pronounce, had a sultry voice with an accent that accentuated a steamy seductiveness. He had to keep himself from laughing all evening as she made him ever aware she was willing to do whatever it took to take her place at his side as queen. She had started subtly, but as the evening wore on she apparently thought he was not getting her messages.

"So," she sighed as she sucked on the end of a strawberry dredged thickly with chocolate, "is this dining area the only place in the palace I get to see tonight. I was really hoping for a tour."

I bet you were. "Unfortunately," he tried to sound sincere, "I could only cut out enough time for a leisurely dinner. Military maneuvers are coming up soon and I have a meeting tonight with the generals to begin planning our missions for the summer."

Her sultry frown, coupled with the strawberry between her teeth, almost made him wish he had carved out more time. She pouted as she moaned, "This is not how I imagined my evening with the strong, handsome, virile Prince Andrew Braisogn would end. You are killing me with this military mandate to leave."

He would most definitely not be marrying this woman, but he wondered if she even cared. He would probably be the ultimate notch on a belt of conquests that he guessed was rather well-marked with previous men.

"Well, what I must do is probably not near as fun as what you had in mind ..." he told her.

"I can guarantee it's not near as fun."

He laughed now. "I can only imagine. However, I need to get going." He rose from his seat and extended his hand to her.

"How sad," she pouted again as she took his hand and slowly kissed his palm.

He smiled politely as he pulled it back and wiped the chocolate she had left behind on a napkin.

"Perhaps," she wondered as she stood slowly, and again, seductively from her seat, "we could leave this evening with at least a kiss."

For a moment he was tempted, but as he thought of Evangeline, the only woman he had ever kissed, the only woman he would ever love, he felt to indulge in Tondra would be traitorous. The purity of Evangeline's kisses would be a passion that could never be matched by Tondra's sensual delights—and he would not pollute her memory with something tawdry and momentary.

Poor Stephanie. Evangeline continued to glare at her worn down opponent across the net at the French Open. This had been the worse match for Stephanie they had ever played. Evangeline couldn't help it—clay was still her best medium. She barely had to think on it. With grass and hard courts her concentration needed to be strong to make sure she never slipped with a shot thus giving her opponent any advantage during play. But with clay, all she had to do was what came naturally. She wished she could enjoy it, but every pounding of the ball was full of hate as she imagined it being one royal head after another.

Andrew, watching the match inside his own room at the military training base, found his mind wandering to many places with Evangeline that had nothing to do with tennis. She had such dominance on the court today that he found himself pitying Stephanie. In fact, the game was downright boring. He tried to concentrate on the match, but with every move of her body he went back over every conversation he had ever had with her. He longed to be with her right now, sitting in her box cheering her on. He longed to celebrate her victory with another night of talking and laughing. He wished he could welcome her home with a warm fire and a cup of hot chocolate or whisk her off to the waterfall where they could be totally alone again. It seemed that the more he tried to push her out of his mind, the stronger his desire to be with her grew.

ℾ Chapter Fifteen ℞

The unsettled feeling in the pit of Andrew's stomach was becoming more pronounced each day. Why his father relentlessly insisted he marry as soon as possible was beyond him. In less than a year he would be crowned king of Braisognia. He would have plenty else to dwell on than trying to build a pretend life with a woman for whom he cared nothing. He was settled in his mind that marriage would never be a part of his life, and he wished his father would take the hint and accept it also. As for an heir, he would worry with that later. Next in line was Gregory Braisogn, his chubby, obnoxious cousin. He supposed Gregory's son would be the eventual ruler. Perhaps with proper training and exposure he could be less repugnant than his father.

As he stood on the balcony off his room staring down onto the lavish gardens, fountain and pond that were the centerpieces of all the connected palace buildings, it only reminded him of how pretentious his world was. He couldn't help but compare it with the memory of the waterfall at the Dorvain property. He wondered why his father had never sought to buy some land and build a private retreat for the family so they could get away from the pressures and microscope of palace living.

Because he had no desire to get away from palace living. Palace living was the only thing that seemed to energize Christopher Braisogn. It certainly wasn't his wife or his children or any other relationship for that matter. The older Andrew got, the more he wondered if perhaps his father had taken a mistress at some point in time. But the man never left the palace. If he had a woman somewhere, even at the palace, when did he spend time with her?

Andrew would welcome summer maneuvers this year. They would

remove him from the constant badgering of his father and keep him busy for two months. The one bright spot would be getting to watch Evangeline play on television during the upcoming days of Wimbledon. It seemed that the harder she played, the more the kingdom and the world loved her. At least in her home she had a solace, a place of true escape. He had considered driving there for a day to just unwind and relax away from the agitated eyes of his father, but with all the rumors flying about on his picking a bride, he knew a trip to Evangeline's would only fuel the fire. He assumed the rumors were part of his father's pressure. If he couldn't force Andrew into marriage, perhaps the nation could compel him to make a choice. In actuality, he had made his decision—he just had no desire to tell his father quite yet. For some reason Christopher felt it necessary for his son to be married before taking the throne, and unfortunately, his son did not agree.

He walked back inside to his massive, monotonous, sterile room. He had lived in this space his entire life. Very little of it had ever changed. The walls were repainted regularly but always the same beige-white color with a military blue trim. The furniture was replaced every couple of years, but always the same type of piece was brought in to take the exact place of whatever had been removed. Fixtures occasionally might be more modern, but usually they were great antique structures used in hopes of filling up the empty spaces in the enormous room. The only section that remotely looked like it might belong to him was the small corner next to the double doors leading to the balcony. It contained his three guitars, a grand piano, and several shelves of music. An area rug set it apart, and often Andrew would lie upon it as he cranked up his stereo to listen in casual comfort to the music that often spoke to his soul and calmed his insecurities.

How he longed for the rustic simplicity of the Dorvain home. It had its rooms of fancy flair, but never once had they been used the week he had visited. All their time had been spent in the kitchen or in the den with the fireplace. Shoes and boots were often removed as people curled up on a couch or chair with a fleece blanket thrown over the feet to keep them warm. Even the hardwood floors held a warm and welcome ambience as compared to the cold, harsh marble laid throughout the palace—including his room.

He thought of picking up a guitar and singing through a favorite song or two, but his heart wasn't in it. Perhaps he should take his Bible back out to the balcony and spend more time in prayer as he did each morning now since leaving Evangeline's, but even that made him restless. What he wanted, what he needed, was to throw off the chains choking him more and more each day, and run free for just a bit so he could focus again on the daunting task that would be his within the year.

He finally decided his best and simplest option would be to saddle up his horse and ride for awhile. He couldn't trot through a forest to a luscious spot holding a waterfall and a swimming hole, but riding around in circles in the large pasture would be better than nothing. He changed his clothes and then made his way through the corridors with hopes of the stable and the field bringing him some sense of release. As he passed by the library, he heard his father call to him.

"Andrew! Where on earth are you headed dressed like that?"

Christopher had a way of making everything seem like an unpardonable sin.

He halted and walked back to the library. "I was going to ride for awhile. Maneuvers will be upon me soon and I would rather my steed not forget me during the long summer months."

The king shook his head in disapproval. "What are you doing, Andrew? With maneuvers so close you should be narrowing your choice for queen. You really should be ready to walk the aisle immediately when the summer is finished. The nation is getting restless."

He wanted to explode but had learned long ago that the only outbursts his father tolerated were his own. "I guess now would be as good a time as any to let you know I've come to a decision concerning a wife." He dreaded actually telling his father because he seemed to put so much emphasis on the need for a queen to bear heirs, but getting it out in the open would at least stop the badgering over this particular subject.

His father's face literally lifted at the announcement. "Well, tell me then. The suspense is killing me! Who is the lucky girl?"

Andrew tried to appear calm, but inside he was trembling at the reaction he knew his declaration would incur.

"Alfred!" Christopher called to the old man as he passed by them in the corridor outside the library. "Come in here! You can get in on the announcement Andrew is about to make concerning a bride."

Alfred stepped into the room and actually had an expression of curiosity, a drastic change from his typical blasé appearance.

"Very good, sir," Alfred responded as he looked expectantly toward Andrew.

"So tell us? Who is the young lady to rule by your side in our kingdom?" Christopher coaxed.

Andrew's first thought was to make a sardonic remark about the ruling by your side comment. No queen had ever ruled by the side of any Braisognian king. But that point would be unimportant once he told them his decision.

"I've decided not to marry," he said forthright. "Maybe in the future I might think differently, but for now I won't take a wife. I know it's never been done in Braisognia before, but it's a new day. I'm sure everyone will grow used to it once it's announced."

His father's face began to grow red, but he remained speechless for the moment.

Andrew confessed, "Well, it feels good to have that over and done with. Now, if you don't mind, I think I'll head on out for that ride."

The explosion finally detonated. "Are you out of your blasted mind?" Christopher bellowed. "What possibly makes you think everyone will overlook protocol just to appease your spineless, sappy, emotional weaknesses?"

"What?" Andrew asked. "What protocol? I've been indoctrinated with royal protocol for fifteen years. Never have I heard anything concerning marriage except the poor girl must be royal of some kind. You can't just create something out of the blue to force me into marriage. I won't do it!"

"Are you kidding me?" His father was still yelling and now beginning to pace. "You're going to stand there and pretend that the entire Section Seven doesn't even exist? I've never actually called you stupid before, but this is borderline moronic!"

"I have no idea what you're talking about."

Christopher spun around to Alfred as he pointed at Andrew. "Did you not teach this boy the rules and demands concerning marriage before taking the throne?"

In a stunning answer, the staunch old man merely replied, "No, sir, I did not."

Now both Andrew and Christopher were shocked. He had been responsible for training him on all things royal yet had just openly admitted his negligence to the king.

The vein in Christopher's forehead pulsed stronger than Andrew had ever seen before as he threatened, "You had better give me a valid reason before I call the palace guard in here to lock you up for the rest of your life."

"I did not," Alfred explained, "because, your majesty, you insisted that I not."

The king shook his head swiftly as if trying to sling out this unbelievable revelation. "I have never … would never … tell you to omit something like this … or anything period … to do with royal protocol. Are you out of your mind, Alfred?"

"Your highness, did you not teach him Section Seven as you demanded I allow you to do?"

"I never demanded any such thing. It's not my job as king to mold this boy into royalty. No time have I ever taken this matter into my own hands! You must have been dreaming or something, but I guarantee you'll be out of this job and out of this palace by tonight."

"If you insist," Alfred bowed slightly. "But you made me sign a contract swearing I would leave the training of Section Seven to you. It never occurred to me that you had not fulfilled your … demand."

"I have no idea what you're talking about," the king seethed. "But if there's a contract, I suggest you produce it immediately. You're dangerously close to committing treason here, Alfred."

"Hang on just a minute!" Andrew stepped in. "I'm completely lost about all of this! Exactly what is contained in Section Seven that I apparently never learned?"

Christopher sighed partially in anger, partially in frustration. "Marriage," he said flatly. "The king must be married before taking the throne. It's been in there since its inception. The writers felt an unmarried king would be perceived too much as a, well, for lack of a better word, a playboy. A married king would seem more settled—more mature." He glared at Andrew. "You must marry before your twenty-fifth birthday or you will not be eligible to rule."

Andrew dropped down onto the closest couch as Christopher returned to his assault on Alfred. "Are you in the process of finding me this supposed contract you claim I've signed? I warn you, Alfred, your years of faithful service will be considered moot if you're lying about this."

Alfred, calm and controlled as always, merely answered, "I can understand, sir. The contract is on its way to the room now."

"Exactly when … or for that matter … why was this contract drawn up?"

"When Prince George announced his intentions to marry Miss Lynette, the non-royal. You were extremely angry with his attendant and fired him immediately. You felt no one but yourself could convey the importance of a prince to marry royalty. Rather than see myself and Prince Peter's attendant fail also, you took the task upon yourself."

Christopher shook his head. "I don't remember such a rash decision." He rubbed his forehead. "Exactly when did I sign it?"

"In your study, your majesty, later that evening."

A page promptly walked through the door carrying a large envelope which he handed to Alfred. The old man motioned the boy to leave as he opened the packet and retrieved the document. He handed it to the king. Christopher carefully read the words and scrutinized the signatures. In exasperation he slammed the papers against his hand.

"This is preposterous!" he yelled toward Alfred. "Was I drunk? Did you consider that? I have no recollection of this whatsoever! If I didn't know better, I would swear it was a prank!"

Alfred, unruffled, merely stated, "I am hoping, your majesty, that you know better." The response was almost impertinent. "I have served you loyally in this position for twenty-two years and seen to it that every wish and desire you expressed concerning Prince Andrew's training was carried out. This was one of those desires, and you were emphatic about it. It never occurred to me that you would not … remember … something so basic and important to the prince's education."

Andrew was utterly shocked at Alfred's almost chiding the king. He wanted to jump up and yell for Alfred to get him as this was the first time ever Andrew had seen anyone put the arrogant man in a catch. Christopher was at a loss. He glanced over the paper again, and indeed it was valid. Andrew saw his father's signature, Alfred's signature, and two recognizable witness signatures.

After much silence, Christopher turned to Andrew and said, "Well, there you have it. Section Seven requires you to marry prior to the coronation. So, unless you intend to abdicate as your traitorous brothers did, I suggest you rethink your decision and choose a bride prior to summer maneuvers so that a royal wedding can be put into planning."

Now it was Andrew turning red. His simple plan to bypass marriage had now been deemed impossible. His head was spinning from the ramifications of Section Seven, and he suddenly remembered Evangeline mentioning it to him back at the Christmas Ball when he had told her of his plan to simply not marry. He could feel his pulse rising and face flushing as the reality washed over him.

"I will not marry," he told his father through gritted teeth. "You can change the rule or I will abdicate. But I won't marry for the sake of the throne. If I marry, it will be for love."

Christopher tossed the contract toward Alfred in rage as he grabbed the lapel of Andrew's shirt and howled, "You will not abdicate! You are a stupid, emotional pansy when it comes to women! You will bone up, stand like a man, like a ruler, like a king, and pick a proper queen immediately! I will not have you sniveling about something as insignificant as love!"

To everyone's surprise, Alfred stepped toward them both and suggested, "What about Miss Dorvain?"

Christopher turned and raised his arm to belt him. "Don't you ever, ever … mention that woman's name in my presence again! How dare you even suggest to him that he marry that … that …"

"Because I know your son better than you do." Alfred was actually being bold. If Andrew wasn't so convinced of his attendant's fierce loyalty to the king, he would almost think Alfred was on his side.

"Don't tell me what I know or don't know about my son!"

"Your highness, I have assumed for years now that Prince Andrew has been merely postponing the inevitable to hold off the disdain you will shower on both him and Miss Dorvain once their marriage is announced."

"What?" Christopher spun around to Andrew. "You've been planning to marry her? All this time you've been lying?"

"No!" Andrew insisted. "I told you I would never drag her into this palace … into this life! She is above this pretentious mess, and I love her too much to subject her to such pompous, substandard living!"

"Then what is Alfred talking about?" The king turned to the servant. "What do you mean, Alfred?"

The old man, calm as ever, spoke frankly. "Andrew is different from you. I have tried to move him in your direction, but there are some things innate within a man that cannot be changed. Andrew will marry no one except for Miss Dorvain ... of that I am certain. Your growing disdain for her has done nothing more than drive them desperately closer. Your misstep, if I may be so bold, was to assume Andrew could deny his heart as you have come to do so well." He stepped back. "I have done all I could do. You have done all you could do. If Andrew is to take the throne, I suggest you open your eyes to this fact."

And with that, Alfred walked out. Both Christopher and Andrew stood stunned. Never had Alfred spoken out of turn or even suggested to tell the king or prince what to do. Andrew had berated him many times over the foolishness of things he was teaching, but never once did Alfred take offense or defense.

"You will not marry that woman," Christopher forbade firmly. "I won't allow it."

"Then you won't have an heir on the throne," Andrew spewed. "It seems you've succeeded in driving all three of your sons from their destiny to carry on your legacy. Congratulations, King—you win, I suppose."

"You will not abdicate!" his father now screamed. "You will stand up and be a man! You will choose a bride or have me choose one for you! You will not ..."

"I don't believe you have any control at this point over what I do or don't do."

"I am your king, and you will obey my command!"

He looked darkly at his father and slowly shook his head. "Not this time."

He turned to go but his father stepped quickly and grabbed his arm, jerking him back. "You will not go to that woman! I won't have it!"

He shrugged off his father's hand and started for the door.

"I'm warning you," Christopher hissed. "I will not allow this to happen."

Fear gripped Andrew as he realized his father was making a threat. He knew he was capable of many things in order to have his own way, but he couldn't be certain how far he might push the limits.

He pointed at his father and clearly stated, "Don't threaten me. Let me make this as definitive as possible—if anything at all happens to Evangeline, or her father, or her friends, I'll hold you accountable, and I'll leave this kingdom, and I'll take you down with me. You don't know the meaning of the word traitor. If she so much as gets the sniffles, I'm gone."

He lowered his arm, shaking with anger and fear. "I hope I've made myself clear."

He walked out of the room but his father yelled after him, "I forbid you to go to her! I forbid it, do you hear me?"

He didn't turn around as he mumbled the words, "Don't wait up, Father."

✠ Chapter Sixteen ✠

"Dang it, Evie!" Terry yelled across the net as she had hit him for the third time during practice that afternoon. "I really don't care for this new approach you've created!"

"Move your feet and get out of the way," she said with no emotion as she walked back to the service line.

"You can't just hit people!"

She tossed the ball into the air then slammed it hard across the net. He didn't try to hit it back—he dodged it by falling to the grass.

"Evie!" he shrieked. "You can't keep doing that!" He got up from the court and began to stomp off. "I think that's enough for the day. I'm heading to my room in town where I'll take a hot shower hoping to soothe these bruises you've given me." He picked up his towel and mumbled, "I ought to sue you, but you pay me too much already."

As he dried the perspiration from his face he noticed Andrew Braisogn walking toward the court from the side of the house. He grabbed his rackets and bag and hurried in Andrew's direction toward his own car.

"Mr. Smith," the prince acknowledged as they met.

"Terry," he reminded him as he shook his hand. "You picked a fine day to visit. If I were you, I wouldn't get closer than ten feet from her. It might cost you your life."

As Terry fled up the path, Andrew wondered what had him so agitated. He looked back to the court and saw Evangeline practicing her serve, still oblivious to his presence. He stopped to take in her beauty, her form, her technique. He still had no idea what to say to her, what to tell her, and whether or not he could do what he came here to do. Being under the world's eyes from tennis had been hard enough on her. What would happen if she became queen? In tennis she was impossible to criticize—she did nothing wrong. As a member of the royal family, every action, word, outfit and gesture would be analyzed, and enemies could always find a subjective way to tear her down if that was their goal.

He ambled toward the court as he watched her take ball after ball from the basket and strategically spin them across the net. He tried to determine from her serve which way the ball would go when it finally hit the grassy surface, but the serves were so well disguised that he missed each call. He shook his head in amazement. Was this the same five year old with shining eyes that used to take his hand and crawl beneath the tables at the Christmas Ball? He never imagined such fierce determination lay within her.

He approached the court, but she still didn't see him, so he finally called to her. She immediately spun around and looked stunned to see him there. She dropped the ball from her hand and started across the court for him. A weary smile began to grow.

"What could possibly bring you out here in the middle of the week?" she asked as she dropped her racket onto a bench and picked up a towel.

He joined her. "You, of course."

She wiped her face and then stared into his eyes. "What's wrong? Something's going on, isn't it?"

He stuck his hands in his pockets and suddenly felt silly and foolish. What *was* he doing here?

"Andrew?" She rolled the towel, placed it around her neck and then reached out her hand to touch his arm. "What in the world has happened?"

He sighed and shrugged. How did he begin? "Can we go up to the house and talk?"

"Certainly." She looked deeply at him, concern filling her expression. "I would say you need a hug, but I'm pretty much drenched with sweat, and I'm sure I smell."

He took her hand and pulled her into his arms. "You can't know how badly I need a hug from you right now." He could feel her stiffen and hoped it was because she felt self-conscious being sweaty and not that she despised being touched by him. He released her finally and motioned for them to return to the house. They walked silently up the pathway and to the series of steps that led to the large back deck. Neither said anything. He wasn't even sure why he was here. What exactly was he about to do? Abdicate? Propose? Run?

"Andrew?" she asked in sudden panic. "Did somebody die?"

"No, but somebody wants to right now."

"Augh! Would you please tell me what is going on? You can't imagine all the crazy things running through my mind right now."

He breathed a deep sigh and raked a hand through his hair. "I don't even know where to start."

"Well, I can answer that one," she said impatiently. "If you were talking to my father, he would tell you the beginning is usually the best place."

"The beginning," he mulled. "I guess the beginning would be the night George announced he would be marrying Lynette." He dropped into a chair as she sat in the swing. "My father, as you can imagine, went ballistic—I remember it well. He blamed everyone and everything on George's impulsive, idiotic decision. He went down the line yelling at one person after another, completely oblivious to the idea that he himself in his egotistical, uncaring fathering could have contributed in any way to George's choice for love over duty. It went on and on—rant after rant after rant.

"Apparently later on in the night, or early morning, he just got drunk. And in his drunkenness he came up with a plan to assure this wouldn't happen to his other two heirs. He called in Alfred along with Peter's attendant and told them obviously no one was capable of teaching his boys proper royal protocol when it came to marriage, and he had some sort of hand written contract drawn up which they both had to sign, along with my father, saying they wouldn't touch Section Seven. The king himself would now be responsible for teaching us all that mumbo-jumbo."

"Well, so far that sounds very typical."

He chuckled at what he was about to tell her next. "But now for the ironic turn in the story—apparently Father was so inebriated that he never remembered the contract—his decision to share with us the joys of Section Seven or his command to our attendants to completely delete that section of protocol in our training."

He stared at her to see if she understood what he was saying.

"So what exactly are you telling me?" she asked cautiously.

"Until an hour ago, I had no idea all that was required concerning Section Seven. No one had ever fully explained it to me. I knew I had to marry a royal—that was made very clear as soon as our friendship began to seem questionable to my father. But the business about having to marry before taking the throne … never heard it before." He closed his eyes, leaned back his head and ran his fingers through his hair again.

"Oh … my … gosh," she whispered. "So your slowness in choosing a queen had nothing to do with just procrastination? You really didn't realize you had to be married before the coronation?"

He shook his head. "No idea. In fact, I had decided not to marry for the time being. Somewhere down the road I would worry about the next heir, but for now, I had put it all out of my mind. I wondered why everyone was so insistent about picking a bride. I didn't care about marrying, didn't want to marry, and probably never would marry. That was my decision, and I told my father today, at which he exploded and finally all this jumbled, drunken mess was revealed."

She gawked. "What are you gonna do? I can imagine what a jolt this was for you."

He stood from the chair and went to the edge of the deck, leaning his body on the weight of his arms as they propped against the railing. "As I see it, I only have two choices. One, I marry some random girl who has no meaning or purpose in my life other than to fulfill a royal duty." He shuddered at the very idea. "Or two, I abdicate."

Evangeline popped up from the swing. "And neither of those is acceptable." She joined him at the rail. "You can't abdicate, Andrew. You are the only hope for this kingdom. If you refuse the throne over this, your snotty cousin—who's not married yet either—would take over. And he would marry ... anyone ... just to get the line away from your family." She shook her head emphatically. "That isn't an option."

"But I can't bring myself to marry any of these women I've been told are great prospects! I can't have a life like that! My father might be able to have a marriage of convenience, but look what that did to our family! My poor mother—no life, no purpose ... and she never even had the chance to be a real mother to us. Father refused to give her any freedom or say-so in our upbringing because he thought a woman's influence would make sissies out of us. And then me and my brothers ... what can I say? We were three miserable, beaten-down boys growing up in that palace. My brothers only found peace when they totally excluded themselves from any hope of fulfilling their legacy to the throne." He threw his hands up in the air. "Is that now my only hope, too? Am I to abdicate and finally find my peace?"

"No," she said more gently than insistent. "Because you know that wouldn't bring you peace. You've embraced your destiny, and this nation has embraced you." She placed her hand on his shoulder. "I don't believe you could live with yourself if you abdicated."

"And I don't think I could live with myself if I married whomever from wherever just to satisfy the idiotic protocol this nation agreed upon over eight hundred years ago."

She sighed as she looked out over the back into the courtyard. "You know there's a third option, and my guess is that's the reason you're here and not packing your bags."

He shook his head. "No. I don't honestly know why I'm here. I just didn't know where else to go."

"Augh!" she screamed out in frustration as she slammed her hands on the railing. "Andrew, this is not all about *you*!"

He looked down at her, shocked by her reaction. "I know. That's why I won't ... can't ... bring you into this."

"I'm already into this!" she replied with great irritation. "I was into this when you kissed me at your sixteenth birthday party! Shoot! I was into this long before that!" She looked at him fiercely with what seemed more like hurt than anger. "If you didn't really want me into this, you should have pushed me away long ago. If you were some college chum or fellow player, I might think you were toying with me in all of it. But I know you, and you really believe that somehow denying me the opportunity to spend my life with you is what's best."

"It is best. What kind of man would I be if I took the person most precious to my heart and dragged her willingly into a suicide mission? I can't do that! If anything, Evangeline, I need to protect you from all the garbage and bitterness you would face if I let you be a part of my life!"

"All the garbage and bitterness is already there ... always has been. That's all I knew growing up in a royal school. And in college, when it came out I was actually of pure royal blood, the disdain became worse. And now," she pointed to the three courts behind the house, "my success on those has only upped the hatred. If I had been a failure and faded into the background, everyone would have been happy. Don't you think I know that? But I chose NOT to bow to them! I won't give in to their snide remarks and hateful insinuations."

He turned his back to the rail and tried to explain, "But can you imagine how much worse it would be if you became queen?"

"I don't care about being your stupid queen!" she yelled at him.

He looked at her in surprise.

She melted and spoke softly this time. "I don't care about being queen," she repeated. "I want to be your friend for life, your soul-mate, your helpmeet, your support, your lover ... in essence, I just want to be your wife, Andrew. That's all that matters to me."

"But you can't be that without being queen ... unless I abdicate."

"And since I have no desire to see you abdicate because I know you'll be the best king this kingdom has ever seen, I will gladly, willingly accept the title and role of queen. It comes with the territory. I've always known that."

He shook his head and walked away. "I can't do that to you. You don't understand the royal microscope."

"Don't you even begin to lecture me on not understanding the royal microscope!" Her voice was rising again. "I'm there right now! I have always been there!"

"But not to the degree they will place on you if you move into the palace!"

She stomped over to him and grabbed his arm. "Stop playing games with me, Prince! I've just always assumed you felt as deeply for me as I have for you. I would sacrifice anything, everything, to be with you! I don't care what the price might be. Obviously, somewhere along the years I deluded myself into thinking you had the same emotions—the same attachment."

She released his arm and headed toward the doors to the house.

"Evangeline!" he called to her. "Stop! What are you suggesting?"

"I think I made it clear. This relationship is apparently more one sided than I believed"

"I'm only trying to protect you," he maintained. "I ... I ... how could you even think I don't care for you?"

"Maybe I'm not the one who needs protecting, Andrew. Maybe that's not your purpose here—protecting me. Maybe your whole reason for existence is to do the king thing. And maybe my reason and purpose is to keep you from becoming your father. What if I'm supposed to protect you? What if all this nobility you keep insisting on is just a trap to keep you from the one thing that will save you—love—if you actually love me ... you've never said it, so I have no idea. Again, I may be presuming way too much, embarrassing myself for the past twenty years."

This time he grabbed her arm. "You're not presuming anything. You have nothing to be embarrassed about. I've never told you how I felt because I've never said those words to anyone." He swallowed hard. "No one." He hesitated. "And no one ... has ever spoken those words to me ... except you."

"I've never told you that I loved you—I've been extremely careful not to."

He smiled. "Yes, you did."

"No, I did not," she was adamant. "I have deliberately avoided ..."

"At the last ball ... in the parlor. You were really sick, talking out your head. Somewhere in the midst of all that nonsense you upped and said that you loved me." He paused. "I thought I would die. I'd always hoped, but never knew for sure."

She blushed and closed her eyes in humiliation. "Did I say anything else during that time I might not remember?"

"It doesn't matter," he smiled as he slid his hand down her muscled arm to find her fingers. "Somehow just knowing that you really did love me—that someone really loved me—was all I could remember."

"So that whole week you spent at my house you knew how I felt?"

He nodded.

"And you didn't think it might have been courteous to let me know?"

He nodded again, but explained, "I just ... didn't want to ruin that week. It was the best ..."

"I know ... the best week of your life."

They stood quietly for a moment. This was awkward. Many years of untold feelings washed between them. He rubbed her fingers as he remembered chasing dragons as children, being kissed at sixteen, being kissed after her mother's death, being told she loved him, and then sitting at the fire learning how to pray from the Bible. With deep emotion, he whispered, "I do love you ... maybe only you." The very words caused him to choke.

She tightened her fingers around his as she put her other hand up to his beard and asked earnestly, "Exactly why did you come here today? Why did you come to me when all of this was revealed?"

He shrugged. "Because I didn't know where else to go."

She turned his face to look at her. "Let me save you, Andrew. That's all I've ever wanted. When I would fly to the palace in my imaginations as a child, it was always to rescue you. Even then I somehow knew how unhappy you were. And when you asked for a kiss at your birthday party, how could I deny you ... even though everything within me warned me I would be giving you my heart forever, believing at that time it would be pointless?"

She dropped her hands to her side. "I'm tired of trying to save you. Either let me do it, let me inside your life, or stop playing with my destiny." She walked back to the railing.

He followed and asked, "But what about tennis? If you marry me, you'll have to retire ... as soon as it's announced."

She smiled and shook her head. "I hate tennis. I think you know that. But the reality is, you still haven't proposed. I won't talk about changing my future unless I know a different destiny awaits me."

He sighed again. "This goes against everything I've forced myself to think about you. It's like asking you to lay down your life for me. That's not who I am."

"You already did that when you asked for that first kiss," she reiterated.

"I wasn't thinking then. I'm thinking very clearly right now, and I'm seeing your life pass before my eyes."

She tried to breathe out the frustration. "Again, why did you come here today? Why didn't you go to someone else—anyone else?"

He turned to her and felt his resolve slowly slip away. Why? He knew why. He came here because the only answer to every question, problem, misery, complaint, frustration and impossibility was Evangeline Dorvain. That had always been the case. He had tried to convince himself that he could live without her, but even in his resolve he had always turned to her with his deepest needs. He could never sever the tie between them even when he had committed to live life alone rather than drag her into his world. He kept creeping back, slowly but persistently, always seeking a glimpse of her light in the midst of his deepest darkness. Maybe she was right—she wasn't the one who needed to be saved.

"You would do this for me?" he asked, wondering if she really knew what she was up against.

She smiled impishly. "I ... don't ... know," she said slowly. "Ask me and find out." She slowly turned her back and walked toward the door.

"Are you leaving?" he questioned as he stayed by the rail.

She looked back. "Give me a reason not to. The ball is in your court, Prince ... and always has been. Either serve ... or default. I would tell you that I won't wait forever, but it seems as though I've already done that. I'd like to shower and change, if you don't mind. You can decide what your next move is while I'm gone."

She reached for the door and turned the knob, but he yelled, "Wait! Don't leave!"

She looked back at him, cocking her head to the side and closing her eyes in frustration.

"If you leave," he continued, "I might lose my nerve."

She folded her arms and he turned back toward the yard, wringing his hands. He faced her, squared his shoulders, took a deep breath, and spoke, "Evangeline, I've loved you for as long as I can remember being alive. You've been my life." He felt so awkward. "I wish I had been ... well ... better prepared for this. I could have sung to you, or presented you with something ... but I'm here ... just empty ... just me alone ... on my own."

"And don't you understand that's all I've ever wanted?"

"Would you ..." he almost seemed to lose his breath, "would you ... marry me?"

When the words finally slipped from his lips, they seemed to hit Evangeline with such force that she gasped. He had done it. Immediately tears began to swell in her eyes, and he could see her legs buckle beneath her. She did the only thing she could do at the moment and that was to slide to her knees as she sobbed out a weak, "Yes."

He stood there watching. "Are you okay?" He wasn't sure what to do. "Did you just say yes?"

She nodded and tried to breathe. He finally came to his senses and rushed to his knees in front of her. Tears now lined his face as he tried to speak, but he was stunned that this had happened. So much in his life would change. So much in her life would change. Then he remembered her tennis career.

"What about tennis?" he managed to get out.

She shook her head as another sob rang through. "It's ... no ... problem. Already ... retiring ... this year." She took a couple of labored breaths. "Daddy and I ... discussed shortly back ... was gonna retire after the U.S. Open."

"We'll wait until then," he said softly as he took her hands.

She shook her head. "No." She squeezed back as she tried to regain her composure. "I'll do Wimbledon." She took a deep breath. "I'm committed to that already. But then I'm through." She breathed deeply again. "I ... will finally ... be through."

He pulled her head to his chest. "Stephanie Bartko will think she's died and gone to heaven when she finds out."

She giggled, "I know the feeling."

He pulled her back and looked seriously at her. "There's so much we've got to discuss because I leave for maneuvers in a week. First thing ..."

She interrupted him immediately. "Andrew Braisogn," she said firmly, "don't you dare start talking about the technical details of this without kissing me first. I've waited many years to do this without guilt or fear."

He stared in astonishment. "Wow ... me too." He slumped. "I'm not very good at all this. You'll have to remind me often when I get things wrong or out of order."

She pulled him to her. "Gladly."

The kiss was more tender than passionate. Years of denial and barriers dissolved within moments, and he couldn't believe he was really going through with it. But at this point, he could never go back. His heart had said yes, and now everything within him and without was about to change.

♉ ♉ ♉

When James Dorvain walked into the house, he was exceedingly concerned at seeing Andrew's car on the front drive. He placed his briefcase on the small table in the foyer and immediately headed for the back deck where he assumed he would find the two of them. He was right. His daughter was sitting in a chair, obviously clean and dressed early rather than still practicing, and was speaking quite seriously to Andrew who was leaning against the railing looking out toward the back of the yard. He tried not to let anger rise in him, but he knew the last thing Evie needed right now was another visit from the love she could never own. Andrew had more or less promised James that after the week at New Year's he would determine not to see her again. With an upcoming marriage and coronation, the need to sever their ties was mandatory. Not only for the sake of Evangeline's heart, but also for the rumors that would fly if anyone got wind that he still frequented their home.

"Is everything all right?" he asked cautiously as he opened one of the double doors to the deck and stepped outside.

Both Andrew and Evangeline were startled.

"Daddy," she said quickly, "I had no idea it was getting so late. Is it six already?"

"No," he replied curtly, avoiding her eyes and directing his stare toward Andrew. "I stopped early today." He got straight to the point. "What are you doing here, Andrew?"

The young man stared in silence for a moment, then managed to say, "Sir, I ... uh ... I came here today ... to ... ask your daughter ..." He looked petrified.

Evangeline saw his fear and stood up beside him, taking his hand. "It's okay, Andrew. Just tell him."

He shook his head. "I don't want to just tell him. It needs to be more than that."

James was still concerned about what exactly was happening. "Whatever is going on, I'd like to know ... now."

Andrew swallowed and squeezed her hand hard. "I would very much like your blessing ... your approval ... your permission to marry Evangeline."

James felt the blood leave his face. "Are you kidding me?"

"No sir," Andrew said quickly. "I've asked her ... and she's said yes, but I really need you to sanction this. It would kill me, sir, if you didn't ... well ... endorse our love."

James shook his head in shock then stared into his daughter's eyes. She was glowing. He looked back at Andrew and wanted to know, "Please tell me you're not abdicating with this proposal."

He shook his head. "No sir. I'm asking Evangeline to be my wife because I love her and can't imagine spending the rest of my life with anyone but her. And I'm asking her to be my queen because, unfortunately, that goes with the territory."

James reached out his hand to Andrew who took it and shook it firmly. "Finally came to your senses, did you?" He smiled.

Still shaking his hand, Andrew beamed with relief. "Thank you, sir. Thank you."

James pulled him into a firm embrace and an overwhelming rush of emotion washed through him. All the years of persecution his daughter had experienced would now be erased, not because she would be queen, but because her love would no longer be denied. He of all people knew the power love held in a person's life. And even though the scrutiny would now be magnified, she would survive stronger than before. How he wished Giselle was here to see it.

✼ Chapter Seventeen ✼

"Tell me you did not offer the kingdom to that woman." Andrew was surprised at the calm in his father's voice as he passed the library. He knew he would have to face him eventually—why not get it over with now while he was still high on love and acceptance from the Dorvains? Cautiously stepping into the darkened room, he stared to where one lone lamp shined. There sat Christopher Braisogn with a glass of brandy and a near empty bottle. No wonder he wasn't yelling—the alcohol had momentarily anesthetized the anger.

"No," Andrew replied. "I didn't offer her the kingdom—I offered her my love. Fortunately for this nation, the kingdom comes with that. Evangeline Dorvain will be the finest queen this country has ever known."

"Don't insult your mother, your grandmother, and every other queen that has worn that title."

He was amazed at his father's control even while drunk. His speech slowed some, but never slurred, his words punctual and articulate. No wonder Alfred assumed he was sane when he insisted on drawing up the Section Seven contract.

"I know you want to draw me into an argument," the prince began. "You want to berate me, demean Evangeline, and bemoan the future of the nation. You want to pile so much guilt and degradation on me right now that you hope I'll somehow cower and cave to your ridiculous ideals. Save your breath." He paused. "It's done. The only way to prevent Evangeline from becoming queen is to prevent me from becoming king. Your decision now, Father, is which loathing emotion you're going to fuel most—your relief at finally having your own heir on the throne after driving the first two away, or your hatred of Evangeline. And I'll say this again—if anything happens to her, her family, or anyone connected to her in anyway, I'll leave it all … and squarely place the blame on you." He turned to leave, then added, "And make no mistake—that isn't an idle threat."

♀ ♀ ♀

"What?" Terry was completely confounded. "How can you think of retiring? And after Wimbledon? Are you crazy? You haven't even played two full years! I knew something had you messed up, but this is ridiculous! What's going on with you?"

"What I'm about to tell you has got to remain confidential," Evangeline began, "at least until it's made public."

"Of course! You tell me to keep it quiet, I'll keep it quiet. But please tell me what the heck is going on!"

"I'm getting married."

His jaw dropped. This was the last thing he had expected to hear. "So you're telling me all this aggression I've had to wade through the past months is because you're getting married. Poor guy. Who is he? I didn't even know you were dating anyone. I thought you were all hung up over the prince fellow."

She smiled. "It is the prince fellow. I'm marrying Andrew Braisogn."

The lights came on. "Holy cow!" He hit his head with his palm. "So that's why he was here yesterday? To propose?"

She nodded.

"You're gonna be the queen?"

She gave a silly shrug.

He shook his head and closed his eyes, totally baffled by this turn of events. "So, what happens to me now?"

"What do you want to happen to you now?"

He held out his arms in total confusion. "I have no idea. I just figured I'd spend the rest of my days riding your glory. The truth is I'm not your coach. You have your own agenda, your own style, and frankly, it's always scared the crap out of me. All I've done is ride your coattails. You retire and suddenly every player in the world is gonna try to hire me on as coach … and I'm pitiful!"

"You're not that bad."

"Yes, I am!"

"You've taught me a lot of technique. I couldn't have done this without your help in analyzing and dissecting the games of my opponents."

"Technique is nothing! Nobody wants me to teach them technique. They're gonna want me to teach them how to win! I can't make anybody do what you do. You're … one of a kind. What else can I say?"

"How about congratulations?"

He tried to calm himself and step outside his own frustration for a moment. "How did this happen? I thought it was like impossible or something for you two to get married."

"It was." She began to grin. "I guess sometimes miracles still take place."

"Wow, girl. You've shaken up my world … in more ways than one."

"If you want, I can get you some kind of job here in Braisognia. You could work at a university coaching or something. You could even work as a coach at the palace if that appeals to you."

He shook his head. "Naw, but thanks. If I play my cards right maybe I can get some kind of media job … announcer or something like that. Your fame has sort of catapulted mine, although mine isn't deserved. Rather than embarrass myself trying to coach anyone else, maybe all this charm and good looks could be put to better use in front of the camera."

"If that's what you want." She took his hand. "I'll give you a significant severance package when it's over to keep you on your feet for awhile. You deserve it after putting up with me this last year."

"So all this madness was about love?" He was still befuddled. "You're the most complicated person I've ever known. You've been beating the snot out of me 'cause you were in love?"

"Well, at that time it was unrequited. I may have just lost my edge now."

"Oh, no," he said quickly. "You can't lose Wimbledon and then just quit."

"Who said anything about losing?"

♚ ♚ ♚

Amy couldn't believe her ears. "You're marrying Andrew?"

Again, Evangeline was beaming. "I would say I don't believe it myself, but I'm so enraptured by it all that it's pointless to question it." She slapped her knee. "I'm marrying Andrew!"

Her friend screamed and threw her arms around her. "I'm so, so happy for you! This is unbelievable!"

"But that means we have a serious decision to make. You signed on to do PR with me as a tennis person. That's going to be over in a month and a half. I'd really like you to consider staying on as my secretary."

"Are you kidding?"

"I certainly don't want someone appointed by the king handling my affairs," she moaned. "You know me better than anyone. It would be a great solace having you walk through all this with me."

"Oh, gosh—I don't think I can adopt that snooty royal attitude."

"Hallelujah! But on a serious note, you'll have to play double duty starting now. I'm supposed to meet with Andrew and his secretary/attendant, the formidable Alfred, tomorrow to discuss dates …

wedding date, date to announce the engagement … blah, blah, blah. I need my secretary with me. Andrew said the palace could appoint someone if needed. I told him no thanks." She smiled at the memory. "He said I was smarter than I realized."

♕ ♕ ♕

Christopher Braisogn stared out the window of his marbled office trying to devise a way to control the situation. His first thought was to destroy the whole family in a freak accident, but Andrew had made it clear he wouldn't allow that. Funny that the boy would finally grow a backbone, but only over the foolishness of a worthless girl. He had to stop this marriage somehow, and his only hope at the moment was through Alfred.

"Do you understand what I'm telling you to do?" he asked the old man.

"Yes, sir," he replied humbly. "Make sure that every date picked for the wedding be unfavorable. Make sure no minister in his right mind be willing to marry them. Make sure I bring up Miss Dorvain's flaws as often as I can. Make sure the prince knows you do not and never will approve of this marriage."

"That will have to do for now." He glared at Alfred. "If you fail me on this, you'll be fired."

"Understood, sir," he bowed slightly. "I will do my best to comply with your wishes, just as I have always done."

♕ ♕ ♕

"And what date are we considering for the wedding?" Alfred asked Andrew, Evangeline and Amy as the meeting began.

Andrew looked to the ladies. "Is there any time in particular that would be better for your schedule?"

The nervous bride shook her head. She hated being in Alfred's presence. His crooked nose reminded her of a buzzard's beak, and she knew he was loyal to the king to a flaw.

"When Wimbledon is over I have nothing else," she explained. "You're the one with the busy schedule, military maneuvers and princey-stuff. I'll be a nobody very soon."

Andrew grinned. "Not for long." He looked to Alfred. "I'd like to set the date as soon as maneuvers are over. How about the second weekend in August?"

The aged man looked down to his calendar for what seemed like only one second and replied, "No. The cathedral is taken that day."

"Ok, how about the following weekend?"

Alfred gave the same quick glance and repeated, "No. The cathedral is taken that day also."

Andrew's brows knit together. "Are there any open dates in August, Alfred?"

He gave another glance and shook his head. "Afraid not, sir. It would appear that the cathedral is generally booked way in advance for such important occasions, as opposed to … well … a shotgun or off-the-cuff affair."

Evangeline's cheeks rushed with heat.

"Let me ask you this, then," Andrew surmised, "are there any open dates for *my* wedding available at St. John's Cathedral, the cathedral where every king and queen of Braisognia have exchanged nuptials?"

Alfred perused his notes again and turned a few pages of his calendar. "It would appear not, sir."

Andrew sat back and stroked his beard while in obvious deep thought. Evangeline knew this was the king's work. He had obviously done something, threatened something, to ensure that an open date for the wedding wouldn't be obtainable.

"As I see it, I have two options then," Andrew finally communicated. "I can either break centuries of tradition and marry Evangeline somewhere other than the cathedral if you and my father persist with this silly game. Or I can give into to this insane whim he has that by somehow blocking my efforts to set a date I'll get the message and not marry Evangeline." He stood from his seat and reached over to take Alfred's calendar. "My choice is really rather simple. As of now, Alfred, you're no longer my attendant. I appreciate your years of service to me, although they were really years of service to my father. But from this point on, you will not move into the role of my secretary. I desire someone who will be loyal to me, not my father. Is that understood?"

Alfred slowly rose from the table, buttoned the coat of his trails, nodded his head and then left the room.

Andrew, Evangeline and Amy remained silent for several moments before Andrew finally confessed, "That felt good."

"Can you do that?" Evangeline wondered. "Can you fire your king-appointed attendant?"

"For my whole life I've always been compliant where my father was concerned. I've buckled under his ridiculous demands and given into his egotistical whims. I've watched him destroy my mother, my two brothers, and anyone who dared question his absolute authority. I accepted the role as heir to the throne more out of pity for him than out of duty. Well, now I stand ready to take on that burden, but I won't do it any longer under his terms. I'd just as soon abdicate this whole mess and walk away, never turning back, but that would accomplish nothing." He turned to Evangeline. "My first step in taking control of my life was to ask you to marry me—I think he hates it more that I defied him than he hates you. My second step is firing Alfred. If Father wants a fight, he shall have one, but on my terms this time. His only option is to either allow me to make my own choices, or to deny me the throne. Frankly, I'd rather he deny me the throne, but his pride won't go there.

"So, to answer your question as to whether I can fire Alfred or not," a smile began to grow, "I can do anything I want."

The girls stared in astonishment.

"Well, if we're voting here," Amy interjected lightly, "could you maybe find someone a little younger this time—someone with perhaps a personality? If I'm going to spend the rest of my life working with your next choice, I'd really like him to be … more … human? Possibly?"

Andrew laughed. "I'll see what I can do."

♙ ♙ ♙

"Jimmy, you have a very important guest here to see you," the page said wide-eyed. "He's in the conference room."

Jimmy Newell shook his head in confusion. Who of any importance would be coming to Greenleaf to see him? Whoever it might be couldn't possibly make his life any worse. He shuffled the papers back into a file, straightened his tie and headed toward the room. When he saw secret service standing outside the door, his adrenaline began to flow. Maybe his life could get worse. He tried to do a fast rewind of the past few weeks, months, years, that might warrant a visit from someone here to reprimand him for some careless deed. Several faces popped up in his head, most involving their daughters.

"Jimmy!" the prince greeted as he walked into the room. "You look sharp, buddy."

Slowly his nerves began to ease and a smile replaced the previous sober frown. "Andrew Braisogn," he acknowledged as he stuck out his hand. "What on earth are you doing here at Greenleaf? Not looking to buy it are you?"

"No. Just came here to see you."

"Well, I'm honored, but all the … uh …" he pointed to some of the security, "… effort it took to do this—you could have just called me to the palace."

"I needed to do this quickly. I've got to stay two or three steps ahead of my father at the moment."

"Okay, let's have a seat and tell me what's going on."

The men sat at the large table as the events of the past few days were unfolded.

"So, you're marrying her? For real?" Jimmy had never expected that.

"Yes, I am. I love her. You know that. And when I found out I had to marry before taking the throne, I had no choice. I just couldn't bring myself to marry another woman."

"Well, I'm thrilled for you, man. I really am."

"Which brings me to you," Andrew redirected the conversation.

"You want me in the wedding?"

"Well, no. Based on protocol you don't qualify. Sorry."

Jimmy held his hands up. "No problem. I'm just trying to guess why you're here."

"My attendant, Alfred, is unswervingly loyal to my father, which, I suppose, he should be. When we began trying to set a wedding date this morning, he insisted no date for my wedding to Evangeline could be made available."

"What do you mean?"

"In other words, he let me know he would not, in any way, go against my father's wishes by helping me set a date and prepare for the wedding."

"He's your secretary! He has to. This will be the social event of the year."

"He doesn't have to any more. I fired him."

Jimmy nodded. "Probably a good idea."

"So I need a secretary, a good PR man ... pronto ... today ... like right now."

His eyes grew wide. "Me? Is that why you're here? You want me to take Alfred's place?"

"Not take his place," Andrew clarified. "I don't need an attendant any longer. He would have eventually rolled over into the role of secretary at my coronation. So, in actuality, I'm just getting rid of him and basically hiring a secretary ... for life, I hope. It needs to be someone I can communicate with easily, someone I trust, someone who will be loyal to me. I need this guy to be as much a friend as he is a capable employee. You were the first one to come to mind."

Jimmy stood from the table and began to pace the room. "Wow, this is something I never anticipated."

"I know it would bind you down in some ways, but you would also have longer periods of free time and vacation. With a new wife and all, I know this could get taxing because the schedule is so unpredictable, but ..."

Jimmy held up a hand to stop him. "I didn't get married."

"You didn't? But I thought that was why you were taking the job at Greenleaf ... you were settling down."

"I was," he sighed. "Didn't work out. It was practically an arranged marriage, and as time rolled closer to the date ... well, it just didn't work out."

"I'm sorry, man," Andrew said getting up from the table and putting his hand on Jimmy's shoulder.

"Don't be. Like I said, it was more or less arranged. Our parents felt we both needed to settle down. They sort of made us a lucrative offer, and we thought it might be a good idea." He smiled. "It wasn't."

"Then maybe my offer is just what you need, unless you really like it here at Greenleaf."

He chuckled at the suggestion. "Right, corporate life. That's really me." He looked at Andrew and leaned in to whisper, "I'm so miserable here I could scream sometimes. Nine to five, every day, the same thing … over and over and over. If you really want me, I'm yours. I just hope you find me capable enough to fill the job."

"I can't think of a better man."

"Consider me your right hand then."

Jimmy offered his hand again, but this time Andrew pulled him into an embrace.

"One hurdle overcome," the prince breathed with relief.

❧ Chapter Eighteen ☙

Nicolas Scott had thought that taking the pastorate at St. John's would be a dream come true. In his mind he had reached the pinnacle of any minister's ideal. He was only thirty-five and had sacrificed greatly to complete his education and move through the ranks of the Braisognian church to become the youngest pastor ever at St. John's. Now he was wondering if this might be more of a curse than a blessing. After being here only three months, he stood on the verge of possibly losing his ministry forever.

The young minister tried to appear calm as he sat across the desk from Andrew Braisogn and Evangeline Dorvain, but he was in the worst imaginable position. Above all, he was a man of God, devout to a life of integrity and honesty, but he had been threatened into a decision that he now regretted more than ever. He wouldn't lie to them concerning what he had been told, but it had been made clear that he was to say nothing if he wanted to not merely keep his position, but ever work in Braisognia again.

"Rev. Scott," Andrew stated gently, "before you start sweating about all this, I want to assure you that I'm not here to cause you any trouble. I've lived with my father, the king, for twenty-four years, and I know what he's capable of. I also know that whatever has been said and demanded of you the past two days have probably got you tied up in knots."

The fact that the prince had some idea of what was going on still did not reassure Nicolas. The old man, Alfred, had insisted that if anything he had been told was leaked, he would be ruined.

"When you came to St. John's," Andrew continued, "I was very pleased. You were like a breath of fresh air, not only into the church, but into my life. Your sermons and your sincerity have done a lot to encourage me in my new walk with the Lord. Evangeline got me started, but you've sort of urged me on."

The pastor shakily nodded and replied, "Thank y ... you. Glad to hear that."

"I also believe that you're a man who lives by what you teach, which means that you would choose honesty and the right thing over deception and the wrong thing on any day."

Nicolas nodded slightly, but his stomach was beginning to churn. He feared the prince was going to question him about the old man's visit, and either he would have to lie to preserve his future, or tell him the truth and forever lose all he had worked for his entire life.

"Because of this," Andrew went on, "I don't want to force you to compromise yourself. The best I can do is just ask some yes and no questions, and assure you that nothing I infer will ever leave this room."

Evangeline reached across the desk and covered the minister's shaking hands with her own. "Rev. Scott, please don't be alarmed. Andrew isn't his father, nothing like his father, and this conversation isn't meant to bring you any kind of harm."

The bile was rising in Nic's throat.

"I'm going to assume that someone came to you and insisted that if you wanted to keep your job, you shouldn't marry us," Andrew spoke plainly. "If that's true, don't say anything. Don't nod, don't blink, don't cough."

The minister just sat there continuing to shake from nerves.

"What I want you to know is that I'd very much like to be married here at St. John's because it is the Braisognian tradition. I'm not generally big into tradition, but this has been my church my whole life, so it carries a little more weight than the average royal ritual. I'd also like for you to be the man who performs the ceremony. You can't know what you've meant to me the few months you've been here. I also think that the exposure you would receive from the televised wedding would make you a household name and boost your influence in the Braisognian church." He paused. "This church desperately needs more influence from men like yourself."

Nicolas didn't know if he was to acknowledge the compliment or continue being nonresponsive. He just sat.

"What I want to offer you is the opportunity for both of us to get what is best here ... to do what is best ... not just for us, but for the reputation of this kingdom."

Nic sighed and finally spoke. "I don't think that's possible, your majesty."

"You don't have to majesty me, Rev. Scott. You're my pastor, and I want to do right by you."

"But you don't understand ..."

"Believe me when I say that I do," Andrew assured sympathetically.

"It's not just about me anymore," Nic wearily explained. "I have a wife, three kids and one on the way. This job was finally a security. We have a nice home at the parsonage, and as much as I hate to admit it, I make a nice salary at last. If I throw all this away, it's not just me who suffers."

"I don't want you to throw this away. Just listen to my idea. It will require some patience on your part, but we'll all live happily ever after once my father is off the throne and I'm king. Just remember that—he won't be king this time next year … I will."

Pastor Scott nodded and unintentionally took a gasp of air. He didn't realize he'd been holding his breath.

"How would you like to move out of the parsonage and into your very own home?" Andrew asked.

Nic shook his head. "I can't even begin to afford that right now, and I have a baby on the way."

"I'm not suggesting you buy it—I'm suggesting that as my gift to you for agreeing to marry us, I give you a home and the equivalent lump sum of what your yearly salary and benefits are here at St. John's. When my father fires you from the position of pastor after performing our wedding, which I assume is what he threatened, you'll have your own home and enough money to last until my coronation. The day after I become king, my first order of duty will be to reinstate you and derail all the derogatory garbage the palace spews about you in the coming months. I'll assure the public and this congregation and the Braisognian church that you are indeed a noble man, a righteous man, and that you chose to do the right thing over intense pressure to bend to the threats of the former king."

Nic tried to breathe again. Could this offer be possible? He would have his own home in which to raise his family?

"I know my father will have you slandered in some way," Andrew warned him, "but I promise you that when I become king, I'll make it all right."

He shook his head in disbelief. "How do you people live like this? The hate, the deception, the covering of truth?"

"Believe me, it's a miserable existence, but it's not a life I've chosen. This is the life that was handed to me, and my father wants nothing more than for me to carry on such a legacy of sham and deceit." He leaned down on the reverend's desk and declared, "But that legacy stops with me. I know this is a tall order for you. I know what you'll have to go through the next months, but if you can just be patient and realize that it'll be made right in the end, your restoration will well be worth the price. If you'd rather not, I understand reverend. I'll find another church and another pastor, but I would really like to begin the start of my legacy here and now. And I would like you to walk this bold path with me."

"Fired?" Christopher Braisogn raged. "He can't fire you! He has no authority to fire you! Until he takes the throne he will abide by my choices and my rules!"

"I beg to differ, sir," Alfred said meekly.

"What?" The king was astonished. "I don't know what's gotten into you lately, Alfred, but you're forgetting your place, I fear! You dare to question my authority over Andrew—over my own son?"

"I am not questioning the position of your authority nor the law of your authority. You surely know that Andrew has never been a fan of filling your shoes as king. As that date approaches closer he may seek ways that would appear to force your hand in his life. He knows your temperament, sir. He knows if he pushes hard enough, you could blow beyond repair and do something so against him that he could validly walk away from the throne."

Christopher didn't like what the old man had suggested. "I am still king—I am still in control."

"But when Andrew, the only remaining heir, turns twenty-five, you will no longer be king. And if he abdicates, then on Andrew's twenty-fifth birthday, your cousin's son will inherit the crown, your family will lose its line, and the monarchy will forever be ripped from your loins."

The venom pulsing through the king was so strong he believed he could literally tear a man apart with his bare hands. He wanted to start with Alfred, breaking him limb by limb, and throwing him from the highest pinnacle of the palace. He had never actually killed a man himself, although he'd had it done many times, but the old man was close to losing his head.

"Do you realize I could obliterate you right here, right now, and no one would ever know what happened?"

"Absolutely, sir," he bowed slightly. "My loyalty is only to you, your majesty. I point these things out not to disturb you but to warn you. I know the greatest meaning in your life has been the kingship. I know the greatest legacy you can leave is a son on the throne. I also know that beneath the lamb's heart of your youngest son lies a strong and fierce lion ... that is who he was raised to be. My desire is to see that lion unleashed in proper perspective, and not toward the father who only wants what's best for him."

Christopher's shoulders finally slumped in reprieve. It was true—Andrew now held over him the very legacy he had fought so hard to preserve. Any irrational misstep and the boy would gladly give up the throne, just like George and Peter. The ultimate insult to the entire life of Christopher Braisogn could be handed to him by his last son.

"I need a shot of bourbon," he said as he walked toward the cabinet, "... or two ... or three ..."

Andrew, Evangeline, Amy and Jimmy sat together for the first time in the living area of Amy's new suite near the palace. The young prince hated to admit it, but he was enjoying the control of his own destiny at the moment. Year after wretched year he had bended to the unreasonable demands of his father, but something within him had snapped. If his father wanted to adamantly continue being the tyrant to his family that he always has been, Andrew would no longer be a part of it. He had secretly envied the freedom and peace that George and Peter gained when they defied their father and left the palace, but his sense of duty to the kingdom could never release him to do the same. He had wanted to, had longed to, but some small part of him was able to pity his father just enough to stay the course and accept his fate.

Now, as he sat together with the only people he could ever truly call friends, Evangeline and Jimmy, he felt a long needed release from the strangling grip of his father. He also felt the need to ensure his own sons would never despise him in like manner. The king had constantly pounded into his head that it was an honor and not a curse to be a Braisognian heir. Andrew hoped his example would be something his sons truly wanted to follow.

"The wedding will be the second weekend in August," Evangeline began the actual business part of the meeting.

Andrew interjected, "Which is going to be a bit of a problem because we aren't even announcing the engagement until after Wimbledon."

"Why not?" Jimmy wanted to know. "Why not just let it out now?"

"Protection," Evangeline explained. "Once it's announced, I have to go into full blown palace level security mode. Hobnobbing at Wimbledon would be practically impossible. It would be more trouble than it's worth."

Jimmy nodded. "I can understand that. I remember college life with Andrew very well."

"Rumors will start flying like crazy because we're getting married so soon," Andrew continued. "You guys," he pointed to Amy and Jimmy, "need to be ready to handle the press and all their questions and speculations. The main thing is that we held off with the announcement because Evangeline had already committed to play Wimbledon and many Braisognians made plans and reservations to attend—we didn't want to inconvenience them. This will be her last tournament and the last opportunity, at least where Evangeline is concerned, for Braisognia to be represented like this internationally."

"Gee," Jimmy grinned, "you're a very noble lady."

Amy chuckled, "She just wants the trophy to balance out her collection. You need to decorate in odds, not evens."

"The people of Braisognia should be proud to know their future queen is willing to sacrifice so much for the cause of interior design," Jimmy smirked.

Amy grinned. "Wow, Andrew … I can see you found some personality here. Can you handle this guy after so many years with Alfred?"

"I'm oozing with personality," Jimmy carried on. "That's the only reason Andrew wanted me. He could care less about my professional skills."

The banter continued on for some time, and Andrew marveled at the promise of his new found life. For the first time he had control of his future rather than sitting quietly while Alfred and a group of various older men and women dictated to him the next days and weeks. When they did come around to finally discussing the plans for the coming months, it was still fun. And the fact that Evangeline was sitting next to him holding his hand and winking at him between laughs almost made him think he was in heaven. As he leaned back and sighed, he wondered if this might possibly be the best day of his life.

ᐃ Chapter Nineteen ᐁ

Evangeline maneuvered through the various locker rooms hoping to find Stephanie Bartko. This was bound to be a difficult conversation but one she had wanted to have for a long time. She didn't anticipate a welcomed reception—in fact, she wouldn't be surprised if she had her thrown out. As she rounded the corner she spotted her sitting on a bench, her face buried in a towel. Somehow her vicious victories over the champion seemed trite at the moment.

"Stephanie?" she whispered.

The weary woman looked up and immediately flushed. "What could you possibly want?"

"To talk … just for a minute."

She stood and threw her towel to the bench. She was intimidating and tall, the muscles glistening in her arms and legs from perspiration. Evangeline was unsettled by her for the first time. "I have nothing to say to you," she mumbled as she threw a few items in her bag.

"But I have something I'd like to say to you." She tried to sound bold.

"I don't care!" She yelled an expletive. "And you shouldn't even be in here! For crying out loud, we have a finals match tomorrow. You have no right coming in here trying to throw me off balance!"

"Do you really believe that's why I'm here?"

Stephanie stared at her then threw up her hands. "I have no clue! All I know is that I have no desire to speak with you for any reason. You've ruined my life, you know? You've desecrated my past, stomped on my present and destroyed my future. I could almost break your neck right now … right here … if it weren't for the fact that it would come off as some maniacally jealous act and make me look even worse than I already do."

"I never wanted to do that to you. All I knew was that I had to win, and

144

unfortunately, you were the one I had to beat."

"Congratulations," she sarcastically spat. "So what do you want? Are you here to gloat? To tease me? To rub it in? I know it can't be to ask me to throw the game tomorrow." She laughed. "That would be hilarious."

"I hate tennis," Evangeline confessed. "I hate the raw competition that it's become."

"You know what," still sarcastic, "I hate it too! But I have nothing else! This is it for me! Since I was four years old, this is the path my father chose for me. I was groomed, coached, trained ... all for this! I never had any other choice. While other girls were roller skating and going to slumber parties and spending their summers at the pool, I was training and playing and competing because my father said all those other normal things girls did were silly. I was going to be the best in the world, and I had to sacrifice my childhood and youth to do it." She dropped to the bench. "And for a small window of time, I was the best." She looked up at Evangeline. "Then you waltzed in out of nowhere ... some no name from some unknown nation. I laughed when I heard you would be my final opponent at the French last year. I was thinking to myself that this had just become too easy." She sighed and closed her eyes. "And you tore my world apart."

Evangeline walked over cautiously and eased down beside her. "I know how you feel ... sort of. Tennis was the only hope to change my destiny. I didn't play tennis because I wanted to be the best—I played because I was the best, and because of that, I had a chance to rise above the doom everyone had pronounced on my life."

Stephanie chuckled. "Ironic, isn't it? The two best players in the world actually hate the sport."

"Do you really hate it? Or do you just hate me?"

Stephanie, who towered over her even as they sat on the bench, sighed deeply and shook her head. "I don't honestly know anymore. I can definitely say that I hate you ... and that at this moment right now the last thing I want to do is play you tomorrow. The thought actually nauseates me. I almost considered throwing my last match because I didn't want to face you again in another Grand Slam final, but then that would make me look weak. It's one thing losing to you—it's another thing entirely ... losing to anyone else."

"I want to tell you something, but I need you to keep it confidential ... at least until it's made public next week."

"Are you joking? You're about to tell me something that I have to keep quiet? Don't you know that the thing I want most in this world is to destroy you? If I were you, I wouldn't tell me anything right now."

"I'm retiring after tomorrow's match."

She stared at Evangeline with raised eyebrows as if she were waiting on the punch line of a confusing joke. "Funny," she finally managed to say.

"Very funny."

"I'm being serious. I'm getting married, but we're not saying anything until after the tournament. That's why I need you to keep it quiet."

"What's the big deal?" She appeared suspicious. "I didn't even know you were … dating. Is it Terry? Are you marrying that idiot coach of yours?"

She smiled and shook her head. "No. I'm marrying the prince—soon to be king—of Braisognia."

"Wo. The dark-haired guy with the beard? The one in your box at New York?"

Now Evangeline was flushed. "That's the one."

"Wow." She sat stunned a moment. "But why do you have to retire? Players get married all the time … sometimes to each other! Marriage doesn't stop your career on the court."

"I can't continue playing as the soon-to-be-queen. There's a lot of protocol that prohibits it plus security issues, but frankly, I really don't care. It's like I told you—I hate playing. The whole reason we're waiting to publicize it is Wimbledon. That's why I need you to keep it quiet until after we make the formal announcement. When that happens you can tell the world you knew before they did. Shoot, you can even tell everyone we were great chums off the court and you knew about it all along. I don't really care. I just mainly wanted you to know that tomorrow is our last match, and I wish that … well … that you knew me as something other than your enemy."

Stephanie shook her head. "I can't believe it." She looked at her with tired eyes. "Everyone kept telling me you were a nice girl. I just didn't want to believe them." She grinned. "Does this mean you're gonna let me win?"

"Not on your life. You won't believe how many Braisognians will be here tomorrow. Nothing like this has ever happened in our country before."

"No kidding. I'd never even heard of your country until last year."

Stephanie reached out her hand and Evangeline stood to take it.

"Congratulations. And for the record, I won't be telling people that we were *chums*. We don't even use that word in America."

"I understand."

"But I will tell them that you were a nice lady, although a fierce opponent." Stephanie reached down for her bag. "And after the announcement … about the wedding … I *might* let everyone know I already knew, just to stir the pot a little."

♉ ♉ ♉

Andrew stared at the screen in amazement as he watched Evangeline take down Stephanie again. If he didn't know better, it almost seemed as though she actually gave a few games to the former champion. She never hit errors, but this match had been full of them. As the final spin from Evangeline's shot twisted beyond Stephanie's reach, he watched the two players approach the net and ceremonially shake hands. Then, for the first time, they pulled each other into an embrace.

"What the heck?" he muttered to himself. Then a thought hit him—she knows. Evangeline told her.

The guys in the room were whooping and yelling. Andrew continued to calmly watch the screen trying to hear the words of the commentators until one soldier made a suggestive remark concerning Evangeline.

"You're way out of line there!" Andrew yelled at him.

All the men got quiet.

"Sorry, sir," the soldier replied meekly. "She's just so ... hot. I mean, she really is."

The guys all nodded.

"That's no reason to speak of her in such a derogatory manner," he scolded. "She's done more for the advancement of our nation in the eyes of the world than anyone in history. She deserves our respect."

"I'd like to show her some respect," another man dared to say. "In private!"

Andrew slammed his hand on the table as he stood to his feet. "That will be enough!"

Again the men became quiet. He looked around at them all. This was unfair. They really were more his friends than men beneath his command, yet he knew each one would lay down his life for him without a second thought. He didn't want to be an unreasonable tyrant like his father.

"Guys," he redirected calmly, "please understand something. Evangeline is ... well ... she's more than just a face on the screen or an icon in a magazine." He hesitated. "She's ... close to me." He looked up at them. "Very close ... to me."

One man asked, "Just how close is she to you, sir?"

He wanted to burst with his news, but he remained controlled and reserved. "We're announcing our engagement next weekend."

"No way!"

The men began to cheer.

Andrew put up his hand to silence them. "Please don't speak of this to anyone until we've made it public. Her safety and security could be at risk. We need to get her back to Braisognia, protected behind her own borders and home again. So when I leave this weekend, you'll all know why. We had to wait until this tournament was over. I know it's against rules for a soldier to leave camp during maneuvers, but it will be a quick trip to the palace and then back again."

"We won't speak of it, sir. You can count on us."

"Thanks, men."

The first soldier then added, "For the record, I think you might be the luckiest man in the world."

Andrew smiled. "No argument there."

♙ ♙ ♙

Christopher Braisogn pulled a knife from his pocket and jabbed it into the table to emphasize the seriousness of his request. All five men jumped. He said nothing for the moment as he stared intensely at each. They knew him well, and they knew why they were here. For lack of a better description they were his lynch men. The details of deeds they had done for him over the years could have sent each one to prison for hundreds of years. They were well paid and always immune to prosecution. When the king of the country who holds fifty-one percent of the rule says a man's charges will not remain and a compensation will be paid to all who remain silent, it's amazing how well a crime can be covered. The only problem with the request he was making now was that no crime could be committed.

"Your majesty," said one man respectfully, "how do you expect us to do this?"

"Exactly," agreed another. "You say to keep the Dorvain lady off the throne, but we can't kill her or kidnap her—we can't make her disappear. So what do we do?"

The king folded his arms and locked his jaw as he spoke. "I have no idea, that's why I've called you here. You guys are the geniuses. You tell me what you're going to do. If I could have hatched a plan myself don't you think I'd be dispensing orders rather than asking your inept advice?"

"How long we got? You want her gone before the wedding?"

He shook his head. "First of all, she can't be *gone*. I thought I made that clear."

One man stood from the table as he rubbed the back of his head. "So you're gonna let the wedding go through? You're gonna let them marry, then you want us to try and destroy her ... only without destroying her?"

"Listen to me!" The vein in Christopher's forehead was pulsing blue. "If anything happens to her, Andrew will blame me and will not take the throne! If you so much as singe a hair on her body, I'll hunt you down myself and put a bullet between your eyes!"

Another man tried to reason with him. "We can't keep her off the throne if she marries your son. There's no way around this. What you're asking us to do is impossible."

He nodded with an evil grin. "That's why I'm asking you," he motioned toward the five as he retrieved the knife. "I could have each one of you arrested before your feet left this room and have you put away for life. I

148

strongly suggest you find a way to make it happen before Andrew is crowned next April. You've got plenty of time, and I assume plenty of motivation. Have I made myself clear?"

"Yes, your majesty," seethed the first man.

❧ Chapter Twenty ❧

Evangeline was thankful Andrew was already at the palace when her limo arrived. She couldn't bear the thought of facing the king without him by her side. Because he was at maneuvers, he wasn't allowed to have contact with anyone outside of immediate family, and only then could it be done via e-mail. Because she wasn't family, he couldn't legally communicate with her. Once their engagement was announced, in approximately thirty minutes, she could officially be put on his list. Of course, she had never been able to communicate with him anyway. Anything prior to today had been done by her father through military channels, until Jimmy Newell had been hired. Now Jimmy and Amy managed to send brief, impersonal messages with certain details concerning the announcement, but any more than that could have been grounds for military punishment.

She wondered what it would be like to be able to communicate with him whenever she wanted. So many times she had actually written him letters but then tore them up because she knew he would never receive them. After today she would have unlimited access to him through the internet—and to her that was a respite she could cling to as she faced the storm that would ensue once the wedding was announced. She would have to remain positive though, and never let Andrew know when she was struggling or suffering because of it. It had taken him years to finally believe she was strong enough to handle marrying him. It would now be up to her to maintain that.

Her father reached for her hand as the car pulled through the gate of the palace grounds. The lawns were filled with people here to see her receive more accolades for Wimbledon—at least that's what they presumed. They had no idea they were about to witness a moment in Braisognian history. Her heart stopped at the thought—she would be officially engaged to the prince of the land, the future king of this country. She dreaded that part of the arrangement, but to know that Andrew would be hers for life, and she would be his, made the unwanted baggage tolerable.

"You okay?" he asked as he squeezed her hand tenderly.

"Nervous. I'll get to see the old familiar glare of Christopher Braisogn—get to feel his contempt."

"Well, be glad that you're marrying his son and not him."

She choked at the thought. "Don't even suggest such an idea! I'm already dreading have to live in the same building with him until the coronation. I sometimes wonder how I'll manage … then I remember—Andrew will be there too."

"And I guarantee you he'll protect you from his father as much as is possible. He'll hover over you like a mother hen."

"No," she countered. "I won't allow myself to be weak. I'm not here to sabotage the kingdom as his father believes. I'm here to love Andrew, to be his solace, his support, his love. He doesn't need to protect me from anything. I'm strong—I've lived through enough royal contempt to have the skin of an elephant."

"But you've never lived under the same roof with that contempt."

"Yes, I did. Welcome back to the memories of my college years."

He made no further comment but nodded toward the palace. When she looked she saw Andrew waiting on the steps. Her heart flipped. This couldn't be happening. She was about to be officially engaged to this man.

"How do I greet him, Daddy? This is so public. Cameras will be focused on us—the nation will be watching. Right now I just want to grab him and hold him forever! I haven't seen him in over a month."

"That wouldn't be my suggestion," he teased. "Take your cues from him. He won't guide you wrong."

As the limo stopped and a guard opened her door, her heart raced and her hands quivered. This had to be a dream, and she was afraid she would wake up before she got to the good part. But as soon as she stepped out of the car, Andrew moved down the steps to greet her. His eyes were bright and his smile excited. She waited for his cue, as her father suggested, and Andrew soon reached out his hand to shake hers. When she took it, warmth flooded her body.

"I want to do so much more than shake your hand right now," he confessed, still smiling, "but until the world knows what's happening, this handshake will have to do."

"The feeling's mutual," she grinned back as she removed her hand. "I hope I can keep up this charade the next few minutes. I'm afraid that everything I feel right now is written all over my face."

"Then you must be feeling lovely, because that's all I can see."

The crowd cheered from behind the gates, and the two responded with waves as they made their way to the steps of the palace. She hoped the people wouldn't be disappointed when they learned she would no longer be their hero, but instead their new queen. She knew the royals would still despise her but would never have the nerve to proclaim it publicly. And once the announcement was made today, she could begin her charity work that had been the real goal of her tennis career from the beginning. She hoped, though futile as it may be, that she could be a step in finally bridging the ridiculous gap between the classes in her nation.

Once inside the palace beyond the views of cameras and people, Andrew whisked her into a small side room. He closed the door for privacy but the glass window through the top made it impossible.

"I just needed a moment with you," he explained as he reached his hands to her face. "I have dreamed of seeing you like this for weeks now. Can I kiss you? Would it mess up your make-up … your lipstick?"

"Who cares?" she told him as she grabbed his collar and pulled him down to her.

His kiss was heavenly, tender, loving. Her body swooned with warmth again as he melted his arms around her. It didn't matter if the whole world was against her now. Andrew loved her and was making her his wife. She could handle the persecution—she could handle anything.

"I don't know how those married guys do it," he whispered as he leaned his face into her hair. "I felt as though I would die over and over if I didn't see you soon."

He kissed her again and held her tight. She wanted this moment to linger but knew the conference was waiting. When he finally released her all he could do was smile into her eyes.

"My lipstick?" she asked. "Did you … uh … rearrange it?"

He examined her lips then gently kissed the top one, then the bottom one, then her nose. "You look beautiful. I wouldn't change a thing."

She reached up and carefully removed a small smudge from his lips. "You only have a tinge here, but I think that got it." She grinned at the memory of his lips gently touching hers. "It was a soft kiss anyway."

"Our kisses are always soft, aren't they?"

She thought for a moment. "I think that's because they're always so short. We're always just catching a moment here or there, on our way to somewhere else or surrounded by people."

"In a month we'll be married. I can kiss you forever."

"I look forward to it."

They stared at each other only briefly because of James' rapping at the door's window. He motioned to his watch.

"And we're off," Andrew sighed. "But one day I'll have you all to myself."

"I look forward to that too."

There was no time for idle talk as they rushed down the corridors toward the balcony where the press had been set up. The king and queen were already standing near the doors as the young couple entered the area. Her first thought was to try and avoid the king's gaze as much as possible, but she didn't want him to think his intimidation affected her. He definitely made her feel like a worthless intruder, but if she didn't show it, he would never know his tactics had worked.

She bowed respectfully before both of them. "Your majesties."

"Evangeline," Julia said warmly as she reached out for her. Surprisingly the queen pulled her into a small hug. "Congratulations on Wimbledon … again."

"Yes," came the snide remark from the king. "I suppose all these accolades are becoming rather mundane for you now. It seems that you are quite unbeatable at tennis."

"I've had a lucky run of it." She maintained her composure.

"Tsk, tsk," he shook his finger. "Don't be so modest, Miss Dorvain. That was no stroke of luck. You decimated many ladies all over the world to do what you've done. It appears you are a fierce competitor."

"Only when it's necessary, sir."

"And in your mind, all this," he paused, "was necessary?"

Was he talking about tennis still, or was he now referring to her relationship with Andrew?

"Would you have rather seen this nation represented as a failure? I'm not exactly sure what you're insinuating."

Andrew, who had been getting directions from the press secretary, stepped into the conversation. "Everyone playing nice?" he asked as he protectively placed his hand on the small of her back.

"But of course," Christopher bowed. "We were just discussing how your bride-to-be seems to be having quite the winning streak lately."

Andrew gave a doubtful smile. "And our nation has benefited greatly as a result. Now, is everyone ready to step outside and give the world a smile?"

No one replied, but they all moved toward the doors and took their respective places, the king in front, the queen her dutiful paces behind, followed by Andrew and Evangeline side by side. Had the king seen it, he would have scowled. She looked over to her father for a sense of commendation, an assurance that she was doing the right thing. James nodded confidently and that was all she needed. They walked out onto the balcony and the crowd immediately rose to a roar. Each dignitary waved as they stood near the railing and then went to their predetermined spaces to stand for the announcement. Reaching into her tote, she removed the folded paper containing her short speech. Never had she been so nervous in her life. Playing tennis on worldwide television with the world's most dominant players was a breeze compared to defying Christopher Braisogn in his own palace by accepting the crown with his son.

At last Andrew stepped up to the podium. "I must say, this is quite a turnout for something so simple as a game or two of tennis."

The crowd went wild across the lawns. He stood back from the microphone and let them yell. Turning his gaze toward Evangeline, he winked as he motioned his hand to the crowd. Her heart skipped. He was assuring her that the people of Braisognia loved her and would accept the announcement soon to be made. She marveled that he had no speech prepared, at least no written speech. Yet he seemed calm and in control as he waited at the lectern for the cheering to subside.

"It would appear that our native girl, Evangeline Dorvain, is a force to be reckoned with." The cheering began again, but he didn't pause as long this time. "We are here today at the palace grounds to offer our nation's congratulations and thankfulness for such displays of strength, confidence and amazing sportsmanship. I assure you that whenever Miss Dorvain steps out onto a court anywhere on this planet, the world is keenly aware of a nation called Braisognia and that powerful things can indeed come in small packages."

The crowd grew so loud again that he had to wait for the sound to subside.

"On this day in July, we," he motioned back toward his parents, "my father, King of Braisognia, my mother the queen, and myself, the crowned prince in waiting," gentle laughter rolled among the crowd, "would like to bestow upon Miss Dorvain a token of the nation's appreciation for her representation and victory in her field." He reached beneath the podium and pulled out a crystal goblet. The crowd sang with delight as he held it up. "Miss Dorvain, would you join me?"

Evangeline had to will her feet to move as her entire body trembled. She tried to walk with grace and poise knowing in a matter of minutes the entire nation would realize she would be its queen within a year. Andrew's smile was full of admiration as he handed her the goblet, and when their fingers touched briefly during the exchange, she felt that immediate warmth again. She could do this.

She placed the goblet on the podium, nodded and waved to the crowd, then unfolded her note. She had never been so nervous, and for a fleeting moment she imagined herself flinging off her high heels and running back inside to her father's arms—but just off to her right stood Andrew. Her father's arms would offer her safety, but Andrew was her destiny, her life, her heart. This was not about her anymore—this was about him. She had sworn to him she had the strength to be what he needed, and that the pressure of palace life would not destroy her, would not clip her wings. Now was the time to prove to him, to his father, but most of all to herself—she could do this. She smiled at him with a confidence she didn't own at the moment and turned back to the crowd.

"Honorable king and queen of Braisognia, Prince Andrew, and ladies and gentlemen of the kingdom, I'm humbled again at your displays of gratefulness for my representation on the court. I've worked hard to make sure that when I step out of the boundaries of this mighty country I embody the character and heart which has made this nation great. As a child it never occurred to me that I would have a future so wrapped up in the public eye. All I ever dreamed of doing was carrying out the work that my mother, Giselle Montevo Dorvain, had begun—to help children in need realize their potential and find the freedom to dream big." She paused as the crowd applauded.

"I confess to you that I am a dreamer. Tennis was never a part of my dreaming, but merely an ability, a gift as my mother called it. I chose to see it as a tool that would launch my dreams. Because of that, and because I never desired to make a life's career out of the sport, that it was merely a means to an end, I am announcing today that I will retire from professional tennis as of Wimbledon this year."

The disappointment of the crowd was obvious. She looked over to Andrew not knowing whether to continue or allow them to moan on. He smiled again and motioned that she finish her speech.

"Please understand that I'm not in any way abandoning this nation. I'm merely laying aside one pursuit in exchange for a greater one. My hope is that rather than me, as one individual standing out from among you—that we will stand together and unite for a greater cause than any sporting event. My dream is that I would be the first of many future players, not only in tennis, but in every other venue imaginable, from sports to the arts, to the sciences … that every child, regardless of their background or misfortune, can have the opportunity to represent this nation on the world stage also. The world now knows who we are. My dream is to make sure that it never forgets. Thank you."

This time the crowd roared and applauded even louder. She took a deep breath and braced herself against the lectern. The speech was over, but the announcement was still to come. She whispered a prayer that this nation would be just as willing to accept her as the wife of their beloved prince as they had her championships. When Andrew placed his hand on her back she exhaled—had she ever been more nervous? She wanted to lean into him and feel his embrace and be assured that she had done the right thing, but she knew it wouldn't be appropriate. To her surprise, however, Andrew pulled her into a hug with both his arms surrounding her, protecting her, promising her that she would be his wife and in a moment the entire world would know.

The crowd responded even more to the embrace. She knew the nation loved her because of her success, but she hoped the announcement of retiring in order to pursue the helping of needy children would endear her more. In her mind, this was a much nobler goal. She hoped they would embrace her as queen simply because she had a heart that loved its most vulnerable.

Stepping back to the microphone, Andrew reached into his pocket and removed a small box which he placed on the podium. She secretly hoped it wasn't another gift from the palace. She had no desire to say or accept anything else. All she wanted was for the announcement to be over so the press conference could end, and she could spend a few more moments alone with Andrew before he was rushed back to maneuvers for the rest of the month.

"Ladies and gentlemen, if I could have your attention for a moment, I would like to add one more event to our agenda today."

The crowd noise subsided as they looked expectantly toward the balcony.

"I am sure that Miss Dorvain has captured the heart of this nation in many ways." He turned toward her and reached out his hand. She took it and he pulled her next to him. "I must confess that she has captured my heart as well." The crowd began to murmur again. "I've known for many years that this woman was uniquely special, that she had a quality about her that was like a breath of fresh air blowing throughout this kingdom. I never knew for sure what her future held, but I knew that whatever it was it would be great." He took the box from the podium and then looked down at her, full of confidence and admiration. He opened the box and revealed a simple diamond ring. "I would get on my knees before this crowd, before this nation, and ask you to become my bride, but no one would be able to hear me or see me, and I want there to be no mistake at what I'm proposing here. Evangeline Dorvain, would you do me the honor of accepting this ring as a pledge to be my wife, to live life with me, and to be the queen of this great nation?"

The eruption from the crowd was now deafening, and she was taken aback by his public proposal. She put a shaky hand to her mouth as tears and sobs began to build from deep within. The emotion of it all had overwhelmed her to the breaking point, and she could no longer control her reaction. He merely took her in his arms again and tenderly held her before the country as the crowd began to chant her name. She tried to regain composure as quickly as possible, but her body continued to shake as tears flowed. She forced herself to pull away from him and looked up into his eyes while nodding. The crowd was ecstatic. He removed the ring from the box and tried to place it on her quivering finger.

He leaned down to her ear and said, "If you could hold still, this would be so much easier."

Looking up at him she replied, "If I could hold still? Are you kidding me?"

And for the first time in Braisognian history, a member of the royal family placed a public kiss on the lips of his intended as the nation watched and cheered.

❧ Chapter Twenty-One ❧

"Where are we going?" Evangeline asked as Andrew hurried her through the halls of the palace.

"For someone with such energy on the court you sure are drained today," he teased.

She pulled him to a halt. "Do you have any idea how stressful this has been?"

He smiled, gently kissed her, and replied, "Yes. The worst is over. But we have to hurry."

"Again, where are we going?"

"I need to show you something, but we don't have much time. The base is expecting me back at a specific time, and cavorting around the palace with my fiancé would be a breach of military ethics. I'm supposed to be here on official royal business—and that business has already occurred." He finally stopped at a large, vaguely familiar, ornate door.

"Your room?" she asked.

"You remembered. I'm impressed since you said it looked like every other place in this sterile building."

She ran her hand across the carved lion on the door. "I could never forget this design. It was the only thing I liked about your room."

"I see. Glad to know something about it was memorable other than it's utter boredom."

He opened the door and led her inside, leaving it widely ajar so no one could accuse them of impropriety. She looked around the room and found it basically identical as fifteen years ago with the exception of one corner where a large area rug and musical instruments were displayed.

"Home, sweet, home," she mumbled.

"Almost."

He led her to a door on the right side of his room, opened it and pulled her inside. It was the same massive size as his but completely bare.

"What's this?" she wondered.

"It's yours," he informed her proudly.

"Mine? For what reason?"

"It's your room. It used to be George's, but no one has occupied it for many years. It'll be very convenient being next to mine."

She shook her head in confusion. "I don't understand. Why do I need a room?"

"Because you'll be living in the palace once we're married, at least I assumed that. You will, won't you?"

She looked around the room still perplexed by the idea. "Of course, I will, but why do I need a room? What am I supposed to do with it?"

He seemed bewildered. "You decorate it—you fill it. You can choose any color you want for the walls and pick out any furniture you desire. When you move in, it'll be all set according to your design."

"Again, for what purpose do I need my own room?"

"You have your own room now at your house. You'll have your own room here also. Everyone has a room. What did you expect?"

"I expected to share *your* room," she said softly. "We'll be married—husband and wife. We don't need separate quarters. Most houses in this country could fit inside your room with space to spare. In fact, you could almost fit my house inside your room, and it's a big house."

"You want to share my room? Where will you sleep?"

Tears began to well in her eyes as she realized how sheltered and unnatural his upbringing had been. Somehow she had imagined that their love could conquer all the abnormalities palace life would bring, but this wasn't an issue she had expected.

"What's wrong?" he sputtered as he saw her on the verge of crying. "I don't understand, Evangeline. What have I done? I've somehow offended you and I'm clueless. I brought you here to make you happy—to show you we would be close to each other. I don't …"

She hushed him with a kiss. "I will not live in a room next to you. I don't know exactly what you were raised to believe about marriage, but in the real world, the world outside these walls, married couples share a room and a bed … always. If you want a place that you can escape to away from me, then you take George's room and turn it into a … a … man cave … if that's what you need. But I won't live separately from you in any way, and I most certainly will not sleep anywhere other than beside you … every night … for the rest of our lives unless providentially hindered."

His jaw dropped. "Seriously?" He swallowed hard.

"When I close my eyes in sleep each night, the last memory I want to have is my head on your chest and your arm around me. When I wake up in the middle of the night, I want to hear you breathing and know that you're still beside me. When I wake up in the mornings, your face is the first thing I want to see." She was still trying to hold back tears. "I don't care what palace marriages have been like before, I won't move on this issue. We'll live in your room … together."

He put his hand to his heart and shook his head. "You're serious." He turned around, looking at the bare room. "Your parents didn't have separate rooms?"

"Of course not." She couldn't imagine him thinking that. "When she was in the hospital dying, my father climbed into bed with her and stayed beside her until she passed. And that's what I intend to do, Andrew Braisogn. That is a *real* marriage—*that* is real love. Are you telling me your parents have separate rooms?"

He nodded. "And I've never slept with anyone in my entire life." He looked lost. "Never."

"Not even your brothers … or your mother when you were sick?"

"Are you kidding? My father would have hit the ceiling. It was something he forbade."

"Why?" She was amazed that such a rule could even exist.

"You've slept with people? Really?"

"Well," she was quick to defend, "not guys, you know, not like that. But Amy and Jenna and I have piled into one bed many nights at sleepovers. Mother slept with me often as a child when I was sick, and I always slept with her when Daddy was away at maneuvers. When cousins would visit, we would cram as many of us into my bed as we could fit."

He took another look around the room, placed his hand in hers, and led her back into his own room. He closed George's door and began to survey his space. "You must change this then," he surmised. "It needs to look like you belong here."

"I don't care how it looks. I just want to make sure I'm welcome here— that you can live with me like this. I couldn't bear it, Andrew, if you didn't want to share this with me."

He smiled. "You have to understand that up to this moment in time I've always been led to believe that people had their own rooms. The prospect of sharing *this* with you is exciting, freeing. I've imagined this past month trying to share my life with you here, knocking on that door and hoping I wouldn't be intruding to just see you one more time before I went to bed." He took a deep breath and ran his fingers through his hair. "Now you've told me that there will be no barriers ever. I'll always be beside you when I'm here. You've handed me the keys to heaven. How could I not want that?"

She reached up and kissed him again, stroking his beard, caressing his hair. His arms entwined around her waist and he pulled her close as he deepened the kiss. She could feel her body begin to lose itself to the emotion and passion she felt for him. She knew she was indeed his savior, and this one thing would be only the beginning of a new life for him. The control his father had once had was beginning to lose its grip. That would be a battle she would have to face often, but the rewards would be well worth the fight.

"Andrew."

They looked to the door to find a smiling Max waving.

"As much as I hate to break this up," he said politely, "we need to move out. Your father would like nothing more than to hear you were punished because of fraternizing with your fiancé during maneuvers."

Andrew sighed. "Agreed." He looked down at her. "Three weeks—I'll see you in three weeks."

"But we can e-mail now," she reminded him.

"Jimmy will be at your house this afternoon to set up the computer and secure all the lines."

"Then you'll hear from me tonight."

"I can't wait." He kissed her quickly and then took her hand to lead her to the door.

"Wait," she stopped him. "Sometime between now and the wedding, you need to talk to your brothers about, well, real married life. I imagine they could share with you a lot of experience that ... uh ... you would find helpful ... considering ... oh ... your lack of exposure."

"I understand," he assured her. "Good idea. Now, let's go before I incur the wrath of the military."

♉ ♉ ♉

"And there you go," Jimmy announced as he pushed back from the small laptop at the table in the Dorvain den. "You're in business now."

Evangeline looked at him and smiled gratefully. "So I can just e-mail him anytime the mood hits me?"

"Yep, but only here at your house. Don't use this anywhere else. Only this wireless station is secured for this address. If you send him something from somewhere else, it can be hacked and monitored. I'm sure the king would love to have access to whatever you and his son will be communicating in the coming weeks."

"Point taken."

Amy stepped up to the table and looked admiringly at Jimmy. "So you do computer stuff too? I'm impressed."

He beamed. "I'm a man of many talents."

"So, I've seen. I'm glad the prince took my advice when I told him to find a good man this time around."

"I aim to please."

Amy grinned. "I'm pleased then …"

Evangeline rolled her eyes. "If we could take a break for a moment from the Jimmy Newell Fan Club, I still have a few questions."

He turned his attention back to Evangeline. "If I must, but I rather like that club."

"I'm sure … however, I need to know if it's safe to communicate with others from this laptop, or do I need to use my old computer for everything else."

"You can do everything on this one as long as you use it in this house only. If you ever leave with it, make sure the wireless receptor is turned off." He showed her the switch on the side of the device. "If you don't and you go somewhere with wireless capabilities, it will try to connect automatically. If anyone outside of here ever gets access, then its security can be compromised. Not that it will be compromised, but that it's possible. And believe me, there will be those always trying to break into your business. Some will just be harmless fans wanting to get as close to you as possible, but others will be more malicious. Don't take any chances."

"What would happen if someone did? All I'm doing is talking to Andrew. Are they gonna publish our conversations? That's not exactly malicious."

"Embarrassing, but not malicious, I agree. The problem is that once someone with enough know-how to break into your computer manages to do that, he would have total access to everything on your computer. He would also have this wireless address and security info. He could create anything he wanted and make it appear on your computer and make your computer send it out."

She frowned. "Heavens, that's a little scary. Maybe I should never even let the thing leave the house."

"It's not a problem as long as you connect to secure wireless networks outside. I know you'll be travelling to the palace some during the next month. You can get online there and it won't be a problem."

"Couldn't the king hack in if I do that?"

"It's secure. He couldn't. But if you were messing with your laptop in the car and it automatically found a network while your receiver was on and you're just travelling around, someone could do some damage. Again, it would have to be someone who knew what they were doing, and someone who was deliberately trying to do it."

"Which you obviously think is possible."

He shrugged, then nodded. "Not all royals are nice people. I think you're already aware of that."

"The generals would like to see you immediately."

This was not the reception Andrew had hoped for as he exited the helicopter upon his return to the base. He was ten minutes later than his allotted arrival time, but it had been worth it. If he was reprimanded he really didn't care. Realizing that he would be living with Evangeline in such an intimate arrangement had occupied his thoughts during the flight back. He was embarrassed as he recalled bringing her into the room and pronouncing proudly that she would be living *next* to him rather than *with* him. He understood her devastation now. Her suggestion that he speak with his brothers concerning normal married life was something he would most definitely do. What else had been hidden from him that every other person in the kingdom considered normal? He knew Evangeline would be patient and understanding as he learned what it meant to be a true husband, but he would never forget the look on her face when he suggested she have her own room at the palace. The truth was if he could have his own way he would leave the palace all together and move into a house of their own, a house like the Dorvain house. But leaving the palace meant leaving his destiny, and as much as he hated the thought of being king, it was meant to be. Until his own child took the throne, he and Evangeline would live in the cold, marble halls of the Braisognian castle. However, they wouldn't be as cold anymore.

He walked quickly toward the conference room as he anticipated the reprimand. He would offer no excuse for his lateness, but take whatever punishment the five generals deemed appropriate. These five men were the only ones who actually had the power to depose the king of Braisognia. The only escape the constitution had made for the possibility of a lunatic tyrant keeping the throne was that the five commanding generals of the military must vote unanimously, based upon clear evidence, to remove the king of his power. It had never happened or even been considered. That one fact had kept even the worst of rulers from crossing a line too far. But Andrew knew the worst king the country ever had was on the throne now, but in less than a year his rule would finally end.

As he entered the building he squared his shoulders with confidence. He respected these men greatly and wasn't proud of his fault in the matter, but he wouldn't cower or plead his case. He had worked with them closely for four years and knew them to be fair and reasonable. In less than a year he would be their Commander, and he wanted them to know he was behind their decision to carry out the law of the military.

Walking into the room, he saluted and remained at attention.

General Sourkis spoke first. "At ease, Captain." Andrew took the stance but would not look any of them in the eye. "Please have a seat."

Andrew spoke respectfully. "I would rather remain standing, if you don't mind, sirs."

"Very well," Sourkis continued. "We've been discussing the events of the day and would like to note a few things concerning all that has taken place." He deferred to General Trakeos.

"You've always been a very outstanding young man," Trakeos began. "From your first year in the military as a young boy you've never failed to follow procedure, been a quick learner, and been compliant in whatever you were asked to do. It was actually a relief to see your brothers abdicate—although somewhat embarrassing—a relief nevertheless. When it was obvious that you were to become king, we collectively agreed that the nation would be in good hands."

"Thank you, sir … sirs, all of you. I hope I live up to your expectations."

Trakeos continued. "Today you revealed the first of many important decisions you'll have to make that will affect your reputation as well as your ability to rule this country. We, as a group, must say we're extremely impressed with your choice for queen."

Andrew was suddenly shocked at the announcement and lost his composure. He looked down at them. "What?"

"Evie Dorvain," General Sourkis said with a smile. "Who would have ever thought that was the course of action you would take? You've made a rather strategic move here, Andrew, and we must say you've already exceeded our expectations of handling this country."

He was still confused. "I don't understand, sirs. What does Evangeline have to do with … this … this meeting?"

General Allen stood from his seat and began to pace leisurely about the room. "The biggest issue this country faces is the continuing divide among the classes—the royals verses the commoners. The biggest internal threat we face is that the ruling class is still very much controlled by the royals while eighty-five percent of the nation is not royal. In truth, probably less than that if we were to know how the bloodlines have been mixed from unknown affairs over hundreds of years. You have singlehandedly managed to choose the one constitutionally eligible woman in the entire world who has the heritage that can actually unite both groups."

Andrew was beginning to wonder if there would even be a reprimand. "Is that why you called me in here today? To congratulate me for my engagement rather than penalize me?"

"Penalize you for what?" General Allen asked.

"For being late, sir."

Allen laughed. "If we had known what you'd been up to, we would have given you the entire weekend off!"

"Andrew," a fourth general, Lewis, tried to explain further, "what you've done today is bridge the largest gap in this nation. I'm surprised your father let you get away with it."

"He didn't want to, sir. He doesn't approve of my choice."

"I'll bet," General Lewis nodded knowingly. "Which goes to prove our point—you're a wise young man capable of making hard decisions when the pressure is on."

Andrew appreciated what they were assuming about him, but the truth was that he loved her and desperately wanted to spend his life with her. It really wasn't a hard decision. Then again, yes, it was. He had gone against his father and against the expectation of every snobbish royal in the kingdom in order to marry her. There would be ramifications for years.

"I love her, sirs," he said weakly. "I admit that it was under great disdain from my father that I chose to marry her, but I'm afraid my heart wouldn't let me do otherwise."

"A king with heart," Trakeos mulled. "Imagine that gentlemen. Personally I find it refreshing as well as promising."

Four of the generals seemed to be in agreement, but General Daniels never commented. He was the youngest of the five, still in his fifties, and a rather hard man in many ways. Andrew had never had a conversation with him or worked directly with him since becoming an officer. He nodded once in Andrew's direction, more acknowledging his presence rather than assenting agreement.

"All we're saying here, Captain, is that in less than a year you will become our superior." Trakeos picked up the next point. "We had no way of knowing what kind of man you really were until today. You showed an independence and a fortitude that will be easy to respect in one so young."

Andrew felt compelled to assure them of his need for their guidance. "I hope sirs understand that I in no way believe I'm capable of running this country or this military without the advice and recommendations of those who have high positions right now, and have had for many years."

General Allen came around and put his hand on Andrew's shoulder. "And that, young Captain, is what makes you a great leader."

ॐ ॐ ॐ

Andrew tried to concentrate on his duties the rest of the afternoon, but Evangeline filled his mind most of the time. Fortunately, the majority of his work was mindless activity. He hoped beyond hope that she had e-mailed something to which he could absorb again and again throughout the evening. He wouldn't even turn on the computer until after he had showered and was ready to retire. He planned to read it, read it again, and read it again. Of course, he would respond, but to just have communication with her would be unimaginable.

His shower over, he towel dried his hair, pulled on his skivvies, and sat down at his desk. He hesitated as he signed into his account, fearful she possibly might not have written, but when the page pulled up, there indeed was a letter. His heart raced.

Dear Andrew,

I can't believe I'm actually writing to you. I'm having to fight the urge to be really sappy and write all this oozing sweet stuff, because that's what's filling my heart right now. Then two fears begin cropping up in my mind. First, what if I say too much and bore you and you begin to think you've made a major mistake? I've insisted on sharing your room and your bed, so you'll have no escape from me! Before we've always had to steal time to be together and there was always so much to say, but now with unlimited communication will I actually say too much? Then what if you reply with two sentences because you don't really like communication, and then I'm devastated!

He smiled at her dilemma. Indeed this would be a learning process for them both.

I find myself overwhelmed as I type these words and see your ring sparkling constantly on my finger. You shocked me with that presentation, you know? Apparently you shocked the nation also. I'm daunted with the task of being queen, but please know that it's overshadowed by the thrill of being your wife. I've had many goals over the years, but have only ever had one dream ... and you have now made it come true.

❧ Chapter Twenty-Two ☙

Andrew needed a contractor to work on a special project —a wedding present for Evangeline. Jimmy's first thought was to locate several and have them bid, but there was no time for that. This was huge. He had to find the best he could who was available and was willing to work endlessly to ensure the project was finished by the end of maneuvers at the last of July. Because of its personal nature, Amy was brought in to secretly oversee the major details and make sure the design would be according to Evangeline's taste.

"I sure am thankful I'm working through this with you and not Alfred," Amy told Jimmy one evening near the end of the construction as they sat in her hotel suite near the palace. "You can't imagine how hard it's been keeping this from Evie. She wants to know what's so important about staying here when she needs me there."

He scratched his head and yawned as he leaned back on the couch and propped his feet on the coffee table. "So what do you say? Do you lie to her?"

"I keep telling her I'm working on wedding details at St. John's and finalizing her move to the palace."

"You're good," he grinned. "'Cause in essence that's exactly what you're doing." He shifted his feet then gave her a sideways glance. "Did you always plan to be a PR person? Was that your course of study in college?"

"Not at all—it just sort of fell into my lap when Evie's popularity got out of control. I actually studied advertising—wanted to do something creative but still business-like. I took one of those placement tests and that's what it suggested. Sounded better than anything else I could think of. What about you?"

"Ha," he chortled unenthusiastically. "I was the typical underachiever. I kept wondering what I could do in life that required no talent from me whatsoever—just ride on the coattails of somebody else. Ba-da-bing ... publicity."

"So how did you manage to get hooked up with Andrew if you were so *unremarkable?*"

"Ah, the prince—the ultimate talent of the kingdom. We had a couple of classes together our first semester, and while everyone else was intimidated by him, I joked with him a lot—especially about his prince-li-ness. If things got really boring I'd suggest he outlaw the subject when he became king. When someone would ask a stupid question and get the professor sidetracked forever, I'd write a note saying he needed his security to have 'em removed. Come to find out ... all he really wanted was to be a regular guy. Seeing that I was as regular as they came and had no desire to be irregular, i.e. royal superior attitude, even to a fault, we clicked."

"And now you're the secretary to the second most powerful person in the kingdom. How unremarkable of you."

"Third," he corrected her. "The queen would be second."

"Really? She would actually rule Braisognia if the king ... uh ... couldn't?"

"You never studied royal protocol, I suppose."

"I am now. I guess I haven't gotten to that part yet. So that's why the king is so bent against Evie marrying Andrew—he doesn't want her to ever have the chance to rule." She looked wide-eyed at Jimmy. "Holy cow! That's a lot of power for someone just marrying into a position."

"Yep."

♛ ♛ ♛

Evangeline hoped one day her overstressed nerves would calm, but for now it seemed everything she did upped the level. Queen Julia requested they have lunch together to discuss the wedding and any other details that might seem pertinent. Considering they would be living under the same roof until Andrew's coronation, she dare not decline. As she waited in the quaintly feminine tea room for the queen's arrival, she tried to settle herself with deep breaths and soothing thoughts. Even though Julia had never been anything other than cordial and kind to her, she was married to Christopher Braisogn, a heartless father and selfish ruler. Did she share his sentiments after sharing life with him for nearly forty years, or was she as much a prisoner in this palace as her sons?

"Evangeline."

The queen's voice startled her. She immediately turned and curtsied. "I'm sorry, your majesty, I didn't hear you enter."

"Oh, please," she threw her hand to the side. "Let's dispense with the formalities immediately. Call me Julia—I insist."

168

She smiled with a small bit of relief. "I'll try, but you have to know it will be difficult."

The graceful older woman motioned for her to take a seat at a glass table. "Not if we become friends." Her smile was pleasant and reassuring. "I imagine you have all sorts of preconceived ideas about why I've asked you to lunch. True?"

She nodded.

"One of those ideas being that I'm about to suggest how to carry out your wedding to my son?"

"I suppose so. You said you wanted to discuss it in your invitation."

The queen leaned into the table toward Evie and gently admitted, "I have no plans or demands for your wedding. It should be exactly what *you* want it to be. I just needed an excuse to officially meet with you, and that was the best I could come up with."

Her nerves returned. Being summoned to a meeting on false pretense seemed worse. "Then why are we meeting?"

Stately, Julia sat back, poised and controlled, as she considered her explanation. For the first time Evangeline noticed a weariness in her eyes and demeanor. Was she as alone here as Andrew?

"I truthfully only want to offer my friendship," she said tenderly. "I was much younger than you when I was married and whisked away to this place. I'd imagined all sorts of wonderful things would happen when I married the handsome prince from another land. I envisioned evening strolls in the gardens, sharing our dreams, our life, and hopefully our love eventually." She sighed. "None of that was to be. I then only hoped that when I had children, I would find fulfillment there—mothering and caring for them instead of loving a husband. But that wasn't to be either."

"I'm sorry—I had no idea."

"Oh, I'm sure you wondered. I imagine Andrew's told you of the heartlessness of his father. I was always so thankful he had you, you know?"

Evangeline shook her head. No, she had never thought that.

"When the truth about your royal heritage was revealed, I actually cried with delight. I knew he could marry you and still keep the throne. He was too noble to abdicate after both his brothers. But his nobility got the best of him, and he couldn't bear the thought of bringing you into this prison." She shook her head and gave a sad smile. "He is so good-hearted."

"I know." She felt the need to speak and affirm the queen's sentiments. "And I want to assure you that his heart is safe with me. I think I've always loved him, but feared admitting it."

Julia nodded as she knit her brows in concern. "Your life here will be unspeakably miserable until the coronation—Christopher will see to that. I assume you've already deduced it?"

"Oh, yes. No surprise there."

"Just remember it's only temporary. Andrew will want to protect you. The more hurt you show, the more you allow Christopher's antics to eat away at you, the more unsettled Andrew will become—and the more hate will fill his heart. When it becomes unbearable, please come to me, not my son. There is nothing you could tell me I haven't felt already where that tyrant is concerned. It's been hard enough for Andrew to keep himself intact all these years and not cower to the overbearing demands of a lunatic controller. But if that controller were to begin damaging the only person who ever gave him hope ..."

"I understand," Evangeline interrupted as she reached across the table and took the queen's hand. "And let me put your mind at rest—when Andrew proposed, I determined at that moment to be stronger in my love for him than in my fear of the king. I know I'll be intimidated, but I'll never let Andrew see the struggle. You do realize that this fight is one I've had to battle my entire life? And it never stopped—not when I was declared royal, and not when I won world championship after world championship."

"But you've always had a reprieve ... home."

"Yes, and I'll still have reprieve," she smiled. "This time in the arms of the one man I would sacrifice absolutely everything for. I'm prepared to be the strongest support he'll ever know in this life."

"And you will always have me. I can't move mountains, but I can listen to a young lady's distress and empathize greatly."

Grinning she replied, "I can move mountains—I've moved them all my life."

The queen's eyes began to fill as she squeezed Evangeline's hand. She couldn't speak but managed to mouth a thank you as the butler brought in a tray of food.

The rest of the visit was easy and wonderful. They discussed the details of the wedding and Julia was thrilled with them all. When Evangeline left that afternoon, she felt as though she had truly found a new friend, a kindred spirit, and someone who loved Andrew as much as she did. She also knew that when things at the palace did become difficult, she would not go to the queen either. This woman needed as much support and assurance as Andrew.

Dear God, help me be what they need me to be in these coming months. Let me be the rock You have formed me to be. I wondered why I was forced to know such persecution and harshness all those years. I now understand—you needed someone to pick up the pieces of tender hearts that this king has shattered for years on end.

♱ ♱ ♱

"Excuse me?" The response sounded strained so Evangeline looked over to Amy. Her friend's expression was one of utter astonishment as she changed the phone to her other hand and began to thumb through the calendar. Amy glanced up toward her as alarm rose in her wide eyes.

"What?" Evangeline mouthed.

She shook her head and continued the conversation. "No, sir. Every booking for Miss Dorvain comes directly through me, and I can assure you we've had no contact concerning this event. In fact, there's actually a conflict—I would have never scheduled an appearance for her on the day maneuvers were finished." Amy remained silent as she listened. She began shaking her head as she looked back at Evangeline. "Could you hold just a second, please?" She pressed the hold button and dropped her head in her hands.

"What is it?" Evangeline was beginning to panic herself.

"Well, apparently someone has been sowing seeds of intentional confusion. You're booked to visit the Northwest Quadrant Children's Home at eleven o'clock on Saturday."

"What? I knew nothing about that!"

"Me either—and I do all your booking! Lucky for us this guy called the official number rather than the one they'd been using for contact all this time—someone misplaced it so he had to look up mine on the internet."

"Of all the dirty tricks ..." She shook her head in disbelief. "Christopher Braisogn is behind this—I guarantee it."

"Can you imagine? All these kids would have been there waiting with signs and a program planned, cameras rolling ready to capture the moment, and suddenly the coverage switches to you greeting Andrew here at your house."

"Oh ... that is evil." She looked up and whispered a prayer—*Thank You, God. What a horrible predicament this could have been.* "I've never been very tolerant of staff losing important numbers before—I'll most definitely learn to be more gracious in that area from here on out." She reached for the phone. "What's the man's name?"

"Edward Carthage."

She pressed the button. "Mr. Carthage, this is Evangeline Dorvain."

"Miss Dorvain! I'm so sorry to bother you. I don't understand what's going on here."

"I'm afraid I do. There are those who would love to sabotage my reputation right now. I'm sure you understand the fact that many royals are not at all happy about me being their future queen."

"To be honest with you, Miss Dorvain, I seldom rub shoulders with royals anymore. They don't offer a lot of support to commoner children who had the audacity to have no parents. We depend on the precious few like you and your mother to help keep us afloat."

"Yes, then you can understand how devastating this would have been had you not called this number. I would have come across as somehow switching sides and abandoning the most helpless in our nation."

"I am so sorry—I had no idea. We can cancel the event."

"No!" she replied adamantly. "Not in a million years! If these children have planned on my visit, I will most certainly not disappoint them."

"You could come the following day ... after church perhaps?"

"How about a better plan?" She smiled at her idea. "Let's not make them wait—let's do it earlier. Is there any time on Thursday or Friday that would work?"

"Friday evening is movie night. We could easily move you in there. I'm sure the children would much rather see you than a replayed film they've viewed ten times before."

"Could I eat dinner with them also?"

"Uh ... well ... of course, but it won't be the kind of fare you're used to."

"If it's good enough for the children, it's good enough for me."

The ladies sat in relief that the situation had been remedied, but they were concerned there could possibly be more.

"Evie, with all the appointments you've got the next two weeks about the wedding, whoever did this could stir up a mass of problems and conflicts."

"I know. I'm thinking."

"Let me call Jimmy to get in touch with Andrew. I'm sure he could put someone on it right away. They could figure out who's doing it and ..."

"No." She was firm. "We're big girls here, Amy—smart too. I'm not gonna run to Andrew for help every time his warped father tries to do me in. We can figure this out."

Amy's eyes widened. "Seriously? You're taking on Christopher Braisogn?"

"You bet." She grinned victoriously. "First, we hire a staff. We need a couple of people to take on the job of answering the phone to confirm dates. I'm sure there will be as many prank calls as genuine. We hire a couple more to put out public service announcements on every station—television and radio. Also we need to make ads available on the major social networking sites. We explain what's happened and suggest they call the right number this time to confirm."

"I'm on it. I'll have ads going before the day is over."

"No."

Amy looked bewildered. "No? We're gonna wait?"

"You bet we are," she raised an eyebrow mischievously. "Schedule all ads and announcements to be posted right after the press broadcasts me walking into the home and greeting the children. We'll give his majesty a double surprise ... have him and his minions scrambling and scratching their heads."

Amy understood and her smile widened. "Oh, my—that's good."

♕ ♕ ♕

"Your majesty!" A page came running into the palace library out of breath and unannounced.

Christopher whipped around in his chair, enraged at the young man's audacity. "How dare you enter in such a manner!"

"I'm sorry, sir," the young man tried to speak through heaves of breathlessness. "Alfred said ... television ... any channel." He swallowed as he leaned his hands on his knees and tried to breathe. "He said ... no time ... to waste."

Still deeply perturbed, the king walked to his desk and removed the remote from its drawer. Turning on the television, he folded his arms and wondered what could be so important that such an ill-mannered announcement was necessary. As he watched Evie Dorvain shake hands with the director of the Northeast Quadrant's children's home, he went pale.

"What?" he whispered at first. Then he began to boil. "What the ...?" He looked back at the page. "Would you mind telling me exactly what is happening here?"

At that moment Alfred walked into the library, calm and controlled. "Somehow it seems that Miss Dorvain's trip to visit the orphaned children was changed to tonight rather than in the morning."

Christopher threw the remote across the room shattering it to pieces. "How did this happen?" he boomed. "She was supposed to be there tomorrow! I thought you had alerted the press and ..."

The sound of Evangeline's voice stopped his rant as he turned to see her face on the screen with a number boldly displayed beneath.

"... so we're asking if you have any kind of appointment where I'm concerned, please call the number listed below to confirm. I would never deliberately disappoint or hurt anyone in this kingdom. And my staff is neither incompetent nor incapable. Whoever pulled this prank could have damaged my reputation, but more importantly, would have hurt the innocent hearts of over a hundred children. Thank you for your cooperation. And I do guarantee—if anything else has been double-booked, I will personally ensure a visit at some point in time."

When the king looked back at Alfred, the old man shook his head in disgust as he said, "Sir, who did you tell that could have possibly given this away?"

The familiar vein began throbbing. "You're blaming *me* for this? Are you out of your deluded mind?"

"Those working on this are very loyal to you, sir. No one would have dared let anything slip. I have questioned each person who knew. The only other one who could have done this is you."

"Fire them all!" he demanded. "Every one of them!"

"They are loyal—I would stake my life on them … and those loyal to the present crown are growing fewer each day."

The king looked for something else to shatter. The nearest lamp felt his blow this time.

✂ Chapter Twenty-Three ✂

"You're nervous, aren't you?" Amy asked as Evangeline tried something different with her hair for the third time.

"Totally. I seldom see him, and when I do I want to be ... memorable."

"Please ... I should actually laugh at that statement. You're memorable period."

She gave up and let her hair drop around her shoulders. "I have no idea what you mean by that, but I don't really care. At least this time we've been able to communicate through email—it won't seem like a blind date or something."

"It's always amazed me how you two seem to pick right up where you last left off."

"And where we left off last was him proposing and presenting an engagement ring in front of the entire nation." The sound of the helicopter threw her into a tizzy. "Augh! I'm not ready!"

"Sure you are." Amy pointed her toward the door. "Let's go meet your prince."

Andrew had written that they should be very staged in their greeting. Cameras would be in the air and they would need to give a bit of a show, but not too much. Since her father and Jimmy would be riding with him, she should greet her father first. After that, they would embrace, give a small kiss, and then head inside the house. Evangeline longed for the day when they could be completely alone—no cameras, no king, no secretaries, no shows—just the two of them sharing life together. It had been that way when he had visited at New Year's. But for the next two weeks Evangeline's every move had to be choreographed. It was okay—at the end was her prince.

They went through the motions as planned and then all had lunch together on the back deck. Soon afterwards everyone made their way elsewhere to give the couple some time alone. As they sat in the swing, fingers intertwined, they shared what little had not been communicated over the internet—which included the almost fiasco with the Northeast Quadrant Children's Home.

"No!" Andrew said in anger. "I can't believe he did that! Why didn't you tell me? I would have dealt with it immediately!"

"Did you not hear what I just explained? I took care of it."

"You shouldn't have to take care of things like that!" He put his face in his hands. "You should never have to deal with anything like that. It's utterly ridiculous."

"True … on the ridiculous part, but not on my handling of it. I'm a big girl—I can take care of myself. There was no way I was going to interrupt your training of new military recruits, and your strengthening of the protectors of this nation because the real Commander-in-Chief chose to sit in his cushy castle and devise a way to hurt the most helpless citizens in our land!"

"I promise you he'll hear about this as soon as I get to the palace!"

"No—don't do that."

"Are you joking? You just want me to let him get away with it? I can't do that!"

She took his hand again and kissed the back of it. "As I see it, he didn't get away with it. In fact, I'd be willing to bet he went ballistic when he realized his scheme didn't work."

"But if we don't face him with it … confront him about it, then he wins!"

"By whose rules does he win? I'm not playing his game. In my book, the one who wins is the one who keeps their dignity and integrity. If I went off on every royal that ever despised me … ever sabotaged me … I'd be so full of hate I could barely function. And what's even sadder about all this is that had his plan worked, the real loser wouldn't have been me—it would have been those innocent children. He chose the most helpless in our nation to use as a target in his personal war." She turned his face toward hers. "You don't confront a man like that, Andrew, and expect remorse. All you do is get pulled into his game."

"So he gets away with it," he said with defeat.

"No! He got away with nothing! Don't you get it? He hates, so he does hateful things. He would love nothing more than for you to slam a finger in his face and demand an explanation. He would get to spew on you about everything he hates again. Don't let him—don't even go there!"

"But we're eating with him tonight!"

"Yes! And can you imagine how irate he'll be knowing we're aware of all this yet silently moving on? Integrity, Andrew. Dignity. That's what makes a king. It's not what flows through your blood, nor is it how much power and control you can wield over others." She now took her finger and touched his chest. "It's what's in your heart that's most important. He hates that your heart isn't black like his. He sees it as a weakness, but trust me—it's your most defining and strongest asset."

He leaned over and tenderly kissed her. "You are amazing ... and strong." He grinned. "And you did beat my father at his own game, even by his own rules. You won."

She shook her head. "The children won. And besides, you and I both know this is only round one. He won't stop. We stay true to what is right no matter what he does."

"Keep reminding me of that, will you?"

♕ ♕ ♕

There would be no more traveling by limousine for Evangeline when going from her home to the palace. It made her too vulnerable, so she and Amy took the first of many helicopter trips to the capitol city. She wasn't looking forward to dinner with the king, but after her lunch with the queen earlier in the month, she had longed to see her again. A small bond had begun, and she now wondered if the nation understood at all what kind of man Christopher Braisogn was. Tonight at the table, there would be three hearts united against one—simply because the one had chosen to hurt all three in devastating ways.

She had noticed the gradual change in the appearance of the military's leadership—many were sporting longer hair and beards, the complete opposite of Christopher's preference. He could make no laws concerning it, but he could most definitely state his opinion. So far he said nothing publicly knowing that the change was merely showing support for the new king-to-be. She imagined, however, that someone somewhere had most definitely heard an earful about it.

Dinner with the king was tense and silent for the most part. He had nothing to say the entire meal, and the queen tried her best to break the awkwardness with small talk. Andrew and Evangeline always responded to her, but it was so shallow that there was nowhere else for the conversation to go.

As soon as Christopher finished eating, he pushed his chair back, stood and said, "I have things to do if you all will excuse me."

No one said a word as he left, but once the door was shut, the queen looked at the two of them and began to giggle. Within a few seconds Andrew began to laugh also, and a moment later they were nearly overcome with hilarity.

"What's so funny?" Evangeline wanted to know. "We went from austere to comedy in a matter of seconds! I'm completely lost."

The queen shook her head—she couldn't stop laughing.

"Never," Andrew tried to explain, "ever ... have we had a meal that he hasn't dominated the conversation constantly. He's either ranted or raved about whatever flew into his head."

"Seriously?" She had just assumed the silence was normal.

"Most assuredly," the queen nodded as she wiped her eyes from the tearful laughter. "I kept expecting him to get cranked up at some point, but he just sat here like a stone!"

Evangeline was stunned. "Why? You think he's that angry with me?"

"Totally," Andrew said with a victorious grin.

She didn't feel nearly as fun about the situation as the other two obviously did. "I don't know that we should interpret that as a good sign. It probably means he's looking for something even more heinous to do."

"Of course he is," Julia acknowledged. "But then that's his modus-operandi at all times. Normally he would be warning you to watch your back."

"He's got nothing ... at least for the moment," Andrew added. "If he had, it would have been unleashed. I believe you knocked him off his game for the first time."

"She's so good at that," the queen winked. "I've watched you do it on the court time and again ... so did the king. He may fear he's met his match."

Evangeline pushed away from the table and dropped her linen onto the plate. "I'm very uncomfortable with this. Someone being silent is not a sign of victory—it's a warning."

They both shook their heads, then Andrew explained, "Not with him. You'll understand better as the months go by."

"Enough," Evangeline shook her head. "I'm a bundle of nerves already."

Julia smiled warmly and suggested, "Perhaps this would be the time for Andrew to show you his early wedding present—take your mind off of all this ... idiocy."

"Excellent idea," he beamed as he stood and reached out his hand to his bride-to-be. "Shall we?"

The queen left them alone to view the gift in private. He led her down what were still unfamiliar hallways until she finally recognized his door again. She became nervous as she remembered the last conversation they had in his room. He had offered her what he thought was a magnanimous gift—a massive room next to his—only to have her break into tears and emotional distress at the very suggestion.

"Something you said," he began, "when we were here last sort of sparked my imagination."

She gulped quietly. "I'm sorry about that ... I didn't realize ..."

"No, don't apologize. What you said was all good. I have no problems with that conversation. In fact, as I said, it lit an idea."

She couldn't help but smile at his enthusiasm. Whatever he had done, he was extremely proud about it. "What is it?"

"Close your eyes."

She did and then heard him turn the handle and slowly creak open the heavy door. Leading her through with his hand on her back, he moved her inside and then whispered in her ear. "Okay ... open your eyes."

Nothing could prepare her for what she discovered. The entire room had been transformed. It was no longer a single, massive room but a place divided into several sections by walls. The first area was directly in front of her—a kitchen.

"Andrew!" she whispered in shock. "I can't believe this!" She walked to the kitchen area and immediately took note of the floor. "Red and white checkered tile? That was always my dream. How did you know? I've never ... ever ... mentioned that to you."

"Have you not?" he teased. "You recall every conversation we've had?"

"Yes ... and I can guarantee I've never said anything about that." She ran her hand over the retro table with the shining red top and thick, matching, red vinyl chairs. "Where on earth did you find this stuff? They don't even make this anymore."

"Amy," he smiled with pride. "I told her to make this your dream kitchen ... just gave her carte-blanche."

She walked into the horseshoe shaped area and ran her hand over the red counters, the new stove, the white cabinets—then stopping, she smelled the bouquet of fresh, red roses in a simple white vase. She turned toward him, almost overcome with emotion again as like last time, only now with pure honor and delight. "This is ... unspeakably wonderful."

He came up and took her hands in his. "That's what I was going for. I know you wanted a real home—a place where you ... we ... could cook our own meals, live a normal life. And I also know you were willing to sacrifice all of that in order to have a life with me. I figured the least I could do was try and give you an almost normal house."

She softly kissed him and asked, "What on earth did I say to spark all this? I don't remember saying anything positive that day. I felt so guilty about it."

"You told me you could fit most homes in the entire kingdom inside the space of this room. That made me think—then make this room a home. Come on—let me show you the rest."

He took her down to the first wall on the right which separated into a small library. She stared at the shelves of books and quickly realized most of them were her favorites. She shook her head in astonishment. Then she recognized the desk as the very one that had been in her mother's office at home. She put her hand to her mouth, overcome with emotion.

"No, don't start that," he crooned softly as he took her hand and led her across the small open hallway to the living area. "You can cry over the memories another time."

The living area was furnished with new, modern leather furniture rather than the antique, stately couch and chairs she had always seen before.

"I'm not against antiques," she told him truthfully.

"Me either, but I'm sick to death of them." He pointed toward the white leather couch. "Amy said you had admired this many times at Jenna's house. I told her to find one and bring it in."

She let go of his hand and plopped onto the couch, raising her feet with the built in recliner. "Very nice. Join me?"

"You keep wanting to stall in each room," he shook his head. "Our time is limited, and there's more to see."

"I want to savor it!"

He held out his hand again. "This isn't the time for savoring—you can do that when you move in."

"All right ... all right." She stood and took his hand. "What's next?"

The last part of the room had been completely walled off with a door. He opened it and motioned her inside. Again, it took her breath away. The bedroom was indeed furnished with antiques. The bed was a massive four poster piece with luxurious, royal blue, satin cloth draping from the tops.

"New bed?" she grinned.

"New life. And I won't sleep in it until you join me."

She raised an eyebrow. "There are still weeks before the wedding. Where do you intend to sleep?"

"George's old room."

"It's not empty anymore?"

"I had Amy furnish that too—as a guest room for when your father or anyone else visits us."

She shook her head as she eased herself down onto the bed. "And Amy told me she was busy here with finalizing the wedding and moving plans. That was very sneaky of her." She patted the bed beside her for him to join her. "It's okay for you to sleep here now. I certainly won't mind."

He sat beside her and took her hand. "No—this isn't at all the same room anymore. Everything about it has changed ... and it's all because of you. I don't want to live here until you're here with me. I want to wake up that first morning, throw open the blinds in this room and let the sun shine in on your face as you awaken. I want to watch you make coffee and bake muffins. I want to sit back on our couch and take in some completely nonsensical television show and laugh beside you." He touched her hair, her cheek, her lips with his hand. "And I never want to know what it's like to be here without you."

"Your father hates me," she reminded him.

"He hates me too." He furled his brow in confusion. "Why would you bring him up right now? I thought we were having quite the romantic moment. Killed the mood, you know?"

"No wonder he sulked at supper. You literally altered your sterile environment—the one I'm sure he demanded you be raised in … no frills … no extra amenities—and you did it all for me."

"I know." He was beaming again with pride. "We both knew—Mother and I. We just didn't want to give it away."

She shook her head and then pushed him back on the bed, leaning over him with a kiss. "I almost feel sorry for him."

He pulled her into another kiss then added, "Never feel sorry for him."

"Okay," she whispered as she touched his beard and ran her fingers through his long, dark locks.

They lingered briefly on the bed, then she hopped up. "There's a space we haven't discovered yet."

"The bathroom and closet?"

"Don't care about those." She pulled him up. "Follow me." She led him back into the main area next to the kitchen where all of his music paraphernalia sat on a plush red carpet. "There's something missing here," she said soberly.

He looked around and shrugged his shoulders. "Piano, guitars, music stand, music … what are we missing?"

"Something wonderfully comfortable for me to sit upon and listen to you play each evening."

His smile grew. "Really?"

"Of course! My own personal entertainment. I want a lounge right here," she pointed to a spot next to the piano. "Do you actually play piano too? I've never heard you … only the guitar."

He snickered nervously. "At the ball—that was embarrassing."

"Not to me … or to anyone else there."

"Yeah … well …"

"Play something for me."

He staggered back. "Seriously? Right now?"

"Absolutely!" She looked around and grabbed one of the red, vinyl dining chairs then placed it next to the piano. She sat, crossed her arms and looked expectantly.

"Well … okay then." He moved out the bench and sat, then playfully cracked his knuckles. "I know just the piece."

She marveled as she watched his long fingers skillfully play the most beautiful melody she had ever heard. He would look at her on occasion as his hands effortlessly floated across the keys, and she wondered who this man really was. Inside him lay an untapped wealth this nation had never seen, she had never seen—and she was determined to get to know every level buried within.

When he finished, he simply looked down at the keyboard as though deliberately avoiding her eyes.

"That was unspeakably beautiful," she said gently as she stood from her chair and joined him on the bench. "What's it called? I think it's the most incredible piece of music I've ever heard."

He looked into her eyes, smiled warmly and said, "Evangeline—it's called Evangeline."

❧ Chapter Twenty-Four ❧

Evangeline had tried to sleep the night before, but it was pointless. Now she stood exhausted next to the long window at the palace believing she could drowse for hours. Unfortunately she couldn't even sit because of the bulk of her wedding dress. Attendants bustled about, taking care of last minute details, and the ever present photographer was capturing every expression and move she, Amy and Jenna made. She knew one day she would be thankful to look through the pictures that had captured one of the most joyous days of her life, but right now all she wanted was to give the camera a swift kick.

"You really don't seem ok," Jenna noted once again—probably for the tenth time it seemed. "You don't have to go through with this."

She shook her head. "I *want* to go through with this—I'm just tired. I wish I could have slept in my own bed last night instead of the hotel suite."

Her friend seemed doubtful. "If you say so. Just know I'm ready to take care of anything you might need me to do."

She now chuckled at the thought of Jenna marching to the front of the church to announce the royal wedding was off. Evangeline was most definitely ready to marry Andrew, but that marriage incurred so much more than just a husband. The weight of it all kept her pondering that night. Had it been a regular marriage, like Jenna's, these thoughts wouldn't plague her. But the fact that the present king would do all in his power to prevent her from becoming queen was a thunderhead ever looming, threatening to burst any moment. Her only consolation was knowing he wanted Andrew, his own son, on the throne when he stepped down. Andrew swore if anything happened to Evangeline or someone close to her, he would abdicate.

Amy took her arm and whispered, "The queen would like a word with you in private. Is that okay?"

She nodded and looked toward the door where Julia stood, elegant and beautiful. Evangeline motioned her over and suggested Amy and Jenna take a final restroom break. She then told the photographer he may capture a couple of pictures, but would have to leave the room and wait for her in the vestibule of the church. He was not at all pleased with the suggestion, but after snapping away incessantly he finally left.

Julia gently touched the lace around Evangeline's collar and smiled almost tearfully as she spoke. "I wanted to thank you for what you've done for my son. He told me about the conversation you had when he returned from maneuvers—about how you handled the Northeast Quadrant fiasco. He said you explained how winning wasn't who upped the other, but rather who maintained their dignity and integrity. He also said you showed him how important it was not to hate, but to move on." She took her hand. "That's exactly what I asked you to do—and you magnificently pulled it off."

"You make it sound way more noble than it was."

"No, it was extremely noble. All his father wants right now is to somehow punish him for this choice, but he can't because he must see Andrew on the throne. The biggest insult that could be delivered to him on Andrew's twenty-fifth birthday would be for someone else to wear the crown. All his years as king would be pointless if he lost the final heir. Because of that he is angry and beyond reason. He has never once had his hand stayed, unable to force his way. Right now he would love nothing more than to engage his son in a battle of hate, but Andrew won't—only because you told him the greater road was to not let it consume him. Only you could accomplish that—and I thank you."

She wanted to confess to Julia how distressed she was, how frightened, how overcome with worry she really was concerning the king, but she remembered her role was that of a savior. She must be strong not only for Andrew, but also for this dear woman who was never allowed to love and nurture the way women are born to do.

"I will always do my best to help Andrew see that hate only clouds the better path."

🎖 🎖 🎖

The wedding was perfect, and from the moment the page announced five minutes, Evangeline's adrenaline kicked in and she had all the energy needed to be the perfect bride, and now princess, the kingdom required. In her mind the present king did not exist this day—only the future one. Andrew wore his military blue, covered with medals and tassels as usual, but he had managed a red tie to match those of his brothers. She wasn't completely sure why she liked him in red—perhaps because it was her favorite color, or maybe it just looked handsome on him. Whatever the reason, she couldn't take her eyes off his beaming face the entire ceremony.

Her father had managed to hold it together until the minister asked who gives this woman to be married to this man. He then gave a small speech explaining that he had to say her mother and I because all the strength, dignity, poise and nobility now evident in Evangeline was because of the mother who had been her biggest influence. Evangeline willed herself to keep back the tears as she smiled gratefully at the man who had always been her rock.

As she and her new husband, along with the entourage of security and secretaries, boarded the jet for a two week honeymoon on a private Greek Isle in the Mediterranean, the exhaustion hit again. It would be a four hour flight. She longed to talk with Andrew and Amy and reminisce about the day, but she felt if she did not sit immediately she would collapse. She dropped into a seat near the back of the jet and was delighted to find it reclined with a footrest.

"Amy told me you had a rough night sleeping," Andrew said with a frown as he eased himself beside her. "Just rest now. I'll wake you when we get there."

"Will we land directly on the island?"

He shook his head. "No, sorry. It does have a helipad so we'll take a chopper from the airport."

She smiled wearily. "That's no problem. I feel guilty that I'm so ..."

"Don't even go there. We have two whole weeks to do anything we want. Tonight we rest and let the stress of the past ... ha, twenty or so years melt away."

Evangeline slept the entire flight, and as they exited the jet, the humidity and rumbling of thunder was ominous.

"Wo," she cringed as she felt perspiration immediately begin to bead. "It's about to pour down rain."

Andrew took her elbow and led her to the helicopter. "I know. The weather's going to be really bad. They're gonna fly us and two security men immediately—our luggage and everyone else will be transported once the storm has passed."

"Only two security?" she asked alarmed.

He smiled calmly. "The island and house are already secured with a trained team waiting. Max and Hampton will be with us on the ride just in case ... well ..."

"Because they need to be."

"Right."

The blades were already whirling and she shaded her eyes with one hand while holding the hem of her dress with the other. Once safely inside and buckled down, they donned their headpieces and were swept off to the island.

☙ ☙ ☙

Amy looked over at Jimmy who was staring at the rain pounding the glass of the airport. She needed coffee if she was going to last the night. Walking over to him, she tapped his shoulder. "You want to try and find something loaded with caffeine to help us stay awake?"

He looked doubtfully out the window again. "I hope they made it okay."

"Someone will contact us, won't they ... to let us know?"

He shrugged. "It's a nasty storm, but it blew in from the west and they were going east. Hopefully they were ahead of it."

"Jimmy, we're talking about the prince and princess of Braisognia. I guarantee the forces-that-be took a good look at all the radars and maps and ... all those things ... and knew exactly how much time was needed and exactly where to fly."

"You're right," he exhaled. "Let's find that caffeine. I have a feeling it's gonna be a really long night."

They roamed through the small airport, only used for private charters, and finally found a food shop at the opposite end. They ordered coffee each and a pastry to share, then sat at one of three tables to wait for the rain to slack.

"So," Jimmy offered in conversation, "you and Evie go back a long time, huh?"

"She and Jenna and I have been best friends for as long as I can remember." She blew the top of her cup to cool the steaming liquid. "I can't recall exactly when we all started hanging out together exclusively, but it was early—elementary school for sure."

"Uh ... didn't that kind of cut in on your royal social life? I mean, I knew who Evie Dorvain was long before I ever remember actually seeing her. I don't imagine the rest of your snobby school took well to the friendship."

Amy swallowed a sip and smiled. "We didn't care. As strong and assured as Evie is now ... she was just like that as a kid."

"That's what Andrew said."

"There was something about her that was so ... I don't know ... magical? We were drawn to her—honored to be her friends. Everyone else made their decisions based purely on their parents' prejudices. Fortunately mine and Jenna's families felt people were worth more than a supposed bloodline."

"Andrew used to tell me in college she was the only friend he had ever really had. When I realized who he was talking about, I felt sorry for him. I knew he was in love with her, but could never marry her because she wasn't a royal … at that time. Then there was the whole dilemma with his two older brothers having abdicated. What a mess. He didn't want to be king, but he had to be king. I felt really sorry for him most of the time."

"So, you're just a big-hearted guy … with no talent?"

"Yep," he shrugged as he pinched off a piece of the pastry. "That's me."

"Hmmm, what did you do between college and becoming secretary to the future king?"

"I did what's only fitting for a guy with no talent—after my mandatory two years in the military, I traveled around trying to find myself … I suppose. At least that makes it sound like I had some kind of goal."

She giggled as she swallowed a bite. "Alone?"

"I was with two guys from my platoon. None of us were really cut out for military life—we basically survived it all by dreaming of taking it easy as soon as we got out. We spent a month with our families and then took off. We camped a little, hoteled a lot, made a few friends along the way that we stayed with—just wasted a lot of time."

"Did it work?"

"What do you mean?"

"Did you find yourself?"

He chuckled and shook his head. "Nope … still haven't. Not really sure where else to look."

She nodded and took another sip of coffee. Jimmy was funny, but closed off. He could talk for hours and have her laughing the whole time, yet through it all never reveal much of himself. This little bit of information only gave her a timeline, but still no link to who he really was. "No women along the way?"

"Ah … a string of 'em. You probably figured that though. I didn't feel it was worth mentioning."

"Actually no—I don't imagine you've ever had a relationship with a woman your whole life."

He put his hand up to his heart. "I'm hurt. You don't see me as the Casanova I really am." He sighed and picked up his coffee. "Actually, it was a woman that put a stop to all my travelling."

She perked up. "Seriously? You met someone? What happened?"

"Well, not really met, more like had known forever. Our parents had arranged a union for us years back. I was traveling, she was in theater—the adults in our lives felt like maybe a marriage would put us on the road to real life."

"You're obviously not married. What happened?"

"We did get engaged, and I got a real job. I was the PR guy at

Greenleaf."

"Wow … you went from vagabond to corporate giant. I'm impressed."

"At last," he said wide-eyed. "That's all it took—a high paying job in a big corporation to impress you?"

She refused to get off track. He was telling her something beneath the surface for a change. "So you got engaged. Was she pretty?"

He cocked his head to the side and replied, "All women are. You're so different from us, you know. The way you think, respond, nurture—fascinates me as a boring, predictable male."

"And you got engaged to a pretty young actress … continue."

"Well, we made some plans, tried to settle on a date, a place to live, but I knew her heart wasn't in it."

"Was yours?"

He shrugged. "I have no idea. I was excited about *attempting* to share life with someone. I had known her for a long while but never spent much time with her. The more we were together, the more I thought it might work—but there was always something hesitant with her. Then one day she just blurted out in tears that she was in love with another guy." He sighed. "You know the law—we could only get out of the contract our parents made if we both declined."

"So you nobly declined and got stuck with your big corporate job and no one to come home to—not to mention a pair of major disappointed parents, I imagine."

"Oh, yeah. I was relieved on one hand because I knew she and I didn't really click, but then few marriages ever do. I figured a mediocre arranged marriage stood as good a chance as a love marriage that eventually went dry."

"True, but at what point in a relationship do you know it's actually love?"

"You're kidding, right?"

She was a little embarrassed at his response. "Well, I know some people fall in love and it's deep and stuff. Evie and Andrew have been head over heels forever, but sometimes I think a lot of that was because of the barriers and boundaries."

"Ah … what one longs for the most are the things he can never have."

"I guess so. And Evie's parents were the most in love people I've ever known. Then again—their love was also forbidden."

He nodded knowingly and rested his finger on his chin. "Maybe … maybe not. I think she touched something deep inside Andrew that no one else could reach. She completed him in such a way that it was almost like she was a part of him."

Her eyes grew big. "That's quite a romantic concept. Do you think there's someone out there for everybody like that? Someone that completes us—that touches us in a way no one else can?"

"Probably not," he shrugged it off. "It'd be an awful waste, wouldn't it, to wait your whole life for that and never find it."

They sat in silence as the rain and thunder sounded through the hallway. Then Jimmy spoke, "What about you? You have a string of men with broken hearts laid out across the path of your past?"

"Seriously?" She gave a sarcastic laugh.

"Sure. You seem like the kind of girl a guy could connect to easily."

Amy really didn't want to discuss her failed love life with him. Perhaps she shouldn't have pried so deeply. "Quid pro quo, huh?"

He raised an eyebrow with interest. "So you do have a life outside of Evie Dorvain."

She felt her cheeks grow warm. "Not a very interesting one. After college I started working at an ad agency and met a few interesting guys there. None of them really took an interest in me, however. We were all good buddies, and seeing that I was the only female on the team, they always came to me with their girl issues. At one of their weddings, I met the groom's brother. We talked a lot that night seeing that neither of us really cared to drink or dance. He got my number and called me the next week. We started dating. After a couple of years he said it looked like this thing was going to work and suggested we get married. I figured why not? No one else was asking or even trying."

"Wait a minute. Are you telling me all it takes to marry a girl is just time? I've been thinking I needed to romance her, make her swoon, and then do something incredibly unforgettable in order to propose. I wish I'd known."

He always made her laugh. "You're too funny. Obviously it didn't work, so keep your game plan. Romance her, moon and swoon over her, then go all out when you pop the question. Had Bill done that I might have stayed with him."

"So, what happened?"

"He wasn't thrilled that I worked with all those guys and suggested I quit. I could stay at home and raise babies. Not that that was a bad idea, it just didn't sound all that appealing with *him*. When Evie won the first U.S. Open, she begged me to work with her. It seemed good to Bill—getting me away from the guys—who didn't care for me, by the way. But as the traveling grew longer, he didn't like it. We started arguing more than getting along. He blamed it on my new job—I blamed it on him. He gave me an ultimatum—leave Evie or him."

There was no need to finish the story. It was obvious what her choice had been.

"You ever regret it?" he asked.

"No, I didn't love him, and I knew I never did. I hoped someday I might, but near the end it was obvious there was nothing that really connected us. I'd rather live alone than marry and live with him."

"Definitely a good move on your part."

His response surprised her. "Why do you say that?"

Suddenly both their phones buzzed with a message. As they opened the link, it was from Max to both of them saying the helicopter had safely landed and the royal couple was inside.

﷽ Chapter Twenty-Five ﷽

The ride back to the palace from the airport in Braisognia was bittersweet. The couple had enjoyed their uninterrupted two weeks on the secluded Greek isle. They never left the island, choosing rather to enjoy the beach, the pool, the tennis courts, and the many other amenities available at the massive compound. Jimmy and Amy spent a lot of time off the island touring the historic sections and countryside. In the evenings, the four of them often played several rounds of cards, laughing and relaxing with no schedule, no overbearing king, and no worries.

But as they pulled through the front gate and headed back to the real world, no one said anything. There were nine months before Andrew's coronation, at which life would take a busy turn for all of them. Until that time, they knew staying one step ahead of whatever Christopher Braisogn might attempt in order to discredit Evie was the main agenda. The nation adored her, but as the almost fiasco with the Northeast Quadrant Home revealed—he would stop at nothing to tarnish her reputation. He was a man used to getting what he wanted, and they knew this gridlock had him stewing and brewing like never before.

Opening the door to their room, their home, Evangeline melted at the incredible transformation. Andrew had gone to great lengths to make this a place she would grow to love. If only he understood that anywhere with him would be a place to love. She walked into the kitchen and checked the refrigerator. Yes, the staff had shopped and stocked it with the supplies she had e-mailed. She then opened the pantry and discovered it also to be full of items she had requested.

Andrew asked, "Are you cooking tonight, or should I tell the kitchen to prepare something?"

"Most definitely cooking." She shut the cupboard and turned toward him. "Should we invite your mother … and perhaps your father?"

Chuckling, he shook his head and said, "My father wouldn't step foot in here for anything."

"Doesn't mean we can't invite him."

"Yes, it does. We're not going to begin our life together here by asking for his rejection."

She put her arms around him and pulled him close. "If we asked and he rejected, would it surprise you?"

"Absolutely not."

"Would it hurt you?"

"No, I'd be relieved actually."

"Then we choose the higher road, we choose not to hate, and we invite him. If indeed he does reject, we've lost nothing, but he loses again. Love is always the better choice, Andrew … always."

♍ ♍ ♍

"Unbelievable!" Amy exclaimed as she sat with the staff hired to ensure no missed or double bookings occurred again for Evie. "One hundred and seventy-three? He booked that many events for her in the next three weeks after her honeymoon? Why didn't you call me so I could have handled this?"

"After the tenth one on the first day you were gone, we realized this was going to be ridiculous," one lady explained. "Obviously someone is trying to wreak havoc here. We immediately changed tactics. We explained she was on her honeymoon for two weeks, that her secretary was with her, and the last thing they would have done is spend their time booking engagements for when they returned. We then started telling them, *You're the thirteenth false booking*, or whatever number, *received today*. People started getting mad—not at Evie, but at whoever was doing this to her." She pulled out a stack of newspapers and began to thumb through the headlines with Amy. "We didn't do this—we didn't go to the Press. The people went. Once they started, it spread like wildfire."

Amy shook her head in disbelief. "Look at these headlines. They know the source comes from the royals somewhere, but if they only knew exactly how high up that source was." She smiled at her staff. "Good job, all. I hate to tell Evie and Andrew, but I probably need to. One more question—when all this hit the papers, did the bookings stop?"

"No, they just keep rolling in."

♍ ♍ ♍

As the first week of November approached, and Andrew prepared to leave for the annual fall military maneuvers, he was extremely unsettled about leaving Evangeline alone in the palace.

"I'm not alone, Andrew," she insisted. "I've got my security, I've got Amy, I've got my staff—I'll be fine."

"But you've been so pale lately." He pulled her close to him in their bed. "I think you've been cooped up in here too long. Why don't you go to your father's house? Take the staff with you. It'll be like a mini-vacation."

"No it won't—not without you." She leaned up and kissed him. "This is my life now. The hardest part in all this is being separated from you for three weeks. If I can live through that, I'll be fine."

"I think you need to see a doctor."

"I'm fine, Andrew! Would you stop worrying? I've never been a morning person."

"Not true. You get up every morning, pray and read your Bible, then cook breakfast for us."

"That doesn't mean I'm a morning person—it just means I'm a disciplined person."

"Well, you've been much undisciplined the last week, and it worries me."

"I've been lazy. We've stayed up late watching silly movies every night. Look at the time now—it's after midnight already, and here we are still awake. That is all that's happened to my crazy life at the moment."

He smiled at the moonlight revealing her beauty in the darkness. "I just worry. I've never worried about anyone before, you know? We've been through so much to get here—I don't want anything to happen to you. And then there's this whole mess with my father. I wouldn't put it past him to … well … to, you know …"

"Poison me?"

"Ugh. Don't even say that, but yes. I told him if anything happened I would abdicate. Surely he wouldn't test that threat."

"Tell you what—I'll make a promise to you. Let me give it another week, and if I'm still struggling, I'll call your personal physician and pay him a visit."

"No, you have him come here," he insisted. "If you go off to a doctor somewhere, the Press will have a field day speculating what might be wrong. He'll be very confidential—not even my father will know who he is or why he's here."

"Okay, okay, okay. Is it a deal?"

"Deal."

⚓ ⚓ ⚓

"Ick," Evangeline moaned as she came back from the bathroom and dropped onto the couch.

"That's it," Amy insisted. "I'm calling Andrew's doctor."

"Give me a couple of more days, please."

"It's been a week, Evie! Andrew made me promise I wouldn't let this continue. And you know what? I'm worried now too! The only person who doesn't seem concerned about this is you!"

"It's a bug or something."

"Three weeks is not a bug." Amy pulled out her phone. "I'm calling now. You can protest all you want, but it doesn't matter. I've seen enough."

She lay back on the couch and felt tears sting her eyes. She knew something serious was wrong, but she didn't want to admit it or even face it. At the top of her list was the thought that Christopher may have found some way to infiltrate her food supply. She trusted the staff who shopped for her, and everything she prepared for herself, Andrew also ate, along with Amy, Jimmy, her father, and Julia at times. How the king could have exclusive access to her, she couldn't surmise.

When the doctor did arrive, he gave her a thorough examination and took blood and urine samples to run through a battery of tests. Andrew had assured her this physician was completely aware of their plight and knew of the king's hatred toward her. Because of that she shared her fears with him.

"I think you might be overreacting a bit," he said with a grin.

"Really? So you don't think I'm being poisoned?" She was relieved.

"No, not at all. Give me a couple of hours, and I'll get right back with you."

"That's all it takes to run these tests? I've waited days and weeks before to hear back from a doctor."

"You were never a princess before. You hold a little more sway now."

She smiled. "Thank you for your secrecy. Andrew felt it was important for the public not to know."

"The prince and I go way back. When he started maneuvers as a ten year-old, I was his military doctor. I was amazed at how determined and strong he was for one so young. I thought then that he was the only one of the three princes really suited to rule."

"Really? When he was ten you thought that?"

He nodded as he packed up his gear. "Yeah. People are more vulnerable with doctors than with others. You get a lot of insight into their character if you observe carefully."

She suddenly felt uncomfortable. "So, were you analyzing me through all this? Do you find me unsettled, paranoid, not fit to be the future queen?"

"Not at all—just a little naïve perhaps."

She was slightly insulted. "Naïve? Why would you think that? Did I not answer all your questions?"

"Yes, and quite adequately. In fact, you answered so well that I've already diagnosed your problem but will wait for the test results before I deliver my prognosis."

"What? You know what's wrong with me?"

"Fairly good idea," but he put up his hand to stop her. "Give me a couple of hours, and I'll be back to deliver the information."

♆ ♆ ♆

"He just doesn't stop, does he?" Evie grumbled as she looked at the latest list of unending bookings the king's minions continued to create.

Amy placed the list back into the folder. "I think Andrew has a good point about stopping everything until the coronation. It's actually having the opposite effect in the kingdom. The commoners are sickened by it, along with a good percent of the royals. Everyone feels more sympathy for you than disgust. If we stopped altogether and then made a public announcement explaining why, either he would have to stop or continue to make the royals look like idiots. And the fact that you're … sick… or something, is a really good excuse to do it."

"No! The people don't need to know that anything's wrong with me!"

"If you're seriously sick, Evie, they're gonna find out eventually."

"So you think I'm next to death too?"

"I don't know. All I know is you're definitely not yourself lately. You're a physically strong person. To see you lying around groaning and griping isn't normal. Never in my life have I seen you so … weak."

Just then a knock was heard at the door.

"I bet that's the doctor now," Amy said as she left her seat to answer it. "Hopefully, we'll know exactly what the problem is and how to treat it … if indeed it's treatable."

"Thanks for the vote of confidence," she moaned again as she forced herself to sit up on the couch.

The doctor followed Amy past the wall that separated the entrance and kitchen from the living room area. He seemed pleasant enough. The news must not be too devastating.

"Mrs. Braisogn," he greeted as he sat across from Evie on the loveseat. "Still lounging on the couch, I see."

"Should I not be? Everyone seems to think I'm at death's door."

He sighed and leaned back on the seat, crossing his arms as he eyed her strangely. "I consider you to be a fairly intelligent woman." Both Evie and Amy registered surprise.

"Do you know what's wrong with me?"

"Absolutely. My most obvious suspicions are now conclusive." He

195

glanced toward Amy. "This ... condition ... of yours is quite personal. You may prefer to be alone when we discuss it."

Amy immediately sat next to her on the couch and took her hand defiantly.

"Amy's my best friend and closest confidante," Evie stated. "Whatever you have to say can be said in front of her."

"Hmmm," he grunted as he rubbed his chin.

"Is it that bad?" Amy wondered.

"Mrs. Braisogn ..."

"Evie ... please," she suggested. "Apparently we're going to be seeing a lot of each other in the coming days. We might as well quit the formalities."

"Actually, you'll be needing to see a specialist in this area."

Amy gulped. "Specialist?"

"Evie, when was your last period?" he asked pointedly.

She shrugged. "I don't recall."

"Have you had one since you've been married?"

"Yes," she remembered that much.

"More than one?"

"I have no idea! Possibly."

Amy's hand came to her mouth as she exclaimed, "Oh, my gosh! You're pregnant!"

Evie jerked her head toward her friend and then turned back to the doctor. "Huh? Really? But I can't be ..."

The doctor smiled and nodded. "Indeed you are. Like I said, I figured you to be an intelligent woman. It didn't even cross your mind?"

She leaned back against the couch. "I never imagined pregnancy would make me feel so ... yucky."

"Have you never heard of morning sickness?"

"Morning?" she laughed, partly from relief and partly from astonishment. "Try noon, afternoon, evening, night, midnight ... pick your favorite time of the day."

"Understood," he said as he pulled a bottle from his pocket and handed it toward her. "It actually tends to stretch itself out. The good news is that for many it only lasts during the first weeks ... or months ... of pregnancy. The bad news is that sometimes it lasts the whole blame time."

She was still stunned. "So I'm not being poisoned and about to die?"

He chuckled. "Not yet. Of course, when the king hears about this, who knows what will happen."

"You're right. Nobody needs to know until Andrew is told. He can then decide what we should do as far as an announcement is concerned." She looked at the bottle. "What's this?"

"Prenatal vitamins. Since you're still struggling to keep down food, these will help keep you and the baby nourished. I know you're a health nut—

read about your strict diet regimens in a magazine. When you get back to normal, you might could go off of these if your doctor agrees."

Amy giggled. "Strict only when she's trying to stay a world tennis champion. Outside of that she's pretty much a pig."

"Hmmm, take it up with your doctor then," he raised an eyebrow.

"About that," Evie said. "When should I see one?"

"Right away. You need to determine how far along you are, how the baby's developing, if there are any complications and such."

Amy pulled out her notebook. "And who would you suggest we call? If we don't take her to a regular doctor, we surely don't need to take her to an obstetrician."

"I can suggest someone … even set it up if you like," he told them. "This will definitely need to be handled with utmost confidence. I know who's loyal and who's not in the medical field."

"Then do it," Evie agreed as she placed her hand on her tummy. "That will be one decision I won't have to worry about. Right now I have to decide whether to tell Andrew through e-mail or wait until he returns from maneuvers in two weeks." She looked at them both. "Any suggestions?"

Amy shook her head. "That's your call … Mommy."

❧ Chapter Twenty-Six ❧

Andrew's heart had never pounded more when leaving maneuvers. As a boy, he had seen them as an escape from the palace. The rigors of intense military living and training were a picnic compared to the ever judging eyes of his father ... and Albert. When he had left from summer maneuvers to marry Evangeline, even then he had a sense of dread. What if he couldn't measure up as a husband? What if all they had dreamed and planned came crashing around them because of some scheme the king would manage to create. But now, after three and a half months of pure wedded bliss, and the only concoction to deal with was the ongoing over-scheduling his father refused to stop pursuing, he couldn't wait to see his wife again. One of the first mandates he would change after becoming king would be the silliness of no weekend leaves. He could understand the importance of new recruits and boot camp trainees remaining on base, but for officers it was pointless.

He had treasured every e-mail from his new wife during the time away. He would have read them over and over again, but she wrote so many throughout the day that it was almost as though she were there with him. After being married, the communication had become much easier and much less formal. He was still concerned about her illness, but she assured him the doctor said it would pass. Within a few months she would be back to normal and all would be fine. For the time being she needed to take things slower. He had insisted she do no more traveling or publicity. They were able to blame it on the continued overbooking—saying that since the perpetrator refused to stop the sabotage, they would. Evie made a formal announcement on television, radio and social media to say any bookings from that day forward were to be considered moot. The king had yet to relent, however.

Andrew had advised Evangeline to remain in their room when he returned, but his excitement escalated as the helicopter began to land, hoping she had ignored him again and would be waiting to greet him. Sure enough, as soon as he and Jimmy jumped out, she came running from the side entrance. Cameras whirred and flashed as they embraced, and even though he told himself to not get carried away, when she kissed him, he gave up. The press literally cheered. She had been out of circulation for two weeks, and the country longed to see their future queen again.

"You're still pale," he mourned as they sat on the couch, fingers and legs intertwined. "I'm not sure the doctor is doing the best for you. Let me see if we can find ..."

"The doctor is wonderful," she assured him. "There's nothing more anyone can do until this thing runs its course."

"And how long is that supposed to take?" he asked in exasperation.

She grinned. "Usually about nine months."

"Nine months?" He was devastated—he had imagined only a few weeks. "This will go right through the coronation. If you're not strong enough, I'll insist you not be there."

"I'll most definitely be there!" She smiled again and kissed his hand. "Nine months ... interesting allotment of time, wouldn't you say?"

"It's a long allotment of time, but we'll get through it."

"It can be reoccurring, you know?"

He furled his brow in disappointment. "No ... please, no. I can't bear seeing you so ..." He stopped talking and just stared at her a moment. "Actually, you seem rather happy beside all the paleness."

"Oh, I'm beyond happy—I've hit ecstatic."

His face began to beam. "You missed me that much?"

She rolled her eyes. "Andrew, are you so sheltered that you really don't understand the significance of nine months?"

He was confused. "Apparently so. There's more to all this than just the illness?"

"I'm not sick," she said as she took his hand and placed it on her tummy. "I'm carrying your child."

His mouth went dry and no words could form. He looked at her—then down to their hands touching her stomach.

"I didn't want to tell you through e-mail. I don't trust anything out of my ..."

"You're gonna have a baby?" He was still bewildered.

"Yes ... *we're* gonna have a baby."

He seldom cried. It was one of those things his father detested most in women and would not tolerate in men. But at this moment, tears began to slide down his cheeks as he cradled her close to him.

"Happy?" she asked as she nuzzled her head into his beard.

"I'm beyond happy—I believe ecstatic would be the better word."

She giggled then pulled his lips to hers. How could life possibly get any sweeter?

☟ ☟ ☟

Andrew raked his beard in concern as he discussed the ramifications of the pregnancy with Evangeline and Amy. "So, only you two know and the two doctors?"

Evangeline shrugged. "It's possible the technicians who ran the tests might know, but you said your doctor was loyal. Surely he knew the importance of secrecy in all this."

He sighed with a nod. "He knows." Leaning back at the dining table, he couldn't shake his apprehension. "No one else is to know."

"You've got to tell Jimmy," Amy insisted.

"No. There's no reason for him to find out." He was firm.

"There's a huge reason," she countered, "the four of us meet together almost daily. There's no way we can be comfortable around each other with something as major as this looming in the silence."

"But the more people who know, the more the chance of it slipping out."

"This is Jimmy—your trusted friend, not to mention your secretary and confidante!"

"Okay, okay. We'll tell him, but that's it."

Evangeline shook her head. "We've got to tell my father and your mother."

"Absolutely not!" He was leaning over the table with a frantic look.

"I am telling my father!"

"No! Don't you understand? What if he was put in some high pressure situation and it was forcefully coerced out of him? This is as much for his protection as ours!"

"I am telling my father."

"Evangeline …"

"Listen, outside of you, he's the only other person who could protect me if something were to happen. What if a major problem occurred and you couldn't get to me? My father would make sure I was evacuated as soon as possible. Believe me—he understands the pressures of living outside the royal blessing."

He stood and walked over to the double doors of the balcony. "The circle can't keep getting larger."

"We won't tell your mother then—but I insist on my father knowing." She stood and joined him, putting her arm on his shoulder. "I understand the significance of this, my father will understand, and Jimmy will understand. We have to trust some people in life, Andrew—and we have to trust God."

He nodded, but nothing could erase his uneasiness. Excusing himself, he walked onto the balcony alone, closing the doors behind him.

Dear God, what are You doing here? We were so careful, even using birth control to prevent this from happening before my coronation. I come home from maneuvers only to find the worst imaginable situation I could face. I am only a man ... and a helpless man right now. I am not like my father—I do not believe, and never have believed, that I can control my world and the people in it. I've come to trust You in many ways, but this is terrifying. Had this been six months down the road, I would be screaming with joy and thanking You profusely, thrilled to know that Evangeline didn't have the same issue as her mother in conceiving. But right now? What are You doing, God? Give me faith that I don't have. Give me peace and wisdom that I don't have. And help me trust You—because right now I don't trust anything or anyone.

🎖 🎖 🎖

Jimmy Newell and James Dorvain both sat stunned at the news. James looked at his daughter with an air of reprimand.

"I was on birth control," she defended.

As if no one understood, he stated, "This is really bad timing."

Evangeline shot up from the couch like an emotional rocket. "Don't you think we all know that? I didn't ask to be pregnant! We took every precaution! What do you expect me to do at this point? You're making me want to hate this child, and it's not even here yet!"

"Stop it!" Andrew yelled to everyone's surprise. He looked at Evangeline and grabbed her arm. "Don't you ever say that again!" His look became less severe as his hand gently glided down to hers. "There is an element we're all forgetting here. We seem to think this is a major inconvenience, a problem, a negative force—but we're not in control, are we?"

Near tears, Evangeline collapsed onto his shoulder. "If you have words of hope, I could sure use them."

He held her close. "We talked about this before the wedding, and we carefully discussed with the doctor the ramifications. He prescribed a reliable birth control, and we followed all directions—I assume." He raised his eyebrows in question.

"Of course," she said weakly. "I didn't *even* want to consider pregnancy right now."

"Okay then—we can't see down the road, but God can," he continued. "What to us may seem like an insurmountable obstacle may be something of divine providence yet to come. We don't create children—He does. He has a purpose for this child ... this baby ... this little person." He reached down and softly placed his hand on her tummy. "We will no longer speak of this precious being as some accidental inconvenience. We don't know the future," he pointed up, "but He does. And when it's show time, God will amaze us all."

Evangeline put her arms around him and let a single sob escape.

James stood and put his hand on his shoulder. "You're right. I apologize for my reaction." He then grinned at his son-in-law. "When did you become such a bastion of faith?"

Without smiling, Andrew told him, "When I had nowhere else to go."

James nodded. "And that, my boy, is usually how it happens." He clapped his hands once. "Now, I think it wise we make some plans—we need to be prepared to move as quickly as possible if a situation should arise."

"Agreed," Jimmy said nervously as he rubbed his hands together. "And despite your reluctance to add anymore to our inner circle here, I'd suggest you call Max in. I'd personally feel better with him in the planning."

Andrew closed his eyes and nodded. "You call him. I need to be alone with Evangeline for a moment."

As Amy, James and Jimmy went to the dining area to discuss what would happen next, Andrew led his wife into the bedroom, closing the door before he said anything more. However, before he had a chance, she began to weep. He sat her on the bed and held her close until the cries began to subside.

"I meant what I said," he assured her. "I had to get with God and try to wrap my understanding around all of this. He quickly let me know I couldn't. He reminded me that His ways are not my ways—His thoughts are not my thoughts." He lifted her chin. "This is His doing, Evangeline. We've got to trust Him."

She sniffed and attempted to wipe a few of the tears. "I'll have to trust your faith in Him right now, because I'm so weak I don't know that I have any ounce left inside me."

"You will. You always have before."

🎖 🎖 🎖

Evangeline never imagined she would stand on this side of the receiving line at the Royal Christmas Ball. She was amazed that the majority of those greeting her seemed genuinely pleased. Only a few showed the polite disdain she had come to know so well over the years. Seeing that every person here was a legitimate royal on paper, she wondered if perhaps the nation was not as divided as it used to be concerning blood lines. Another obvious observation was the longer hair and beards on not only most of the military men, but also on many of the government representatives. It was four months until Andrew's coronation, and the leadership in the kingdom was showing its clear support of the future king.

When Jenna and her husband came through, Evangeline swelled with envy at the glory of her friend's pregnancy. At seven months, she was glowing. How she wished she could tell of her own child inside, but the need to keep the secret was still dangerously strong. Since she was not overtly showing, there had been no problems, but as she had put on her dress that evening, she noticed a small bulge for the first time. Four months now—she knew it wouldn't be long before her situation became obvious. At least Christmas would be at her father's house—the one truly safe place for her in the entire kingdom.

When the receiving was finally over, Andrew excused himself to greet some of his close military buddies. Hoping to spend the evening with Jenna and Amy, Evangeline was caught off guard when the king grabbed her arm and pulled her aside.

"It would appear that the princess has been neglecting her appearance of late," he said quietly in her ear.

"What?" She whipped her head around in confusion and surprise.

"One thing that's always been true of you, Miss Dorvain," he still refused to call her anything else, "has been your impeccable beauty and figure. It would seem that you're putting on a little weight."

After years of dealing with Christopher Braisogn's disapproval, her calm and collected guard went up immediately. "I suppose palace life is agreeing with me … or perhaps maybe I should say marriage is. Everyone's always said I was too thin to be healthy."

He shook his finger at her like a metronome. "One must not let one's self lose control while living in the public eye. One sure thing that could always be said of the present queen—she never let herself go. She always remained thin, shapely … perfect really."

"Oh, I think a lot more of the present queen could be said than that." She needed to think quickly, sharply and clearly, ignore that her heart was banging. "She's a delightful and competent woman."

"Hmmm, so I've been told. However, I'm wondering if I should make a royal mandate that you stop cooking in that … whatever it is you live in … and begin dining on a strict diet prepared by the royal chef."

Smiling, she looked directly at him and replied, "Is it really my figure you're concerned about, or just simply that you miss me at the dinner table each evening? I'm sure Andrew and I could accommodate you on occasion if it means that much."

"I'm not fond of indigestion, dear, something dining with you would surely bring about." He touched her chin. "Just watch the weight. There are too many perfect ladies out there deserving of your position."

"Yes, your majesty." It wasn't worth the fight. "I will surely keep that in mind. I had no idea you were watching me so intently."

"Always."

☿ ☿ ☿

She expected Andrew to explode when she told him about her exchange with the king, but he calmly pulled her closer in the bed.

"I've told you a thousand times—we do our best, but whatever happens, happens," he said simply.

"Do you think he suspects?"

"What did he tell you about my mother's figure?"

"Basically that she has always had a perfect one."

"Yes—and how many times has my mother been pregnant?"

"Three ..."

"Yes ... and did he happen to qualify that her figure was less than perfect during those times?"

She was confused. "Where are you going with this?"

"Face it—you have a tiny bump down here." He gently patted her stomach. "He's so concerned with pointing out any imperfections in you, that he isn't thinking about pregnancy. He just noticed something wrong and took great delight in pointing it out to you personally. Had he suspected you were pregnant, he would have said nothing. He also would not have compared you to the queen—pregnant three times. He wants you to think you're getting fat and that he somehow has control over that." He chuckled. "Welcome to my world."

She sighed. "And what a world it is. I'm really looking forward to going home for Christmas."

He sighed this time.

"What?" she wondered. "Why the sad sigh?"

"Will you ever think of *this* as your home?"

"That's not what I meant. I told you before my home would be wherever you are."

"The truth is—home is where you feel the safest ... the most comfortable."

She leaned over and kissed him. "Which is with you ... always."

"I appreciate the sentiment, but the reality is that with me you are at your most dangerous and vulnerable. Until I'm king ... and you're queen ... we'll never be safe."

"But my heart is safe—that's all that matters."

"Your heart most definitely is safe. I would never do anything to hurt you."

"Exactly," she smiled in the darkness. "I can live with everything else knowing that I'm here right now ... beside you ... where I belong."

℘ Chapter Twenty-Seven ℘

This time Christopher Braisogn brought a more foreboding weapon—a small revolver. The dim, smoky room resembled more of a pub than a place for important conferences. This was a secret area the king had established decades before to meet with those who would handle his *dirty work*. Very few at the palace even knew it existed. It was located at the end of an ancient wing used more for storage than anything else and was hidden behind a dusty bookshelf that contained volumes that were centuries old.

He reached into his coat pocket and produced the miniature gun, small enough to fit entirely in the palm of his hand. He placed it on the table then gave it a spin. The five men stared wide-eyed back and forth from the gun to their boss.

"You know of Alfred, I assume," Christopher motioned toward the old man standing discreetly in the corner. "He's shown himself to be rather smart at times … and extremely loyal. I'm beginning to think you men might have lost your edge and need a little more help in your work." He picked up the revolver. "Or perhaps just a little more encouragement."

"Your majesty," the man nearest him addressed, "you've asked an almost impossible deed of us here."

"It would seem that way, wouldn't it?" The king quickly pointed the revolver at the man's forehead. "This little thing is kind of worthless if you're going for distance. Short barrel, no useful aim on it. However, at point-blank it will do an amazing job."

The man trembled and darted his eyes to the others in the room.

"Sir," another of the thugs called out, "you've tied our hands! We've done all we can do!"

Christopher pointed the gun at him. "And to be honest, the little deed you thought up—double booking the woman everywhere—frankly it's been rather humiliating for me. I'm beginning to believe you gentlemen—and I use that word loosely—are losing your touch. That makes me slightly apprehensive. I pay you good money to settle my problems. If I have to hire more to take care of my business now, it will be to replace you—not help you. And my, my, my—what business you gentlemen have done. Surely you don't imagine I can let you live with such knowledge?"

"Your majesty," the first man ventured again, "if you just let us…"

"Enough!" the king roared, putting the revolver on the man's forehead again. "I've made my point! This first stint is marked well as an abject and humiliating failure. I will not accept a second one."

"If I may, sir," Alfred humbly approached.

"Ah, yes … Alfred. You mentioned there might be a way of impeding this mess for a while. Frankly, old man, I half blame you for the whole marriage. If, however, you can give us something that will stall the process of that woman becoming queen, you could possibly redeem yourself. What have you got?"

The aged man seemed almost wizard-like in his appearance. If he had long hair and a flowing beard, it would have perfectly matched the hooked nose and knowing eyes. He stepped up to the table and bowed slightly before the king.

"If there is a war, sir," he began, "the coronation cannot take place. According to paragraph twenty-seven of the constitution, a king who has declared war cannot be replaced until the war has been decided."

Christopher's eyes grew wide with amusement then he laughed mockingly. "Are you kidding me? This is you answer, old man?" He now moved the revolver directly to Alfred's shirt pointing at his heart. "You would have me declare war on some unsuspecting nation over that woman? You are out of your demented mind!"

Slowly, almost brazenly, Alfred took his finger and moved the point of the pistol away. "Not unsuspecting, sir, but rather provoked."

"And what little idiotic, pathetic country would dare challenge the military of Braisognia? They would be out of their minds! And I certainly wouldn't dream of attacking anyone without a valid reason!"

"As I said, your highness, if they provoked our nation, we would have no choice but to respond. And the smaller and more unprepared the nation, the easier to dominate and keep up a presence there for as long as necessary—even years perhaps."

"And how do you propose we provoke a nation to provoke us?"

Suddenly the first man who had had the revolver at his forehead jumped to his feet. "We steal their military uniforms!" He came around the table toward Alfred. "We have people dress in them and attack us! We get footage—do it somewhere with security cameras all over!"

Another man popped up. "The armory—ammunition storage! We break in, steal a few things … just make it look good. Then you got your reason for a war!"

The king thoughtfully played with the weapon as he considered the idea. "And what nation would possibly want to do such a thing—dare to do such a thing?"

"Aicirtapvakia," another man suggested.

"Oh, that's good!" the first man nodded. "They just had that massive blizzard! They're starving and struggling—national disaster going on."

Another man added, "They're weak and vulnerable. It would be a brash decision on their part, hoping to bolster their affected military, but it would be believable."

Christopher slowly replaced the revolver to his pocket as a sinister smile began to spread. "And to think I almost gave up on you guys." He looked to Alfred. "You're just full of all kinds of surprises, aren't you, old man?"

♉ ♉ ♉

"Augh!" Evangeline yelled as she tried to fasten the pants over her ever-growing belly. "I can't do this much longer."

Andrew tenderly took her hands. "Then don't. At some point the world is going to have to know. Maybe this is that time."

She shook her head. "No, not yet. I'm sorry." She headed back to the closet to find a loose fitting dress. "I can barely breathe half the time even with loose fitting clothes. Then when I go out in public and spandex myself up, I'm so miserable it's a wonder I can concentrate on whatever the task at hand is."

"Again, maybe it's time to stop the charade."

She gave him a weary nod. "I'm five months. All this tight fitting clothing can't be good for the baby either. If nothing else, it stresses me out which has to stress him … or her also." She squinted. "Are you sure you don't want to know if it's a boy or a girl."

"No," he asserted. "This is the first birth I've ever been a part of, and I want to experience that joy of surprise."

"Can I found out?"

He raised an eyebrow. "No. I want to share it with you."

"Men" she huffed as she pulled the dress over head. "You plant your little seed then we get to do all the lugging around."

"Agreed, you do get the short end of the stick as far as bearing the burden goes."

"Ah!" she screamed suddenly as she jerked her hand toward her tummy.

"What?" He rushed toward her in alarm.

"Give me your hand!" She placed it beneath hers on her belly. The baby gave another weak kick. "Did you feel that?"

He turned pale. "That was the baby?"

She grinned and looked whimsically at him. "Or the worst case of indigestion ever recorded."

♉ ♉ ♉

Jimmy rushed to the door of Amy's hotel suite after being summoned frantically a minute prior. She opened it and motioned him in and toward her dining table.

"What's wrong?" he asked uneasily as he took a seat and glanced down at the papers spread over it.

"I've been informed it's time to reveal the pregnancy."

Jimmy sucked a huge breath hissing between his teeth. "Already? I mean I knew it was coming soon but kept hoping we could hide it a little longer … like four more months."

Amy's nervous chuckle didn't make the situation any lighter. "Could we whisk them away somewhere for a few more weeks? Like maybe that Greek isle we went to for the honeymoon? Andrew doesn't have any more maneuvers until summer, right?"

"Well, he can't just take off like that three and a half months before his coronation. He's being trained in leading congress, presiding over legislative activities, Commander-in-Chief duties with the generals—in a word … *no*. There's no way he can go anywhere right now."

"Eh, it was a thought." She scratched a line through it on her notepad then scribbled down a few more ideas.

"She's really getting big," he noted. "I'm surprised nobody's noticed anything.

"Thank goodness it's winter and she wears those massive coats."

Jimmy snickered.

"What's so funny about that?" she asked him.

"When she's out she never takes them off. Did you notice her in church Sunday? She was sweating like crazy."

"And it was hot in there too. That old preacher they got to replace Rev. Scott must have really thin blood."

"And a really bad memory."

"I know, right? He reads all his sermons, not that there's anything wrong with that …"

"Until he loses his place."

"Exactly." She jotted a few more things on her pad then looked at Jimmy. "What are we going to do? How do we make this announcement?"

Shaking his head he held up his arms in question. "How we make the announcement isn't important. How we protect the future queen is the real issue."

♔ ♔ ♔

Two weeks later Andrew entered his home after a grueling day of training to find Evangeline in the kitchen cooking and swaying to music blaring through the speakers. She hadn't noticed he was there. He stopped and took in the sight, smiling at her sweet form so obviously pregnant in her smocked shirt and stretchy pants. She wasn't a large woman, so the tiny baby was very prominent at the front of her frame. She did a twirl to the beat of the song as she moved toward the stove and gave out a startled scream when she saw him standing there.

"You could have warned me," she scolded as she turned down the music with the remote before going over to the stove.

"But then I would have hindered your interpretive dance session. I happen to like this song very much, and after what I've just witnessed, it might possibly be my favorite piece ever now."

She stirred the pot then walked over to him, lifting herself on her tiptoes to kiss his cheek.

"That's it?" he complained. "After the day I've had that's the kiss you choose to give me?"

She shook her finger at him. "Learn to weigh your options, Princey. You want a deeper greeting? Don't sneak up on a pregnant woman dancing."

"I'll remember that," he noted as he marked an invisible line in the air. "I've had an awful lot to learn about this marriage thing."

"And I'll give you an A for effort."

"Thank you. Now, what's for dinner? I'm starving."

"Shrimp Scampi."

"Really, you can cook that too?" He was constantly impressed by her culinary skills.

"Cooking channels, internet, cookbooks—I can cook anything," she boasted. "What do you want tomorrow night? You name it—I'll cook it."

"Oh, that's right." He grimaced. "Father saw me in the corridor and asked if we could dine with them tomorrow evening."

"Ugh ... I'll have to wear something tight and eat at the same time."

Andrew shook his head. "He was a bit too gleeful about it all."

"Gleeful?"

"Almost gloating. Makes me wonder if he knows something ... you know ... about the pregnancy."

"You think he'd be gloating if he did."

He looked out toward the balcony and nervously chewed on his bottom lip. "No, he wouldn't. But he's got something up his sleeve."

"Maybe tomorrow night is when we need to reveal the pregnancy

209

then—take whatever that wind is out of his sails. Tell him at dinner and then announce it the next day to the public."

Andrew looked over at her sternly. "Something's going on." He pulled out his phone and punched Max's name. "And I intend to find out before tomorrow night."

🎖 🎖 🎖

"I've got nothing for you," Max explained as he detailed his snooping at the palace after Andrew's earlier call. "Then again, here at the palace there are more loyal to you than to your father. If he were up to something, I seriously doubt these would be the people pulling it off."

Andrew watched his breath in the frigid air as he stood on the balcony to take the call. "That's an even scarier thought. What kind of people would my father use if he wanted to do something dastardly?"

"Dastardly people, I guess."

"Exactly." He dredged a finger through the frost on the railing. "My instinct tells me to be prepared."

"For what?"

"I have no idea, but I'm not going to face whatever it is blindly. My first concern is Evangeline. Notify her father and have a chopper on standby at all times these next few weeks. If something were to go down, I want her immediately evacuated to his house, and I want a security team headed by *you* to remain there at all times. Is that clear?"

"Perfectly," Max affirmed. "And for the record, I agree with you. Hamilton will take my post as your personal bodyguard and I'll stay with the princess. Also, I'm gonna put a few men on twenty-four/seven alert, manning television and internet sites. If any chatter develops, they'll alert me immediately."

"And then you'll immediately alert me."

"That goes without saying."

❧ Chapter Twenty-Eight ❧

Andrew hadn't slept anyway, so when the siren went off shortly after midnight, dread rushed through his body as adrenaline kicked in. He looked over at Evangeline and she was sound asleep. This pregnancy had exhausted her, and when she fell into bed each night she slept deeply. He didn't want to startle her, but they needed to move quickly.

"Evangeline! Wake up!" He was half-whispering, half panicking.

She merely rolled away from him.

"No, no, no, you can't do that!" He reached for her arm and rolled her back. "We've got to get you out of here now!"

"For crying out loud, Andrew," she shoved his arm away. "Turn off the alarm! It's still dark outside."

"You've got to wake up!" He sat erect and then tried to drag her up too. "That's not an alarm. It's an emergency siren which means something really bad is happening. In all the years I've lived here it has never sounded."

She shrugged his arms off her and placed her hands over her ears. "Can you please turn it off?"

"You don't understand!" He hopped from the bed and moved toward the desk for his phone. "It's a warning, and you have to get dressed and ready to leave right now!"

"Ugh …" she groaned as she awkwardly eased herself to the floor. "Do I have to wear tight clothes? I don't think I could stand tight clothes this time of the night."

Grabbing his phone from the charger with one hand, he took her hand with the other and led her toward the closet. "It doesn't matter! Just get dressed … now! … quickly! … please!"

"Okay, okay," she mumbled putting her hands back up to her ears. "Relax, would you? And please turn off your alarm."

211

"Hurry," he sighed as he slid up his phone's screen to call security. Before he could finish, the phone lit up with Max's name. He answered instantly. "What the heck is going on?"

"I have no idea, but my guys who are monitoring broadcasts are telling me to turn on the television—apparently the king is about to make some kind of pronouncement."

"Great," Andrew mumbled as he snapped his fingers at Evangeline to hurry. "Please tell me you've got a helicopter ready to leave this place now."

"With two security men already there. They're firing it up as we speak."

"Good job. I'll turn on the television and see if I can catch the announcement while Evangeline finishes dressing." Someone began pounding on the door. "Are you at my room?"

"No, on my way to the hangar to wait for you and Evangeline."

"Okay, I've got to get the door then."

"Andrew, be careful," he warned. "I've got six men headed your way to escort you to the helicopter, but they couldn't have made it there yet. I don't know who it is, but I wouldn't trust anyone until we know what's happening."

"Understood. We'll be ready soon."

He threw his phone on the bed and opened the bedroom door.

As he walked out of the room, Evangeline yelled. "What do you mean we'll be ready soon? You're running around in your boxers and a t-shirt!"

"True." He turned around and threw on a pair of jeans and a pullover sweatshirt as the pounding got louder. "Turn on the television," he commanded as he ran from the room. "Hang on! Hang on, whoever you are! I'm on my way!"

When he finally got to the entrance, he demanded to know who it was. Julia.

He unlocked the door quickly and pulled it open. There stood his mother, horrified and out of breath.

"Mother!"

"Andrew, what is going on?" she whispered in horror.

He pulled her inside and locked the door behind her. "I don't know. Father is supposed to be making some kind of announcement about something. Let's see if that gives us any answers."

They scrambled to the living area where Evangeline had just turned on the television.

Julia shook her head. "What on earth has he done? I knew something was astir."

"Me too," Andrew admitted. "I wish I would have caught wind of it before today."

"He's too smart for that," his mother reminded him. "He wanted us to worry, wanted us to anticipate, but not until he was ready to act. You've managed to cut off his every move since the engagement. He knew exactly what he was doing."

Andrew reached his arms around Evangeline who was wearing a sweat suit with a big, bulky jacket over it. Smart, he thought. Loose clothes but still camouflaging the pregnancy. He pulled her close and rested his chin on the top of her head as they all watched the television. Within a few seconds the emergency sign flashed.

"Here we go," Julia sighed.

A very disheveled king appeared before the camera. He looked as though he had been up for hours on end.

"That's odd," Andrew noted. "He was well dressed and rested when I saw him this evening."

"Please," the queen rolled her eyes. "It's make-up—it's all a show. He's about to give us quite a performance."

Evangeline glanced at her mother-in-law in astonishment. "Are you serious?"

"Oh, I can guarantee it—just watch."

"Ladies and gentlemen of the kingdom," Christopher began, "I have been notified of an atrocious invasion taking place right now against the welfare and security of our nation. As I speak, a small militia is trying to subdue a group of foreign soldiers who have broken into one of our arsenals. We're not sure who these men are, but we can only assume they are attempting to pilfer weapons from our military storehouses."

"No way," Andrew scoffed as he grabbed the remote and turned up the volume. "No one would do that! That's a suicide mission!"

"Wait a second," the king put up a hand. "They're claiming to have video footage." He paused as he looked off camera and then began to nod. "Yes, here is security footage of the attack." He glanced back to the camera and shook his head in disdain and anger. "I warn you—I've not seen this so I can't say how violent it might be."

Julia seethed under her breath, "Oh, I bet ..."

Evie turned to face them both. "You think this is all staged? He made this up?"

"Oh, I'm sure it's real," Julia confirmed. "Staged is the wrong word. Engineered would be more appropriate."

Footage came up and they stared in horror as they watched blurry soldiers in strange uniforms mercilessly slaughter Braisognian guards. Next, they battered through the doors of the armory and began to remove containers. The men worked fast as trucks pulled in and were filled with Braisognian artillery. Suddenly the building exploded and flames took over the scene. Within seconds, the footage went black as the camera was engulfed in fire.

The king was back on the screen, now with tears welling in his eyes.

"Why?" he cried through trembling lips. "We are a peaceful nation." He slammed his fist on the news desk and pointed into the camera. "Whoever did this will pay. I swear to this nation there will be revenge, and it will taste of blood just as has been done to us!"

He looked off screen and shook his head as he received more information. "Unbelievable," he snarled, glaring back at the camera with a ferocity that sent chills through Andrew. "I've just been informed that the uniforms have been identified as Aicirtapvakian."

"No," Andrew objected in shock. "They wouldn't dare. That's a lie."

The king now stood and pointed his finger defiantly at the camera. "As Commander-in-Chief, I now declare war on the nation of Aicirtapvakia. May God grant us revenge and victory and may he have pity on your destitute souls!"

Julia fisted her hands and slowly seethed, "He ... did ... not ..."

"Yes, he did," Andrew confirmed.

"What exactly just happened," Evangeline wondered. "Did we not get attacked?"

"By Aicirtapvakia?" Andrew shook his head. "Not in a million years."

"Then what is going on?" she wanted to know.

Julia put a hand on her shoulder and stated, "Christopher Braisogn has just found the only way he can remain king and keep you and Andrew off the throne—he declared war."

Andrew's phone began to sound from the bedroom. He bounded through the door and jerked it up. General Sourkis.

"Yes, sir," he answered.

"Have you seen this mess?" the general asked.

"All of it. What's your opinion?"

"You don't want to know," Sourkis barked. "But I'll tell you one thing—before I send my highly trained military out to decimate a nation as pitiful as Aicirtapvakia, I'd better have a whole lot more undisputed evidence than a crying king and a convenient video. I'm calling the generals together and I'd like you to be there. I've had it with this charlatan of a ruler—I'm ready to use my power and depose this man once and for all. How convenient that he declares war three months before your coronation."

"I don't want to believe this is happening, sir, but I'm afraid I agree with you. Let me get Evangeline on a chopper to her father's house, then I'll be on my way to headquarters."

"Send the queen with her."

"Send Mother to the Dorvain house?"

"When we oust your father, she takes ruler-ship until your twenty-fifth birthday. If the man thinks nothing of murdering his own military guards and blowing up one of his country's arsenals, I seriously doubt he'll have any conscience about taking out the woman who would replace him."

Andrew trembled at the thought. "Agreed. I'll get them off and meet you as soon as I can get there.

"Mother," he yelled above the siren still sounding. "Go grab a coat from your room! You're going with Evangeline to the Dorvain house until all this is settled."

A knock sounded at the door.

"That will be your security escorts." He looked to Evangeline. "Go get Mother one of your big coats. You both need to get out of here *now*."

Julia grabbed his arm. "What is about to happen that you feel I should leave?"

He paused, swallowed hard, then revealed, "The king is about to be deposed. Your safety is mandatory until he can be contained."

She nodded. "I understand." She looked to Evangeline. "Are you ready, dear?"

She shook her head. "Are you not coming with us, Andrew? I thought you were coming too!"

"I have to meet with the generals—I need to be a part of this decision. The nation needs to know that their future king was completely aware of what the generals are about to do tonight."

She reached up and caressed his beard. "Then when it's over will you come home to Daddy's? Please?"

He took her hand and kissed it tenderly. "Absolutely. And we'll stay there a few days to let all this blow over."

She smiled through her tears and reached out to embrace him. The door pounded again.

"You've got to go," Andrew commanded. "I'll be there in a few hours." He reached for his mother and hugged her tightly. "This nightmare of a life you've had is about to finally end."

She pulled back and gave a weak smile. "I'll believe it when I see it."

Max's security team identified themselves with a safe word and then Andrew opened the door and ushered the women out. As they hurried down the long corridor, he wished he could see them off, but he needed to grab a coat and take another flight to headquarters. He retrieved his phone, pulled out his warmest military jacket, and set out for the hangar.

Once inside the helicopter, the women were flanked by three security men as they donned their headphones and closed the door.

"Max!" Evie yelled above the noise. "Why aren't you with Andrew?"

Max shook his head. "Hamilton's with him! I've got princess duty!"

She nodded and gave him a thumbs up as the chopper took off. It wasn't long before the heater warmed the transport and Evie asked permission to unbuckle her seatbelt so she could remove her jacket.

"Be quick about it," Max urged.

She nodded, undid her belt and removed her jacket. The queen stared completely stunned.

"Oh … my … Lord," Julia barely managed to say. "You're pregnant!"

Trying to maneuver back into the straps, Evie smiled and shrugged. "I forgot you didn't know. I suppose this wasn't the best way for you to find out."

"On the contrary," Julia countered, "it probably was. If I didn't pick up on it, then Christopher didn't either. Heaven help you if he finds out!"

"I know."

"You're a much smarter girl than I realized.

Ꮽ Chapter Twenty-Nine Ꮕ

When Andrew reached headquarters, he moved quickly to what was termed the *War Room*. It was where all activity was monitored whether during maneuvers or actual combat. Filled with screens for radar and camera footage, it was used for posting whatever plans, activities or information was necessary. Four of the generals were already there—Sourkis, Trakeos, Allen and Lewis—and he found it disconcerting that Daniels had yet to arrive. The fifth general's quick rise and sudden appointment after the retirement of General Edwards had been questioned among the military's leadership. Most believed he was a puppet of the king and was placed there to be more of an informant than a true leader. If that was the case, the purpose of this meeting might be seriously hindered.

"Generals," Andrew said soberly as he approached the men who were watching a replay of the attack video which had been broadcast an hour and a half earlier.

"Captain," Sourkis replied, motioning Andrew to join them. "We've been reviewing this footage trying to make sense of it all."

Trakeos added, "It makes *no* sense! Aicirtapvakia is so destitute right now I can't even imagine them having enough fuel to drive those huge trucks across the border."

"Where's General Lewis?" Andrew wanted to know.

Sourkis shrugged and shook his head slowly. "No idea. He should have been here before you."

"That's not very encouraging."

"You're telling me."

The men turned their attention back to the screen as General Allen pointed out one of the better views of an attacking soldier. "Is that a mask?"

217

"Pause the footage," Sourkis commanded.

The technician stopped the recording.

General Allen touched the screen. "Back it up until you can see the face of this guy." He slowly moved the video feed backwards until Allen told him to stop. "Right there."

"That's a mask for sure," Trakeos agreed. "Why would foreign soldiers raid a place with masks?"

"It's cold?" Andrew suggested.

Allen turned to him. "If you were doing a quick raid would you suggest your soldiers put on full faced coverings which might hinder the speed of the operation and obstruct their vision?"

"No, sir."

"Exactly."

Suddenly the door burst open and in walked the king with General Daniels and several heavily armed palace security guards.

"Now, that's what I like to see!" Christopher roared out as he ambled toward the generals. "My military leadership planning the strategy of attack for their king."

No one commented.

"That is what you're doing, right?" the king queried. "I mean, immediately after I've declared war on a murderous band of foreign invaders it would only make sense to see my generals discussing how best to carry out our combat." Still silence. "Am I correct, gentlemen?"

Sourkis stepped forward and squared his shoulders. "Not exactly."

"Hmmm," Christopher responded as he slowly removed the fingers of a glove. "That doesn't sound very hopeful to me, general. What exactly are you doing here in the War Room … if not planning a war?"

"We've been examining the footage and discussing the circumstances because we have strong doubts as to the validity of this attack."

The king bellowed out a long laugh. "You doubt the validity of this attack? As you watch soldiers thoughtlessly take out your own guards and loot your ammunition you stand there and doubt the validity?" He turned to Daniels. "General Daniels, do *you* have a problem with the validity of this attack?"

Daniels took a deep breath, gave a brief glance toward the other generals, then looked back at the king. "No, your majesty. I can't imagine questioning such a brutal onslaught."

Andrew's heart sank. It was obvious at this point there would not be a unanimous five vote decision for the removal of the king.

"Well, generals," Christopher continued, "since I am Commander of this army, and you are under my leadership, I suggest you stop questioning my declaration and begin creating a plan of attack. I want this to be swift— to show that no one defiles the nation of Braisognia when the mood hits them."

Sourkis looked back at his fellow leaders and raised an eyebrow in question. Each man, including Andrew, shook their heads slightly. Sourkis turned to the king and stated, "No."

Christopher's first expression was one of shock, but then it began to morph into something more stern, even sinister. "Are you defying my order, general?"

Without so much as a blink, Sourkis replied, "That's exactly what I'm doing."

Trakeos stepped up next to Sourkis and added, "Me too. I will not support a hasty decision until all the facts are in."

Allen and Lewis joined the other generals as a show of support. Andrew knew at this point whatever happened would not turn out well. He had two options. One, he could side with his father, make sure the attack or war or whatever was to take place went quickly so he could take the throne as soon as possible and then pardon the generals that were about to be court-martialed. Or two, he could stand with them and endure whatever punishment his father threw at them.

He stood straighter and taller than ever before and took a step up beside Sourkis. His father merely raised an eyebrow at him.

"Really?" Christopher scowled. "You will cast your lot with these men against your own father, even though I have visual evidence to support my decision to protect this country ... *your* country?"

He stared directly into his father's eyes and declared, "You are no father. You're not much of a king either. I will take my place next to these men of honor in a second before I will stand with a man of selfish and questionable character. I will gladly bear the punishment you hand down to them before I will bow to your delusions of grandeur—king."

Christopher loosened his collar as he considered what should come next. "Very well, then. Arrest these five men for treason against the crown and have them transported to Razewwell immediately."

General Daniels stammered, "Ra ... Razewwell?"

"Is there a problem Daniels?" the king grunted.

"Well, that's not a prison, sir—it's a stone dungeon ... an abandoned hole in the wall."

"Exactly. The only fitting place for five dangerous, insubordinate criminals."

Andrew's stomach lurched at the thought, but he maintained his cool exterior. He took his cues from the men with which he had sided. They didn't flinch in any way when their sentence was pronounced, nor did they take their eyes off the king.

Christopher stepped down from the upper level and approached his son with an icy stare. "I almost hate to say I'm disappointed in you because that would mean at some point I must have believed you were better than this. I guess the best I can do is to admit my instincts were right—you are nothing more than a spineless, sniveling, traitorous being just like your worthless brothers."

Sourkis dared to interject, "He is an outstanding man of character!"

Christopher immediately backhanded the general, sending him sailing into Allen and Lewis. The soldiers and technicians monitoring the room were obviously torn about the exchange. Their true leaders, the generals, were being dishonored and lied about by their highest Commander. One man finally jumped from his seat and ran to Sourkis. When he knelt down to help him up, Christopher kicked his head and sent him flailing to the floor holding his ear as blood began to spew forth.

"Arrest him too," sneered the king with a careless wave of his hand. "Razewwell has many rooms."

The armed guards approached the generals with caution, but they willingly held out their hands to be cuffed. Andrew offered his also, staring at his father the entire time. There was nothing the king could gain that should be worth the arrest of his only heir left to the throne. All the prince could figure was that the man was so ridiculously blinded by pride that he would sacrifice everything of true importance to have his way. And he knew that when it came to the bottom line, it was all about Evangeline—nothing more. Because Andrew had defied him in that area only, the king was determined to punish him no matter what. He had at last succeeded.

"By the way," Christopher added as the prisoners were being moved toward the exit, "make sure you shave all their heads and get rid of that ridiculous facial hair. Maybe if they all looked less like women they'd stop acting like them."

♈ ♈ ♈

James was amazed at the strength of both his daughter and the queen as he explained what had happened. Rather than fall apart emotionally, they sat quietly considering the ramifications.

"You ladies took that well."

Evangeline exhaled deeply as she placed her hand on her swollen belly. "I was prepared for the worst—at least he's still alive."

James was stunned. She actually had expected him to be killed?

The queen stood, however, and was quite animated as she explained, "We have a secret weapon, though." She smiled as though victory was inevitable.

"And that would be?" he wondered.

The queen reached down and touched Evangeline's tummy. "We have another heir."

The impact began to dawn on them.

"Holy smoke," James gasped. "I didn't even think of that." He looked at his daughter. "If Andrew is not released by his coronation, because you bear the heir, you will become queen."

Evangeline raised a finger. "Only if the war is over."

"There will be no war," he assured them.

Julia reminded him, "But he declared war. They have to fight."

"The only soldier willing to fight this mockery of a war is General Daniels—no one else will pick up arms against Aicirtapvakia for any reason. The generals expressed utter doubt as to its validity—and then the guys who were in there have already divulged how Christopher handled them. There's not a man with any character in that army that would dare fight this battle."

"Then what happens?" Evangeline wanted to know. "Are we at war simply because the king declared it even though the military refuses to fight? Or are we not?"

"Interesting question," he acknowledged.

Julia sat beside Evangeline and concluded, "The only option is to try and prove that this whole attack was concocted by Christopher to delay the crowning of Andrew because he despised Evangeline." She looked intently to James. "Colonel, you have your work cut out for you." She then turned to Evangeline. "And you, dear, are to stay out of sight at all costs. You, as I said before, are our secret weapon. As long as the king is clueless about this pregnancy, he will leave you alone and focus on scrambling around the military fiasco. Once we have evidence that this invasion was created, we present it to the nation. Any general that would not depose a king after that would be considered a gutless, worthless, cowardly pawn."

James was impressed. "Sounds like a plan. I'll get on it immediately, but don't expect quick results. Whoever carried this out knows their heads are on the block. It won't be a simple matter of hide and seek."

Evangeline reached for her father's hand. "Just remember—my husband … and four noble generals as well as another brave man with enough backbone to take action … they're sitting in cold, dank cells probably close to freezing to death. Don't take too long."

"I'll do my best," he assured with a squeeze of his hand. "And meanwhile, you do as the queen said—you hole up here, inside, out of the sight of anyone—until we have something solid to go public with. Stay off the porch—stay off the deck."

She chuckled as she came to her feet. "Well, I wanted to spend some time here—wish granted, I suppose." She moved toward the hallway. "Excuse me, please. Another potty break. Take heart with that. I couldn't go too far if I wanted. I have to be near a restroom every thirty minutes it seems."

When Evangeline closed the door, the queen turned to James. "Please call me Julia. I have no intentions of leaving here until I walk out with Evangeline. If I'm living under your roof, I believe a first name basis is completely appropriate."

"As you wish … *Julia*."

♉ ♉ ♉

It was nearly nine o'clock the following evening when the king returned to the palace. He went directly to the library and buzzed for a servant. Exhausted from not having slept for nearly forty-eight hours, he fumbled with the latch on his liquor cabinet. Once open, he fingered the bottles trying to decide which would be most appropriate for the occasion.

"Scotch," he mused as he removed the bottle and reached for a glass. "Time to tie up my most annoying loose end, and then I can get some much needed rest."

"Yes, your majesty?" a page bowed as he entered the room. "What may I do for you?"

"Please bring Evie Dorvain to me at once."

The servant hesitated.

"Is there a problem?" the king asked as he raised the glass to his lips for the first swallow.

"She is not here, your majesty."

He drank a long swallow and waited for the burn to ease. Looking back at the page he asked, "What does that mean, *she is not here*?"

"We've not been able to locate her all day."

This was not what he had hoped to hear. With Andrew being gone he could now do what he liked to the pompous princess … and he had many things in mind. "Then find Andrew's muscle man … what's his name … *Max*, and bring him in. He'll know."

More hesitation, then, "He's not been located either."

He now became slightly alarmed. "You're saying Miss Dorvain and Andrew's head of security are nowhere to be found?"

"Yes, your majesty. We have no idea where they are or when they left."

He took another swallow and emptied the glass. "Well, is there anyone else you can't seem to locate today?"

The young man wavered, obviously delaying his response. "Uh … yes, you majesty."

Christopher glared at him. "And who might that be?"

He swallowed. "The queen."

ℬ Chapter Thirty ℭ

Partly because he had seen the cameras installed, but mostly because he refused to let this situation break him, Andrew never showed emotion of any kind during the first month of his imprisonment. The cell, if it could even be called that, was nothing more than a cave made of hewn stone. There was a small window near the top with iron bars not more than five by ten inches—not even large enough for a head to fit through if the bars could be removed. A large wooden door with a small drawer at the bottom where food and water was passed was the only other exit or entrance to the room. His bed was a smelly, stained, three inch mattress on a raised concrete slab with no sheets but several thick, scratchy wool blankets provided for warmth. And they were desperately needed as the bitter cold of winter was almost unbearable, especially at night.

Andrew had kept up with the date since the arrest mainly to keep his mind attentive on anything. He was totally isolated, having no idea where the generals were—or even if they were still alive. Once a week two men came into the room. First, they would lug in a heavy wooden chair to which they would handcuff Andrew. Next, they would remove the two buckets he used for bathroom purposes. When the buckets were returned, they were always filled with hot water. A small sliver of soap and a clean towel were laid on the bed. They would then proceed to shave his head and beard.

Each time Andrew would ask them one question to which one man would always give the same reply.

"How is my wife?"

"She's dead."

Andrew never reacted to the response because he knew it was a lie. Evangeline was pregnant, obvious by this time, and had the king killed her, he would have gloated over killing her heir also. He would have taken great pleasure in holding that over Andrew's head, hoping to force the guilt of his murdered child on the imprisoned prince. As long as the response remained *she's dead*, Andrew knew she was still safe at her father's house.

With nothing else to do, he focused on strengthening his body. He knew the two cameras at either end of his cell gave his father visual access any hour of the day, so he would work out as much as his stamina would allow. He was fed three eggs each morning, along with two pieces of bacon, two pieces of sausage, and a slice of bread. He would receive nothing else until late in the afternoon when he was given two more pieces of bread and some clear broth. He had to be careful to not overuse his energy and thus destroy his body. Push-ups, pull-ups to the iron bars on the small window, lifting the cinder blocks that held the concrete slab for his bed—he did this several times a day, but more in the mornings after having his only real meal.

When he had pushed his body to its limits, he would lie on his bed and imagine anything he could to keep his mind occupied. He thought mostly of Evangeline, and relived over twenty years of their lives together. He built a house—nail by nail, brick by brick—near the waterfall on the Dorvain property. He imagined raising their child, maybe more than one, and living a normal life outside of the palace with the only person he could truly say he ever loved. He wrote songs, melodies, lyrics, guitar pieces, piano pieces, and went over them each day, humming to himself, hoping he could sing them to Evangeline eventually. He imagined her delight and fought tears each time he saw her in his mind touching his beard or gently kissing his cheek in adulation for his creations. No wonder his father had always hated her—she was perfect—and no one in the kingdom was allowed that honor except him.

Andrew also knew that she was under the protection of her father. With Max forging a security team along with the impenetrable walls of the Dorvain estate, the only way to possibly break through that fortress would be to bomb it, and he knew the king had to be on shaky ground already after what had happened. To forcefully obtain Evangeline might possibly cause a revolt, which, Andrew considered, might not be a bad idea.

♉ ♉ ♉

"This ridiculous insubordination must end now!" the king wailed to the only man in the military who would even listen to him. "What kind of general are you if you can't control your troops! Maybe if we threatened to imprison the ones refusing to comply we could get a better response!"

General Daniels, weary from a month of useless command, tried to explain. "Then you would arrest every soldier but me. There's not a single man or woman prepared to carry out anything that has to do with your war."

"*My* war?" he shrieked as he sent a bourbon glass across the room smashing into shards against a shelf. "This is a war against the reputation and dignity of this nation! How dare these people question my authority and ability to maintain the self-respect we deserve?" He glared at Daniels. "Perhaps I should start with you." He grabbed his lapel and yanked him close. "Why don't I have you arrested? I could start by replacing everyone—from the top on down!"

The king threw him off and Daniels attempted to straighten his jacket. "Go ahead. I'd rather be in jail than go back and face the glares of your army again."

"You're as worthless as the rest of them," he spat, proceeding toward the liquor cabinet for another glass.

Daniels ripped the stripes and tassels from his uniform and dropped them to the floor.

The king ambled over with a fresh tumbler and stared down at the pile. "And what is this."

"I resign," he answered simply. "You obviously chose the wrong man."

He turned to go, but Christopher caught his arm and wrenched him back around. "Obviously. And when I make such a horrendous mistake by choosing a coward to lead my military, I must rectify it as quickly as possible."

"Good luck with that."

"No problem." The king reached into his pocket and retrieved the small revolver. "This mistake will be permanently erased, I assure you."

Daniels didn't even gasp. He merely took a step toward the king, closed his eyes and begged, "Please, put me out of my misery."

This only angered him more. He wanted him to grovel, to beg for his life. He harshly rammed the pistol at Daniels' forehead, but rather than flinch, the general gritted his teeth and said, "Just ... shut ... up ... and ... do it."

He hadn't really desired to murder the man, just scare him. He wanted him to understand that when you worked for the king of Braisognia, you never quit. Christopher had done many wicked things in his life, including having men killed, but he had never pulled the trigger himself. His hand began to shake and sweat as he tried to hold the revolver still. The glass of liquor crashed to the floor, but Daniels never moved.

After about thirty seconds, the general opened his eyes and stared at the sweating, trembling king. "Tell me who's the coward now?"

Christopher gawked as the man turned and headed for the exit. How dare he? He raised the revolver and forced himself to squeeze the trigger. It hit the man's back, but nowhere close to his heart.

Daniels fell to his knees and laughed. "Is that all you've got, king? That's the best you can do?"

Enraged, he walked in front of the kneeling man and stuck the gun to his forehead again.

"Do it," Daniels gritted. "And I'll see you in hell."

With a yell of anguish, the king closed his eyes and firmly pulled the trigger. Daniels fell backward, and blood began to pool on the plush Persian rug. With trembling hands, he placed the revolver back in his pocket, took a deep, cleansing breath, and walked out of the library. Heading down the corridor he saw Alfred coming toward him.

"There's a mess in the library you need to deal with," Christopher told him.

"Very good, sir. I'll get on it at once."

♉ ♉ ♉

Max sat at the Dorvain dining table with James, Julia and Evangeline shortly after dinner. He was seldom seen in person, but his ability to protect those under his watch was obvious at every turn on the estate. The fact that all three of them had not been pursued in any way was evidence of his proficiency. To have him actually meet with them meant something dire must have taken place.

"It appears the king has murdered General Daniels," Max explained soberly.

"Oh, good lands," Julia muttered. "The man is crazy."

James wearily rubbed his fingers across his newly acquired beard, grown to show support for the imprisoned prince. "His list of loyal people just decreased by one. There can't be many left."

"Very true," Max agreed. "In fact, the only one left at the palace that seems to have any affection for him is old Alfred. They claimed he discovered the body and began barking orders immediately to get the place restored. Hamilton said had the circumstance not been so dire and bloody, it would have been humorous. No one knew why Alfred should be in charge, but he assuredly was."

"Traitor," Evangeline muttered. "He was supposed to be on Andrew's side."

James shook his head. "Not really. He was chosen by the king for the purpose of turning Andrew into the next king. His loyalties have always been the crown—then and now."

"I'm serious," Julia stood and began to pace as she continued with her previous train of thought. "I think the man's gone crazy. Shoot! I think he always has been crazy! Something in his brain is not wired right—that's all there is to it."

"Perhaps," James doubted, "or maybe his hunger for power and control and his incessant pride have finally pushed him over the edge."

"Exactly!" she reiterated. "He's gone crazy!"

James crossed his arms and leaned against the back of his chair. "Did you know his parents at all?"

"Very little. As soon as he was crowned he insisted they leave the palace. He never invited them back."

"They were fools," James remembered.

"Daddy!"

"It's true," he insisted. "They wined and dined, partied, orgied— basically made a mockery of the crown. There was nothing stately or respectable about them at all. Luckily, as the world fought its wars, no one really cared about this tiny nation with little influence. The wars were over before they got close to Braisognia, so fortune was on our side. Christopher considered them an embarrassment and was determined to reclaim the dignity of the throne."

"He more or less banned them from the palace," the queen added. "They never attended another ball or royal event once Christopher was crowned. I remember when they each died he made an appearance at the funerals but refused to have anything to do with the arrangements. In fact, could he have had them buried anywhere other than Capitol Gardens, he would have done so. He more or less erased them from his life."

Evangeline looked at her father. "Were they really that bad? There were only a few sentences about them in Braisognian history. They were fun-loving and celebratory if I remember correctly."

"That about sums it up," he nodded. "They married very young, fifteen and sixteen, and had children right away, so they only ruled seventeen years."

Touching Evangeline's shoulder, the queen added, "I was not allowed to fraternize with them in any way or form. In his mind they were poison … a joke. We were to have nothing to do with them even as we lived with them in the palace that short year. They never saw their grandsons, never celebrated any milestones with us. They were an anathema in his mind to the whole kingdom, and he just wished to erase them from it all."

Easing up from the table to make another trip to the bathroom, Evangeline concluded, "So Christopher became as opposite as he possibly could from the parents he so despised. And in turn, his own children became as opposite from him for the same reason."

Julia nodded. "Very unfortunate."

"Yes," Evangeline chirped as she hustled down the hall. "For everyone involved—even the king."

Andrew compliantly wrapped his arms behind the heavy chair and the man placed the cuffs on each wrist.

"And how is my lovely wife these days?" he asked cheerfully, offering an insincere smile.

"She's dead," the man with the buckets gagged as he carried the waste out the door.

"Still?" he mused. "I guess I was hoping for a resurrection maybe."

This took the men off guard. Andrew never said anything other than to question about Evangeline.

"Just curious," the prince continued, "are these cuffs for my safety or yours?"

"Beg your pardon?"

"Well, it would be utterly foolish for me to attempt anything with either of you. Suppose I overpowered you both and managed to escape this cell? What next? Surely there are armed guards out there ready to remedy an attempted break out."

The bucket man walked back in with the hot water. "Don't listen to 'em, Jarvis. He's just trying to yank yer' chain."

"No, seriously," Andrew goaded. "Let's be realistic—what would I gain by strangling or dismembering you with my bare hands and then running off as though I were a free man in the middle of an arctic wasteland?"

"What do you want from us?" bucket man questioned as he pulled out the clippers from a bag.

"Well, to be honest, I'd first like to know if you washed your hands after emptying my toilet. I've always been a little on the nice-nasty side. Call me a sissy if you must."

"Wise guy, you're bein' today, eh?" He turned on the clippers and started the shearing.

"You guys are my only friends," Andrew taunted.

"You hear that, Jarvis? We're friends with the prince now? Who woulda thought it!"

Jarvis fidgeted with the key to the handcuffs. "I don't trust him. He's trying to get information."

"Duh," bucket man continued clipping.

"I'm hurt, fellows," Andrew continued. "The only information I really want is the condition of my wife, and you guys lie about that every week."

"How you know we're lyin'?" Jarvis shot back.

Bucket man stopped clipping long enough to belt Jarvis in the nose. "Ya idiot! I toldja he was fishin' and now you've done gone and made him think we've been lyin' to him. Dang, shut up already!"

"Wait!" Andrew shrieked. "I was just making small talk? Evangeline's okay? She really is alive?"

"Idiot," bucket man growled as he went back to buzzing.

Andrew looked at Jarvis and winked. He hoped the king would watch the entire exchange and know that Andrew Braisogn was nowhere close to defeat.

✂ Chapter Thirty-One ⊱

It had been twenty-eight days since Andrew had last seen Jarvis and bucket man. After his over friendly conversation with them, they were replaced by two new flunkies, neither of which would utter a word. Each week when they came in, he faithfully asked about the condition of his wife, but there was no response now. His three egg breakfast had been reduced to one egg, and there was only sausage, no bacon. It had become more and more difficult to keep up his morale as well as his strength. He had been horribly sick, both diarrhea and vomiting, and the fact that both were going into the same buckets added to his distress. He exercised as much as he could tolerate—he wanted to guarantee that if he ever got out of this hole, he would have the muscle to lift his father off the floor and slam him into a wall.

He no longer thought of music or hummed on his bed. The hunger, the sickness and the isolation were eating away at him, and he knew his body was losing weight and muscle now. He wondered if his father was actually pulling the strings, watching him through the cameras, and then deciding when to deprive him of something else. Or had he hired some sick brain who dabbled just enough in psychology to know how to slowly drive a man insane. He also questioned *why* the king felt it necessary to bring him to such a point. What did he hope to accomplish? Did he somehow think that after such treatment he would fall at the man's feet and beg for his life?

Throughout the first month he had thought mostly of Evangeline and how sweet life would be when he was released. But that had changed. Now the main thought that kept him going was an overwhelming desire to see his hands on his father's throat, feel the crushing of bones as he squeezed harder and tighter, and watch the life slowly fade from his eyes.

The Lord is my Shepherd, I shall not want. Andrew had refused to pray from the day he entered the prison. He refused to acknowledge the God who took the side of the evil king and dismissed the men of character with one, sweeping blow. But now Scripture was pounding in his head and he couldn't turn it off. *He maketh me to lie down in green pastures—He restoreth my soul. Yea, though I walk through the valley of the shadow of death, I will fear no evil, for Thou art with me.*

As he lay on his bed, scratchy wool wrapped around his freezing body, he pulled his knees to his abdomen as high as possible hoping to relieve the pain and cramping. His stomach was lurching again, and he knew if he couldn't keep his breakfast down, there would only be broth and bread at the end of the day for nourishment.

Dear God, he whispered in desperation, *This has to be the valley of the shadow of death.* His quiet voice quivered from weakness and his body trembled with pain. *Are you with me? Are you really? Will you restore my soul? Will I ever lie down in green pastures again on this side of death? I would beg you to take me, but I must see her again … must see my baby at least. Please, God … please.*

He could feel his breakfast at the edge of his throat. *Thou preparest a table before me in the presence of mine enemies.* He forced himself to sit up and drag his legs to the edge of the bed. *Will you do that for me, God? Prepare a table for me before my enemies? I don't want to die here. Not yet, God, please … not yet.*

Unable to hold it down any longer, he shuffled to the buckets and gave up his breakfast.

♉ ♉ ♉

Christopher stared at the television screens displaying the man he barely recognized as his son. He was vomiting again. His body was gaunt and sharp with angles of bone and muscle. His movements were slow and deliberate as if every action was a painful effort. The doctor insisted that as long as he had water he could survive several weeks. When he remained chipper and undaunted the first month, the king had his food reduced. Surely he was miserable … close to his breaking point. And then what? Did he really believe Andrew would see the error of defying him? Would he repent of his sins and seek absolution? He had the power to destroy him by simply withholding more food, even water—he could kill him slowly and painfully. But that's not what he wanted. He wanted his insolent son to break just enough to realize his only hope was the mercy of his father, his king. He wanted to be acknowledged as the sovereign he was, not a mere man who could be trifled with or cast off. Andrew had seen the cameras installed so he had to know Christopher was watching, but he never made any attempt to plea for food, sanitation, warmth … or his life.

Tired of the monotony, the king rose and moved to the window. Snow blanketed the grounds and ice filled the fountains and ponds. With no heat in the prison cell, he wondered how the boy ... the man ... could survive. To occupy his time he thought perhaps he could go back to the library now, have a page build a roaring fire, and maybe read something to escape the boredom. No. He still couldn't enter that room. Why had the execution so disgusted him? He had ordered them done many times prior, but to pull the trigger and watch the life leave a man had been overwhelming. The library had always been his favorite place.

He had not left the palace in a month. The military still refused to fight, and the nation itself was demanding answers about the attack at the arsenal. Why did no one believe their king? What made them so sure the military was right? Hoping for a new plan, he had met with his men to do some strategizing, but they had been no help. Perhaps he should have brought his revolver to the meeting again—mentioned the deed with General Daniels. His face contorted at the thought.

How would the nation feel if they ignored their king and another attack happened? A personal attack? An attack on citizens—not the military. What if their families or businesses were in peril? That was it!

Throwing open the door he rushed into the hallway. "Alfred!" he yelled. "Someone find Alfred and have him come to my personal study immediately!"

A young page who had been reading a book jumped to his feet, threw the book on the bench, and nodded as he ran down the hall.

"They'll be sorry they ever doubted me ... extremely sorry."

🎖 🎖 🎖

Evangeline and Julia stared expectantly from the front window as the limousine barreled down the driveway.

Evie giggled. "I didn't know a limo could move that fast."

"It almost took the curve on two wheels."

"Do you think he's really found something tangible this time or is there the chance of another dead end? What exactly did he tell you?"

"He said to rouse you from your nap and be ready for big news—they've got the evidence they've been looking for."

"My heart is racing at the prospect of this nightmare finally coming to an end." She grabbed Julia's arm. "Then this other part of me is saying to not get my hopes up again."

Patting the younger woman's hand, the queen assured, "There wasn't anything doubtful in his voice. Your father is a very reasonable and rational man. He usually precedes his information with, *Don't get overly excited because this might be another dead end,* but ... there was none of that this time."

They watched James literally jump from the car and run to the house with his laptop in hand. Leaving the front room the ladies hurried to the door just as he burst through.

"Eureka!" he exclaimed practically dancing into the foyer. "We've got him! We've got him! We ... have ... got ... him!"

Tears immediately began to form in Evangeline's eyes. "Are you certain?"

He stopped his animation and gave her a bemused glance. "Do you think I would be acting a fool like this if I had any doubts?"

Julia intervened, "I certainly don't. I've never seen you so ... un-colonel-like."

He winked and motioned them toward the den. "You won't believe this." He sat on the couch and the ladies parked on either side. Opening his computer he gave another excited yelp, startling them both. "Sorry—but I'm saying it again, *you won't believe this.*" He opened a media file and the footage of the alleged attack began to roll.

"Oh, great," Evangeline mourned, "I don't think I can stomach this again."

"Keep watching. This is an enhanced video. One of the techs has been working on this for several hours. He had told us from the beginning he believed he could zoom in with greater detail if we could find the original recording rather than one of the hundreds of copies floating around. He explained that the security cameras were high definition for the very purpose of something like this."

"Why didn't they do this before?" Julia wondered.

"Because they couldn't get the original." He paused the video. "They had tried to zoom in on many of the copies, but the results were always the same—just a bunch of blurry blah ... almost as if the resolution had been deliberately diminished. They searched everywhere imaginable for the actual recording, but nothing could be found."

"Someone had to have it," Evangeline insisted. "I'd guess the king since he showed the footage that first night."

"Yes!" James concurred. "The palace is turning against the king at an alarming rate, so one of the techs we've been working with took a chance that an old classmate whom he knew worked video security at the palace might be able to find something."

"Good lands," the queen gasped. "He'll lose his head if Christopher finds out."

"No," he said firmly. "The only head lost over this will be the king's—he's going down. Once this is released, there will be no doubt this was rigged—and since the video was in the king's possession, locked up tight protecting all the evidence, any general who would refuse to dethrone him would be considered so corrupt the military would probably shoot him immediately."

"Daddy!"

"Listen—this is a major breakthrough—it's irrefutable!" He pressed the play button to continue the footage. "Just watch. First, look what happens when he zooms in on the license plate of the truck."

"It's Braisognian?" Evangeline questioned. "Really?"

"Oh, yes—and registered, believe it or not, to the palace."

"You're kidding?" Julia gasped. "How could he be so careless? That's not like him!"

"He wasn't," James noted. "Remember, he had the original footage and only released video that would render any zooming useless." He pointed back to the screen. "Now watch this guy."

"I can't watch this again," Evangeline nearly gagged. "He point-blank shoots that guard in the head."

"You won't see that. Watch what happens when you zoom in on his eyes."

The ladies watched as the man's face grew larger and larger on the screen.

"Oh, my gosh!" Julia exclaimed. "That scar on the bridge of his nose... and the glass eye—I know that man!"

"... so does every person who ever worked at the palace. It didn't take fifteen minutes to get a name and a location. But look at this." He pointed to a gun as the screen's view grew closer. "See the emblem?"

Evangeline scrunched her nose. "I know I've seen it, but I don't know where."

But Julia gasped again. "I can't believe this—it's a palace guard insignia."

"Yes!" Evangeline shrieked. "I remember now! All their rifles, swords, uniforms ... they all have that crest thing on them!"

The queen shook her head doubtfully. "As incriminating as all this is, it still seems circumstantial to me. All he has to claim is that someone stole all this stuff to implicate him, and he would even go so far as to blame it on the man with the scar and the eye. And that man would take the blame, assured that Christopher would have him released and sent off to some other country—along with a huge stipend for his allegiance."

James raised an eyebrow. "Dear Julia, do you not remember my profession?"

"Actually, I do, which is why all this surprises me. You obviously don't know the king as well as I assumed."

James started the video again. "Watch this. See the man riding shotgun in the truck? Feeling assured no high resolution video would be found, he obviously thought there was no need for a mask at that distance."

The computerized program kept creeping closer and closer until a face was clearly recognizable.

Both women gawked in unison, "Alfred!"

"Bingo!" he clapped. "You can dismiss the other evidence, but when you add Alfred to the mix, the king's right hand man, all of it comes together. And remember, we're not taking this to a court—we're not taking it to the king. We're presenting it to the nation—every station will show it at the same time. It will not be a king's twisted explanation that will hold the sway. Most people have lost their trust in him after the deposing of four generals and the prince—then the questionable disappearance of General Lewis."

Evangeline broke in, "And you're sure they're all still alive … that Andrew's still alive."

"Yes, our contact assured us they're all alive."

"But I wonder in what condition," Julia grunted.

"That we don't know. Our man's not actually at Razewwell, but knows someone who does a weekly supply run. He didn't want to ask too many questions and raise suspicions—just enough to assure they're alive."

"So," Evangeline wanted a timeline and a plan, and wanted Andrew home as soon as possible, "what happens next?"

James closed his laptop and moved to warm himself by the fire. "You ladies get dolled up for a public announcement to be made early this evening."

"What?" Evangeline hadn't imagined she would be the one going public. "I can't hide the pregnancy anymore under a bunch of thick clothes and coats."

Julia gracefully stood and shook a knowing finger at James. "You are good, colonel. You don't intend for her to hide it, do you?"

"Not at all," he confirmed. "You two make the announcement together, a unified front of the two who will inherit the throne when Christopher is removed. Julia, you will be queen until Andrew's twenty-fifth birthday, and Evie, since you are pregnant with the next legitimate heir, you will take the throne in place of Andrew if he is not released … or alive."

"Alive?" Evangeline panicked.

"I'm just saying that the king—and the nation—will realize for the first time that you carry the heir. When he is blasted with the video evidence and blamed for the feigned attack, his first order of business might be to … punish everyone in some way by …"

"Harming Andrew?" she choked.

Julia picked up the thought. "But when he realizes that you … *you* … will actually take the throne after me—that will be the final, defeating blow. To remove Andrew would not put his cousin on the throne any longer. To remove Andrew would put—and I apologize for this—the person Christopher most hates in this world on the throne."

Evangeline rubbed her hands on her thighs as she took in a deep breath. "I sure hope this works. I'll be nothing more than a pure bundle of nerves the rest of the day. Are you saying that it's possible Andrew could be here this time tomorrow?"

James looked to Julia. "That might depend on the queen. Hopefully after you two do your televised announcement, the nation will demand a vote from the generals—one that removes the king at last. Once the king is ousted, you, dear lady, will be the ruler of this country. As with every coronation, the queen takes the oath also with the new king as second in command. Julia immediately inherits the crown. I suppose your first rule of order—of course, I would never impose on the queen—might be to pardon the prince, four generals, and one very brave technician."

Julia grinned. "Oh, you can count on it."

Evangeline drew herself up from the couch and moved toward the hallway. "Sorry … bathroom … again."

James' phone rang. He pulled it out and glanced at the face. "Great! This may be more good news." The queen headed toward the kitchen, but a loud yell of *Yes!* made her turn back to the colonel. He shut off his phone and pumped his fist in the air. "They found the trucks—still full of the stolen ammunition!"

"No way!" she exclaimed. "Where?"

"It's unbelievable—in a locked garage at the palace's hangar."

Her jaw dropped and she put her hand to her head in disbelief. "I suppose I need to find something to wear. I have an announcement to make in a few hours."

❦ Chapter Thirty-Two ❧

Christopher took his dinner in the personal study next to his bedroom. He had grown tired of the suspicious looks from everyone at the palace. They would all be sorry in a few days when another band of Aicirtapvakian soldiers would invade a local shopping plaza—using stolen Braisognian arms—and slaughter innocent civilians in order to loot the two electronics and computer stores. After this, the nation would mourn and fall at the feet of their king demanding vengeance at last. How dare they doubt his sincerity and commitment to the protection of his people—his nation?

He took the final bite of his steak, a bit too overdone and tough for his liking, and blotted his mouth with a linen napkin. After the next attack, he could fire the cook who had become inattentive to his tastes and choose from what he knew would be an extensive line of chefs longing to cater to the king—the sole individual who knew the truth about the attacks yet was discredited by his people over the lies and dishonor of his own military. In fact, there would be many in the palace that would be fired—some even imprisoned over their disloyal and careless actions the past two months.

Thinking he might shower and turn in early this evening, he started to rise from his desk when the door burst open and a page ran in uninvited.

"What the devil do you think you're doing?" he bellowed at the breathless boy.

"Alfred, sir—I mean your majesty," he tried to catch his breath. "He said ... turn on the television ... right away." The boy swallowed. "Big announcement coming."

"Big announcement? Who on earth from?"

"Don't know," he panted. "Just ... Alfred said ..."

"You realize you will be punished for this outburst," the king said sternly as he sat back at his desk and removed the remote from his top, middle drawer. "I will not tolerate impertinence in any form at the palace, regardless of what Alfred might have directed you to do." He glared over at the boy. "Do you understand?"

He nodded as he bent over, still trying to breathe.

"Straighten up, you disrespectful degenerate! You are to never take a relaxed stance in the presence of your king!"

The boy immediately came to attention. "Sorry ... your majesty ... I was just ... doing as Alfred said."

Alfred rushed in through the open door. Christopher had never seen him move so quickly.

"Ah," the king clucked in revulsion, "and now Alfred runs in unbidden! I have had it with the brazenness of this palace!"

Without acknowledging any wrong, the old man merely pointed to the screen and asserted, "Turn it on immediately, sir."

"How dare you!"

"Sir!" Alfred raised his voice to their dismay. "The queen is about to speak!"

Christopher gaped. Slowly he looked down to the remote and then up to the television.

"Sir!" Alfred repeated. "Must I do it for you?"

Christopher pressed the button and turned his attention to the screen as he slowly sat back in his chair. A reporter's face appeared outside what he knew to be the Dorvain residence. His assumption had been right—Evie and Julia had somehow been ushered there shortly after the attack. He never imagined Andrew would act so quickly.

The reporter spoke hurriedly as snow blustered around him. "We've been given no information as to the reason for the queen's announcement. We do know that this is her first appearance since the alleged attack of the arsenal by a supposed ..."

"Alleged!" the king screamed as he threw the plate across the room. "How dare they continue to speak of this as some deception!"

The page ran from the room in wide-eyed terror.

"Bring him back!" Christopher ordered Alfred. "I did not dismiss the brat!"

"Sir!" Alfred was loud again as he attempted to redirect the king to the television. "There she is!"

He looked fiercely back at the screen. He wasn't sure exactly why his heart was racing—it was either the impertinence of the young man or the audacity of Julia to do anything which he had not ordained. "She'll pay for this," he seethed.

She looked directly at the camera and displayed an unusual air of confidence. "Men and women of Braisognia, I come to you this evening with an urgency like never before. There has been some doubt the past weeks concerning the declaration of war and the inactivity of the nation's military over the questionable act of terrorism supposedly committed by the struggling nation of Aicirtapvakia. Tonight I ask that you bear with me as I replay a few pieces of footage from the video of the incident."

"Seriously?" the king laughed. "She's going to attempt to sway the nation over something that's been unsuccessfully combed through again and again?" He glanced at Alfred. "I should just turn this off except for the desire to see the woman make a fool of herself."

Alfred attempted a half-smile, but turned his attention back to the screen.

She continued. "We have unsuccessfully tried to zoom in on various aspects of the video knowing that the cameras were extremely high definition, but the only copies that had been offered from the king were particularly low quality."

"What?" he shrieked. "The king! How dare she accuse me!"

"Finally a person from the palace was able to locate the original video yesterday which allowed technical specialists to use the expertise for which the cameras were set up—to be able to pinpoint anyone who might attempt to sabotage our nation's military."

The king now turned pale as the blood rushed from his face. He said nothing more, but someone in the palace would die in a matter of minutes when he discovered who procured that footage—and he, the king, would execute personally again.

She carefully read the descriptions as the video zoomed—there was the well known palace guard with the scar and fake eye, the obvious emblems, and the Braisognian trucks which had now been located at the palace hangar along with video footage showing them presently parked. But lastly was Alfred's face as he leaned from the window and pointed toward the arsenal.

The king had no words. He stared at the evidence and shook his head in astonishment. He had to think fast, and he needed Alfred to pull it off. After this, the old man would be of no use to him because of the video. He would have to deal with that later. He had only a few minutes to set off the second attack.

"Alfred, call the men immediately!" he panicked. "Step two goes down tonight!"

Instead of responding, the old man nodded toward the screen. "Miss Dorvain, sir."

Christopher looked back to the television and slowly came to his feet as an obviously pregnant Evangeline stood before the camera.

"No," he barely breathed. "No, she can't be." He turned to Alfred. "Did you know about this?"

Shaking his head, he replied, "Not at all, sir. Not at all."

"No wonder Andrew evacuated her so quickly. Now I know why he never believed them when he was told she was dead." He slammed his fist on the desk. "I should have known something was going on—I should have sensed it! They were going to mock me with her on his birthday! Show up and have that Jezebel of a woman claim the right to the throne!" He jerked toward Alfred and pointed his finger. "Phase Two goes down now! Assemble the men and have this executed within the hour!" Wringing his hands together he sneered, "We'll see who gets mocked by the end of the night. Get moving, Alfred!"

The man merely stood there and shook his head.

"I said to get moving! Now!"

Alfred stepped toward the door, locked it, and then drew his hands together. "Sir, surely you know the moment I step foot out of this office, I will be arrested. I would even surmise that the queen already has law enforcement heading toward this corridor."

"Then move!" he demanded.

Alfred shook his head. Very carefully and deliberately he stated, "I'm afraid it's over, sir."

Slamming his hand on the desk he bellowed, "Over? Over? Over my dead body!"

The old man breathed a deep sigh and nodded slowly as he approached the desk. "That would appear to be your only *respectable* option at this point."

"What? What are you even suggesting?"

Alfred opened the top, right drawer of the desk and removed the small revolver. He placed it in front of the king and stood back.

Christopher glared at him in shock. "Are you out of your mind? I am no coward! I will not take a coward's out!"

"Then you will go to prison—possibly replace your son at Razewwell. The queen will not take his treatment lightly once she sees him."

That point brought the reality of his position to light at last. As his heart hammered relentlessly, the king forced his trembling hand to the revolver. Touching the cold, metal handle, he tried to summon the same courage as when he had faced General Daniels in the library. The revolver had been an extension of his anger then—now it must become an extension of his determination.

❮❮❮

Andrew refused to open his eyes. He knew the yelling of his name was only another hopeful dream. This time it had been Max's voice calling to him. He hadn't realized he had dozed off again. Pulling the abrasive blankets up to his neck, he tried to warm his chilled body. If only they would give him one more blanket. He used the bath towel left for him each week to wrap his feet, but lately that was useless as he often pulled his knees to his chest in cramping pain. He hadn't eaten since yesterday morning, and since he had thrown that up, his stomach gnawed for food.

"Andrew!"

There was the dream again, but he knew now he wasn't asleep. Was he imagining, delusional? Is that where this miserable condition had finally led him?

"Andrew Braisogn, where are you?" The voice was closer, and it was unmistakably Max.

Rather than get his hopes up, he looked to the cameras. This must be some demented joke or test his father had created. He was probably watching some screen in a warm, hidden room waiting to see the prince jump to his feet in excited expectation only to eventually discover it was a recording.

I won't give you the pleasure of a response, he gritted as he rolled over to show his indignation at the trap.

"Dang it, Andrew, answer me! I have no idea which cell you're in!"

He put his hands to his ears. He would not play this game.

"Look," another voice yelled. "There's bread in the tray of that drawer."

"That must be the one!" Now they banged on the door. "Andrew, are you there?"

He pushed his hands harder against his ears. *No! I won't let him do this to me! I will not respond!*

"Move away," Max's voice boomed. "I'm gonna have to shoot the lock!"

Bang!

Andrew bolted up. That had been a real gun, and it was just outside his room. He heard the rusty hinges of the ancient door creak to life and he stared fearfully at who might be entering to bring some new form of torture. Within a few seconds Max appeared, quickly shadowed by Hamilton. Both men abruptly halted when they saw the prince.

"Andrew?" Max grimaced from the smell as he squinted from the threshold.

"Max?" he replied, wondering for the first time if maybe this was an actual rescue.

"Andrew!" he yelled with recognition, now dashing toward his friend. "What the heck have they done to you?"

Max and Hamilton immediately flanked him and pulled him to his feet.

"He's freezing," Hamilton noted. "Let's get him out now to a heated room."

Andrew glared at him. "They have heated rooms here?"

"Good lands, man, what did they do to you?" Max questioned again.

"Wait." Andrew had to understand this was for real. "What is going on?"

"Sorry, man," Max apologized. "My first thought is to just get you out of this sewer, but I guess you're pretty confused." He looked directly at Andrew. "The short version is that it's over—the king is gone, your mother is taking the throne, and in one month you and Evie will be the crowned rulers of Braisognia."

Andrew shook his head. This couldn't be real. "What's the long version?"

"Let's get you warmed up and showered and then we can tell you the whole story on the flight home."

"Evangeline!" he gasped suddenly. "Why are you not with Evangeline? I told you to stay with her! You shouldn't be here! Is she okay? And the baby?"

"Better than ever since they know you're coming home."

Tears grew in his eyes as he released a deep sigh. "My mother too?"

"Yes," Max affirmed. "They've been well kept at the Dorvain house. Your mother is waiting to head back to the palace after she sees you. Although, you are quite the sight, my man—a rather hard sight."

"The generals? Are they still here too? Are they all okay—alive?"

"Yes, and in much better shape than you."

"I want to see them."

"Andrew, man, please let us get you warmed up and cleaned."

"No!" he cried. "I have to know! This could all be another sick trick! Show me the generals—now!" He wrestled with what little strength he had to get released from their grip. They easily let him go.

"Andrew, no problem," Max assured him. "They're at the opposite end—in another whole complex. I just thought you'd rather be clean and warm before venturing out in the cold. It's been snowing like crazy all night."

Shaking his head he repeated, "I have to see them first, please."

Hamilton noted, "At least it's heated there. Let me grab a blanket to wrap him in."

"No," Max countered as he began removing his coat. "He can have mine—boots too."

They bundled Andrew and then rushed through the outside to the wing were the generals had been kept. When they entered the building, he was overcome with the warmth. "They had heat …"

"Yes," was all Max would say.

"Bathrooms?"

"Look, we had no idea the conditions you were …"

"Did they have bathrooms … and showers?" he demanded to know.

Max hesitated. "Yes."

Andrew smiled, closed his eyes and nodded. "Thank God."

After several turns they approached a large, central room where Andrew again was overwhelmed. There stood all four generals and the man who had jumped in to help Sourkis—all with shaggy hair and long beards. When they saw Andrew, they rushed to him and took turns hugging.

Trakeos surmised, "He punished you by shaving your head and beard, I see. He punished us by refusing to since we had declared our loyalty to you."

"I'm so glad you guys are alive," Andrew choked. "I had no way of knowing and no one would tell me anything."

"They told us you had been executed that first night," Sourkis explained. "We had no idea until these guys came that you were even alive. We wouldn't believe them, but they assured us you were."

Hamilton clarified the situation. "We had an informant who brought supplies here weekly. Here's a real friendly guy and managed to eke out a little more information each time he came. He didn't push it because he knew if they caught on, he'd be arrested too and then we'd have nothing. The second week he got word that Andrew was being held in a different part of the prison."

Andrew looked around at the modern conveniences and sighed. "You have no idea how different."

"You look bad, Captain," Trakeos noted. "Apparently they took better care of us."

The prince raised an eyebrow as he looked over the men. "You're no picture of beauty either, sirs."

They smiled and agreed.

The warmth of the shower infused life back into Andrew's weakened body and spirit. He let it pour over his head and race down his shoulders as he stood still and basked in the sensation of comfort. His body was covered with sores from the inescapable filth he had lived in as well as the scratchy wool blankets he had wrapped tightly around him. He hated to face Evangeline in such a deplorable condition, but she had promised for better or for worse, and this had to be the worst.

After a much longer shower than he had intended, he dressed in winter military camouflage they had brought from his room at headquarters. The clothes swallowed him as he had lost much weight, but the warmth and softness enveloped him like a comfortable bed. He had never been much for headwear, but he gladly donned the knit hat and was thankful for something to cover his shorn head. Now that their prince was clean and dressed, the generals said their goodbyes and left in transports to their homes as Andrew, Hamilton and Max boarded the chopper that would take them to Evangeline.

"The long story," Andrew spoke into the mic of his headset. "I want to hear it now. What am I facing? What's happened the past two months?"

Max divulged all he could remember with help from Hamilton concerning facts. When he finished with the queen's announcement and Evangeline's appearance, he told the next horrifying details.

"Apparently your mother's information and the obvious new obstacle of an heir to the throne finally pushed your father over the edge," Max revealed cautiously. "It seems he … shot himself … suicide. It had to have been instant. There was no getting away from the evidence, and we suppose he figured death would be the better of his options."

Shocking both security men, Andrew yelled an expletive for the first time in his life. "How dare he! How dare he take that escape rather than face his accusers like a man! After all the dastardly, twisted, wicked things he's so brazenly done, how dare he just step away from it all rather than face his consequences!"

"At least those he tried to ruin can live in peace now."

"Peace?" he mocked. "You think there will be peace? You think I'll be able to lie down at night and not dwell on how my father locked me away in a freezing, stone-walled cave with two buckets for my waste and two pathetic meals a day? The only pleasure I can imagine at this moment is throwing him against a wall and beating his face until there's nothing left but …"

They made no comments. They wouldn't even look at him.

"Sorry," he regretted as soon as he realized how he was spewing. "I just … for all that time …"

"We understand," Max assured. "If I could face him myself I would gladly do it for you."

಄ Chapter Thirty-Three ಇ

"I hear the chopper!" Evangeline exclaimed, throwing off a blanket as she managed to joggle from the couch.

Julia stood gracefully and followed her to the foyer with James close behind grabbing luggage from the hallway. He would accompany the queen to the palace to assist with funeral arrangements and ease some of the pressure from all that had to be done. Evangeline would stay here with Andrew until he felt able to return to the royal residence.

"You ladies stay in the house," he suggested. "I'll take our things out and make the last of the security arrangements with Max."

"Can we still not go outside?" Evie wondered with alarm. "I thought all the hiding was over!"

He set down the luggage and pulled her into his arms. "You can go outside ... anytime you want. It's just extremely cold, and since Andrew's on his way inside, I think it would be best if you waited here—that's all."

She breathed deeply. "Sorry, Daddy. I just need to see him ... be with him ... now."

"And you will be ... very soon." He kissed her forehead then turned to the queen. "How are you holding up?"

"My biggest blight in life is gone," she sighed. "I'm rather daunted about the prospect of learning how to live."

To Evangeline's shock, her father reached over and gently touched Julia's cheek. "You're a strong woman, your majesty," he assured. "You'll find your new life quite refreshing—I have no doubts about that."

She blushed, and shook her finger at him. "We will not be going back to *your majesty* after all we've been through."

"Publicly we will. I prefer everyone to see that I honor my queen—just setting a noble example."

"And you are most certainly the noblest of the noble."

Before Evangeline could process their intimate exchange, the helicopter flew over the house and came into view as it set down on the front lawn.

"Let me get these loaded," James said retrieving the luggage and opening the door. "I'll bring Andrew in directly."

He shut the door quickly to keep the blustering wind and snow from invading the foyer. The ladies watched through the side windows as he moved against the whirling blades and saluted the pilots. The first to exit was Max and then Hamilton followed by a thin man Evangeline couldn't recognize. Her father shook hands with the security men then reached his arms around the third one. They all talked for some time as the ladies waited for the prince to emerge.

"Where's Andrew?" Evangeline asked worriedly. "He's supposed to be on this one, isn't he?"

"I believe so. I thought Max and Hamilton were escorting him here."

James finally put an arm on the shoulder of the strange man and began to walk him toward the porch. The reality then slammed onto both ladies.

"Oh … my … gosh," Evangeline gasped as a sob escaped her throat. "That can't be Andrew! He's so thin … and where is his beard … and hair?" Another cry.

Julia grasped her shoulders and turned her toward her. "Do you remember the talk we had before you married? When I told you to be strong and not let him know that the circumstances were overwhelming you?"

She nodded.

"You did remarkable … but now you must do it again." She wiped a tear from the young woman's face. "He knows what he looks like and I imagine is struggling to face his wife in such a condition."

"I would never condemn him!"

"No, I don't believe you would, but right now, even though pregnant and excessively emotional, you need to stand strong and help guide him through this. We have no idea what he's been through, but if that's what he looks like after only two months, I would say he's just spent hell on earth— all at the hands of his father."

Evangeline nodded again as she quickly wiped another tear.

"Talk to me … or your father … or Amy or Jimmy or even Max if it gets too much. But you stay strong for Andrew."

Giving a final nod she squared her shoulders and stood straight. "I will," she resolved, knowing it would be difficult.

"You're an amazing woman, Evie—I've told you that many times. You'll get through this fine, I promise. You're as much a daughter to me as my sons have been sons. Living with you and James like this … out here … away from the insanity I've dwelt in all these years … has been the only thing that kept me going. I look forward to the future with you, watching you grow, watching you raise my grandchildren—life will be so much different now … in a good way."

Evangeline reached out and hugged her tightly. "Thank you," was all she could manage.

The door swung open and Andrew stepped through followed by the colonel and Max. Julia moved to him quickly and threw her arms around him. She then pulled back and stared into his eyes. "I cannot tell you how relieved I am to see you again. I've never in my life known such fear and worry."

He offered a slight smile. "Believe me, I understand. I honestly didn't know if this day would ever come."

She took a deep breath and reached up to cradle his cheek. "Well, it has, and I'm sure you've been given all the gory details of our lives right now so I won't hash them out with you. I've got to get to the palace and try to bring some kind of order and closure to all this mess."

He smiled bigger and shook his head. "I'm honestly glad it's you and not me right now who's taking the throne."

She gave him a quick once over and said, "Me too. Now … I've got to get to the palace. Stay here as long as you need. There's no reason for you to hurry there or make any kind of appearance until you're rested and composed."

"You're wrong," he disagreed. "This nation needs to see what a king with too much power is capable of. They need to see me now—see what he did to me—and realize that no one had the power to stop him." He clenched his jaw and then added, "And they need to make sure this never happens again."

"If that's what you want," she acknowledged. "You do whatever you feel is necessary, but at least get a decent amount of rest before you take on the world. Promise me?"

"Promise, but we may disagree on what defines decent."

She pulled on her coat and grinned. "Very well—I think you're a big boy now, and I'll trust your judgment." She nodded her head to Evangeline. "Now, go spend some time with your wife and perhaps let her help you decide what *decent* might be."

James and Max followed Julia out and then Andrew slowly turned to Evangeline. Nothing about him was recognizable except for his eyes, and even they had changed—something darker shone through them now, something less innocent and hopeful. He reached up and removed the knit hat revealing not only had his hair been cut, but had been shaved. It had been years since she had seen him without a beard, but now all that was there was a few days' stubble. Knowing he must be self-conscious, she finally held out her arms and offered a tender smile.

"Hello, Princey," she said warmly. "Welcome home."

He swallowed then moved toward her slowly as though drained of life. She put her arms around his neck and pulled him close. He merely laid his head on her shoulder, nestled his nose in her flowing hair as he let out a single, heart-cringing sob. Everything within her wanted to break, but she held him tightly, rubbing his back, willing her own tears to stay subdued.

After a minute or two, he slid down to her belly and reached his arms around her. "Hello, baby," he whispered. "I was so worried—didn't know if I would ever see you, if you would ever even know who I was. But I'm home now." He looked up at Evangeline. "I'm really home."

She cupped his cheek with her hand and pulled him back up to her. "There's no way to tell you how thankful I am right now."

"Trust me, I understand."

She pulled him down and kissed him softly, painfully, overcome with everything they had ever been through. She knew for some that passion was all they craved, and this moment would have been powerful and strong. But her prince was a man of tenderness who had lived on the edge of brutality all his life as his father had tried to sharpen the gentle curves. All she wanted now was to nurture and heal whatever was broken in him so that he could finally be the man he was born to be.

"What can I do for you?" she breathed against his lips. "Anything …"

He pulled back and gave a weak smile. "I hear the fire crackling. Just to sit there in the den in front of that warmth would be a dream come true."

She took his hand and walked him to the couch. Reaching down for the blanket she had tossed earlier, she placed it over his legs. She then kneeled on the floor and removed his boots so she could prop his feet on an ottoman. Surely he was tired and ready for bed seeing as it was the middle of the night, but that had not been his request.

"What else?" she urged, wanting to somehow make up for two months of hell.

Another feeble smile. "You don't happen to know how to make your father's hot cocoa, do you?"

She clumsily leaned on his legs to push herself up from the floor. "Well, don't ever tell him this, but I actually have the formula down. You know men—so proud of themselves."

He nodded. "Your dad's a good man."

"A very good man," she acknowledged. "So, you want some cocoa?"

"That would be wonderful."

She braced her hands on the couch and pushed herself up. He immediately tried to help, but she insisted she was more than capable. "How about I bring you one of my big, fat muffins, warmed in the microwave and slathered with butter? Banana nut?"

"Please. Maybe I can keep something down this time."

"You've been sick?" she worried again.

His weary eyes, darkened with thick bags and red from sleeplessness, fixed on hers as he disclosed, "You have no idea how sick."

❦ ❦ ❦

Although they hadn't been in bed long, Evangeline awoke for one of her frequent bathroom trips. She rolled over to reach for Andrew, but he wasn't there. Alarmed that all this might have been a dream, her heart began to race as she pushed herself up in the bed. Searching the room, she noticed him sitting in the window seat staring outside. She wanted to go to him immediately, but the bathroom was the first order of need. When she returned, he was still sitting there in only his boxers and a t-shirt. She grabbed a throw blanket from across a chest and wrapped it around him as she joined him on the bench.

"You're going to freeze and end up even more sick," she scolded as she took his icy hand.

"No, I kept the muffin and cocoa down. That's a good sign."

"What are you doing up? Is everything okay?"

"Okay," he sighed. "That's such a relative word—*okay*. I'm no longer in prison but here with my wife sleeping in a warm room and a soft bed. I sat by a fire, I ate and drank pure deliciousness—very *okay*." He squeezed her hand and pulled her to him. "My father put me in a dungeon, no heat, no sanitation, fed me twice a day—barely. Now he's killed himself so he never has to answer for his sins—I can never confront him about the wickedness of his actions—not *okay* at all."

She nodded, but held her tongue from saying he would pay for his sins in eternity. Right now this broken man wasn't thinking in that realm. She also knew that he would need to talk through many things before he could think clearly again. In one month he would be king and would need to be in much better mental condition than he was at the moment.

Standing, she pulled him to his feet and dragged him toward the bed. "Come lie beside me and at least stay warm," she pleaded.

"I haven't seen the outside in two months ... not really. I had a tiny opening at the top of my cell. I would jump and grab the bars on it, just wide enough for my hands, then do pull ups. The first week I could see the landscape. After that, they put a bucket in front so I could see nothing." He sighed as they climbed into bed. "Why?"

She wanted to answer him, but there was no answer. Instead, she pulled the covers over them and suggested, "Turn toward the window and you can at least see the branches swaying in the moonlight. I'll snuggle up behind you and keep you toasty until morning. If you really want to get out, we can ride to the waterfall for a little bit tomorrow."

"No! You can't ride a horse this far along in the pregnancy!"

"No," she agreed, "I meant take the buggy."

"Oh," he relaxed against her. "Sorry, but still *no*. We need to get to the palace as soon as we can get moving tomorrow. I'm sure Mother will make some sort of announcement, and I want to be there."

"Andrew, you need to rest."

"No, I need to expose the lunacy of this nation's predicament. They need to understand that when I step into power, things are going to change—and in a big way. I will never be like my father, and I would hate to think that any of my own children or grandchildren might be, but there are no guarantees. What my father did must never happen again—*never*. And that change begins tomorrow when the nation sees the evidence stand before them in flesh and blood."

℘ Chapter Thirty-Four ☙

Andrew could take no more. He rose to his feet as quickly as his strength would allow and declared, "I will not agree to any of this, nor will I remain silent if this lie is perpetrated!"

The advisory council that had more or less designated themselves that position was meeting with the queen and Andrew to offer a more favorable version of the king's demise. They were a group of royal politicians who believed to announce the king's suicide would be a great blot on the nation.

Andrew was dumbfounded. "To claim he had some kind of brain cancer which caused him to act unreasonably would do nothing more than pardon his inexcusable behavior!"

Representative Averill Braisogn, a distant cousin of Christopher's, put up a gentle hand to explain. "We're not wanting to pardon or defend the king's actions—we merely want to protect the reputation of Braisognia which has been so greatly brought before the world stage by your incomparable wife, your highness."

"No," Andrew countered fiercely. "You want to protect this continuing farce that somehow royal blood has more nobility and worth than any other. You want this nation to believe that only a man with a sickness in his brain would be capable of the things my father has done. You want to erase the evil and whitewash the darkness in hopes that you all can continue to look down your noses from your pretentious, unearned seats of honor."

Averill tried a different approach. "You really need to understand that we have the heart of the nation in mind here. It's not the king's legacy we want to protect—it's the reputation and stability of our own country. If people are led to believe that one man can create such disruption …"

The prince interrupted, "Then they would know the truth." He gazed at each of them. "Bastards." The entire room gasped, including his mother and Colonel Dorvain. "And I mean that in the literal sense, not the profane. You have no way of knowing how pure or impure your bloodlines are anymore. Evangeline is perfect proof of that. She and her mother were disdained because of a lie, a deception created by a royal to save his selfish reputation. Yet when the truth came out, the disdain deepened because each of you in this room knows there's a huge possibility, that after 800 years of protecting bloodlines, there have been many, many, many indiscretions. And who knows just how pure or impure any of us are by this time."

Andrew removed his jacket, unbuttoned and stripped off his shirt, then his undershirt. The group stared in distaste at the starved form and the oozing sores. "This," he motioned over his torso, "is the deliberate work of your king ... your pure, royal bloodline. And don't think he was unaware of my condition. He had cameras installed the first week of my capture. Palace staff has told me he spent hours in that room watching ... gaping ... smirking at the condition of his son ... your prince. I knew he watched, so I refused to give into hopelessness. I physically pushed my body and did every mental exercise possible to keep my mind alert ... all this in a room with no heat during the dead of winter, two buckets for my excrement which were emptied once a week, and two meals a day—three eggs, bacon, sausage, and a slice of bread for breakfast—broth and another two slices of bread at night. I had a bucket of water given me daily to drink. When he saw I wouldn't be defeated, he cut my breakfast to one egg and sausage with the bread."

The men now stared in horror. He went on, "My body broke long before my mind. Had not my mother and Colonel Dorvain spent tireless hours trying to prove the king's fraudulent claims, I would still be there ... and no thanks to any of you who were more than willing to let him have his maniacal way for the sake of the precious reputation of this country." He grabbed his shirt and put it back on. As he buttoned the front, he dared the group. "You carry out the lie, and in one month when I'm king, you'll have the opportunity to understand what it's like to be on the unfavorable end of a controlling monarch." He picked up his coat and undershirt, and laying them across his arm he added, "Welcome to the new regime, lords of Braisognia."

♉ ♉ ♉

Evangeline was deplete. After the queen's announcement of Christopher's suicide and the immediate pardoning of the six prisoners, Andrew had taken the lectern. She imagined the shock of the nation as their future king stood before the cameras and explained in detail the ordeal of his imprisonment. Formerly, a man so handsome he could have been a celebrity in any nation just from looks alone, he now was pitiful and almost despicable in appearance. He had shaved the beard but left the mustache in hopes of some help for his face. He spoke not so much with confidence, but with determination. She knew he had no plan as to how change should happen—only that it must, and that it be as quickly as possible.

Being back at the palace was bittersweet. She had enjoyed her childhood home again but hated being there without Andrew. Her home now truly was wherever he would be. And with only two months to go in the pregnancy, the palace was the best place for the moment. Her doctor had already checked with her that day and assured her the baby was fine. That gave her some sense of relief in the midst of such chaos. And even as she sat in the strangeness of the home Andrew had tried to create for her, she couldn't help but smile at the details. He had battled with the fear that their marriage would destroy her, but he had never considered the depths to which his father was willing to go—destroying his own son and final heir— over a woman he hated.

Planning to cook for just the two of them, she sat on a reclining end of the couch to make a grocery list. She had no idea she had drifted off until Andrew came in and found her asleep. He insisted the chef prepare them a meal and bring it to them. She tried to protest but was actually relieved over the thought of relaxing. The day had been more taxing than she realized. Her father had divulged the meeting with the advisory board and how Andrew had faced them down with his insistence on the truth.

"It makes me wonder," James had told her, "if during all those years of training and preparation, the heart of a lion was lurking, waiting, biding his time until he could pounce and show his strength. I hate to say it, but his father would have been proud of him today. He would have hated his stance, but would have been proud of his delivery."

"Is that good?" she wondered. "Andrew, a lion like his father?"

He laughed. "Christopher was no lion—he was a vicious weasel. He imagined himself a lion but never was. I believe those men thought when Andrew took the throne they would have someone they could finally manipulate. When he left that room today, I don't think they knew what to do. They had been so sickeningly placating in their presentation I feared Julia would take the bait. She never had the chance. Andrew ... roared and they shook."

"What did she think? How did she react to his ... roaring?"

"She whispered to me that she hopes this last month passes quickly because it's time for a true ruler to own the throne."

At supper they ate quietly, both weary from not merely the day, but from two months, or perhaps even twenty years of unending stress. She wouldn't say it, but she was elated to watch him eat so eagerly. She had feared it might irritate whatever had made his stomach sick the last days of his imprisonment, but his strength seemed to return with his appetite.

"How are you?" she finally ventured as they had their dessert on the couch.

"How am I what?" he replied. "Physically, emotionally, royally?"

She giggled. "Yes."

"Ah, well," he mused, "I'm rather ugly at the moment ... on all levels."

"Stop that! I won't have you talking about yourself that way."

"Oooo," he teased. "Getting bossy and demanding now, are you? The princess is giving the prince a taste of his own medicine?"

"As I see it, you did nothing more today than put out a few pointless fires."

He sighed and laid back in the recliner. "There is so much to do in this kingdom—I don't know where to start. What's even step number one? I'd love to fire every one of those self proclaimed aristocrats and send them out on the streets, but they were elected by their own kind, so I'll honor that. But I don't have to honor them or bow to their sticking their royal noses into my mother's business."

"Hear, hear!" she clapped. "I wish I could have been a fly on the wall when everyone left."

"What angers me more, though, is that many of the royals will blame *you* for this. They won't think I have the fortitude to decide this on my own. They'll spin it all around until they've concluded I've been poisoned and blinded and am nothing more than a puppet of some subversive agenda."

"I don't care what they think about me—I never have. But what do you want them to think?"

He looked over to her wearily and shook his head. "Something they won't—that I'm smart ... capable ... totally aware of their delusions. But that, therein, is where the real problem lies. The royals are pampered and blind and somehow believe that's how it should be. Their whole way of life is based on pretense at this point. It's a joke really, but no one ever laughs. The commoners are forced into a substandard existence—they don't it funny. The royals cling to a past of bloodlines so polluted but ignored—they dare not laugh for fear of investigation." He chuckled. "Maybe we should have mandatory blood screenings and post the results in the newspapers."

"Oh, that would stir the pot for sure." She ambled up from her seat and crawled into his lap. "It seems you've had a lot of time on your hands lately to think about things."

"A couple of months," he shrugged. "Had nothing better to do."

She ran her hand over his prickly head and then traced it down his smooth cheek. "Daddy says you've become a lion." She growled softly in his ear.

"Did he now? Is that good or bad?"

"I just think the cub has finally awakened." She drew her finger over his lips. "He's been there all the time but somehow knew his roar would only be wasted until the pride recognized him as king."

He pulled her into a kiss, deep and long, shifting their bodies on the seat until they were side by side. "I'm so thankful I have you," he breathed. "Because right now ... there is no crown, there is no roar, there is no nation—there's only us. And that's the only thing I've ever really wanted."

"Well, then," she gently touched his nose, "wish granted."

U U U

The group of men sat around the den of Averill Braisogn with their brandies and long faces. Their plan to keep the suicide of the king under wraps had utterly failed, and they wondered if this would now be the way of things. The discussions were bleak and fearful as they processed the unexpected behavior of Andrew Braisogn earlier that day.

Averill addressed them soberly, yet hopefully. "I think what we must keep in mind is that the boy has been through an overwhelming experience. I don't believe this is necessarily an indication of how he plans to rule. Let's face it—he was awakened last night from a prison cell. That has been his life for two months. Once his routine gets back to normal, I feel he will be more reasonable and accepting of how things are. He's never expressed any real desire to rule—it's rather opposite his nature. He's the artistic-musician type—a creative temperament. Politics, I imagine, is far from his interests. I'm sure he'll be pleased to have a council of experienced men who can guide him in directing the country."

The men nodded in support. This was what they wanted to believe.

Mortimer Cunningham, however, would not let the suggestion settle. "I think your first mistake is referring to the crowned prince as a boy." He stood, placed his glass on the mantle and stuck a hand in his pocket. "That was no boy we faced today. That was a man who had been utterly humiliated and degraded by his king ... who unfortunately was also his father. And while he froze and starved in that cesspool, we, gentlemen, sat in our comfy rooms drinking our expensive liquors discussing how we could continue doing that for centuries to come ... never lending a hand to the search for proof of his innocence via proof of the king's guilt and deception."

"But we didn't realize the king had lied," a man defended.

"Please," Mortimer quieted him. "We all knew—we ... all ... knew." He took his glass and emptied it before continuing. "Our strategy from the past is going to have to change. If we want to continue in this," he motioned toward the luxury of the room, "then we are going to have to play a new game."

Averill questioned him warily, "And what game might that be?"

He sighed and shook his head slowly. "I have no idea. Most of us were the peers of Christopher's parents. They gave us free reign—literally. They had no cares for politics and considered it a relief of a great burden to let us have our way. Then Christopher was so bent on restoring the nobility of the royals his parents had made a mockery of, any suggestion we made was always accepted." He toyed with his empty glass, running his fingers around the rim. "If a worst case scenario could have been drawn, I believe this would be it. The present king mistreats the future king and then leaves the mess unanswered. The future king comes to power with a vendetta, and the only ones who can pay are those who supported his enemy."

"Good gosh!" another man exclaimed. "Christopher was his father! Everyone makes mistakes! Surely the boy has some affection for the man and will let this all go!"

"Tsk, tsk, tsk," Mortimer clucked. "I heard no affection in his voice today. I'm afraid, however, that I do hear the winds of change, gentlemen. Prepare yourselves."

Averill stood abruptly and pointed accusingly at Mortimer. "Whose side are you on exactly?"

"My side! I have lived comfortably with my head in the sand assuming things would always be as they are! Don't accuse me, Averill, of switching loyalties here! I am simply facing the facts which the rest of you seem to be ignoring! Andrew Braisogn has no desire to cater to bloodlines or royals or affluence or privilege. For mercy's sake—he married Evie Dorvain! If nothing else, that woman could convince him to imprison us all after the way she and her mother were treated!"

"No one knew they were of royal blood!"

"Exactly! Yet they were disdained by us all!" Mortimer shook his finger. "We have been shamed, gentlemen. And we were shamed again today. Were Christopher Braisogn still here with us, we would have no worries. He would snap a finger and all our problems would magically disappear." He grabbed up his coat and stated, "But he is gone, and he has left us with a massive mess to deal with. We have no absolute monarch in our corner any longer to cater to our whims and wishes." He gave them a nod. "Good day, gentlemen—or should I say, good luck."

☙ Chapter Thirty-Five ❧

Andrew had not wanted excessive pomp and circumstance surrounding his coronation, but other than the pardons, his mother had done nothing as queen for the month. She insisted the event be memorable, and as she was still in control of the nation, she would do as she wished and he would comply. Begrudgingly he went through the motions yet found vindication as Evangeline also took her oath and received a crown. Although very pregnant, she dazzled the nation with her grace and beauty, and the pregnancy only added to her glow. Thankfully his mother understood how he detested receiving lines, so hours of meaningless greetings were dismissed once the crowning had taken place.

Had the coronation occurred even a hundred years ago, the entire nation would have celebrated for days with feasts and fairs and well wishing for the new king and queen. But the last deeds of Christopher Braisogn still hung heavy in the air. The commoners were affronted at the brazen deception and uncensored control he had wielded. The royals were terrified that their privilege was about to be stripped away and their influence greatly diminished. The biggest burden, however, was on the new king as the fate of the nation lay in his hands. Change must come, but it must be slow, calculated, decisive and above all, fair. He had to set aside his ache for vengeance and simply embrace what was best for everyone.

♉ ♉ ♉

"You're going to do fine," Evangeline assured her husband as he prepared for his first congressional address the day after the coronation. "You've thought this through and have come up with a perfect solution."

"Not perfect, just workable."

"I disagree—it's the perfect solution toward a definitive change."

The door sounded.

"That would be Max and Hamilton," he breathed nervously. "I hate thinking I must be escorted by security to simply travel across the street to the capitol."

She gave him a quick kiss and a warm smile. "Stop being negative—it could be worse."

He raised an eyebrow. "How?"

She reached up and ran her fingers through his perfectly combed hair. "You could still be bald."

He chuckled and removed her hand, then kissed it and headed back to the bathroom to brush through his hair again. "Get the door and tell them I'm on my way ... just having to fix my wife's messes on top of the nation's!"

"A king's work is never done!"

♇ ♇ ♇

"Gentlemen," Andrew began, "and ladies," he nodded to the only two women in congress, both commoners as the royals had always felt that taboo, "I welcome you to a new regime. I know this must be difficult for many of you seeing as you have served this country for decades, and then you must sit respectfully under a man more than half your age who just walks in with the power to change your destinies." He paused and looked across the great chamber. "I don't find that quite fair myself. However, be assured that from the time I was five years old all the way to yesterday, I was tutored, drilled, rehearsed, mandated, lectured, exercised and trained to take this place ... on this day ... to lead this nation in greatness.

"I know many rumors have been thrown around over the years, one being that I'm merely *the third king*, the flunky beneath two brothers who should have ruled instead." Many shifted at the thought of his knowing that nickname. "However, they chose their paths, and I have accepted mine. Therefore, by constitutional right, I am no flunky—make sure you understand that right now. Should a more noble man be in my place? Possibly. But as fate would have it—whether you believe in fate or not—I am here ... and I am your king.

"I also know there are concerns that my wife will have a huge effect on my ideas and thinking, and that somehow whatever decisions I choose to make will be unfairly predisposed to her rationale. Let me assure everyone here today—the biggest influence on any decision I will ever make as your king will be none other than your former king, Christopher Braisogn. Trust me when I tell you that anything I ever do in regard to this nation, this government—it is directly related to him."

The shifting began again coupled with murmurs this time.

"Having said all that let me make it clear that I believe the time has come for change."

"Hear, hear!" yelled a man from the back. The murmuring grew louder.

"Please," Andrew commanded as he put up his hand for silence. "When one man has fifty-one percent of the power in a country which claims to be a constitutional monarchy, what you have is a joke."

Averill Braisogn stood to his feet and declared, "A joke doesn't run a country effectively for over eight hundred years!"

Murmurs of agreement sounded. The king waited for the room to quiet before he continued. "Representative Braisogn," he addressed directly, "how about I show you personally the effectiveness of a supreme monarch? You've disrespectfully interrupted my speech. Suppose I call the guards to arrest you then haul you off to Razewwell where you will be isolated in a damp cell with no toilet. Then I will command they feed you twice a day—an ample breakfast, but only broth and bread in the evening. Your head will be shaved, your clothes will be changed once a week, and you will be allowed a bath once a week. And when I see no sense of remorse for your action today, I will give you even less food. And when your body can no longer stand the physical limits it's been subjected to, I will offer no relief as you vomit in one bucket while sitting on another with diarrhea." Neither the king nor the representative moved as Andrew paused. "Fortunately for you, it would be the middle of April and not winter." Andrew stepped away from the platform, and resting his hand on one side of the lectern, he added, "That is the nature of our eight hundred years."

Much shifting and whispering started as he walked back to his notes. He looked down at Averill who was still standing. "Be seated, sir, and be glad I'm *not* my father. You condemn me for a desire to change because you have never known what it's like to be on the wrong end of our constitution. You've never been denied anything because of a status you inherited as a result of these eight hundred years. But just now you should have shaken in your shoes as I, the supreme ruler, suggested a tortuous punishment simply because I found you to be insulting. Be glad I question our constitution. Be glad I believe that all men should be treated equally and should be treated fairly, regardless of who they are or what their status of birth or bloodline might be."

All order was gone now as it melted into rantings of chaos. He hadn't meant to state that so soon in his address, but as he had stared down the defiant man who was making his own statement of resisting change, Andrew released it.

He held up his hand again as men argued across the aisles. Slowly they retreated and went to their seats.

"Please understand that I am not proposing a Robin Hood mentality here. I have no agenda to strip anything from anyone. I just want to be assured that if a man—or woman—sits on that side of the aisle," he pointed to the House of Commons, "he has the same opportunity and chance for advancement in life as a man who sits on that side." He pointed to the royals.

The entire House of Commons jumped to their feet, yelling and applauding with unbridled glee. To Andrew's surprise, many in the House of Royals did the same. Only a somber few sat stoically as if oblivious to the clamor.

The cheering went on several minutes. He allowed them time to process what he was suggesting before he began his proposal. Even with the obvious support he still felt guilty because no matter what anyone thought, the choice boiled down to him. He suddenly changed his speech.

"I wish," he began to speak. They quieted slowly and began to sit. "I wish," he repeated, "that things were already different. I wish this wasn't my plan that is being offered today. I wish that someone had paved the way already and that a vote would be taken which would be fair and measurable and would truly represent the heart of this nation. Unfortunately, that isn't possible … yet."

Again most of the room came to its feet. Men began to stomp in rhythm and chant Re-pub-lic! Re-pub-lic! He let them continue. For eight hundred years this government had been a sham. It was time to turn the page, and it was time to reveal the strategy.

"For fifteen years I have been schooled and groomed by the military to become a decisive and competent Commander in Chief. I have no desire to weaken this nation or make it susceptible to anything other than greatness. As I prepared for today, I wanted to assure you that nothing brash, thoughtless or instantaneous would take place. I also wanted to make sure that the creation of a new government would not be formed out of the mind of one man only. However, with two hundred of you here, it would be impossible to attempt. My suggestion … no, out of fairness lets call it what it is … my *mandate* is that each house elect six men who will serve on a committee that will examine the rule of law in other nations, that will determine what in our own constitution has worked for all men, and then create a new system of government."

The shifting and murmuring started again.

"The committee will also determine a time frame for which it can be properly instituted, deciding what is reasonable to allow for the change of power to occur. Elections for members will take place tomorrow …"

"That's too soon!" a royal yelled. "We need time to evaluate the thoughts and directions of each man."

"That's exactly why I'm giving you only twenty-four hours. Those of you planning to bribe and manipulate will only have a short time in which to do so. Hopefully we will have twelve representatives more concerned about the future of this nation than merely the placement of their bodies another term in this chamber."

The speech was over and the cheers were deafening. However, Andrew refused to either gloat or bask. He wanted out of the room immediately. Max and Hamilton flanked his sides as other security surrounded him and moved him toward the hallway. A few yards down the corridor, a man standing next to the wall gently lifted a finger to get his attention.

"May I have a word with you, your majesty?" he asked as he bowed low.

"I'd rather not," he replied.

"I'm sure, but a little advice from a royal might go a long way in helping you accomplish your goal."

Andrew had seen the face, but couldn't place him. "What's your name?"

"Mortimer Cunningham, your majesty, a representative in the House of Royals."

Andrew continued to stare. The man had to be in his late fifties or early sixties, but was very fit and impeccably groomed. "Where have I seen you before?"

"Unfortunately … at that little fiasco of a meeting prior to your father's funeral."

Andrew nodded as he remembered the group of men attempting to publicize his father's death as a brain disorder rather than suicide. "I don't know that I care to speak with you," he stated frankly.

"I'm sure, considering that particular meeting." Mortimer carried an air of confidence that Andrew found fascinating considering the man was obviously a part of the inner royal circle which he had just thrown to the dogs. "I'm just saying that a few allies on both sides of the aisle could go a long way in helping smooth over any wrinkles that might buckle up in time."

Andrew was curious, mainly because the man appeared so calm and assured, but he knew the style of the royals. They were deceptive to a fault, just like his father. What this man really wanted was an inside track to Andrew in order to manipulate and stay informed. This was exactly what he was hoping to destroy.

"I don't think so, Mr. Cunningham. I'm not going to be playing any sides here"

"That's what you hope, but unfortunately, not everyone will see that." He nonchalantly smoothed his designer jacket. "Right now you're being viewed as very one-sided, and if you hope to have the cooperation of both houses, it will require a little more finesse than just some heartfelt words and a stirring speech."

Andrew passed Max and walked up to the man. He carefully touched Mortimer's lapel, brushing it off as though a piece of lint were there. He then grasped the edge and pulled him directly up to his face. "Right now, I am the king. I don't need the cooperation of both houses. And sir, I most assuredly don't need *you*. I will be in no one's pocket. If you want some kind of inside track during this process, I strongly suggest you head back to the main hall and try to get your name on the ballot for a vote tomorrow. The day of clandestine meetings and secret exchanges is over. This government will be run as a government and not a farce, and men like you are going to have to learn how to fit into the machine instead of trying to drive the whole thing in the direction of your personal preference."

He let go, smoothed Mortimer's collar again, and started down the hallway. All he wanted right now was to see his wife, not his queen, and to dream about the day when he no longer was the king.

෨ Chapter Thirty-Six ෬

(Eight Months Later)

"Shhhhh," Evangeline shushed as she nuzzled her giggling seven month old hoping he would either go back to sleep or nurse a while longer. "Your daddy has a big day today and needs his sleep. He's going to be awfully grumpy if you wake him up."

"Da-da-da-da-da," the baby cooed loudly, his favorite word.

"No," she whispered. "Let Dada sleep."

"Too late," Andrew groaned as he joined them in the living area.

"I'm so sorry. I tried to keep him quiet but it appears he's intent on joining the sunshine this morning."

"Good for him." He reached over and tickled his son's tummy. "I couldn't sleep anyway—doubt I've slept more than two hours all night."

"Da-da-da-da!"

Andrew held out his arms. "Come here, Gabriel. Give Dada some advice today."

"You know he's not really saying *Dada* yet," she informed him. "He's just trying out syllables and apparently he's fixated on the D's at the moment."

He tossed the baby into the air and caught him on the fall. "Keep telling yourself that. I never pegged you for a sore loser."

"I am not a sore loser," she gave him a gentle punch. "I'm just helping you be realistic."

"Da-da-da!"

"There you go," Andrew laughed as he tossed him again. "You know who your Dada is!"

"Da!" the baby giggled again.

Evangeline stood and stretched. "I suppose I should go ahead and start some coffee. Want me to make breakfast now?"

He rose and whirled the baby around a few times as he followed her into the kitchen. "Might as well. I'm not going back to sleep, and apparently this little guy isn't either."

She smiled as she removed the eggs, bacon and bread while watching the two interact. Maybe this was the best start for Andrew's day after all. As he faced the congress with the new constitution and moderated the vote, he needed to remember all of this was to protect the right of every father to share mornings like this with their children. Christopher had never teased or played with his boys. He'd never sneaked eggs to them at breakfast, or taken them outside to watch the birds and squirrels, or rolled a ball across the floor with them. His only goal had been to prepare them for the crown—a goal at which he had utterly failed.

"You know today's going to be a breeze," she tried to encourage. "The discussion and the vote are just formalities you insisted upon for the sake of fairness." She grinned as she set a cup of coffee before him. "You're still king, remember? Just forget it all and say, *Hear, ye! Hear, ye! I now declare this constitution constitutional!*"

He took his coffee and shook his head as he wrestled the mug from Gabriel's exploring hands. "Such a comedienne you are. As tempting as that is, I wouldn't dare."

"You could always take my tablet and play games while the royals argue their points."

"Oh, no—I intend to listen, take notes, and respond to every attack. I will not passively force this through. If they want a final fight, I will certainly grant them that."

She sipped her coffee and ran her fingers through her tangled hair. "I think I'll just stay in my pajamas today, play with my baby, and then nurse my Candy Crush addiction when he naps."

He grunted. "Aren't you supposed to be making my eggs, woman?"

"Aye, aye," she saluted with a spatula. "By the way, your mother will be spending Christmas with us."

"I thought we were spending Christmas at your father's."

"We are."

His brows furrowed. "That's a little ... *creepy* ... isn't it?"

"Andrew Braisogn! You did not just say that! Your mother deserves to have a Christmas like never before this year."

"Well, I guarantee if she's at your father's it will be like never before."

"I thought you enjoyed Christmas last year?"

"I loved it," he assured her as he pushed his mug away from Gabriel's reach. "We used to literally dress in military attire, Mother in a formal gown, as a page read the names on the gifts and passed them out one by one. At your father's we stayed in our pajamas until lunch!"

"And wasn't it wonderful?"

He gazed up to the ceiling mulling the memories. Looking back toward her, a gentle smile evolved. "One of the best days of my life."

"As I said, your mother deserves a Christmas like that."

"I suppose," he was doubtful. "It'll just be …"

"Don't say it," she pointed the spatula at him. "It won't be *creepy*. Maybe you deserve the day you're about to have with that kind of attitude."

"Ugh, nobody deserves the day I'm about to have."

Handing the baby to his mother, Andrew excused himself to the bathroom. She put down the spatula and rumpled his dark head. "You did good, little one. Dada—we've practiced hard on that."

"Da-da-da-da-da!"

"That's right … keep it up. He needs all the support he can get right now."

What could have been a one hour presentation and vote, turned into a ten hour drudge match. Seven persistent men led by the sober face of Averill Braisogn, all from the House of Royals, debated every item of the constitution that had been changed or added. True to his word, Andrew granted them the fight. The congress had been given notes of all the meetings, and at the beginning of the week had received a copy of the completely revised constitution. They had been allowed to debate all points already during the eight months of its modification, and he had carefully organized his notes from the past to reiterate what had already been discussed. Patiently he listened to each argument—again—and jotted thoughts to add to his notes. Occasionally he would allow a member from the committee to address a certain point, but he wanted this group of rogue representatives to remember that Christopher Braisogn was the ultimate reason behind the change. No matter the debate, the former king was used as an example of how each supposed protection could be overrun simply because he had the power to do so.

"I believe that covers everything," Andrew proclaimed when the last issue had been defended. "It's now time to put it to a vote. And yes, we are seeking a majority, not a plurality. We will not make this change if it isn't what the country wants. You've talked with your constituents, and if you are truly men and women of character, today you will vote according to their desires. As I said from the beginning, I will not cast a ballot. The desire of the king is not what's at stake today. If I voted, this would pass with an overwhelming majority considering I carry fifty-one percent." He turned to the dissenters. "You and your consorts, Representatives Braisogn and Cunningham, should take great comfort in that, if indeed it is your genuine wish to do what's best for this country."

He motioned for the technician to start the voting. The young man smiled knowingly as he pulled up the program on the central computer and pressed the launch button. Immediately the congress began making their single choices, and within ten minutes the result was ready. He printed the final count and handed it to Andrew.

With no showiness but great control, the king announced, "The motion carries with eighty-eight percent." The room roared, and the seven royals who had fought the process prepared to exit. "Don't leave just yet." He quieted the room quickly and continued reading from the paper. "The breakdown was one hundred seventy-six for, sixteen against, and eight abstaining." Andrew stared soberly at the men who had stood their ground against the change. "Gentlemen, this was not a vote against you. You nobly held your position and valiantly fought for your preference. You are to be applauded for following the process of a true republic." He then looked up toward the risers where the rest of the houses sat. "As for those who abstained—shame on you. I should release your names to the nation and let them know that you are not representatives who vote the will of the people. Instead you are cowards, or even worse, spoiled brats who would prefer to take your toys and go home rather than participate in this historic experience.

"As agreed, for the next two years you will all remain as the legislative body, each house holding one-third power. I will act as sitting president with the final third of the vote through veto power, however, there is provision to override that should both houses concur. After two years, having made any amendments we as a group deem necessary, we will prepare to launch national elections within six months of that time."

Cheering began as most were ecstatic with the results. The committee had labored for eight months, often working late into the evening, sometimes even morning, to accomplish this. It hadn't been easy considering two of the men were staunchly against it. They had learned early that nothing would be unanimous, but it was actually beneficial to have a couple of devil's advocates to present obstacles for each consideration. The result was a constitution for a full republic and the abolishment of even a constitutional monarchy at the insistence of Andrew. It would serve no purpose except to perpetuate the division of bloodlines, and he was ready for him and his family to disappear into anonymity.

"Ladies and gentlemen, my last order as king is that you all have a joyous and merry Christmas. We'll resume at the start of the new year and begin a new order in the history of Braisognia. I declare this session over." He sounded the gavel.

Julia seemed overwhelmed as the final gift was opened. She had been pleasant throughout the holidays, but now a tear escaped and Evangeline was confused.

"Julia? Is everything all right?"

The gracious woman smiled and nodded as she caressed her grandson who was desperately trying to get wrapping paper into his mouth. "Oh, yes," she choked. "This has been unspeakably wonderful. Last year it was just Christopher and I. I thought it pointless to even attempt a celebration, but he insisted. He spent most of his time ranting about his ungrateful sons and the made-up impropriety of his daughters-in-law." She gently kissed the top of Gabriel's dark hair. "This actually reminds me of Christmases growing up—the informality, the personal nature of the gifts," she wiped the tear, "and the sweet expressions of love."

Evangeline noted, "You never speak about your family. Why haven't you visited them this year?"

Sighing, the former queen explained, "Because they no longer exist. Mine and your situations were similar. My parents struggled for years to have a child. When I was finally born, a girl who could not inherit the throne, they kept trying for another child, but to no avail. The line would end with my father. He had no siblings so a new legacy began with a cousin. They thought marrying me off to the handsome crowned prince of Braisognia would be the perfect solution to their dilemma. I would still become a queen and be able to perpetuate the royal lineage—just in another country—and they could move in with us and we would all live happily ever after. Within a month of my marriage, Christopher forced me to cut all ties with my parents."

Evangeline seethed. "Are you kidding? Why would he do that? How could he do that?"

She shook her head. "It was the beginning of his ability to control, and he relished it. My parents were quite aged, and within ten years they both had died."

"From broken hearts, I would imagine."

Julia shrugged. "That possibly added to it. My mother had always been very sickly, and my father was extremely overweight—something of which Christopher often reminded me. He controlled my eating from the day we married, always concerned that I would pack on the pounds like my father and become a source of embarrassment for him."

James interrupted, apparently wanting to lighten the mood and change the conversation. "Well, there will be no monitoring of food intake at the Dorvain house. In fact, as I smell the roasting turkey, I suggest we clean up this mess, head to the kitchen and then stuff ourselves to the point of misery."

Andrew stood in agreement. "Hear, hear! The man makes an excellent point." He then turned to his wife. "Don't eat too much though. When Gabriel goes down for his nap, I want the two of us to ride out to the waterfall."

She frowned. "I'm not really up for a horse ride today."

"No problem," he piped. "We'll take that motorized contraption of yours instead."

♉ ♉ ♉

Sitting beside the warming fire and staring out toward the majestic Braisognian Mountains behind the water, Andrew gently kissed his wife. "This is the most awesome place in the whole world. Thanks for coming out here. I could never find it on my own."

"We can't stay too long, though. Gabriel will be up in a little while and will want his mommy."

"And he's got two adoring grandparents ready to take his mind off his mommy for as long as is necessary."

"True," she smiled peacefully. She looked up at him and asked, "So of all the places you've been to in this world, this is your favorite?"

"First, I haven't been to many places—that was *your* family," he reminded her as he thought of all the photographs throughout the house of wondrous sites and smiles. "Second, how could anything compare to this?"

She nodded. "It is beautiful—probably my most favorite place too, come to think of it."

He stood and offered his hand to help her up.

"We're leaving the fire?" she grumbled.

"I just wanted to dream with you a moment."

"You can't dream by the fire?"

"Stop whining," he retorted as he pulled her up and began walking away from the waterfall area. "I'm serious. In two and a half years this whole royal thing will be over. I won't be anything—not king, not acting president—nothing. We've got to make plans about what happens next."

"We can move in with my father. You love it here."

He shook his head. "That's your father's home—your father's legacy. We need our own." He held out his hands to a small rise in the forest. "Right here," he beamed, "this could be *our* legacy."

"What do you mean? Here? This? You want to live in the shed back there?"

"I want to build," he revealed, "and I want it here on this small hill. I want to sit," he pointed up, "in a gabled nook on the second floor with my piano and guitar overlooking this scene as I write music. I want a balcony," he pointed up to a different side, "right off our bedroom there where I can gaze at the moonlight reflecting on the snow-covered peaks, or on the

268

water," he turned to her and lifted her chin, "or in your eyes." He softly brushed his lips across her forehead. "I want peace, I want love … I want this … and that's all I'll want."

She stroked his beard and then ran her fingers through his flowing, dark locks. Smiling, she kissed him deeply, pulled back and touched the end of his nose. "Wish granted," she whispered. "But we'd better make it a big house."

"As big as you like."

"Well, it appears Gabriel's going to have a brother or sister this next year."

His eyes grew wide and his heart swelled. "Really?" He stared for confirmation.

"Why else would I give up a horse ride?"

"We'll have a big house for a big family—a really big family."

Touching his nose again, she affirmed, "Wish granted."

℘ Chapter Thirty-Seven ℘

(Two Years Later)

As thunder threatened in the background, Gabriel ran through his home blowing a wooden flute and singing sweetly, "Toot, toot! Wake up, Michael! Wake up, birds! Toot, toot! Mommy's gots eggs, Michael! Toot, too! Wake up!"

Evangeline looked at her husband over the rim of her juice glass and pleaded, "Tell me you did not get him an actual horn for Christmas."

Andrew grinned sheepishly. "Okay, I won't tell you ... again." He swallowed the last of his coffee.

A flash of lightning pierced the room followed by another explosion of thunder.

"Mommy!" came a sweet cry from the room that had belonged to George.

"Michael's awake—what Gabriel couldn't accomplish, Mother Nature did. I'm not sure which to blame this morning," she quipped as she pushed her body from the table trying to avoid scraping her increasingly growing tummy against it.

"Hey, I wanted girls, remember? Quieter, sweeter ... you know ... more feminine and less rambunctious."

She glared at him before moving to the door. "And I had no control over that. Just wait—in six months you'll be home with all of us ... all the time ... and this one will be another loud part of it all by then."

He stood and gave her a quick kiss. "And you can't imagine how I long for that." He glanced at the clock. "I've got to move."

"Yeah, yeah, yeah," she caressed his beard. "It's always something. Where are you off to today?"

"Not sure—Jimmy said I had a strange meeting request. With the vote up tomorrow and then Christmas vacation, my window of time is limited."

"Strange?" she scrunched her nose as Michael gave another yell for Mommy.

"My reaction too," he said turning toward the bedroom. "That's why I'm meeting early—curious to hear about this."

Another crash sounded from the impending storm, and the lights flickered.

Evangeline opened the door and shrieked at the sight of her youngest son. "What on earth have you done?"

Gabriel ran to the scene. "Thatsa lotsa poop, Mommy."

The baby had removed his diaper and painted himself and his crib in deep brown.

♗ ♗ ♗

Having learned the request was from Alfred in his prison cell, Andrew had initially declined. The last thing he wanted was a reminder of his father at this historic time. Tomorrow the congress would vote to officially instate the new government and abolish the monarchy. Whatever the old man had to say could wait until after Christmas, but his curiosity got the best of him. If nothing else he could let him know that he had risen above the system his tutor had so vehemently embraced and was about to abolish it forever.

As barred doors slid open and slammed shut, he had to fight the sick feeling rising from his stomach at remembering his own imprisonment. He had been so busy the past years working toward the changes, he had thought little of his father and Alfred—two men who had supposedly cared for him yet thrown him into an inhumane hell-hole simply because they could. Not anymore. No one man was perfect, and power left unchecked could drive the best of men to heinous sin.

Alfred hadn't changed. The only difference was that he was wearing prison blues instead of the black tux and tails he had always donned. Andrew had never seen him in anything else until now.

The guard asked, "Would you like to visit in the cell, sir, or remain outside?"

Andrew moved to the metal chair beside the bars and took a seat. "Outside will be fine—I won't be here long."

A long roll of thunder sounded and rain began to pound the roof and windows.

Alfred stood, perhaps a little more feebly than before, and requested, "May we be left alone, please?"

Andrew raised a suspecting brow.

"That would be up to the president," the guard replied. He looked to Andrew. Another crash of lightning.

Shrugging, he motioned him toward the exit. "Why not? You guys have cameras, right? In case he pulls out a gun or something?"

The guard sternly assured him, "I guarantee he has no gun or weapon of any kind."

"I'm good then," Andrew smiled. "You may leave."

The guard eyed Alfred warily then opened the door to go, deliberately letting it remain ajar. He looked back in and offered, "I'll be just out here. Yell if you need me."

Andrew nodded then looked back at the elder man with a cautious expression. "I don't have a lot of time, Alfred, so say what you have to say—quickly." The rain grew louder.

"Understood, sir." Still respectful and soft spoken. "There are some things I feel you should know just out of honor for who you are and all you've done."

That caught him by surprise. "Honor?"

"Of course, sir. I have nothing but respect and appreciation for all you've accomplished after all you've been through."

Nodding carefully, he urged, "Go ahead."

"What you are about to do, you think is the result of two and a half years of hard work and planning. But the ground was laid decades before." Alfred took his own chair and set it directly in front of Andrew. "Shortly after your father became king, it was obvious to many on the inside of the palace and the government that this was a man with a short fuse and a long agenda. We knew we were in for many years of tyrannical decisions and illogical leadership. We were powerless to do anything. Our generation, under your father's whims, was helpless, but if we could possibly mold the next monarch to think openly and compassionately, change was a possibility. Because we accepted that this would be an unbearably slow process, we had to commit to incremental steps toward the goal—a true republic in Braisognia."

Andrew gaped at what the man was suggesting. "You're saying you're directly responsible for what's about to occur in the government tomorrow? You? My father's right hand man?"

Boom! Both men jumped from the storm as the lights dashed off for a second.

"I am only one of many," he continued. "We strategically placed men as tutors and mentors to the three princes in hopes of molding one to the throne with ideas very different from his father. George and Peter lacked both the compassion and fortitude to carry out what we needed."

"What just a minute." Andrew snarled. "Are you taking responsibility for my brothers' abdications?"

Giving a slight nod to the side, he admitted, "Yes. It wasn't difficult. Your father had so berated them that planting the suggestion of his watchful eye forever condemning any leadership they might offer ... well ... it was quite simple. Then bring along a beautiful, sympathetic young woman into the picture—the deal ... and the abdications ... were sealed."

Andrew's heart pounded, his insides quivered. He willed himself to remain in control and not let Alfred see the frustration reeling through him. He clasped his hands together then swallowed hard. "And me?" he wondered fearfully.

"Ah," the old man smiled warmly. "You were the perfect prince. You were handsome, pliable, eager to take up the slack of your brothers. You were compassionate, and with a bit of suggestion and influence, you were able to see the plight of the commoners. For you, yourself, were the victim of a vicious royal."

"You never once told me to feel sorry for the commoners! In fact, you made it clear—every day—that I was above them and their kind! You showed disdain for anyone who dared think a commoner should rise above his circumstances or ever be more than a lowly non-royal bloodline!"

"Of course, that was my duty as your mentor ... as the man your father chose to direct you to the throne. I also made sure you abhorred me as much as you abhorred your father. He had the eye of a hawk, and one small slip would have sent me ... well ... probably here." He motioned to the cell. "And I would have accomplished nothing. However, your tutors in both school and the military were carefully chosen. The men who would influence your ideas the most were very different from your father ... and supposedly me."

As the rain grew louder, Andrew actually wondered if he had heard the feeble voice correctly through the noise. He began to replay the years of training and schooling. Many faces stood out—good men with high character whom he knew believed things they never directly said but often alluded to.

"And then there was the matter of," Alfred paused and looked at him painfully, "Miss Dorvain."

Crash! Boom! Lights flickering.

Andrew snapped his head up. "What about Evangeline?"

"Your father wanted the entire Dorvain family banned from the palace after the first ball where you played together so innocently. We realized that *she* could be a major key in the whole setup."

Sweat was now forming inside his collar and the quivering of fear was morphing into anger. "What key? What are you saying?"

"Convincing your father that such a ban would be an affront to many royals and possibly cause a revolt of some whom he desperately needed to remain on his side was complicated. We managed ... and as we hoped, the friendship blossomed.

"Then when Giselle died, a plan we had been working through—the

273

issue with Dexter Braisogn … well … the timing was perfect. We had to concoct some papers quickly, but when you have people desperate for change, you can make things happen."

"What papers?" he gritted.

"DNA tests, of course—undeniable proof that Giselle was Dexter's daughter."

"But she was his daughter, right? You just needed the evidence immediately."

Alfred sighed, leaned back and crossed his arms. "No. It was a well executed plan, and timing was in our favor. Who would have thought, however, that you would have been so noble?"

For the second time in his life, Andrew uttered a profanity. "You are lying!" He stood and ran a shaky hand through his sweaty hair. "I suppose you're going to say James Dorvain was in on all this too!"

"Actually, he was clueless. The fewer we brought into the scheme, the less the chance of discovery. James honestly believes his half-blooded wife and daughter are the descendants of Dexter." He offered an almost wicked smile. "He deserves to believe that, however, considering all he was put through. We would appreciate you keeping that our little secret."

Another string of thunder roared, and Andrew looked to the window. The rain escalated his apprehension. Balling his fist as he tried to control the overwhelming impact this information was having, he asked, "And the whole marriage disinformation issue concerning Section Seven? Was that real?"

Alfred shook his head. "That was created after Peter's abdication. Your father was indeed drunk beyond reason. I planted it in his mind, and he took the bait. All I had to do was steer you away from the information as long as possible."

Andrew now began to pace. All his life he had thought one thing—if he became king, he would change Braisognia. Now he realized it was possibly a ploy. He had been nothing more than a pawn in an extremely long game, and everything he had done was at the bidding of men who had manipulated him since a child. He felt like a fool. He'd rather have never known than to walk into that chamber tomorrow realizing he had done nothing. "Why exactly are you telling me this … now?"

"As I said, I respect you too much to not have you know the truth. What you are doing is a very good thing, but you indeed were used as a means to an end. If you signed that document tomorrow, ending the monarchy and declaring Braisognia a true republic without knowing what I have revealed to you, it would not be of your own doing—and you deserve that honor. Tomorrow needs to be *your* choice, not mine nor any of the others involved. I merely tell you this because I believe you are a good man with a good heart and you deserve to make this decision without any hidden guile."

"And you expect me to believe this? You? The man who led the slaughter of innocent Braisognians that sent me to Razewwell? You, who sat by and watched my father bring me to utter humiliation? Why should I believe a word you've said?"

"Because I'm the one who executed your father to prevent him from carrying out a second attack—this time on innocent Braisognian civilians—to force his war and keep you off the throne."

"Executed? He committed suicide!"

Alfred shook his white head. "I knew it was over. I knew the country and the military would never support him after the video's release. A second attack would have been purely murderous. I knew the time had finally come."

Andrew collapsed into the chair and placed his head in his hands.

"One other thing," Alfred added cautiously.

Andrew looked up hesitantly. "What else could you possibly tell me?"

"It's only fair that you know everything." His pause was foreboding. "Miss Dorvain has been in on this since she was fifteen. We chose her to be your bride."

Boom!

♔ ♔ ♔

Andrew burst through the door of his home as another crash of lightning lit up the room. Evangeline had only seen him look this determined when he had addressed the nation about his father's death after his imprisonment.

"You!" Andrew bellowed at her. Both boys, asleep on her lap, jumped from the yell.

"And good morning to you too," she said with sarcasm as she pulled a now whimpering Michael up to her shoulder. "Do you know how long it took me to get them to sleep in the midst of this storm?"

"You!" he screamed again. "How could you … why … I …" He sputtered and stammered as he began to pace in the living area.

While Michael continued crying, Gabriel rubbed his sleepy eyes and observed, "Daddy mad."

Andrew glared at him and commanded, "Shut up!"

Crash! Lightning surged again, causing the lights to dim a few moments. Gabriel screamed.

As quickly as she could manage in her condition, Evangeline maneuvered herself and Michael up from the couch. "That's enough! Whatever is irking you has nothing to do with these children!"

"Don't you tell me anything!" He looked to Gabriel. "Go to your room!"

"Why?" the toddler wondered.

"I said to go to your room! Now!"

The little boy began sobbing and ran to the door of his and Michael's quarters as another peal roared. He screamed in terror.

"It's okay, sweetie," she assured him. "Play with your flute and Michael and I will be there in just a minute. It's only thunder. It won't bother us." He opened the door and rushed inside as she turned back to Andrew. "What in heaven's name has gotten into you?"

"Alfred just told me everything! *Everything!* How all these men pulled strings and made me a mere puppet all these years in order to bring down the monarchy and do exactly what I plan to do tomorrow!" He glared at her with pure hatred. "And he told me how you were a part of it all."

Her jaw dropped as her heart sank. "I have no idea what you're talking about."

"Really?" He took a step toward her and grabbed her free arm. "So you're denying it?"

She jerked free and stepped back. "Explain to me first what you're accusing me of so I can know whether I'm guilty or not!" Her loud voice caused Michael to cry harder.

"When you were fifteen, were you approached about trying to seduce me into a relationship and then woo me into marriage so I would have deeper sympathy for the mistreatment of commoners?"

"What?" She couldn't believe what he was asking. "The only thing that happened to me when I was fifteen where you were concerned was that I fell in love and lost my heart to a boy I knew I could never be with!"

"Then you deny it?"

"Of course! That never happened! No one ever approached me about such a thing."

The rain was loud taking the level of their arguing even higher.

"And what about the whole business of your mother being Dexter Braisogn's daughter? Did you know that was a fabrication? Did you go along with that too and find yourself disappointed when I chose to protect you rather than cage you?" He turned away and slammed his palm into his forehead. "What an idiot I was! Every one of you played me for a fool!"

Rocking Michael in her arms, she shook her head in astonishment. "And Alfred told you all this?"

He spun around. "So it's true, then!"

Lightning lit through the room and knocked out the lights completely a few more seconds as the crash sounded behind it.

"No!" she exclaimed. "None of this is true! At least where I'm concerned! For crying out loud, Andrew, I would have told you up front if someone had ever even suggested such a thing!"

"I don't know what to believe anymore—I don't know who to believe." He fell to the couch and cradled his head.

"Andrew," she eased herself down beside him. "You can always believe me. I've never lied to you, and I've certainly never used you." She touched his arm. "I love you."

"Don't!" he burst as he sprang from the couch. "I have twenty-four hours to decide whether my life has been one big game … or even worse … one big joke!"

"Are you saying you might not sign the vote tomorrow?"

He whipped around. "That would bother you in a big way, wouldn't it—seeing as you gave up an actual life to play house with me and persuade me to change our world!"

She stared in shock. "You don't believe me, do you? You think I'm guilty."

He merely stared, eyes dark, jaw tensed.

"Answer me," she demanded. "Do you think my love for you was real … or just some award winning performance seeing as I gave up everything to be with you … to bear your children?"

His expression remained unchanged.

She left the living area and started toward the bedroom.

"What are you doing?" he demanded to know as he followed.

"Something I never thought I would do … never thought I could do." She turned back toward him. "I'm taking the boys and I'm leaving."

"Leaving? Where?"

"We'll go to my father's house."

"For how long?"

She gave a chuckling gasp and shook her head. "I'm leaving *you*. I'm gone. It's over. The most real thing in my life has always been my feelings for you. If you don't accept that, I will not live a farce as your parents did." She placed Michael on the bed and headed for the closet.

"You will not turn tail and run out of here! I am still king and I can demand that you do exactly as I say!"

She slowly turned and gave him a defiant stare as disdain pulsed through her. "Congratulations, your majesty. Your father should be applauding from his grave right now because, for the first time in your life, you are behaving just like him. And let me be the first one to point this out to you—seeing as you've chosen to believe a man who's done nothing but sabotage the best things in your life—they lived by a code of deceit and manipulation. I know the part about me is a lie—therefore I'm convinced it all is. And the timing? Are you so blind to not see what Alfred and your father are doing?"

"My father's dead—it's only Alfred, and he felt I should know the truth! He respected me too much to let me do this without understanding the years of manipulation!"

"Them—Alfred and your father!"

"My father is dead!"

"Not today, he isn't! I'm staring straight at him! Apparently Alfred knew the single key to his resurrection, and he unlocked that unfortunate door this morning."

Boom! The lights finally surrendered.

⚉ ⚉ ⚉

Amy and Jimmy sat in candlelit darkness, stunned from Evangeline's call. They had gone from the incredible high of anticipating the signing of the new constitution to complete horror at Andrew's reaction to Alfred's revelation.

"Do you believe it's true?" Amy asked, shaking her head at the very idea. "Was all this some sort of game? I know the part about Evangeline is a lie. Jenna and I cried with her through all those years of trying to deal with her feelings."

Jimmy rubbed his temples. "I can't imagine it being true. Sure, we had a lot of progressive thinking professors and military leaders, but didn't you too? I figured any guy with half a brain in the twenty-first century would have to consider the whole class division thing an archaic joke."

"Absolutely! Anyone with a decent amount of education was actually humiliated by the whole mess."

Jimmy sighed and closed his eyes as he leaned back on the couch. "Do you have any aspirin? My head's killing me."

"Sure," she hopped up and proceeded cautiously in the darkness to the kitchen. "Something to drink with it?"

"You probably don't have what I'd like to drink right now."

"You're probably right." She hunted the aspirin and managed a glass of water then maneuvered carefully back to the couch.

"This is so disheartening," he confessed after swallowing the pills. "I had made some plans—really thought my life was shaping up. Now I don't know what to do."

"In what way? You'll still be his secretary. He's got six more months to be president before the election."

He gave her a hopeless stare. Even in the dimness she could make out his helplessness. "I can't work for him after this." He rubbed his aching temples again and squeezed his eyes shut. "He loved her—she was his whole life. If she had said the word he would have left everything for her."

"And she felt the same way. She couldn't believe he refused to marry her simply out of nobility. She even wondered if maybe he didn't really love her after all."

"Oh, he assuredly did—I knew him well. He said she was a butterfly, beautiful and free. Marrying her would have clipped her wings and he didn't have the heart for it. He didn't just love her—he adored her—he breathed her in as though she were the epitome of life itself." He turned back to Amy. "I wanted that too. I believed it was real."

"It was real. He's under a lot of pressure and isn't thinking clearly right now."

"No—you don't do that. You don't believe the buzzard over the butterfly."

She snickered, and he gave her a shocked stare.

"Amy, I'm serious! I was gonna propose to you tomorrow after the signing."

Her eyes grew wide and she grabbed her chest attempting to catch her breath. "What?"

"I know it's crazy. We haven't even dated or anything, but you're my butterfly. I'm sure of that. I thought we'd plan on having the wedding after the elections in the summer."

"Wait!" She put her hand up to stop him. "I'm totally baffled by your … wanting to marry me?" She shook her head. "Where did this come from?"

"We fit," he shrugged simply. "From the moment we met I knew we fit. Every conversation, every meeting, every stroll, everything—we fit."

She stood and began to pace as she rubbed the top of her arms. "Why didn't you tell me this before? Why now, or tomorrow, as was your plan? Why not years ago when you first thought we fit?"

Putting his head in his hands he tried to apply more pressure to his throbbing forehead. "Because I still felt like a worthless vagabond—a ne'er do well." He looked up at her. "I didn't believe I was worthy of you. But now," he stood and stepped toward her, "I've been a big part of something great. I've fought the system, I've stayed away from old habits—I've grown up." He sighed as he peered through the rain to the capitol. "And I've watched Evie and Andrew grow deeper in love than I ever thought possible."

He turned back to her and finally reached down for her hands. "If you don't feel the same, I understand. I'm totally prepared for your rejection. I'll move off somewhere so we never have to see each other again. But I have to take the chance that you love me too." He squeezed her hands. "I have to believe that you felt the connection."

The corners of her mouth edged upward and she shook her head in disbelief. "This is certainly a day for surprises. I didn't think anything could top Evie's call, but this … you win."

He placed his forehead down against hers. "I only win if you agree to marry me." He sighed. "If you don't, I should probably jump off the building or something to preserve my dignity. However, I'm nowhere near that noble, and I'm a big chicken—it would hurt really bad."

She chuckled. "If you lived through it."

"Oh, I'd live through it—that's my luck."

Still holding hands, she stepped back to see up into his eyes. "We *do* fit. I would never let myself accept it, though. I just figured you were friendly with all the girls."

"Nah, I don't really like girls much," he teased. "They're mostly weird and kind of mean, to be honest." He pulled her closer. "Except you." He looked deeper into her eyes and stopped smiling. "But then, you're not really a girl—you're a butterfly."

She whispered, "Oh … my … gosh—you're gonna make me cry."

"That's not what I was going for. I was hoping for maybe a nice smile and a simple Yes, Jimmy, I'd love to marry you."

Easing her arms up around his neck, she smiled through tears and breathed, "*Yes, Jimmy, I'd love to marry you.*"

Without hesitation he kissed her and pulled her close. "Thank goodness—I really didn't want to jump out the window in the middle of this storm."

❧ Chapter Thirty-Eight ❧

When Andrew signed the vote, the previously solemn chamber was filled with shouts of celebration. *How many know?* he wondered as he made his way from the platform toward the exit. *How many in this room know that I'm nothing more than a puppet?*

"Excellent thing you've done here," a young representative told him as he walked through the door. "Our nation now offers hope for everyone, not just a select few."

He nodded. That much was true. No matter the method that brought it to this point, the reality was it was best and fair for everyone. "I agree," he acknowledged as he started back down the corridor.

"But you've got to know, we're all a bit puzzled as to why you pardoned Alfred before the vote."

Andrew stopped a moment, but did not turn back to face him. "It was my last act as king. I just felt it was the right thing to do."

"Nobody understands why you did it."

"You're wrong there. It's just nobody wants to admit it."

▉ ▉ ▉

Jimmy had barely looked at him or spoken to him since Evangeline had left, but he wanted a meeting now. Andrew wasn't sure how much he knew, but the tension was becoming unbearable. For nearly four years Evangeline and Jimmy had been the rocks of his life. They had been the ones to push him forward when he felt the strangling grip of his father pulling him down … even after the suicide—or murder—as Alfred had revealed. For three weeks he had been alone as the holidays came and went, and he wondered if his father had ever known this kind of helplessness. Supposedly he was planning another attack to slaughter civilians rather than admit defeat. Was there ever a time in the man's life that he had thrown up his hands and admitted things were beyond his control? Apparently not. He was decidedly unlike his father.

He looked to the Christmas tree he had helped Evangeline and the boys decorate. It was so different from the others in the palace. It was filled with memories in homemade ornaments and treasures of love and hope from their past together. The gifts were all still there, some wrapped carefully by mature hands—others the obvious handiwork of Gabriel. His heart ached to see them all, and he knew he had visitation rights, but he couldn't bring himself to face her. Whether she was guilty or innocent was pointless by now. He had condemned her, and he would have to stand by that verdict until proven otherwise.

A knock sounded and he caught his breath before facing his best friend … his former best friend. As much as he had done to save the state of his nation, it had cost him everything in the end.

"Come on in," he gestured after opening the door.

"No thanks," Jimmy shot with a polite, lopsided grin. "I just wanted to give you this and then I'll be on my way." He handed Andrew an envelope.

"And what is this?"

He drew in a deep breath, squared his shoulders and said, "My resignation."

His heart fell. He should have expected it. "At least come in so we can talk about it."

"Not really much to talk about."

"You're resigning—we need to talk."

Cocking his head to the side he asked, "Is that a command?"

Andrew didn't even want to dignify it with a response, but he managed to say, "I'm no longer king—I can't command you to do anything."

He nodded, pursed his lips, then walked through the door.

"Would you like some coffee?" Andrew offered as he went to the kitchen for a cup.

"No."

Ok, he's not even going to attempt to be cordial. "Why are you resigning now? You know I need you for the next six months in a big way. After that, you're a free man."

Jimmy was standing by the tree staring down at the unopened gifts. "Did you do anything for Christmas?"

Pouring his coffee, he confessed, "I looked through the library and my father's old study hoping to find some of that liquor he used to drown himself in all the time." He added sugar and cream, another delight Evangeline had introduced to him. "No such luck. It appears my mother had it all done away with when she took over."

"Look," Jimmy turned around to face him, "the bottom line is—I don't want to work for you anymore. You've become a heartless, selfish, stupid man."

Andrew chuckled as he took a sip from his mug. "Good thing I'm not king. I could have your head for that."

Nodding, he replied, "Or just throw me into Razewwell and slowly freeze and starve me to death. That's what heartless, selfish, stupid men do, or did you forget that?"

"For heaven's sake, Jimmy! I was a puppet! My whole life was a sham!"

"Says Alfred! *Alfred!* The man you fired and replaced with me because his loyalties lay with your father and not with you! Or did you forget that too?"

"He had no choice," he defended. "If he didn't appear loyal to the king, my father would have axed him and no one would have had inside information."

"He led a mocked up raid dressed in Aicirtapvakian military attire against innocent Braisognian soldiers, ordering them slaughtered so your father could remain on the throne a few more months!" He bounded in anger towards Andrew. "He could have waited a mere three months when you would have legitimately taken the throne! Whatever he said to you from that prison cell was either a great distortion or a full out lie!"

Andrew slowly pulled out a chair from the dining table and sat. It was too late to consider all that now. He had been so consumed with the idea of being manipulated that he hadn't thought to reason through the evidence before jumping to emotional conclusions.

"What part of you took over when you left that jail cell and headed home to Evie?" Jimmy queried. "Years of never measuring up to your father, feeling condemned by the haughty, disapproving looks of the buzzard, and the constant insinuations that you weren't worthy to bear the crown—all of that was shoved to the side and the love and support Evie has always given was trampled like dust beneath your feet.

"So," Jimmy finished, "consider my resignation final." He darted to the door then stopped to add, "And by the way, your latest baby was born two nights ago … at the hospital here … if that even matters to you." With that he closed the door.

U U U

With a dry throat and shaking fingers Andrew rapped lightly on the hospital door. He carried a balloon and a bouquet of assorted flowers because in all the years he had known Evangeline, she had never expressed what her favorite was. She said in a world with so much wrong, the choice between one beautiful thing or another seemed trite.

"Come in." Her soft voice sounded warm and sweet.

Slowly he opened the door and eased inside. When she saw him her expression never changed. She merely looked back down at the new baby and continued nursing.

"I just found out today," he began. "I didn't know or I would have been here sooner."

Without looking up, she said, "I didn't expect you to come at all."

A pang thrust through his heart. He knew he deserved any punishment she might offer, but he couldn't understand why no one seemed to recognize his dilemma. "Look, Evangeline, I know things are tense and confusing right now, but they're still my children."

Now she looked at him. "Really ... I thought we were all disowned. We're the result of your false life, remember, the one that took you away from whatever destiny might have been yours had I never done whatever Alfred claimed. I've accepted my senseless punishment ... senseless seeing that I'm innocent of whatever the crime was. Your children, however, don't deserve this. Too bad you're not as free with your pardons when it comes to your family."

He looked down and sighed. That was a low blow. "I just don't know what to do right now. I'm still not sure of the truth. I still don't know what really happened or ... well ..."

"What was made up?" she offered.

He surrendered. "I guess." He placed the flowers and balloon next to the sink. "I don't know if it was the timing or just the information itself, but it all sent me spinning and I had no place to land."

She shook her head. "Yes, you did. You've always had a place to land. Unfortunately, you allowed your enemies to set it afire."

"I don't know that he's my enemy. What he said made complete sense." He struggled to explain. "As I looked back through the narrative he took me through, it all fit so perfectly. Even now I'm in a complete blur." He looked helplessly at her. "I don't know if I actually did something truly noble, or if I merely played the hand that was dealt me by those men ... whoever they are."

She wouldn't respond. Instead, she stopped feeding the infant and closed up her gown. "Would you like to burp her?"

His eyes grew wide. "Her?" He gulped. "It's a girl?"

She nodded as he approached the bed. "And a very good little girl too."

He gently took her and gazed into her petite, alert face. "Her eyes are so light. They're going to be like yours."

"Probably."

"Hello, little angel," he cooed. "You are so tiny, so precious." His defenses were crumbling. He could feel them peeling away layer by layer. He wasn't sure he was ready for that. "I know we need to work through some stuff, but ..."

"No—*you* need to work through some stuff. I know exactly where I stand, and it's the same place I've stood for as long as I can remember. You are the one who's changed."

"I understand how you could feel that way, but it's affected us both. You walked out on me ... that hurt."

"Don't even talk like I had a choice. You basically called me a fraud and accused our entire relationship of being some pretentious sand castle. Did you honestly think I could stay in that?"

More layers peeling, melting away. "Look, I'm sorry."

"For what?"

He was perplexed. "That you were hurt in all of this."

She nodded as she looked out the window toward the ancient, regal skyline of the capitol city. "That's not enough."

He was empty. "That's all I've got. There's nothing else I can say."

"There is, but you haven't seen it yet." She sighed and lay back against the pillow. "Maybe one day you will, but I'm beginning to think you're not the man I believed you to be."

He was too choked to argue, too overcome at holding his baby daughter to find words for fighting. This was all he had ever wanted—Evangeline, a family, and to no longer be king. What had he done, and how could he reclaim it? There was only one man who could give him the beginning of the truth, but he had to find him first.

"What's her name?" he asked as the baby gave an adorable yawn.

"Andrea."

He glanced up at her quickly in question.

"You always wanted a girl," she spoke sadly. "How could I not name her after you?"

♛ ♛ ♛

Gasping from shock, Dexter Braisogn could not believe Andrew was standing outside his door. "How did you find me?"

"I may no longer be king, but I still have some pull."

"Come on in, I guess." He motioned him through a small foyer into a humble sitting room with a gas fire, a television and a glass of brandy next to a comfortable recliner. "I don't imagine my whereabouts came easily for you, so I'm assuming whatever the reason, it must be important." He pointed to a hard, high backed chair. "Have a seat." He held up his glass. "Would you care for some?"

"No."

"I see—all business." He took a swallow then grimaced as the alcohol burned. "So tell me, to what do I owe this pleasure?"

Andrew wasted no time explaining his meeting with Alfred and detailing the events of his life and how they fit into the scheme of the revelation that day. He grumbled through his frustrations with his father, his suspicions about his wife, and his resentment at being a mindless toy to Dexter and Alfred and whatever other men had been involved. The older man listened quietly as the ranting went on and sipped his glass while nodding through it all. When Andrew finished, he glared at one of his supposed puppet-masters waiting for a response. To his surprise, Dexter broke out in roaring laughter.

Offended, Andrew complained, "You find this humorous?"

"You have no idea how much," he smirked making no effort to stifle his amusement. "So, that's why Evie left the palace and then you pardoned that old geezer. The rumors are all over, but no one knows why. It makes sense now." He raised his glass to Andrew. "Congratulations, boy, your father won anyway. After all you did to break away from his strangling hold he still managed to one up you."

"This has nothing to do with my father!"

He laughed again. "What kind of man are you exactly? After all you've been through, after all the fights you've won, you would give up everything in your life that has been truly noble and fall at his feet like a sniveling puppy?"

"What? You must be drunk!"

"I would say the same of you except the whole kingdom knows you despise liquor because your father was such a controlling lush."

"I came here for answers, not insults." He stood to leave. "If you can't offer me anything other than mockery, it's obvious I wasted my time."

"Sit down, boy," Dexter commanded darkly. "Let me clear a lot of things up for you, and then hope you have enough brains left to put your life back together."

Andrew sat, easing his arms on the rests of the stiff chair.

"First, let's make it very clear that I have never … ever … in my life … collaborated with Alfred in any way, shape or form. And as for Giselle, she was every bit my daughter—you can take blood or whatever samples you want and compare them anew with Evie. I gave up my life, my entire future, in order to see my granddaughter rise above the pretentious sewage she had been inundated with all her life … only to watch the one man she ever loved throw her out with the trash just like the rest of his royal buddies."

"That's not what happened!"

"Shut up and listen or I'll gladly pop your insolent mouth until you can't utter another word!"

Andrew swallowed and sat back.

"This has Christopher Braisogn written all over it," he continued. "I knew it was too good to be true, but this confirms it."

"I have no idea what you're talking about."

"Your father isn't dead. He's living it up on some eternal holiday getting a stipend just like me—from somewhere and someone. And you," he pointed an accusing finger, "fell for his final attempt at revenge. Not only did he make you doubt your initiative in changing all that's wrong in this country, he also managed to pry you away from the one person he hated most—Evie. And like a sniveling child you fell for it all."

As the man paused to pour more brandy, Andrew revealed. "Oh, my father's dead all right, but it wasn't suicide."

Dexter raised an eyebrow. "Really?"

"Alfred killed him."

"Bwah ha ha!" He spilled his drink from the bellowing. "You really are a fool, aren't you?"

Jumping up, Andrew yelled, "I've had enough of your mockery!"

"The only mockery in this room right now is you." He slammed the glass on the table. "You have been played like a witless instrument. I knew Alfred long before he became your attendant. He was of the old, hard line. The man was loyal to the monarchy to a fault. He would have no more killed your father than … well, I can't compare to anyone else in the kingdom, because by that time, the only person still loyal to him was Alfred!

"Can't you put it together, boy? The timing was too perfect—the day before you sign the law banishing the crown forever! And to add insult to injury, they managed to destroy the one thing that actually saved your life, the one thing that gave you a heart above the power, the one person in this whole kingdom who had the nerve to defy him … and all because of you … all because she loved you more than her own life." He shook his head and downed another gulp. "They won, after all. They lost the monarchy, but at least they took you … and her … down with them." He raised his glass. "Congratulations Christopher and Alfred, wherever you old boys are!"

✂ Chapter Thirty-Nine ❧

"You're not welcome here." James Dorvain spoke sharply to his son-in-law as they stood on the porch with snow blowing all around them. "I didn't want to allow you through the gate, but when you asked to at least let you speak with your mother, I couldn't deny that. She's my wife now, so this is as much her home as mine—and I insist she have the freedom to live her life without being under anyone's control ... ever again."

"And I appreciate it. She's lucky to have you."

"No, son, I'm the lucky one. Rarely does a man find true love once in a lifetime. I've found it twice, and I'm wise enough to know that it's too priceless a commodity to toss aside when others begin to cast stones of doubt."

Andrew closed his eyes against the biting cold and swallowed his pride. "I realize I've been a fool. I don't know what else I can say."

"That's a pity."

As he explained the details of the past month, his mother listened stoically, allowing him to freely express his explanations and excuses. This was the first they had spoken since the visit with Alfred, and this was the first time he had actually verbally expressed everything he was feeling to anyone.

"Are you quite finished?" she asked curtly when he finally stopped talking and turned his face toward the fire hoping to thaw not only his body, but his raw, cold heart. He nodded. He had nothing more. "Good. Are you ready to listen to reason yet?"

"I'm just ready to know the truth," he conceded. "Whatever it is, I'm ready."

"Do you still not know the truth?" She threw her hands up, exasperated.

"After all this are you actually clinging to the idea that something in Alfred's words might have had an element of truth?"

"I don't know!" he cried. "Why would he say that? Why would he call for me after two years and drop such a bomb? He was my mentor, for bloody sake! Why would he try to destroy everything that made me who I am?"

He tried to hold back the tears threatening to push through, but his confusion and frustration had reached their limit. The fact that she was condemning him also only doubled the pain. He had nothing to cling to, and his last hope had been the understanding heart of his mother.

She gently put her arms around him and turned him to face her. "Andrew, Alfred was an ambitious man who had been overlooked twice. He had put in to tutor both George and Peter, but your father wouldn't even give him a second look. He considered the man old, second rate, not worthy to train a king—and he bluntly told him … twice. No one ever imagined *you* would be the one to take the throne, so when your brothers abdicated, Alfred's job became the most important in the entire kingdom."

"But he defended my marriage to Evangeline!" he protested. "I heard him myself—he stood up to Father and told him if I married anyone it would only be Evangeline! I always wondered about that. What he told me from his cell finally made sense of it all."

Sighing, she took his hand and led him to the couch. "My dear boy, he merely knew your heart—everyone knew your heart! Your father knew your heart. Your love for Evie was the most prominent thing about you … for those who knew you best. Tell me this—after learning about Section Seven, had you not married her, what would you have done?"

"Abdicated," he mumbled without even needing to think.

"Exactly. Alfred knew that. He had groomed the king—he wanted to see you on the throne. And even if Christopher had fired him, he would always be credited as the one who trained you. Believe me, there was nothing noble in that man's actions. He was as devious and snide as your father."

"Then why would he make up such a story?" Andrew wanted to know. "Why would he call me in and spill such a preposterous lie?"

She shook her head. "You are so not your father's child." She ran a gentle finger down the side of his beard. "He wanted to punish you. He wanted to make you doubt all the things you had traded for the kingship. As he sat in that cell over two years, his devious, angered brain worked overtime planning the perfect moment to make his attack and watch you crumble to the ground." She stood and made a startling statement. "And … like Dexter … I would be willing to bet he had help."

He grunted a sigh and moaned, "Father? You can't be serious!"

She chuckled. "Somehow I always doubted the reality of his suicide. It would be so unlike him. He thought much too highly of himself to take his own life. And the idea of Alfred actually murdering him is completely preposterous!"

"But the body … we saw it in the casket."

"But not at the palace or in the morgue." She paused and turned to him. "I actually asked to see it before they sent it to be prepared, but they assured me it was so gruesome and disfigured that I mustn't. I had my doubts at that moment that he wasn't really dead, but if that was the charade he wanted to play, I was more than willing. I gladly accepted the roles of widow and queen over the years of hell he had put me through."

"But we saw his body," he repeated.

She sat beside him again and took his hands. "Andrew, there are wax figures of your father in museums all over this country. It would take less than an hour to have one procured and placed in a casket. Who knows what other prosthetics … or … I don't know. With your father, where there's a will, there's always a way."

He stood and ambled toward the glass doors to the back deck. What had he done? "Why did I believe him … or them … so easily? Why did I cave instead of stand?" He looked back at his mother, emotionally deplete from the psychological ride he had taken.

"Because deep down somewhere," she stood and came to him, "in that big heart of yours," she softly placed her hand on his chest, "you wanted to believe that you could please the men who raised you. You wanted to make them proud, make them believe you were strong and smart and capable of the task fate had handed you. All they ever gave you was how far short you fell of their expectations. Your only salvation was the love of a woman who believed you could do anything, so in order to truly destroy you, they had to destroy that love."

For the first time since speaking with Alfred, the dam broke. Every frustration and fear and loss and question began to pour forth from him in sobs. Julia grabbed him and pulled him down to her shoulder as he wept with long, deep wails. She comforted a crying son—something she had never been allowed to do before.

Finally pulling out of his breakdown, he asked, "Where's Evangeline? I have to see her—I have to make this right."

James, who had watched the whole exchange from the hallway, spoke. "She's at the waterfall with the kids."

"What?" Andrew was confounded. "It's snowing! It's freezing! Is the baby there too?"

"Yes," he nodded. "I can take you there if you want."

"We have to get them!" He rushed to the foyer for his coat.

"Andrew," James assured, "they're fine. The situation isn't what you're imagining. Do you think I would let my only daughter and grandchildren stay outside in weather like this?"

He shook his head, still confused and overwhelmed, then grabbed his father-in-law into a hug. "I'm sorry, sir," he cried again. "I'm so sorry ... so sorry." He pulled back and boldly stared into the man's eyes. "Can you ever forgive me? Can Evangeline forgive me?"

James took his time responding. "I can forgive, because not forgiving would make me no better than your father or Alfred. Unforgiveness makes a man bitter, hard and vengeful. I have too much to live for to be consumed by the darker side of life." He paused and sighed. "As for Evie, I can't answer. She's stronger than any of us could ever hope to be, yet everyone has a breaking point. Maybe this is hers—then again, maybe not. I've never been able to read her mind, but one thing I do know."

Andrew looked hopeful. "What's that, sir?"

"Her love for you superseded everything rational in her life. She defied her parents, her enemies, her future, and even her king to be with you. Had anyone else treated her the way you did ..." He made a slashing movement at his throat. "All I can say is go to her."

He nodded. "Then let's go."

Ӱ Ӱ Ӱ

"When did you pave a road to the waterfall?" Andrew asked as James headed through the thickening snowfall on solid blacktop.

"Last year—when Evie asked me to."

After several minutes of winding through the forest, lights began to sparkle through the trees and snow. He squinted, trying to see exactly what the source was. "Did you get electricity out there?"

"Yes."

He gave the older man a quizzical glance. "When?"

Chuckling, "When Evie asked me to."

Rounding the final curve, he was shocked at the sight. There on the hill exactly as he had imagined stood a towering house. Each window was lit up with a red candle and Christmas wreath, spotlights beaming as though a holiday party were showing guests the way.

"Wow," he breathed in awe. "When did you build this?"

"I didn't—Evie did." He pulled to the front and stopped before a massive porch, each pillar wrapped in garland and red ribbon, and a stained glass door with designs of musical instruments and notes woven throughout.

"I had no idea ..."

"This was to be your Christmas present."

He winced. Could he possibly feel any guiltier? He stared a few moments more, taking in the incredible design and decorations, then finally reached for the handle. "I would say wish me luck, but I don't know exactly where you stand in all this."

"I stand with Evie," he replied plainly.

Nodding, he opened the door. "I understand." He left the vehicle and started up the walk to the porch. James pulled away. That was a bit disconcerting because his only way home had just disappeared through the snow and forest if Evangeline refused to let him in. Taking a deep breath, he continued up the walk to the door. He stopped a moment to notice the details of the stained glass—a guitar, a piano, a flute like Gabriel's, a trumpet like the one still wrapped beneath the tree at the palace. He smiled and shook his head. What a fool he had been. She had done this all for him—built a house, designed it personally, made a place where he could go when his final duties in politics had ended. And what had he done? Accused her of playing a big game and treating him like a puppet.

He rang the doorbell then stepped back and pulled the collar of his coat up around his neck. The wind was howling now and the snow was becoming thicker. He smelled burning hardwood and knew she must have a fire inside. He smiled at the thought. With all the effort she took in making such an amazing house, she kept the simplicity of a wood burning fireplace. He knew it had nothing to do with practicality—it was all about home. He remembered her before the fire as he secretly watched her pray and read Scripture. He recalled warming himself and sipping hot cocoa the night he had been released from prison. It held warmth that went beyond the physical—it warmed the soul.

The door opened slowly and a surprised Evangeline looked out. She had a fleece blanket around her shoulders and a steaming mug in her hand.

"What are you doing?" she asked with furled brows.

"Hoping you'll let me in so I don't freeze to death out here seeing as your father dropped me off and then just left. I didn't know that was the plan."

She opened the door fully. "Sure—come on in."

He walked through and stood in the midst of pure architectural splendor. The vaulted ceiling was covered in unstained wood with many angles and layers of design. He followed her past the open foyer and into a cozy area with a glowing fire, a blow up mattress on the floor, and a rocking chair with a face-downed book in the seat. He walked to the fire and warmed his hands.

"Uh …," he was nearly speechless because of the house, "where's the baby?"

"Asleep in her room."

He nodded. "And the boys?"

"In the playroom building a time machine."

He raised an eyebrow. "Really?"

She smiled slightly and shook her head as she took a sip from her mug. "It was a joke. They're one and two—they're probably emptying every box I placed in there. I found some old toys of mine in the attic at Daddy's and thought I'd let them play with them until I can get back to the palace and get all their stuff."

He cringed. How did he begin? "I want to do this right, Evangeline, but I don't know how."

"Then you'd better figure it out."

He looked up quickly. "Can you give me any clues? I've apologized before, but you said it wasn't right. I don't know what else to do. I'll apologize right now. I'm sorry."

She picked up the book from the chair, closed it and sat down with her cup. "What are you sorry for?"

"Augh!" He put his hands to his head. "I'm sorry for how all this hurt you! I'm sorry that in the midst of all this mess you …"

"Wrong," she interrupted flatly.

"What?"

"That's still the wrong answer."

"Then what's the right answer? I have no clue! Can you at least give me a hint or move me in some general direction?"

She sat back, crossed her legs and took another swallow. "All you're telling me through that apology is that I was somehow collateral damage in all this—I was just caught in the crossfire and managed to take a bullet or two … that's all."

"Huh?" He had no idea what she meant.

"You're sorry that I was hurt in the middle of all that happened, but you've taken no responsibility for that hurt. You've placed the blame on everyone else involved." She paused and he could see the hurt growing on her face. "I don't care what Alfred said, or what any other man said. I don't care what your father did or didn't do. I don't even care if you were some pitiful puppet whose strings were pulled over the years to carry out the schemes of manipulative men. None of that matters to me, and none of that hurt me. Those bullets might have pierced your heart deeply, and I would have gladly empathized and helped nurse you through them—but those are not the bullets that hurt me."

Slowly he began to understand. He turned toward the fire and shut his eyes as he prayed for the first time in months. *God, why is it so hard for me to do this? I don't want to take this responsibility. I want it to be their fault, not mine.* He ran his fingers through his snow-dampened hair and tried to summon the courage to crucify his pride. If he didn't, he would be like his father—a man bent on being right, willing to sacrifice everything to that end, yet never finding real fulfillment. The only life that had ever had meaning to him was life with Evangeline, and she was right—it was the bullets he had fired that had hurt her most.

Before he could speak, the boys came barreling into the room.

"Mommy! Mommy!" Gabriel yelled as he burst through the archway raising a small toy to the air. "Look what we found!" As soon as he saw his father, he stopped and lowered his hand. Michael, however, kept running to his mother and jumped into her lap.

"Horsie!" Michael squealed. "We gots horsie!"

Gabriel slowly moved to his mother, but never took his eyes off Andrew. The last time he had seen him, he had yelled for him to go to his room and had never made it right.

"What have you got there, sweetie?" she asked as she reached out her hand.

Finding his excitement again, Gabriel looked at his mother and placed the toy in her hand—a small, blue horse. He then whispered, "Dis da horsie you tell about in dose stories." His eyes grew wide. "We finded him in dat box."

Andrew put his hand to his heart as he recognized the horse as the one he had colored and given to Evangeline when they were children. She had promised that in their dreams she would ride to him in their secret room on her blue steed, and they would always be together if they just imagined it.

"Hey, guys," he said as he kneeled next to the chair. "Do you have any idea how special that horse is?"

Gabriel nodded enthusiastically as he whispered, "It's magic!"

"Oh yeah," he agreed as he took it from Evangeline's hand. "Very much so." He held it up toward the light and every defense, every excuse, every justification finally melted. "Tell you what, you guys run back to the playroom for a little bit, and when I finish talking with Mommy, I'll come in there and tell you another story about the blue horse."

The boys grinned as Michael climbed off his mother's lap. They grasped hands and trotted like horses out of the room, giggling all the way back.

Andrew took her hand and prayed that he had the right apology this time. "You have always been my reason for living as far back as I can remember. I'll never forget sitting alone in that odd shaped room as I remembered everything about you—your bright eyes, your warm smile, your pink skin, even the way you smelled. I'd imagine you flying to me when things got so horrible I wondered if I could even live through the day, and you'd always smile and tell me it was just another ugly dragon to kill. Somehow believing that you were out there thinking of me too gave me enough strength to get through one more day, one more month, one more year.

"And when you became my wife, I felt like nothing could ever hold me back again—could ever really hurt me again. And it was because you always infused me with strength and confidence." He let go of her hand and got up, moving back to the fireplace. "When Alfred told me what he did, I was so hurt and angry—to be honest, I just felt violated by my world. Because you were the biggest part of my world, I lashed out at you too." He gazed over at her. "Those were my bullets. I fired them deliberately and wanted you to hurt just like I was hurt." His jaw tensed as he pressed on. "And then I hurt my boys, abandoned my little girl—I did everything to those I loved the most just like my father had done to me." He looked back to her. "Is that who I really am inside? Am I like my father after all?"

She drew in a deep breath and slowly released it. "Andrew, no one wears a black hat or a white hat all the time. No one is perfectly good, never making mistakes in judgment or never hurting those they love most. And no one is thoroughly evil either—not even your father or Alfred. As we move through life, though, we grow and we learn about who we really are and not just who we wish we were. Your father wanted to be powerful so he put on the black hat and barreled over everyone to prove it. But at the end of the day, he would escape to his liquor, remove the black hat, and try to anesthetize the part of him that was standing there holding out the white hat.

"And you wanted to be good and right and fair, so you put on your white hat and determined never to wear the same hat as your father. You just didn't realize there are many different black hats out there." She finally stood and moved to him. "No, you are nothing like your father. You hate the black hats—he embraced them." Then she smiled. "And yes, that was the right apology."

His eyes brightened with hope and his heart skipped a moment as he stared in astonishment. "What?"

"That's all I wanted." The green in her eyes sparkled from the fire and her smile was the warmest he could remember. "I needed to hear you admit responsibility for hurting me. No one else mattered. What mattered was that you doubted me, you doubted my love, you doubted the sincerity of all I had ever given you—and I gave you everything, every part of me. Your doubt was the deepest blow I'd ever received."

"I'm sorry," he breathed with desperation.

"I know." She put a finger to his lips. "I also know you were hurt, and I know Alfred crafted a perfectly devious lie meant to destroy you to the core. I just wish you would have trusted me and not him. I would have gone to him myself and worn my own little black hat for a few minutes as I told him my thoughts. But he had won. He had made me your enemy and no longer an ally." She touched his beard. "Always remember—I am your biggest ally. I will face any dragon with you or for you as long as I know we ride off together at the end of each day on my blue horsie."

He melted into her hand and closed his eyes in relief. "Is it over?"

"Look at me." He did. "It's over."

"Do I have to leave … tonight?"

She moved closer. "The storm's getting worse. It'd probably be best if you stayed here."

"I can sleep on that air mattress if you need me to."

"Oh, believe me, I need you to." She put her arms around his neck. "I refused to buy bedroom furniture until I knew you were home for good. I've been sleeping on that for a month."

"Am I home for good?"

She ran her hand down his beard then buried it in his hair. "You'd better be."

She pulled him down and kissed him. This was different. He had changed. He had faced his biggest fears and thought he had lost the battle and her too. Instead, in his vulnerability, he had only come to love her deeper. Overcome with passion, he moved her toward the mattress.

"Daddy?"

He looked to the archway. Gabriel and Michael stood there with expectant smiles.

"You gonna tell us 'bout da blue horsie?"

He let go of Evangeline and straightened her sweater. "Oh, yeah. I was tired … was gonna go to bed."

Evangeline chimed in. "I have an idea—let's get you boys in pajamas and then Daddy can make it a bedtime story."

"Hurry din!" Gabriel exclaimed as he took off for his bedroom.

"Horsie!" Michael whispered and then turned to follow his brother.

Andrew looked back to her and she placed a chaste kiss on his longing lips.

"Welcome home, Daddy," she said smiling.

Nodding, he took her back in his arms. "This is all I've ever wanted. I'm sorry I lost sight of it."

"You didn't lose sight. You wouldn't be here if you had." She kissed him again.

"Did you know I would come back? Did you ever stop believing?"

She motioned her head toward the mattress. "I didn't buy bedroom furniture, did I?"

He grinned. "You didn't buy anything for this room either except a chair."

"This house was your Christmas present. I thought you should have some say in it."

She closed his hand around the little blue horse and turned him toward the archway. "Go tell your sons a story. I'll have some cocoa waiting for you when you finish."

He looked back. "The only thing I want waiting for me when I finish is you."

She reached up and touched the end of his nose. "Wish granted."

☙ Chapter Forty ❧

(Ten Years Later)

After packing the last few items, Andrew zipped his luggage and turned to his wife. "I think that's it. Have the boys gotten their things together yet? The car should be here any minute."

"Are you sure you want to go through with this ... all of this?" she worried. "You can still take the boys to America and see the sights you'd promised—just forget about the visit."

He smoothed his hand down her cheek and gave a gentle kiss. "I'm sure. Trust me, I've gone back and forth with it in my mind more than you can imagine. I feel like it's something I need to do ... as much for me as for him."

"I hope you're not expecting anything different. Your father was a master manipulator. This may be nothing more than one final attempt to shame you for all you've done."

"Do you actually think that's possible?" He pulled her down to sit with him on the bed. "For ten years this country has been run smoothly and fairly with a new government I initiated. I have seven incredible children whom I get to spend my days with ... as well as the most beautiful woman in the nation who I get to spend my nights with." She punched him playfully but then leaned her head on his shoulder. "I write and arrange music in my second story bay window as I look out over the most inspiring view in all of Braisognia, and then I get to direct the national symphony as it plays *my* pieces." He reached for her chin and tilted her face toward his. "What could he possibly do to make me regret any of this?"

"He's your father—enough said. I wonder if George and Peter didn't make the better decision by refusing his invitation." She closed her eyes and threw back her head. "And you're taking my two oldest babies! No telling what kind of stuff he might try to pour into their innocent little brains. They don't even know the whole story."

"I intend to tell them on the flight there," he explained as stood and began moving his luggage to the door. "I'm not totally sure I'll let them meet him or not. I may leave them at the hotel."

"Alone?"

"Gabriel's a very mature twelve year old."

She nodded. "Just keep in touch with me … at all times … so I won't think unspeakable things are happening."

"Dad," Michael called as he gave a short knock on the open door. "The car's here."

"Are your things packed?" his father asked.

"Mine and Gabe's are at the door already."

"Let's do this then."

Michael left and Andrew turned back to Evangeline. He took her hands and assured her, "Everything will be fine. I really believe I need to do this or else I wouldn't be going. I'll be back in a couple of weeks, hopefully with a great tan and a lot of stories to tell you and the girls about our adventures in the mythical land of America."

"I'm counting on it," she whispered as she pulled him down for a goodbye kiss.

☿ ☿ ☿

Christopher Braisogn's house in Palm Beach, Florida, was more modest than Andrew surmised. Although it sat in the midst of expansive, walled estates, this was only one story, no fence, but with direct access to the beach. The yard was perfect with its thick grass and royal palms, and tropical flowers were bursting with color at every corner from uniquely designed beds.

"This place is cool," Michael marveled as they ventured up the concrete path to the front door. "And you can just walk across the street and take those stairs down from the wall to the beach." He looked up at the tall palms. "Why didn't we just stay here? He's your dad, isn't he?"

Gabriel jumped in to answer. "Because he's a mean tyrant. Did you happen to miss that part of the lecture?"

Andrew stopped them. "I didn't *lecture* you—I just asked you to listen to everything until I finished before you asked any questions … then I said *like* a lecture at school."

Michael pointed toward a large bush with bright, red blooms. "What kind of flowers are those? They're huge!"

"I don't know," his father replied. "We'll get a book or something that tells us about the trees and flowers around here." It was a strange country so everything about it seemed odd—the birds, the cars, the plants and especially the accents. The people were friendly, however, and they carried their freedom with ease. Braisognia was still adjusting to the loss of classes and the mixing of education. He realized it might take a generation before things settled completely into normalcy.

As he approached the door, his heart raced. Maybe he shouldn't have brought his sons. What if Evangeline was right and this was nothing more than a final attempt at degradation? He hated for his boys to experience that kind of venom after having such a wonderful grandfather in James.

"Guys," he said firmly, "if at any point I tell you to leave, I want you to do it without questioning me. Just come out here and wait. Is that understood?"

"Yes, sir," Gabriel replied, respectful as always.

Michael gave an animated salute and retorted, "Aye-aye, matey!"

Andrew chuckled, "At ease, private."

"I'm not a private, Dad—I'm a pirate. I think I should get an eye patch and freak Mom out when we return. Maybe a machete too!"

The door opened, and to Andrew's surprise, he recognized the woman. She had been a maid at the palace years back and had often cleaned his room.

"Uh, hello?" he offered. "I … um … didn't expect to see you … here."

She smiled. "I imagine not. Please, come in. Your father will be ready in a moment. The nurse is changing him and getting him all cleaned up for your visit."

This took him by surprise. "A nurse? Is he not well?"

She shook her head. "No, he's not. He's been sick for some time now." She looked at the three of them. "Thank you for coming. You have no idea how much this means to him. He's disappointed George and Peter didn't come, but he understands."

Michael popped out the question they all were wondering. "What's wrong with him? What's he got? What kind of sickness?"

"Cancer—it's his liver." Downcast, she explained, "His appearance will be quite … daunting. He's jaundiced and rather bloated, especially his abdomen."

This had been unexpected for Andrew. "Does he have all the medical help he needs?"

She was obviously grieved over his condition. "He has all the medical help … he wants." She looked away as if to gather her emotions. "He's ready to go, if you can understand that."

He nodded. "I guess I can." He sighed awkwardly, not knowing really what to say next. "And have you been with him since he left Braisognia?"

"Yes. He had two …" she paused and glanced to the sons, "… lady friends at the palace, myself and another. We came with him. She left after only a few months. He eventually married me."

"Lucky you," he noted snidely.

"Actually ..." The nurse came out before she could finish.

"He's all ready—spiffed up and handsome," the nurse informed them with a slow southern drawl. She reached out her hand to Andrew. "You must be the good-lookin' son he talks about all the time." What a strange accent she had. "And you fellers have to be the grandsons."

True to form, Michael piped out, "We're the good-lookin' grandsons."

The nurse wondered, "Are there some ugly ones out there?"

"Absolutely!" he grinned. "Uncle Peter's boys are red ..."

"Michael!" Andrew stopped him then looked back to the nurse. "He's very free with his words."

"Good for him!" she laughed. "Learn to use those words, boy. Too many people are 'fraid to say what's on their minds these days. They think someone's gonna snap them up and arrest them for an opinion." She pointed her finger at Andrew. "Still a free country last time I checked, and I stand on my first amendment rights." She turned to the other woman. "I'm heading out unless there's something else you need."

"No, we're good. Thank-you so much."

When the nurse left, the wife motioned them toward the bedroom just off the front den where they had been waiting. She said nothing more, but turned to leave them alone as they entered.

Walking into the room, the smells of disinfectant and medicines along with the sounds of machines were most prominent, but when the door was fully opened, the bed next to the large window became the center of attention. There lay the former king, a full head of gray hair, but a face filled with pain ... yet happiness somehow. He looked on his son and broadened his smile. It almost seemed there were tears growing. As the woman had said, his appearance was sickening. He was very yellow and very swollen, and Andrew found it difficult to see him in this condition. He motioned his sons on in.

"Andrew," his father spoke, his voice still strong. "Thank you for coming." He looked past his son to his grandchildren. "And you must be Gabriel and Michael." They nodded. "I understand you are both quite talented in your own rights. Gabriel, the musician, and Michael, the athlete."

Andrew was surprised he knew so much about his children. He wondered who kept him informed about things in Braisognia.

"And you, Andrew, are quite the impressive leader of the Braisognian National Symphony. Your compositions and arrangements are beautiful, and your directing is so fluid and smooth. It's as much a thing of beauty to watch as it is to hear."

Andrew swallowed. "Thank you. I didn't realize you had access to all things Braisognian."

He chuckled. "Satellite and internet are wonderful." He motioned toward three chairs beside his bed. "Take a seat, if you will." He looked out his window to the colorful landscape filled with birdhouses and baths and a wide array of winged creatures taking advantage of the offerings. "I confess to watching this," he pointed to the window, "more than television, however. It's more soothing. The birds, coupled with my favorite music," he pressed a button on his remote, "make life somewhat bearable for me."

"Hey, Dad!" Michael chimed as he plopped into a chair, "That's your music!"

Andrew recognized a piano piece from one of his CD's. He looked to his father as he took a seat, baffled that he would choose to listen to his music.

"What can I say," Christopher grinned. "My tastes have improved over the years."

"Wo!" Michael yelled out as he jumped from his chair and pointed toward the largest bird either boy had ever seen. "What on earth is that?"

"Ah," the older man nodded, "that would be the pelican—his beak can hold more than his belly can ... the pelican."

"Huh?" Michael questioned as he went right up to the bed.

"He's got a huge bit of flappy skin beneath his beak there. If he were on the ocean, you might see him swoop down into the water and drag his beak like a net. When he comes up, that skin fills with water, and hopefully a fish or two. It hangs way down like a big pouch."

The boy's eyes grew wide with wonder. "Really? Could I see that on your beach down there? The one across the road?"

"It's not actually *my* beach, but yes, pelicans often fish out there from the pier."

He turned to Andrew. "Dad, can we go? Me and Gabe? I want to see the pellycane fish!"

"Leaving me so soon," the grandfather complained. "You barely just got here."

"Awww, Grandpa ... or Grandfather," Michael paused. "What do we call you anyway?"

He laughed at the unashamed attitude. "What do you want to call me?"

"No idea. Didn't even know you were alive until last week."

"What do you call James ... and Julia?" He slowed through her name, obviously overcome with emotion.

"Papa and Nana. They're pretty cool."

"Well, then, Papa's taken, so just go with whatever moves you."

Michael pondered hard as he stared at the aged man. Cocking his head to the side, just like his mother often did, he finally declared, "Captain—we should call you Captain."

Gabriel jumped in. "That's not a grandparent name."

"So what?" Michael returned. "He looks captainish to me and he lives here right by the sea. Bill Omers calls his grandpa Dooda. What the heck kind of grandpa name is that?"

"Hang on," Christopher stuck up a finger. "I kind of like that—Captain. I can live with that if you can, Gabriel."

Ever the voice of reason, the older boy doubtfully acquiesced. "Just be glad he met you here and not at a zoo, then. Who knows what he might have come up with?"

The Captain laughed heartily and lay back in his bed, weary from such an outburst. "You guys run on down to the beach awhile. Maybe I can persuade your father to stay for lunch and we can visit later in the day."

"Awesome!" Michael beamed. "Aye-aye, Captain!" He saluted his grandfather. "Come on, Gabe! Let's check out the pellycanes."

With the boys gone, the silence was magnified. Andrew had no idea how to start a conversation.

Finally his father spoke. "I wish my window overlooked the beach. I'd love to watch them."

Andrew nodded. "Do you have a wheelchair or anything?"

He shook his head. "I'm way beyond that now." Sighing, he expelled a long cough, then turned his attention to his son. "Thank you for coming. I wasn't sure you would, but I had to at least try. There's so much I've left undone and so little time to make any amends."

"Is that what this is—making amends?"

"I know it's too little too late, but I had to attempt it before I died."

"So, is this a conscience clearing or cleansing? You want to be absolved of all your ..." he struggled, "heavens, Father, I don't even know how to describe the things you did."

"Agreed. And *no*, I could never be absolved by any man of the things I did. My life became nothing more than one criminal act after another. After a while, you get so used to a certain behavior that you begin to believe simply because you *can* do a thing, it's acceptable to do it." He shook his head in remorse. "I had the world at my feet—well, a nation, at least—and I foolishly squandered it like the prodigal son with his inheritance. It never occurred to me in those early years to be anything other than an absolute ruler. And once the die was cast, and I saw men of noble rank melt at my feet, I never looked back." He turned his gaze out the window. "When I had sons, all I could imagine was molding them in my own image—a household of leaders, strong, unmovable, fighting each other for the throne." He chuckled as he shook his head and looked back at Andrew. "Your boys love and respect you. I wanted that too but didn't understand it until it was too late."

"And when was that?" Andrew wondered. "When did all this epiphany occur? Certainly not while you lived at the palace."

"Oh, no," he agreed. "Not until two years ago." He pointed out the window. "See the flower bed over by the little wooden windmill? I worked on that several weeks."

"It's quite beautiful. I never realized you had a green thumb … or a desire to have one."

His father gave a slight laugh. "Never did, or at least never considered it. I loved the grounds at the palace and insisted on perfection. Perhaps that was why—perhaps not. But I found, after moving here, that the warmth and the beauty of this area just drew me outdoors. I started working on projects here and there and discovered I had an actual hobby." He coughed again. "It was … fun."

"I've done a lot at our home, too. Maybe it's hereditary."

He shook his head. "Thank God that's the only thing you inherited from me." He smiled. "Your house is beautiful, by the way. Evie has good tastes."

Andrew tried not to react, but it was impossible. "That's a statement I never thought I'd hear from you."

"I was the worst man I could imagine, son," he regretted. "And yet you managed to rise above it all. You deserve so much more credit than anyone will ever realize—except maybe Evie … and Julia."

"And George and Peter."

"Yes. Anyone close to me knew the monster I was."

"But … you're not that monster any longer?" His tone was skeptical.

Pointing back outside, Christopher continued. "I was working on that bed when this man, younger thirties, walked up. He was starting a church in an old historic hotel they were renovating. He invited me to come, and I politely declined. I figured after all I had done, I deserved hell and everything that went with it." His appearance was sober as he pulled up his blanket. "That little preacher never gave up, though. He said it was my accent and my gardens, but he showed up every Saturday morning, talking about my flowers, my landscape, his church, my lawn, his God, my house, his forgiveness. One day, just feeling sorry for his sincere efforts, I invited him out to the Florida room and offered him some iced tea. I then told him my whole story."

"Wow." Andrew couldn't imagine the preacher hearing about the supposed suicide of a king who ruled with unfettered ferocity. "Did he believe you?"

"He knew of Evie. Tennis is big here in Palm Beach. Everyone and their brother play, have courts in their backyards, send their kids to summer tennis camps. They study Evie's bizarre methods and try to emulate them hoping their kid will be the next rising star. He remembered you from the year you went to Flushing Meadows for the U.S. Open." Coughing and smiling, he pushed himself up straighter in the bed. "When he realized you were my son, the pieces of the stories he had heard over the years began to come together. I thought that would run him off … at least scare him a little bit. You know what he asked me instead?"

Andrew shook his head.

"He wanted to know if I'd confessed all that to God and found freedom or if I was still carrying the baggage around with me. I told him I was taking it all with me straight to hell. Persistent fellow, he was. I told him I'd try out his little church, but I wasn't too keen on a God willing to overlook the sins of a man like me. He assured me God overlooked nothing, but instead would wash me, clean me, then make me new from the inside out." He paused as emotion overtook him.

Andrew found the idea unbelievable. "Are you telling me you became a Christian?"

"Not at first, but yes … and not because I wanted to go to heaven." He now stared directly into Andrew's eyes. "I still told God I deserved hell. But when I realized He bore my sins," he choked, "*my sins*, Andrew—what kind of man throws that into the face of God? I didn't turn to Him because I needed my demons gone." His lip quivered as he explained, "I turned to God because a love that great deserves a response. Son, if He willingly took the wrath meant for me on that cross, how could I turn my back on that?" He pulled the cover higher as his body began to shiver.

"Andrew, I deserve nothing from you—I want you to know I fully accept that. But something else you need to know—I ask you to forgive me, not to absolve me, but for your own sake. To live with vile bitterness as I did all those years is a miserable path. The way I treated you, your brothers, everyone, was inexcusable and inhumane. In fact, after much prayer … a lot with my little pastor … I'd determined to return to Braisognia and face whatever sentence might be pronounced."

This was more mystifying to Andrew than anything said yet. "What? You would return?"

"That was my plan—then I became sick. I ignored it at first, but when it became overwhelming, I had to see a doctor. His diagnosis was my death sentence. And returning to Braisognia was meaningless then. If I went back, the ones who hated me would be forced to care for me." He coughed. "I couldn't do that. Corin and I agreed to stay here and take one day at a time." He glanced up to his son. "It didn't take long."

"But what about treatments?" Andrew protested. "Surely there is therapy or some kind of transplant that can be done. If money's a problem, I can certainly …"

His father held up his hand. "No, trust me when I say we've tried what we could. Money's no issue—it's beyond treatment at this point."

"But," he wanted to offer something, give some ounce of hope. "Not even a transplant?""

"You don't put a fresh liver in an old man's body when the waiting list is long." Gazing at him again, he asked, "Extending my life means nothing to me. All I want to know is can you forgive me?"

"Father, I forgave you long ago, for the very reason you explained." He stood for the first time and moved toward the bed. "After Alfred's false disclosure in his prison cell the day before I signed the new government into law, my world almost fell apart. I nearly lost everything."

"That was my fault too—it was my suggestion."

"Funny, everyone else kept telling me that same thing. They said you were punishing me and that you were still alive out there somewhere … still pulling Alfred's strings." He shook his head. "I didn't believe them … until I saw Dexter Braisogn."

Christopher nodded. "I imagine he set you straight."

"Oh, yeah. I realized then I'd been played … but not as Alfred had said." He actually reached for his father's hand. "Evangeline helped me forgive—she helped me realize there wasn't enough room in a man's heart to nurse bitterness and nurture love at the same time. She said the bitterness was a weed that would eventually overtake everything else. The only chance I stood of rising above the mess you had placed on me was to realize that only a sick, twisted man could do such a thing."

"She was quite right." He chuckled. "She always had me figured out, and I knew it."

"I had to forgive, believing your dark heart had made you ignorant of what really mattered. It wasn't immediate, but in time the hate, the hurt—all of it began to fade. When I got your invitation, Evangeline was worried it might set me off again, but I felt no malice. I assured her that no matter what you did, it couldn't hurt me again, because I had found a life that was worth living, worth fighting for, worth defying you over … again, if I had to."

He squeezed his son's hand. "Good for you—good for you."

๛ Chapter Forty-One ๛

The flight home had been somber. Christopher Braisogn was a winsome man with a mischievous sense of humor that his grandsons found magnetic. After their first day with him, the boys had wondered if they could spend their entire vacation there and return to America another time to see the geological sights. Astonished by their suggestion, Andrew agreed.

They managed getting him into a wheelchair and outdoors for several days. It took a lot out of him, but he insisted he would rather die of exhaustion than boredom. He told the boys tales of history from the area as well as Braisognia, and regretted having no stories to share of their father growing up. They attended his church and spent some time with the pastor who had refused to give up on the king who had refused to let go of his past. At the end of the two weeks, it was an emotional, tearful goodbye. Corin assured Andrew she would let him know when his father passed. He offered to have his body placed in his own grave back at the Capital Gardens, but Christopher insisted that not happen. He was a new man—he wanted a new grave.

Barely a month after their return, Andrew received a large envelope from Corin. It contained a letter from her informing him that his father had passed exactly two weeks from the day they had left. She explained how at peace he was after finding forgiveness from one son and spending time with the two boys. Included in the envelope were hand written letters from Christopher to his three sons and all his grandchildren. Knowing his brothers would probably not come for any type of memorial service, he invited them to a family picnic at the waterfall where he gave each person their letter as they sat around outside after lunch.

"So, this was a setup?" George asked snidely.

"Not at all," Andrew wanted to assure them. "I had my family over for a summertime celebration, and I'm merely delivering these in the process."

"Well, you can keep mine," Peter mumbled as he tossed it to the ground next to Andrew. "Anything he had to say to me isn't worth the paper it's written on—he said plenty before he died the first time."

Andrew didn't want to push the point, but he knew the bitterness his brothers held would only hurt them. He glanced at Evangeline, knowing she well understood the depth his own hatred had once been.

"He has letters for your kids too" he informed them.

"You can keep those also then," Peter told him. "He never acknowledged my children when he was alive—why should I let him now that he's dead ... again?"

George held his letter up toward the sun and said, "Here's what I think about all of this." He slowly began to rip it in half.

Suddenly Gabriel jumped from his seat and ran to George, snatching the letter before he could completely tear it. "Stop it! All of you!" Everyone stared in astonishment as tears brimmed at the edge of the boy's eyes. "He was trying to make things right! Can't you at least give him some credit for that?"

George sighed and tried to explain. "You don't understand the man he used to be ... the way he treated us, put us down, nearly destroyed us."

"Yes, I do," Gabriel insisted. "Dad told us all about him before we met him, and then he told us himself what a horrible dad, a horrible man and a horrible king he had been." He reached up to wipe his eyes. "He wasn't that man anymore and felt awful about the things he had done."

Peter told him, "You don't even know half of what he did."

"You're right, but you don't know who he became," Gabriel continued. "You all buried that man years ago, so this doesn't mean anything to you. I'm having to bury him now, though, and it hurts ... it really hurts." He fought to hold back more tears. "We're his family here, and we all get along good. We have fun and laugh and eat together a lot. We play, we hang out, we pile into beds and pallets and we feel close ... like a family's supposed to." He swallowed hard and tried to stiffen his lip. "If you want to punish him, then he's punished 'cause he's not here. He knows he threw all this away. We'd tell him about the crazy things we do and all the stuff that's happened over the years, and he'd just say he was glad that we had a family that could do that even after the junk he did. And we tried to tell him to come back with us so he could see it all, but he'd just say no and tell us he really wasn't a part of this family. He said he killed his family, and that what we all had together wasn't because of him." He sniffed. "He wasn't stupid—but he really was sorry."

He looked at the letter then glanced over at George. "I don't know what it says, and I don't know what he wrote to all your kids, but he was your dad. And no matter how much you might hate him, he's always gonna be a part of this … our family. And every time we get together, there's gonna be someone who says something about him or thinks something about him. If you keep acting like he's poison, then we all stay infected because of him. And that's what he didn't want. He wanted everybody to think differently because he wanted you to stop hurting, not because he wanted you to forget how crazy mean he was. He knew the past would never be changed, but he hoped big time that you could all think good stuff so you could live with memories that would help … and not hurt anymore."

He could hold it back no longer. As his sobs emerged, he quickly left the lunch area and went to the house. Evangeline followed him, but everyone else sat still.

After a few moments of silence, Andrew spoke. "That basically summed up all that Father wanted. In fact, that was how he had described it to the boys … poison. He knew what he was, and the only reason he asked forgiveness was for our sakes … to stop the poisoning. He said forgiving him would never justify or absolve him—he got away with nothing. Forgiving him was about letting go of the sickening poison he had injected into all of us so we could move on and be all God created us to be." He held up his own unopened letter. "If I refuse this, then the infection continues. If I embrace it, then healing begins." He smiled at his family. "I'm healed. I hope you guys get there too."

♊ ♊ ♊

"Are you going to let me read your letter?" Evangeline asked as she and Andrew sat by the river watching the moon over the waterfall later that evening. It had been an emotional afternoon as each person opened the words of Christopher Braisogn and sought healing.

"Did anybody else let you read their letters?" he teased.

"Yes, Victoria and Clarissa," she replied with a pout.

"Ah, our three and five year olds—the two who can't read."

"They were very sweet. I'm going to put them away and save them for when they're older and can really appreciate what he had to say."

"Good idea," he thought, leaning back in his chair and crossing his arms. "I will tell you one thing he wrote. Guess who he said was the strongest person he had ever known?"

"Alfred," she giggled.

"You're not even funny." He reached over to thump her arm, but she grabbed his hand and kissed it instead. "He said you were."

"*Me!* Are you kidding?"

"He said you were the catalyst for everything positive in this family and nation."

"That's a major stretch, don't you think?"

"Actually, I tend to agree with him. You stuck with me through all the sneers and condemnations, you became the queen against every imaginable opposition my father could throw at you, hid a pregnancy, bore up under my imprisonment ... you stood strong through it all." He then gave a sad sigh. "You even forgave me when I accused you of ... well, all that mess with Alfred." He pulled her hand to his chest. "You are an amazing woman, Evangeline Dorvain Braisogn—strong, brave and beautiful."

"I thank you for the compliment, but the truth is I only followed my heart ... sort of like your son this afternoon." She shook her head in amazement. "Gabriel is a passionate boy, but I've never seen him so intent on communicating something like that ... especially publicly. He would have made a great king."

"I don't know about that. He has too much of his father in him."

"And his father was the greatest king this nation has ever seen!" she protested.

He gave her a grave glance. "His father gave up the crown."

"No, his father handed the crown to his kingdom so they could choose how to rule themselves." She stood from her chair and pulled him up beside her. "There was never a more nobler act done for this country."

"Still, I think Gabriel would prefer to simply find a beautiful maiden, ride off into the sunset with her on a blue steed and live happily ever after."

She gave him a gentle kiss. "So that's all you really wanted?"

"That was it."

"It almost all came true."

He pulled back and eyed her quizzically. "Almost? What did I miss?"

"You never had a blue steed."

"On the contrary," he grinned mischievously as he reached into his pocket and pulled out the tiny colored horse from years ago.

"Where on earth did you find that?"

"Over by the waterfall this afternoon. Apparently the girls were playing with it."

She took it and held it up to the moonlight. "Of all the toys we've indulged them with, and they still choose to play with this old thing."

"I think we sparked their imaginations with all our made up fairy tales about it."

"Did you know that I kept it on my bedside table every night until I married you?"

"Seriously? Why?"

"So you would be the last thing I thought about before going to sleep each night. And I would beg God to strengthen you through every struggle and trial you had to face."

"Well, He answered all those prayers." He looked down at her, overcome again by her heart as well as her matchless beauty. "All I did every night was wish that you would love me and that we could live together someday … happily ever after."

"Well," she kissed him again and then reached up to touch the end of his nose, "wish granted."

Spectrals of Time

Raised on the mission field, Caroline Wallace only had one dream—to return someday and teach other missionary children. As her brother's sickness becomes more grave, she decides to delay her return to Africa and takes a position teaching the three children of a brilliant, yet eccentric, inventor who lost his wife to suicide years earlier. As she tries to teach the free-spirited children in unconventional ways, hoping to make up for lost years from the previous instructors, she and the father butt heads on a regular basis. She could not imagine things being worse until she inadvertently involves herself in one of his experiments. Suddenly time and reality are knocked out of whack, and as she and the doctor try to find answers, they are thrown into a journey that forces them to work together and examine everything they ever held as true.